CUR

Curious, indeed, a bodiless voice spoke from somewhere near at hand. *Inside my head!* Judson thought wildly. He turned toward Cookie to call a warning, but the wiry little chef was already halfway to him, running hard.

"Get back, Cap!" he yelled. "Thing'll get inside yer head, mess up yer brains!"

. . . these entities appear to be self-oriented, even conscious, and—can it be?—motivated by an impulse to assist me, who will undoubtedly destroy them the instant I can control my substance.

Judson had halted and caught Cookie's arm as he came up, panting. "I can hear it talking, Cap!" the cook gasped out. "Talking about killing the both of us!"

"I don't think it will," Judson reassured the man calmly, "once we've explained matters."

"What 'matters,' Cap?" Cookie yelled. "It said, 'I'm gonna kill 'em as soon as they fix me up.' "

Impossible! The silent voice sounded shocked. *They can read my mind!*

Other Books by Keith Laumer
Available from Baen Books

Zone Yellow
The Compleat Bolo
The Stars Must Wait
The Ultimax Man
Time Trap
The Star Treasure
A Plague of Demons
Dinosaur Beach
Chrestomathy
Earthblood (with Rosel George Brown)

The Retief Series:
Reward for Retief
Retief and the Pangalactic Pageant of Pulchritude
Retief and the Warlords
Retief: Diplomat at Arms
Retief: Emissary to the Stars
Retief: Envoy to New Worlds
Retief in the Ruins
Retief of the C.D.T.
Retief to the Rescue
Retief's War
The Return of Retief

KEITH LAUMER

JUDSON'S EDEN

A Baen Books Original

Baen Publishing Enterprises
P.O. Box 1403
Riverdale, N.Y. 10471

ISBN: 0-671-72038-4

Cover art by Keith Parkinson

First printing, February 1991

Distributed by
SIMON & SCHUSTER
1230 Avenue of the Americas
New York, N.Y. 10020

Printed in the United States of America

PART ONE

Prologue

The man had gray hair, but he was husky, tall, with massive shoulders and a slim waist. Below a heavy overcoat, his legs and feet were bare. He was leaning against the wall, looking back along the shabby street in the gray dawn. The cop watched him push off from the wall, stagger, almost fall, then catch himself and set off more steadily toward the well-lit commercial street ahead, away from the grimy port area.

Lazily, the cop fell in behind him, giving his electro-club a practical twirl to seat in his palm with a soft *smack!* At once the suspect halted, stepped into a deep doorway, and was gone. The cop lengthened his stride, came abreast of the doorway, and started, "Hold on, there, zek, I—" He fell abruptly silent as he realized there was no one there; the drunk was gone! It was as if he had disappeared into the air. The cop reached out and tried the door, a weathered metal-clad fire door with a polished brass plate reading "Private Space, Ltd." The door was locked.

"All right, zek!" the cop said wearily. "No games. Where are you?"

The cop stepped back and peered at dark windows

through heavy bars. Above, the tarnished Kawneer facade, in the stark style of a century ago, loomed impassive. No lights showed beyond the dark glass, below the curved-under aluminum storefront. Ghostly outlines of long-gone letters spelled out "Hawkins & Sons—Provisions." The cop unshipped his hand-light and studied the door's keyhole: no scratches indicating forced entry. He knocked on the door, then pounded. No response. He shone his light through the adjacent window, saw covered shapes that might have been furniture or crouching aliens. But—across the room something moved. He set his light up to high intensity and played it over the far wall, a hundred feet away, just in time to see a door close. He was sure of it—well, almost sure. The drunk was in there! Breaking and entering, bold as brass, on Norm Shelski's beat! He'd soon straighten this wise guy out! Breathing hard as if from climbing a steep stair, Shelski got out his tool kit, looked the lock over again, and selected a wire instrument. A moment later the antique lock said *cluck!* and opened.

Inside, the place smelled like a museum, or at least what Norm Shelski thought a museum would smell like. There were large shapes that could have been packing cases or something under plastic covers. He went right across to the door he had seen closing and opened it. Narrow stairs led up. Norm squinted up into the near-total darkness, grunted, settled his gunbelt, and started up. Halfway, he paused to listen and was rewarded with faint sounds. *Some*body was moving around up there! He went on up, making plenty of noise with his boots on the wooden steps; he wasn't interested in surprising the sucker and maybe getting a panic-shot in the belly. At the top, he stepped out into a big office full of desks with papers on them ranked in rows and filing cabinets against the wall. It looked like a place that was in use. The drunk—or was he?—was sitting at a desk at the far end, sorting through papers stacked in the in-basket. He looked up at Norm and said, "No problem, Chief, but thanks for looking in."

Norm took his cap off and slapped his thigh with it.

This was a cool one. "Just doing my job—sir," he said. He got out a pad and pencil. "Could I have that name, sir?" he grunted.

The man rose—definitely not drunk—and said, "Certainly; I'm Marl Judson. This is my office. I own the building."

"Well, *excuse me* all to hell," Norm said, but not aloud. Aloud, he said, "Any proof on you, Mr. Judson?"

"I don't carry the title around with me," the man pointed out. "But I can turn up a tax receipt here." He rose and went to a filing cabinet.

"Hold it, Mr. Judson," the cop said, sounding a little sharper than he'd intended.

Unperturbed, Judson withdrew a folder, took out a folded paper, and laid it on the desk for the cop's inspection. Norm looked it over, nodded, and said, "Now, some personal ID, Mr. Judson, if you don't mind."

Judson handed over a pilot's license, Class One Commercial, with his hologram likeness. The cop nodded again, put his cap back on, started to turn away, and hesitated.

"Now, just what were you doing out in the street at night, Mr. Judson? Down here in the port area, that's not safe."

"I have great confidence in our vigilant police force," Judson replied coolly.

"Yeah, sure, sir, I didn't mean—I mean I meant—"

"Don't we all, Lieutenant?" Judson agreed urbanely, and started past the cop.

"Now, just a minute here, Mr. Judson," Norm protested. "What's that you're wearing under that overcoat?" He frowned as Judson halted and opened the coat, revealing a regulation hospital gown.

"Kind of nippy to be going around barefoot," Norm commented. "You from St. Anne's, up the street? How come no clothes? You kind of left on your own, or what?"

"I was as fully recovered as one could expect, in that institution," Judson told him. "They were unconscionably slow with the paperwork, so I simply walked out. Nothing illegal in that, I presume, sir?"

"Naw." Norm made a throwing-away motion. "I got no beef. Just kind of curious-like, why a gent in your position'd be down here in the middle of the night."

"It's almost morning," Judson pointed out. "I was close to my office, so I came in to attend to some matters that require my attention. I also intended to call my car." He reached for the phone.

"What kind of sick were you, Mr. Judson?" Norm wanted to know.

"They were a little mysterious about that," Judson replied. "Nothing catching, I assure you. Something to do with my immune system, I understand. The symptoms were mild: nausea, and a general debility. My doctor insisted I go in for tests. They did the tests; I left."

"You get some kinda release, or like that?" the cop asked.

Judson shook his head.

Norm came closer. "I guess maybe we better go back up to St. Anne's and straighten out the paperwork, Mr. Judson," he said lazily.

Judson shook his head again. "Not this morning, Captain," he objected. "I don't owe them any money, if that's what you're thinking."

It was Norm's turn to shake his head. "Naw, Mr. Judson. A fellow owns a whole building, even a old dump like this, don't need to skip out on no hospital tab."

"Of course not," Judson confirmed impatiently. "I had important business to attend to, and instead I was merely sitting around that sterile institution doing nothing at all. The physicians agreed they were through with their tests, and the paperwork authorizing my release would be along promptly. After two weeks, it was apparent that their concept of 'prompt' differed from mine. So I walked out. They'd hidden my clothes, except for my overcoat."

Norm nodded thoughtfully. "I know how you feel,

sir," he conceded. "My brother-in-law—" Norm broke off abruptly as Judson put a hand out as if to steady himself, then sat, or fell, into the chair.

"You all right, sir?" Norm demanded. "Maybe you better go back to the hospital after all."

"I'm quite all right, thank you, Sergeant," Judson replied. "And I am *not* going to return to the pest-house."

"Well," the cop said, moving in, "I never said about no pest, sir; I been tryna be nice to you, sir—"

"Is there any reason you shouldn't?" Judson snapped. He waved the cop away. "I'm sorry," he said in an even tone. "Just go away now, please."

"Mr. Judson," Norm said reproachfully, "I'm tryna help ya. If you're sick . . ."

"I told you I'm not contagious," Judson reassured him.

"It ain't that, sir," Norm protested. "I can't leave a citizen here, sick, in this old dump, alone, in the middle of the night."

"I had something important to do here, Corporal," Judson said steadily. "It's very easy; it won't take long."

"What was that, sir?" Norm inquired earnestly. "Maybe I could do it for ya."

"The thought does you credit, Constable," Judson told the cop. "But I'm afraid that's impossible."

"How come, sir?" Norm persisted. "What is it you got to do?"

Judson was looking Norm full in the face. "I came here to die," he said.

1

Norm recoiled as if from a blow. "Now, you hold it right there, Mister!" he said harshly. "What's the idea, talking like that, a man in your position!"

"And what *is* my position, Chief?" Judson asked.

"You're a lucky man, Mr. Judson," Norm protested, waving a hand. "You own this here building, you got plenty scratch, you got everything to live for!"

"I quite agree, sir," Judson said solemnly.

"Then what's this about eating one?"

"You misunderstood me," Judson corrected. "It's not suicide I'm talking about. It's murder."

Norm looked around, moved closer to Judson, his hand on his sidearm. "So who's gonna try to knock you off, Mr. Judson?" He was asking, as he scanned the big, empty room for the threat. Then he turned to give Judson a hard look.

"Your idea of a gag, or what, Mr. Judson?" he demanded in his best cop-voice. "I guess you and me better go downtown." He reached for the middle-aged man's arm, but somehow the arm—and the middle-aged man—weren't there, but two feet away. "Here, you, don't horse around!" Norm commanded. "Yer unner arrest!"

"Not tonight," Judson said quietly. Norm fell silent, staring. He had never seen anyone move like that. Jeez! He'd reached for the suspect's arm and *zap!* the guy sort of turned, and all of a sudden he was out of reach. Must be some kind of circus acrobat or like that.

"Be nice, Mr. Judson," he pled, "and we can straighten this out, OK?"

"There's nothing anyone can straighten out," Judson said doggedly.

"Come on," Norm urged and again moved in for the pinch. This time the citizen fended him off with an arm that yielded not an inch when Norm's weight came against it.

"I have very little time left," Judson said steadily. "I will not spend it in dismal surroundings."

Norm stepped back and hitched up his shiny plastic gunbelt. Again his hand strayed to his gun-butt.

"Don't point that thing at me," Judson advised. "Or I'll have to take it away from you and jam it into a delicate portion of your anatomy."

"Don't go talking mean, Mr. Judson," Norm protested, holding out his hands, palms toward the old goof, and backing away.

"I guess I better call in on this," he told himself sternly. He used his lapel talker, got Chief Kell and said, "Got a feller here talking suicide or maybe murder, won't come in peaceful—yessir. About fifty, I'd say, five-ten, Caucasian, blue eyes, dressed up funny in an overcoat and a hospital thing, you know, open up the back; nossir, got this overcoat over it, nothing like that; nossir, over here portside, St. Anne's, not a mendle ward. A Mister Judson, seen some ID, nossir, just talking crazy down here Portside middle o' the night. He talks crazy, but he don't talk *crazy*. Yessir." Norm returned his attention to Judson. "Got to take you in like I thought, so let's—"

Judson shook his head. "Kindly go away," he said wearily. He put a hand to his forehead. "Fever's getting higher," he commented. He pulled the swivel chair closer and sat in it. "Just go away and leave me alone," he appealed. "I'm so *tired.*"

"Look here, Mr. Judson," Norm tried again. "You tell me there's gonna be a murder and you think I'm gonna waltz outa here and fergit it?"

"Not 'going to be,' sir," Judson corrected. "It's already happened. About an hour ago. In the pest-house."

"Then where's the body at, huh?" the cop challenged. "Wheresa victim o' this here murder, eh?"

"That's me," Judson said as if explicating the obvious.

"You're dead, that it?" Norm came back, but he felt the hairs on his scalp tightening upright. "You tryna tell me yer some kinda ghost or like that?" Norm tried a surprised expression which, alas, made him look like an imbecile.

Judson smiled wearily, "No, Commissioner, I'm not dead. Just dying. Like you, only faster."

"Who you calling me now, wise guy?" the cop demanded. "I'm Patrolman Norm Shelski, OK? And I ain't dying. Ye'r starting to get my goat, Mr. Judson. Now let's get outa here and go down the presink, you'll like it there. They got a nice little room fer you. Come on, now." As he stepped in, the suspect half turned, appeared to lose his balance, and grabbed for support, accidentally catching Norm's arm. Somehow, Norm slipped and fell heavily against the desk and to the floor. Norm's first impulse, as he lay on his back with his ears ringing from the accidental impact of his skull against the desk, was to blow his stack, cuff the suspect, and take him in. But wait a minute, he cautioned himself; he couldn't hardly tell Dutch on the desk this old guy had thrown him on his ass. Naw, it was an accident; he slipped was all.

Norm got up, muttering. The old guy offered a hand up, which was impatiently brushed aside. Norm peered at the suspect, who seemed a bit flushed, Norm thought. "You OK, Mr. Judson?" he inquired. "Prolly we better get you back to the hospital, now."

"Forget it," Judson said firmly. "I left that place

because I didn't want to spend my last hours—or minutes—among incompetent hypocrites. I'm not going back. Just go along and forget you saw me. I'll take care to dispose of the body in a way that won't reflect on your competence, I assure you."

"Now you're talking dead bodies again!" Norm charged. "That ain't nice, Mr. Judson, a responsible citizen like yerself, you know better'n . . ." Norm fell silent. The old guy wasn't listening anyways.

2

Judson was sitting at Mel's desk. He didn't feel a bit well. He put a hand to his forehead; it felt hot. Abruptly he realized it was late, after office hours. Why was he down here, alone in the middle of the night? Not quite alone. A tired-looking patrolman with a baggy uniform and a face to match was leaning a hip against Doreen's desk a few feet away, staring at him with a grim expression.

"You gonna be nice now, Mr. Judson?" the cop inquired in a whine which combined truculence with servility. He was holding a club in his hand, and Judson had a feeling he was thinking seriously of using it. He rose to his feet, felt a momentary vertigo, put a hand on the desktop to steady himself. What the hell was wrong with him? Then he remembered. The hospital, the unctious quack . . .

"What is it you want?" Judson asked the cop. "Is something wrong?"

"What I been tryna fine out," the cop grumbled. "You always come down here at midnight, or what? These streets ain't safe after dark; seen you out there, alone, look like you maybe had a few, or maybe sick, hah? You feeling sick, Mister Judson?"

"How do you know my name?" Judson asked. He was feeling more puzzled by the second. He looked around; the big office was deserted. Why had he come here at this hour?

"You tole me," the cop was replying to his query. "Showed me some ID. I ast what's the idea, down here middle o' the night, and all you done, you wised off at me."

"I don't recall," Judson told the cop. He was feeling definitely bad now. Better get out into the fresh air. He started across toward the double doors.

The cop fell in beside him, thought about clamping a hand on his arm, decided against it. "You want I should see you back to the hospital, sir?" he asked deferentially.

Judson halted. "What hospital?" he demanded sharply.

"You know, St. Anne, up the block, here."

"Why would I want to go to a hospital?" Judson asked. This whole situation was getting more nightmarish by the moment. What was there about a hospital . . . ? He frowned in concentration, abruptly looked down, saw his bare feet. He twitched the coat aside, saw the cotton hospital gown, a garment designed, by being open at the back, to deprive its victim of dignity, and thus, of identity. Yes, he'd been in a hospital. Horrible place. He turned to the cop, who was wiping an unmanicured hand across his lumpy face as if to wipe away the puzzled expression.

"Why was I in the hospital?" Judson asked.

"Beats me, sir," the cop replied. "Sick, I guess. My bet is ye'r still sick. You almost fell down a minute ago. You feel OK, sir?"

Judson shook his head. "No, I don't, Norm," he said. How did he know this cop's name was Norm? He looked; there was no nameplate.

"Actually," Judson went on, "I feel a little lightheaded." He had started to say "terrible," but for some reason had used the milder expression. "I'd appreciate it if you'd call my car," he said.

"Well, I got—I mean—" Norm temporized. "—We could just walk over presink, oney a coupla blocks; if you want I can call a black-and-white."

"Just call my car, please," Judson urged. "One, seven hundred-thirteen."

Jeez, Norm thought, a seven-hundred number! "Sure, Mr. Judson," he said, and picked up a phone from the nearest desk, punched in the code. A man's voice answered.

"Send Mr. Judson's car over the office, pronto," Norm said. "Bring a doctor," he added on impulse.

Judson had moved on to the door. He found himself waiting for the cop to open it, frowned, and pushed the door open. Norm arrived in time to hold it.

"Onna way," the cop said. "Better take it easy onna stairs, Mr. Judson."

"We'll use the lift," Judson replied. He used a key on a blank door and it opened silently. The cop seemed a little nervous getting into the car. They rode in silence down to the street.

A big black car rounded the corner as they stepped out on the pavement. It eased to the curb. A wiry little man in a Private Space cap came around to open the door. He looked curiously at Judson as he got in. "You all right, Mr. Judson?" he asked. "Wherat's yer shoes, Cap?"

"Mister Judson ain't feeling good," Norm grunted. "Wherat's the doc?" He had peered into the gray-lined interior in vain.

"Couldn't get one this quick," the driver said. "Got a call in. He'll be waiting at home—at the apartment, I mean."

Norm started to get in, then paused and looked in critically at Judson.

"You going to be OK now, sir?" he asked. "I guess you don't need me no more."

"I'll be fine, thanks, Norm," Judson replied. "Thanks for being on the job."

Norm straightened up and almost saluted. "Sure, sir, glad to do my job," he said. "I hope you got no beef."

"Not at all," Judson reassured the cop. "In fact, I'll write the Commissioner personally, to express my appreciation."

"Gosh, sir, that ain't necessary," Norm gobbled. Now he'd have to write a report, all right. "Just fergit it, sir, if it's OK with you," he said to the closing door. The driver gave him a stern look and went back around the car.

Once at ease in the car, Judson waited until the small man got behind the wheel, then said, "Cookie, nothing serious, I hope, but I'm feeling very strange. I seem to have amnesia—just a touch, you understand—I have apparently been in a hospital, and left on my own and came down here and went to the office. I came to myself with that policeman standing over me."

"Yessir, you was at St. Anne's, private room, round-the-clock private nurses, doing good, that was after you, uh, fainted, I guess you'd call it, in the garden, after dinner. You remember the dinner for the senator, right, Cap?"

"No," Judson said, "I don't remember any dinner. In fact, I'm hungry. What senator?"

"Well, Jeez, Cap—I mean Mr. Judson—*you* know; Senator Dodley, you been tryna get aholt of for a year—the guy pushing the commerce bill, that'd let the gubment take over what's left o' the business."

"My memory seems a little vague, Cookie," Judson said, thoughtfully. "By the way, I'm not going to the apartment. Just let me out right here." He indicated a stretch of bare loading-platform ahead.

The driver pulled in, protesting. "Now, hold on a minute, Mr. Judson! I got to get you to the doc! What—" He broke off as a police car rounded the corner and put the spotlight in his face. The black-and-white slowed, but went past.

Cookie braked to a halt at the curb, watching the fuzz in his mirror. "Right here, Mr. Judson?" he queried uncertainly. "Those cops are stopping at the building." He shot a look at Judson. "Them guys after *you*, boss, or what?"

"I've changed my mind, Mr. Murphy," Judson said. "Go around the next block and come back up on the other side of the street."

"What's this 'Mr. Murphy'?" the chauffeur asked, sounding resentful. "You mad at me, Cap?"

"Why do you call me 'Cap' one minute, and 'Mr. Judson' the next?" Judson countered.

"Beats me, sir," Cookie grunted. "I guess it kinda depends . . ."

"Yes? Go on," Judson prompted.

"It depends if— Wait a minute, Cap, they're coming back."

"All right, Cookie," Judson said quietly. "Move on—come back up on the other side—and do it quickly."

"They're fingering us, all right, Cap," the driver said after another glance at the rear-scanner. He pulled away, took the corner abruptly, gunned the big car quietly to the next corner, hung a left, and accelerated down the block. He did the left and the next one, then eased back toward where the cop car had been parked. It was gone; no police in sight.

"I guess we lost 'em," he muttered, then twisted in his seat to look at his employer. "What's up, Cap? I leave you all tucked in snug in the ICU, and the next thing, you're down here, portside, in the middle of the night. You feeling OK now, Cap? You looked kinda green around the gills when I taken you in. Huh? OK now?"

"Not too bad, Cookie," Judson told the solicitous driver. "Pull over now, and if you see the police again, lead them on a chase."

"Wait, boss," Cookie blurted. "You can't— I ain't tryna tell ya what to do, natch, Cap, but if you don't feel good, you got no business being down here, on foot—bare feet at that—after midnight!" He was pulling off his shoes by then. "Here, Cap, better'n nothing—if you got to do this."

"Thanks for understanding, shipmate," Judson said, and put on the worn but sturdy shoes. He got out, looked up the block, saw no one moving on the bleak street, and went along beside the high chain-link fence to the shadow of the nearest building, a sagging warehouse as grimy as the rest of the street. His car paced him until he waved it on.

There was a narrow alley cutting back into the masonry block. Beyond the gate at the far end, the harsh light of the polyarcs glared at the tarmac. He went quickly along, past shoals of drifted trash, to the gate. He really wasn't feeling at all well, he realized as he clutched at the wire mesh for support. This was a crazy idea, Cookie was right, he ought to go home and rest and eat, then try again later. But even as he had the thought, he was getting out his key, inserting it in the massive lock-block. The mechanism *whirr*ed and the gate popped open. Judson went through, squinting against the sudden actinic glare from the pole-mounted lights. As always, the sight of the space-burned tugs and shuttles in their ranked cradles in the ready area gave him a lift of spirits no less than the majestic bulk of the great deep-space hulls across the field, before the bright-lit service hangars. There were no lights showing in the line-hut off to the right, backed up against the rusty brick wall of the warehouse. He went past it to the equipment shed, where a yellow glow from inside confirmed that Matt was on duty, as always. He reached the door, pushed into warmth and the sour-sweet odor of Matt's pipe. Matt himself laid aside the pictonews he had been gazing at sleepily.

"Well, Mr. Judson!" he said in his surprisingly small voice, the result of a bout with laryngeal cancer. "What brings the Man himself out in the cold night air?"

"Unfinished business," Judson replied shortly. "You happen to have a pair of ship-boots in my size lying around back there?"

" 'Ten and a half, Cee-A,' " Matt recited. "Sure have, Mr. J," he said, almost reproachfully. "You know I keep yer gear ready any time you want it." He looked the older man up and down. "Looks like you'll need yer A-suit, too, sir. What's up tonight? You wanta look at the new mods on *J. P. Morgan*?" He handed over the gear. Judson sat down on the bench provided and began changing shoes.

"*Morgan* on-line?" Judson asked casually.

"Mr. J," Matt said in a tone of mild surprise. "You know Tiny keeps her at minus five day and night. Sure she's ready. Heard about the gubment tryna take over the firm, sir," he went on in a more subdued tone. "That mean some bunch o' bureaucrats are going to start messing around with ops, go aboard *Ford* and even *Carnegie*?"

"That's what they intend, Matt," Judson said heavily. "They've already notified me, officially, to turn in *Carny's* papers."

"They can't *do* that, Mr. J!" Matt blurted. "Why, she's the vessel you built Private Space on! The one brought you and yer crew in safe and sound after the rock hit her! Some paper-pusher messing around with *Carny*!" The stock-man's face was red with indignation.

"Before that," he went on, warming to his theme, "there wouldn't of been any Lunabase One if you hadn't build *Carny* with yer own dough and *showed* em! And without L-1—no dome program, no bases on Mars and Callisto and the rest! She's a national treasure, like the tube says! They got no right! Sorry, Mr. Judson. I guess I feel pretty strong about all this 'collectivization' stuff; sometimes I think the gubment's going too far, tryna suck up to them Rooshians!"

"Have they grounded *Carny* yet?" Judson inquired.

Matt shook his head. "I guess even them bureaucrats ain't got the nerve fer *that*."

"They don't need nerve, Matt," Judson told him. "They've got regulations they wrote themselves."

"Trouble with this country nowadays," Matt muttered. "A man on his own ain't allowed to do nothing. And a bunch o' men—call 'em a committee or a union or a gang—whatever—*can't* do nothing! They're tryna kill Private Space, is what they're tryna do! Then where'll we be? Waitin' for the Rooshians to invite us out for a guided tour of the Lunar Collective, I guess!"

Matt squinted at Judson. "What you got in mind,

Cap?" he inquired nervously. "They had a ten-man detail on *Carny* all day. Only one guy out there now," he added doubtfully. "You got too much to lose to try anything dumb, Mr. Judson." This sternly.

"Call Ops," Judson directed. "I want *Carny* signed-off and cleared and in position in five minutes. Log her out on Special Official Business."

Matt peered over Judson's shoulder. "Wherat's yer crew, sir?" he wondered aloud, then went to the red talker and passed on Judson's order.

". . . talking about, Matt?" a reedy voice came back. "There's a hold order on that tub you couldn't break with a SWAT division!"

"Just *do* it, Fred," Matt came back. "You don't need to ast no questions. That hold order don't take effect until oh-one-hundred, and you know it! You want to interfere with a official operation here, dum-dum? I told you 'Special Official.' "

"Oh, I didn't get the Notam; sure, Matt, excuse my boner. If the senator—"

"I said nothing about no senator," Matt came back. "Don't try to think, Fred! Five minutes—make that four and a half!"

"Damn paper-pushers," Matt said to a corner of the room. He looked at Judson, now wearing the A-suit, and clipping on the Group One harness. "What's it all about, Cap?" he asked earnestly. "You thinking about pulling a fast one, or what?" He moved closer. "You can count on me, Cap, you know that," he said in a stage whisper. "If there was to be a flash fire over Stores, it might keep the Security boys busy fer a few minutes, hey?"

Judson nodded, but said, "Don't do it, Matt. You'll get in trouble."

Matt said, "Nuts," and went over to his repeater console, stood for a minute studying the big board, then began punching in a complex sequence.

"Rigged some o' this stuff fer drills, time they was talking about taking over the field," he muttered. Judson glanced out through the window beside him. Over behind Ops, an orange glare was visible, with smoke as dense as black whipped cream. A siren *whoop!-whoop!*ed. Men could be seen running from the hangars.

Judson stood. "Thanks, Matt. Time to go."

"Take the line-cart, Cap," Matt urged. "Right outside." Judson nodded.

He went out; it seemed colder, and he was suddenly aware of dizziness; he was confused, he realized, hardly aware of where he was and what he was doing. But he got on the cart, eased it forward, scanned the far side of the field for *Carny*'s berth, saw the old vessel standing by her tender, lit from end to end. The cool breeze on his face felt good. A car was coming across the tarmac, its reddish searchlight probing. Judson veered left into the shelter of the row of old aboveground tanks, and floorboarded the cart. He came up on *Carny* from her port quarter, with the foot-high letters reading "ZY-60."

The police car had swung over toward *Carny*. It was creeping, playing its searchlight over the tarmac. While the car was busy investigating the tender's base, Judson gained a few more feet, keeping the cart in her shadows. The lone sentry was starting across toward the hubbub at Ops when Judson glided silently to a stop near the cargo on-belt. He waited until a little man with a clipboard and a self-important look had disembarked down the personnel ramp and hurried away; then he rode the belt up and into the aft hold. It was dim-lit here, and smelled like a grain and feed store, Judson thought, not for the first time.

He proceeded forward, rode the lift up to the COC and looked around at the familiar, crowded space, grinning from ear to ear. "Damn fool," he said, almost aloud. "This can't work. Get out now and take your chewing from the senator like a good boy, and retire to the estate and let the future happen." But, ignoring this excellent advice, he punched in his personal code to the Pilot's Position, and the fitted chair deployed, its contours writhing into the correct configuration for his unique body contour. He sat, enjoyed the caress of the perfect seat, took a moment to code for the Checklist–

Final, then slapped down the big flat lever, punched in the lift sequence, and poked the comm button, just as it blared out:

"—tower to Zee-Why-Six-oh. Report! An explanation of apparent violation of Category One is required. Kindly pass authorization code. Over to you, Zee-Why."

"Forget all that," Judson said into the talker. "I'm operating under congressional license number one, on Exempt status. Over and out."

"Zee-Ell One is carried as revoked, Six-oh. You will abort at once. You are under arrest—" The voice was drowned by static; the burst of noise expressed Judson's feelings precisely. He laughed.

The rest was lost as *Carny*'s antiquated but still potent helix uttered its preliminary *BONGG!* and threw the vessel upward at a major fraction of escape velocity. Thanks to the superbly-engineered chair, Judson retained consciousness as the breath was expelled from his lungs in a great "hah!" He was remotely aware of the chair shifting minutely under him as it adjusted to his involuntary muscular response to the incredible impact; then he let it all go and slid down into nothingness.

3

Well, not quite "nothingness," he became aware of some aspect of his mind objecting, at the same moment that external sounds impinged on his awareness:

A steady blatting from the talker:

"—compliance with Interim Code paragraph nineteen, Section Two! This is your final notice. Failure to comply—"

"—unauthorized vessel will alter course at once! Repeat, alter course for rendezvous with escort at locus ninety-four/oh-three/fifteen!"

"You'll have to catch me first, Senator," Judson said in a voice that surprised him by its weakness. He drew a deep breath, switched on the space-to-base, and said clearly, "When I rise, you may kiss me."

4

As the old merchant vessel hurtled outward through the rapidly attenuating atmosphere, the howling of battered air molecules and the screech and clatter of the vessel's vibration gradually faded, as did the chatter of planet-based radio traffic. Judson switched frequencies and the Lunar Patrol came in, loud and demanding:

"—unidentified vessel, reply code fourteen. You are not, repeat *not* cleared for Lunar approach! You will resume the following re-entry orbit at once!" A string of numerals followed, which Judson ignored.

"—fire on this clown, or what?" a different voice blurted. "I got to do it now or I lose my sonic! Lunapat, come in, Pat one, operational urgent!"

Judson fired up the extreme-range scanners, saw a scattering of blips representing Lunapat units on routine patrol. There was more excited conversation between Pat One and Lunar Command; in the end the order to open fire was given. Judson ducked instinctively as the red blips of hot warheads winked on, converging on him. The voice of Lunapat became more strident: "—responsible for consequences! Take up orbit Ninety-one, forty-two, zero, at once! This is a category ultimate directive. Zee-why-six-oh! You will—"

Judson cut the sound, watched the incomings.

"The damned fool," he muttered, grinning. "He must be reading his ops tactics out of the textbook! What he's forgetting is that even though *Carny*'s no warship, I fitted her up with the best state-of-the-art junk clearance circuitry the labs could come up with. These boys want to play rough, so be it!" He slammed down a big red-painted knife-switch marked OUTER SCREEN-ACTIVATE. A bare instant later, the orderly arc of incoming warheads dissolved into confusion as the leading units winked out of existence and the others took up a standard, and thus predictable evasion pattern. More of the frantically darting missiles disappeared; collisions occurred. Only three widely spaced warheads made it past the Outer Screen. Judson shook his head and threw in the secondary intercept unit, a seldom-used but uncompromising array of linked sensors and hard-shot projectors that would form an almost solid barrier to any incoming rock—or missile. He watched the screen as one of the three persistent warheads dropped from view, followed almost instantly by another, then as the lone survivor homed on him, he reopened the contact and heard a self-important voice which he recognized as that of Commissioner Spradley of the PSB:

"—know what kind of damn foolishness you have in mind, Mr. Judson, but I can assure you—" The bureaucrat's meaty voice was overridden by another, harder voice:

"—no choice, Judson. The taxpayer—hell, Jud, call it off, you've already run up a bill that even you will have to appeal for an installment payment plan on; go inert, and I can still salvage a little face for Fats Spradley!" His tone changed: "Tell you what, Jud, why don't we talk, just you and me? Pick up course for Farside Station, and I'll personally escort you in."

"Just what I had in mind, Commodore," Judson replied wearily. He squinted at the screen. "If I can pick off your last Assegai Nine here—" He reached to lock-in Final Screen and the panel flashed red and went out as the vessel rang like a bell struck by a hard shot. That had been close—maybe too close! Judson, his ears ringing, punched in the Red checklist, started to get out of the chair and felt himself falling.

5

"—the damnedest old fool in the world!" Commodore Coign was yelling in his face. Judson reached to push him away, but his arm barely twitched. He tried to sit up—dizziness, disorientation. What in hell had happened? Where . . . ?

Judson made an effort to get it together. Coign was still yelling at him, but not as loudly: "—temperature of a hundred and four! What are you trying to do, Cappy—kill yourself? You picked a damned expensive way to do it! I had to mount a full Category Two defense effort to get close enough to talk to you! That's a hundred million guck for openers! Lunapat is on my ass! I've got a report from Earthside—'unauthorized departure from a court-ordered detention in a Class Five facility;—some kind of faked-up hospital. Can't blame you there—but, man, you *are* sick! My own personal doc said so. 'Massive anaphylactic shock,' he says, whatever the hell that is. What did they do to you in that damned St. Anne place? Cap!"

Judson got his shoulders under his eyelids and heaved. The light hurt. He could barely make out Goldie's red face.

"I'm back, Goldie," he said, and heard a blurry sound like a nine-day drunk trying to order one more.

"You clobbered *Carny* in on the VIP pad at Secondary," Coign was telling him sternly. "No real damage—you built the old bitch to last, Cap. But what am I supposed to do with you? I've got Lunapat and Interdict Command and the local security boys on my neck, not to mention a hot-line from the chairman, personally! And *he's* getting it from Zoggy and Sinjin, too! You're a one-man interplanetary incident. If you hadn't been running that one-oh-four, you'd be in the local back-up right now. I used up twenty years' accumulated brownie points to get you remanded to my personal custody.

"So no more games, Cap! Take it easy, and I'll see if this mess can be sorted out, which, frankly, I doubt. The senator's got the media foaming at the mouth about the 'enemy of the people'—you of course. You twisted his nose in the full glare of all the coverage there is. I see old age hasn't made you any smarter than you were the day you came down that ice-mine shaft after me and Flathead! You look bad, Cap! Come on, fight, man! Hold it together! Use your head!"

"M'okay," Judson said, almost clearly. "Doe rember—remember—wha—Cookie said, 'go with 'em, Cap—it's just a hospital'—hah! Some hospital. Sick as a dog—said I signed some kind of papers—unique opportunity, the head quack said. Never have another chance, great boon to mankind or something."

"I don't know about that part, Cap," Coign put in. "All I heard was about the accident—if it *was* an accident—six months under a half-R, was the story, a miracle you were alive—this story about breaking out of the tight ward, beat up some cops, they said. You had 'em all talking at once—and that was *before* you stole Communal Property and wasted the people's money on this crazy expedition! What were you thinking about, Cap?" Coign's voice was pleading for an explanation, even more than his words.

"Had to get . . . clear," Judson managed. "Goldie, do you realize what it means if they close Private Space?"

"Damn right I do, Cap," Coign said tightly. "But what do you mean, 'if'? Expropriation passed unanimously. The Council—"

"Damn the Council!" Judson snarled, or whimpered.

"Why didn't you play it smooth, Cap?" Coign entreated. "You should have accepted the honorary admiral-general's stars, given the interviews, made the expected noises—and today you'd be a national hero instead of a hunted-down felon!"

"I don't know, Goldie," Judson replied, shaking his head. "I can't remember anything but an ugly old dame in a white uniform with a piece of twisted-up white cardboard stuck in her black wig—looked like they'd swiped it from a cocker spaniel—the wig, I mean—trying to supervise me taking a leak—that and waking up with a needle in my arm every time I managed to get to sleep. Then there was a cop, nice fellow—wanted to throw me out of my own office. What the hell, Goldie, did I design and build *Carny* after NASA folded up quietly, and did I start up Private Space and put up the dome on Farside, or—?"

"Sure, sure, Cap, I know; you established the first permanent station on a trans-Martian satellite—gave man the first foothold for the exploration of space—you did it all, damn near single-handed—"

"Don't forget yourself, Goldie," Judson put in, "and Hake and Crusty and a few dozen more—all good men—"

"All dead men," Coign corrected. "The Council in its wisdom determined that space was too dangerous for people. That's why they started AutoSpace, as the media call it; and there was no place for an unofficial one-man show called Private Space. So—Expropriation. You knew the score. Then—you dropped off the big screen. What happened?"

"It's not very clear, Goldie," Judson told the puzzled commodore. "The Foundation approached me last month—very hush-hush. The pitch I got was about my hundred thousand hours plus, deep-space time; all that exposure to cosmic radiation made me uniquely qualified to help them with some new line of research in long-range effects of the Move Into Space . . ."

"Sure—'MIS,' we've heard plenty about that," Coign put in. "Our remote ancestors crawled out onto land—and underwent drastic modifications before they could exploit the new world they'd opened up. Now the species is ready to take the next step—on the same scale as life-on-land. Life in Space—so we can expect some profound changes. Listen, Cap: I have some sources of my own. The Foundation is still on the square, Cap. Hell, *you* founded it!"

"Had an idea we could research aging," Judson managed. "But— "

"They're still on our side, Cap," Coign cut in, "After all, there are plenty of people who don't buy the Council's AutoSpace. Some of 'em have a lot of money, and a lot of 'em have a little money. What they've come up with is the biggest news story that a bureaucrat ever smothered!" Coign shifted in his chair, paused to light up a jasmine-scented dope-stick. "What's the biggest obstacle—at a theoretical level, of course—to the idea of populating the galaxy?"

"Too damn far away," Judson grunted. "Thousands, or millions of years for the one-way trip, even if we attain near-C velocities."

"Right," Coign prompted. "And what's the answer?" He paused for effect: "Longevity, Cap! A man who can live only a hundred years or so can't handle a fifty-thousand-year turnaround time—so we have to live longer. A thousand years as the normal human life-span is the figure I've heard." Coign looked expectantly at Judson. "That's what they wanted you for, Cap! They're ready for the first preliminary tests! And you—damn you, you old reprobate—as if you hadn't done enough for humanity—*you* were in a position to make a vital contribution. And you ran out on it! I'm not blaming you, Cap," Coign assured Judson more mildly. "You didn't know what was going on—"

"Damned Council, I thought," Judson said. "I was a

sick man, no doubt about that. I decided they meant to kill me under cover of trying to help me! I heard 'em talking, knew I had no more time—maybe only a few hours—so I left. No security worth a damn—just walked out. You sure the Foundation hasn't been quietly taken over? It started ignoring my policies a long time ago. I say to hell with committees and Councils and all the rest, trying to control a man's life! Humanity didn't fight its way up from the primordial slime by being told what to do by some damned windbag petty official!" Judson subsided with a groan. "I don't *want* to take on the world, Goldie," he appealed. "I just want them to leave me alone!"

"Some of them aren't so petty," Coign countered. "The senator has a lock on the Council; you know that as well as I do. He parlayed a name and a fortune into a one-man rule like Adolf only dreamed of. How the hell did you expect to buck *him*?"

"I didn't," Judson objected. "I just wanted to go on minding my own business and have others do likewise."

"But your business just happens to be the biggest, most powerful private enterprise ever conceived, Cap. You control—or you *could* control—the whole damned planetary economy! Even the senator felt the bind! The Irresistible Force and the Immovable Object with a vengeance! So you end up on the rug—what else did you expect, dammit?"

"I didn't 'expect' anything, Goldie," Judson said patiently. "I was delirious, I suppose. I felt terrible. I only knew I had to get out of that trap."

"You were lucky," Coign snapped. "The word was passed to the Metro Police about five minutes too late. That cop, Norm, you mentioned—he's in the fax as the 'Hero Who Didn't.' His chief has been fired and is under investigation."

"It figures," Judson said wearily. "Somebody has to be the scapegoat; those men did their job."

Coign made soothing sounds. "All right, Cap. I'll see what I can do for them. But what about you? You know it's my duty to turn you over to Lunapat as soon as your doctor releases you."

"Why wait for that damn fool?" Judson inquired. "He was running late for his foursome; he told me so himself."

"They went a little too far, Cap," Coign told the patient. "They sent me special word via a Lunapat Security man to dope you and ship you back in 'close confinement'; that means cuffed in a cell, dammit—and the Mooncop was standing by (with an extra set of cuffs, I suppose) to make damn sure I did it."

"Pretty dumb way to handle you—a ranking commodore with more decorations than General Margrave has stars," Judson grunted.

"Sure," Coign agreed. "I put in my time as a Spac'n Last Class. If they think I'm going to sit still for this, they can rethink the problem. I sent the pet Mooncop back on an ore-hull, without his sidearm and ID."

"Got you in the ego, eh, Goldie?" Judson almost chuckled. "Lucky for me. They've got one more in the eye coming to them, eh?"

"Bet on it, Cap," Goldie advised. "Unfortunately," he went on, "it seems that our Mooncop left hurriedly: after he formally took over security here, but before he got the sick-bay staked out. After I visited you, you got up and walked out. You took a staff car that was parked just outside that door over there, and made it to the (former) Private Space dome where *Rockefeller III*'s cargo was being modified by Council order to deep-space specs." He turned and walked away.

Judson lay for a moment looking after the trim, immaculately-uniformed man. When the door closed behind Coign, he moved an arm tentatively; it worked. He tried his legs; they responded. He sat up and looked around the spartan room. His shipsuit and boots had been tossed onto a table.

The low Lunar G helped a lot, Judson reflected as he made his way across the room, feeling, he decided, light-headed, but *better*. Yep, he was feeling stronger; the dream quality was gone. He knew exactly where he was and exactly what he had to do.

6

Rocky's aft cargo hatch was open and her loading belt in operation, delivering what looked like an endless stream of square cartons marked "COUNCIL PROPERTY—OFFICIAL CATEGORY ONE USE (see codes 12-29)." The men at the fore belt were engrossed in their work, tallying cargo and comparing readouts. Judson tumbled two of the remarkably heavy boxes off the belts and lay full-length on it. No one yelled. It was strangely quiet here under the dome—no, not strange, Judson corrected himself. Just that it had been a long time and he'd forgotten the enveloping silence.

He waited in the Class One cargo bay for a few minutes, assessing his own bodily sensations. They were other than normal, he decided, but not really bad. In fact, he felt damn good. His breathing was easier than it had been for years. Maybe stale dome air was good for him.

He undogged a hatch into the axial tube and listened. Faint sounds from aft were audible. He started forward.

Fifty feet along the head-ducking passage, he heard footsteps approaching from forward. He stepped into a narrow niche, and felt over the plasticoated bulkhead, found a soft spot and pressed. A panel slid aside, revealing the check-panel, station twelve aft. He slid his hand under the overhanging cover-plate, and tickled a projecting wire, pulled in his arm, and held both arms close to his side. The patch of deck he was standing on rotated silently until he was facing a dark opening. He stepped through, flipped the reflex switch, and the opening closed behind him.

He waited for a moment, heard nothing, and proceeded through the tight aperture into a short, cramped passage which opened into the central operating compartment, where there was barely sufficient space for a man of Judson's physique to squeeze into the G-chair.

Briefly, Judson remembered the day when the designers had tailored the space-buck to him as he sat in the dummy chair in the big, airy drafting room. For a moment, he relaxed utterly. Then he set about examining the complex array of computer readouts, old-fashioned LEDs and LCDs mostly, with only a few of the new SSFs. All that low-tech stuff was beyond him, Judson thought, almost contemptuously. Was he contemptuous of the FINIAC boys who spent their time tending computers, he wondered briefly, or himself for his ignorance?

"Ignorance, hell," he said aloud, then made an effort to refocus his attention on the CURRENT STATUS panel. He knew nothing about solid-state fluctuators, he acknowledged to himself, but he knew about Brownie. Good thing he'd never reported the discovery. He remembered the ninety-nine hours he'd spent on continuous con aboard *Carny*, bored, waiting to run out of air and die, killing time by running a close scan on the anomaly—the not-yet-officially-detected body apparently orbiting the brown dwarf star which, some theorists believed, had made a close approach to Sol four billion years ago, thereby initiating the formation of the planets. They had calculated its mass from its perturbation of the Oort Cloud, but couldn't find it. Judson remembered the thrill, even then, as it had occurred to him that the perturbing body might be bodies, plural, too small to distinguish from the star.

He knew where they were, and he knew how to get there. At that point, the STG idiot light winked on and an uncertain voice said, "Uh, Nine-five-three, commence preliminary idling test sequence. Do you read, Five-three? Over."

Good old Goldie! Once in, he was going all the way, Judson exulted. "Test sequence," eh? He'd test her all right, right past their damned containment. With no further reflection, Judson slammed down the big COIL HOT switch. They'd wanted to complicate that with a sophisticated relay circuit, he remembered, with contempt. Trying to make a space captain into just another button-pusher like themselves. He'd put an end to that in a hurry. When a man fires himself into space, by God, he wants a trigger to pull that he can damn well see! The deep-in-the-bones vibration permeating the vessel and himself intruded on his thoughts. The whirlybirds were on-line, building up the particle-density in the helix, and in a moment the red HOT light would glare. It did. No more stalling, Judson! Have you really got the gall to commit to deep-space orbit, all alone? A crew of three superbly-trained men was well-known to be the theoretical minimum, not that anybody had ever tried it. But then, nobody else had conned a crippled Class Two back from T-P space alone and with a busted femur, either. So screw em! Here goes. He tripped the interlock. Just as his hand went to the DRIVE ENGAGE lever, a voice spoke behind him.

"Permission to enter, Cap," it said uncertainly. Judson twisted to look over his shoulder.

"Cookie!" he blurted. "What in nine hells are *you* doing here, you damned old fool?"

"Knew you'd need at least one good hand, Cap," the little man apologized. "Better not hit the Ponds until I unlock aft."

Judson sat dumbfounded. He'd been *that* close to blowing *Rocky* and himself into a rapidly dissipating gas cloud. "She's engaged! She's lovely! She uses Pond's," the old gag went, so "Ponds" it was, and he'd absent-mindedly disengaged the safeties—

"Welcome aboard, Space'n Second," he said calmly, as if he hadn't almost put an earth-visible crater where the Private Space dome used to be.

"Yessir," Cookie said, and withdrew. A minute later, the green CLEAR FOR ENGAGE light went on. Judson waited another minute, to give Cookie time to get into his launch pocket, and threw in ENGAGE. As always, his mind's first response was absolute panic as its universe exploded in the overwhelming assault of a thousand contradictory fatal sensations as the coil took hold and threw the hundred-ton vessel outward along the strike-slip fault in the space-time continuum. Then *Rocky* settled into her accustomed transit mode as her sensors and autostabilizers recreated Earth-normal conditions aboard.

The talker gave a final drawn-out *squawk* as *Rocky*'s velocity passed point nine light:

"—final warningg," it moaned. "Nessesarreee agzyunnn . . ."

Judson smiled, noting on-screen the detonation, far in his wake, of two final missiles dispatched too late to overtake him. He checked the boards, made final adjustments, and extricated himself from the clutch of the go chair.

Aft, in the galley, he found Cookie, busy tallying stores. The little man looked up, said;

"You better get some rest, Cap. You look a little green. Feeling better?"

"Dial me up a thirty-eight ounce porterhouse, Space'n. That's how I feel."

"A gray Q-ration OK?" Cookie asked as he punched it in.

"Anything but a blue," Judson replied. "Space oysters just don't qualify as human food with me."

"I remember, Cap," Cookie said. "Just let me check that Pand Rand basal." He reached, took Judson's wrist and pressed the sensor against it.

"You're reading on the edge of pink, Cap," he told his boss. "Good show. I guess their dope's wearing off."

Judson sat down and looked the little fellow over.

"Cookie," Judson said carefully, "just how much do you know about the Foundation's operations and my midnight trip to St. Anne's?"

"Me, Cap?" the lone crewman blurted as if surprised. "You didn't look good, Cap. You keeled over right there on the grass, got a green stain on the elbow o' yer dress whites took me a hour to get out. Senator was pretty upset. Called in his own personal doc and who'm I to say no? Said they had this special unit working at St. Anne's. Just the ticket. Wanted to wait and take you in the senator's whirlygig, but I bluffed 'em and old Bette and me got you into the car and I taken you in myself. Acted like they knew what they was doing. Had you breathing good in about a half a minute. Said about taking you to that Rooshia to some Academy, but that's where I stuck a oar in. I called that head quack things I didn't know I knew. They kept shushing me. Seemed to me like they wanted to keep the whole thing quiet. That's how I got away from them. Had special cops, tried to put the arm on me, I give 'em a line about how everybody at home knowed where you was at, and got out. Thought it was best, Cap. Remember, you wasn't breathing good when I taken you in."

"You did fine, Cookie," Judson told the distressed chief.

"About the Foundation," Cookie resumed. "A couple fellers had on ID's said 'Future Foundation,' that's not the name you give the one you set up yerself, is it, Cap? Place's been took over. Thought they was OK, but seemed like they wanted to take you someplace on their own. I played like I'd he'p em, and soon's you were walking good, I foxed em and snuck you into a cargo lift, and then you foxed *me*. Slammed the door 'fore I could get in, and I took the ramp down-cellar and when your lift came along, you walked out and dern nigh busted my jaw." Cookie cradled his mandible gently in both hands. "Thought you was out on your feet, Cap, and taken yer arm, like, to he'p you over to the door, and next I know I'm flat onna deck. Couldn't find you, sir. Went back, and pretty soon you called in."

"I'm sorry, Cookie," Judson said. "I didn't know what I was doing. All I remember is being out in the street."

"Cap," the little man said earnestly, "what you got us into now? You really gonna try to con *Rocky* out to Oort Base, just the two of us?"

Judson shook his head. "I've got another idea, Cookie, maybe worse. You remember the brown dwarf we found last cruise?"

Cookie looked confused, and Judson reminded him of the occasion. "I have an idea," the captain confided, "that dwarf star once made a close pass at Sol, about four billion years ago. Dot and I ran the best numbers we could get through the big box, backtracked it. A near miss. It's an old-fashioned idea, but the planets had a father as well as a mother."

Confused, Cookie opened his mouth to speak, but Judson held up a hand. "Just a minute, Spac'n Murphy. We did an analysis. It seems that in such an encounter, Pa would have held onto most of the heavy matter; that's why we have mostly gas giant planets and an Oort Cloud. But Brownie should have heavy planets. We couldn't detect any—too much glare off Sirius, you know. She's right on the line-of-sight from Sol to the Big S. But, given planets with the same chemical composition as Mercury through Mars, there's a good chance one of those planets, if they exist, could be made to support life. I've waited to make the trip for a long time. That's why I never went public with the discovery. Now's the chance—but of course, you're not obligated to join in—"

"Skip that part, Cap, if you don't mind, sir," Cookie put in. "I'm signed on for the cruise, sir. Now, with the Cap'n's permission, I got work to do." He twisted to exit through the obstructed hatch.

7

Twenty hours later, having handily outstripped the lone DOL vessel that had attempted an intercept, Judson and his volunteer crewman wedged themselves into the relatively spacious, at six by six feet, galley and sat at the unhandy but necessary-for-morale table, then dialed-up and sipped hot coflet from old china cups, also contributory to a sense of well-being and relief from the stark utilitarianism of the rest of their tiny universe.

"Kinda pitiful," Cookie commented, "watching that cop-boat trying to herd *Rocky.*"

Judson nodded. "It's ironic," he remarked, "that I first knocked heads with the senator when I was lobbying for an adequate Observer Corps against his budget plan."

"I always wondered, Cap," the little man put in, "what got the Council down on you. At first, there was the invitation to address the Council, the reserve appointment as six-star admiral-general; all the media coverage was favorable—practically made you out another Lindy. Then the complaints, the court order closing the labs, the thing about monopoly and all—and fin'ly they went ahead and collectivized Prispace, even taken *Carny*—or tried to. Now you really done it, Cap. What you got in mind, running off like this? Oort Base wouldn't provision you even—" he broke off as Judson shook his head. "I know, you said You don't plan to ask 'em," Cookie resumed. "But, Cap, that's awful lonely space out there, trans-Pluto. You really think you can find a landfall?"

"I have a reasonable expectation, Cookie," Judson told him. "Frankly, if I hadn't been delirious—and if that Nurse Frunkle hadn't been hovering over me day and night—I'd probably never have tried it."

"Kind of a weird idea, Cap: Earthlike planets around this here Brownie. But you know more about that than I ever will."

"I expect you'll be pretty well-read on the subject, Cookie," Judson commented, "by the time we have our destination in view on the little screen."

"How long you figure, Cap?" Cookie queried casually. "Couple years, maybe?"

"Six years, minimum," Judson replied. "It's not going to be fun, Spac'n Murphy. You can take to a lifeboat now, if you like, and no hard feelings. You'll make it to Io Station in a few months."

Cookie shook his head. "Not me, Cap. I'm on for the cruise." Just then a shudder went through the ship, rattling the fittings on the panel. Both men glanced at B panel: *Rocky* had just destroyed a fractional megaton missile inside the one-hundred-yard perimeter.

"Old senator's mad," Cookie commented. "Won't quit, neither. Even if he has to chase you all the way to the Cloud."

Judson nodded. "But I'm the fellow who mapped the Passage into Judson's Division, Cookie; I'll bet he can't catch me there."

"What about clearing the Cloud, Otherside?" Cookie pressed. "Ain't never surveyed no Passage that side."

"There's always a first time, Cookie," Judson reminded the man. "Don't worry about that. Worry about whether we have enough stores aboard for the cruise."

Cookie nodded vigorously. "Already done that, Cap. We're stocked to A level with Class One: Council said they meant to use her to resupply Io, you know. Want me to rustle you up that thirty-eight porterhouse, five minutes on each side? And maybe a Beaujolais to go with it. Some o' that First Crop from Lunar Station."

"Save the wine, Cookie," Judson said. "Some day your great-grandchildren will sell it for a few billion."

It was a monotonous routine aboard ship, after the tenth day. Two more extreme-range missiles had been destroyed by the old vessel's automatic S and D gear.

"The senator can't afford much more of that," Cookie commented. "Them E-R fish will wreck the budget. Heard someplace they run over a trillion apiece."

"He's just grandstanding, Cookie," Judson told him. "The real strike will come as soon as we get within interdict range of Oort."

Cookie nodded. "That won't be long now, if they're on the ball with their long-range stuff."

"They will be," Judson assured him. "I estimate another ten hours until C-board picks up an incoming, probably a beam, from Outpost."

"Old *Rocky* equipped to handle the R stuff, Cap?"

Judson shook his head. "Not really. We'll have to rely on our detect-and-avoid capabilities. The beams were just coming on-line when *Rocky* was launched. We stuck in the D and A as an afterthought. We'll have to start bleeding-off some velocity soon, too."

It was nine hours. Both men aboard the antiquated vessel became aware simultaneously of the impingement of the shaped-wave energies known in the more sensational media as a disruptor beam. Photons cannot exceed the limiting velocity, but a sinusoid Fourier transform imposed on the beam can travel as rapidly as it likes, being an immaterial pattern. Its immediate effect was to engender a profound sense of malaise in the protoplasm of the men in its field.

"Me, puke?" Cookie muttered and hurried away to do so. Judson got to the duty officer's cubicle and into the snugly-woven launch pocket before consciousness faded.

8

"Cap!" Cookie's frantic voice cut through a vari-colored haze where Judson had been wandering for a long time now, searching for . . . what . . . ? Then he heard the voice faint and far away; he struggled toward it. It was Spac'n Murphy. He sounded upset. Judson tried to speak, to reassure his shipmate. Must be in deep trouble, he thought numbly, to sound that worried.

"That's right, Cap!" Cookie urged. "C'mon, say something! Yer heart's going good again. You'll be OK, Cap. I can't handle it out here all alone!"

"Take it easy, Cookie," Judson snapped, amazed at the man's insistent nonsense. He slipped, almost fell, heard the dry croak he uttered, and decided to get hold of himself before he scared poor Cookie worse. "It's . . . all . . . right . . . Murphy," he said carefully.

"That's it, Cap!" Cookie yelled. "I heard you say 'Murph' real good. Now breathe again, OK?"

"You talk as if I wasn't breathing, dammit!" Judson barked, then realized that no sound had emerged from his dry throat. He tried again, heard, "I'm alive," almost clearly.

"Course ye'r alive, Cap," Cookie came back, sounding more cheerful. "Yer too tough to die on me. So quit clowning and breathe!"

Judson worked on his breathing, felt air move in his throat. He tried to brush away some encumbrance on his face, but felt his arm grabbed and held.

"Let that breather be, Cap," Cookie pled. "You got to have it right now. I'll take it off soon's yer breathing good."

It was too much trouble to protest, Judson decided quite consciously. Whatever was happening, Spac'n Murphy would take care of it. Now he could rest. He decided to take a deep breath, felt something break and spill boiling-hot fluid over his chest. The sensation faded and he got interested in the rhythmic counterplay of his diaphragm and intercostals, which alternately expanded his lungs, causing air to rush in, and compressed them, pushing the used air back out. Time passed. It was rather pleasant, drifting here in space in his cozy cocoon, all alone in the vastness, rushing toward the distant ice-clumps of the Oort. . . .

He opened his eyes, saw a glint of light nearby, and simultaneously became aware of pain, pain that burned in his body like hot needles, that lanced through him like a spear, that beat in his head like hammers. He heard a groan, which went on and on. . . .

He tried to tell Cookie about it, but Cookie wasn't there. He had been beside him before, but now he was gone. With an effort like putting the capstone on Cheops' pyramid single-handedly, Judson opened both eyes. A crudely lettered note was in front of him. Judson squinted and tried to read it:

Captain, sir, I got to get for'd to A deck now. We been taking some flack, space-junk, I'm pretty sure, but I got—

The input face of a command talker, apparently removed from an A-suit, dangled from its wires beside the note. Judson cleared his throat, eliciting a stab of pain, then said carefully, "Cookie, I think I'm awake now. Get me out of here."

He was pretty sure his voice had worked, and a moment later, Cookie's voice crackled from the output face: "On my way, Cap! Be ten minutes; I was just leaving when I heard the talker."

It seemed to Judson that a very long time passed before light abruptly flooded the compartment and Cookie's monkeylike face hove into view.

". . . knew you could do it, Cap. 'Dead,' the readout said. But you *can't* be dead, Cap. I threw in the emergency life-support circuit and right away you tried to blink. Knew you'd be OK, then. Had us a tough run, Cap. Funny, except for a couple passes with that disruptor thing, all we had was a few old-timey converts the junk-busters handled easy. Must be that admiral pal o' yours, Coign, ain't on the ball."

"Quite the opposite, Cookie," Judson croaked. His throat felt as if it were lined with dry cornhusks. "Goldie let us through. Now he'll never make vice admiral. Good man, Goldie."

"Yessir," Cookie agreed. "Got to get some nutrients into you now, the medic box said. First, I'll get you to yer quarters, like *you* said."

Later, after the exhausting trek, half carried, half dragged by the wiry little cook, Judson lay in his bunk and attempted to organize his confused impressions of what had happened after the first disruptor beam had made contact. Cookie stayed nearby, talking excitedly.

"It was like a EMS at first," the cook said. "After I come unfed, I felt awful, and so did *Rocky*, Cap. None o' the E-gear worked. They coulda took us then. You was the worst. Got the diagnostic gear on you and it said you's dead." Cookie paused to snort. "After a while, we all felt better, and I started tryna get you to wake up, and you did. No flack from Oort Station since then. Reckon they think we're done for."

"Space'n Murphy," Judson said carefully, "do you know about Judson Station?"

"Sure, Cap," Cookie responded. "I was wondering—"

"Can you conn her in there, alone?" Judson cut him off.

"Don't you remember, Cap?" Cookie urged. "I was with you the time we stocked her as a Class One depot. I don't even need to look up the numbers. Never forget that trip, dodging icebergs all the way."

"I remember, Cookie," Judson reassured his crewman. *Not my "crewman,"* he reflected. *My crew.*

"I was wondering, Cap, if maybe that's where you had in mind to go," Cookie chattered on. "Old O-station'll be pretty startled when we just drop off their screens."

Judson glanced at the chronometer mounted on the bulkhead that held the repeater board. "Time to start the MCM, Space'n," he said. "We have to cut this close. We need to use the clutter to screen us; that means plenty of sub-D impacts. Just don't allow any over the D-line."

Cookie nodded emphatically. "You got it, Cap'n, sir," he said, and backed out of view.

9

In the next three hours, Judson forced himself to stay where he was; resting, at least physically. From time to time, watching the repeater board, he used the talker to give Cookie a suggestion, but in the main the spunky little spacecook managed on his own, vectoring the vessel, now barely creeping at sub-Einsteinian velocity, along the crooked lane of Judson's Passage to the old Station, never completed and thus never reported to AutoSpace. Judson was up and ready when Cookie's exultant report came over the squawk-box: "*Mission accompli*, Cap'n!"

Judson Station was a standard cargo pod, converted for use as a "remount station," as Cookie, who was fond of ancient westerns, liked to call it. Inconspicuous among rock-and-ice masses of comparable size, it drifted close to the Passage, a naturally-occurring corridor of irregular and constantly-shifting form, which, however, was constrained by complex gravitational forces to retain its basic configuration. Judson docked *Rocky III* to the artifact, which was almost as massive as the ship itself. The two men transferred to the Station, enjoying the relative spaciousness, and after running a cursory inventory and equipment check, Judson went to the inspection blister and examined *Rocky*'s exterior for any damage not apparent to the ship's own internal sensors, and to his surprise found all shipshape.

"Tough old bitch," Cookie commented, and pointed out to his captain that dinner was served in the "main lounge," a reference to the cramped personnel chamber. They then indulged in the luxury of a sonobath and clean clothing.

"Bring on the super-dreadnoughts, Cap," Cookie proclaimed. "In a clean set o' skivvies, I'm ready for em!"

"Not too loud," Judson suggested. "They could swat us like a fly, if they thought to look for us in the Passage."

"But they won't, Cap'n, sir," Cookie reminded his chief, " 'cause you was cagey to not mention it to 'em."

"I wasn't being cagey," Judson objected mildly. "At the time it seemed like a personal matter; didn't think anybody would care."

"So we're in the clear," Cookie concluded.

"We could be picked up by a standard detector field."

"But they's no AutoSpace personnel out here to have the idea," Cookie mentioned. "Too dangerous, remember? So what are we waiting for, Cap?"

"That's a big jump, Cookie, from the Cloud to Brownie; lots of very empty space out there, and no fire escape, no return. We'll exhaust our reaction-mass accelerating away from the vicinity of Oort Station."

Cookie nodded, his grin somewhat faded. "If you say so, Cap'n, sir," he commented.

"We need all the acceleration available to make the voyage in our lifetimes," Judson explained. "Even then, it will take a lot of luck. I'm going to use the rotational energy of the Cloud for a boost. That means we'll have to work our way out to the fringe of the Cloud without attracting any attention from Base."

The latter maneuver took two ship-days in increments of one millisecond of arc, after the precise numbers had been divulged by the big box. Then Judson fired-up the coil and *Rocky* hurtled outward at a minor angle to the ecliptic at a velocity of over point-nine light.

Shipboard routine fully occupied the time of the two fugitives. After one ship-month, the dim spark that was Brownie had emerged sufficiently from the glare of Sirius to be discerned as a separate body.

"Don't look like much," Cookie commented when Judson showed him the spark which was their destination on the printout. "Reckon that little old star will be hot enough to do any good, if we *do* find a planet?" he queried dubiously.

"It depends on the distance, Cookie," Judson pointed out. "At a half AU, surface temperatures ought to be in the Terra-normal range. I'm still looking for a planet. We can't observe any perturbation of Brownie yet. But I think we'll find it's there. We need a few weeks' run out-system to clear the Sirius-glare enough to see detail."

10

"It's been a ship-month since we lost the last traffic from Lunabase," Cookie remarked one day. "Good thing we got the A-list library aboard. I'm getting real interested in wave mechanics, Cap. Lots o' interesting stuff if a feller had time to read all of it—and time we got. Whatta *you* think about Crumblnsky's Hypothesis, Cap?"

"I never got past Schömburg," Judson admitted. "When time stands still, and distance is zero, how can you talk about velocity, which is distance over time?"

"Well, Cap, the way I see it is, we got to try not to put it in terms of Euclidian space/time. I mean, at those high sub-C velocities, space and time are the same, so it's like tryna measure the mass of a year, say."

"Time does hang a little heavy, Cookie," Judson remarked. "And it's all relative, anyway. Who's to say, in an absolute sense, whether we're moving relative to space, or it's moving relative to us?"

"Not me," Cookie acknowledged.

"Einstein postulated a Cosmological Constant," Judson ruminated aloud. "A finagle factor to make his equations come out right: a repulsive force between masses which increases with distance. He made it up, but consider this: In deep space, suppose you have two featureless masses, connected by a cable, rotating around their common center. There'll be tension in the cable—centrifugal force, tending to throw the masses away from each other. But suppose you consider that the 'fabric of space' is in rotation, and the masses are stationary. Then you have a repulsive force between the masses which increases with the length of the cable; that is, the distance between masses. The rate of rotation of space/time required to produce the observed centrifugal force is very, very low. It hasn't yet completed one revolution since the Big Bang."

Cookie was silent for a while. Then he inquired, "Cap, you heard o' the Wizard of Oz. Did you know there was more than just the one book about Oz? About forty or so, most of 'em wrote by a lady, after old Baum died. I been reading them books, Cap. That's the kinda place I'd like to live in, Cap. I don't mean all the magic and witches and stuff, I mean the easy, kind of friendly way folks act. They ain't hustling nobody, except o' course old Ruggedo, and Mombie the bad witch, and even *they* don't ruin things. Ever'body's happy in Oz. Maybe, if we make it, and find a new world, we could make it like that. You think maybe, Cap? Could folks live together and like each other? Ever'body'd like that. Why didn't we do it?"

"It's a dream worth having, Space'n Murphy," Judson replied. "Let's start by forgetting all about AutoSpace and the Council and the senator, and just concentrating on what's ahead for us."

"Folks never die in Oz," Cookie remarked. "Don't hardly see how that could work out. Place'd be full o' ever'body's ancestors."

"Space," Judson told him. "The excess population settles new worlds, and *more* people are always needed."

Cookie grinned. "That's what you said all along, Cap!" he exulted. "I reckon maybe we're on to something!"

It was late in the following watch that Judson observed Brownie and found the small star was now clear of the primary glare of Sirius, so far beyond the dwarf.

By naked-eye (well, almost) observation on the DV screen a large planet was at once obvious. Cookie's excitement died after he had studied the new find for a moment.

"Too big, Cap," he remarked. "Surface G would squash *Rocky* flat."

"Big box says fifty percent more massive than Jupe," Judson told him. "And it's emitting more heat than it's receiving from Brownie. It's almost a second sun in the system."

"Scratch one planet," Cookie commented glumly. "We got to find another one. Must be more'n just the one planet, Cap, don't you think?"

A few hours' examination of the system, with steadily improving resolution as the apparent angular displacement of Brownie from Sirius increased, revealed a major satellite of Big Boy, and three lesser planets, closer to Brownie: Eenie, Meenie, and Miney. They called the large moon "Junior."

"Looks hopeful, don't it, Cap?" Cookie suggested anxiously. "Them three smaller planets could be about the right distance from old Brownie, dim like it is. And even that moon of Big Boy, you s'pose?"

Within the hour Judson altered course to head directly toward the Brownie system. The dim sun grew steadily on the screens, some sunspot detail becoming apparent on the third day.

"You don't think she's too unstable, do you, Cap?" Cookie worried. "The spots'll be throwing out plenty o' the hard stuff."

"Big Box says no," Judson reassured him. "At one AU, about where Miney is, conditions solar-wind–wise are down to Earth-normal. Out near Boy, it's peaceful. No Northern Lights there."

"Eenie and Meenie are still possibles, I guess," Cookie offered, "but someways I'm liking Boy's moon better'n Miney, even."

"That's my thinking, too, Space'n Murphy," Judson agreed. "It means we'll have to adjust to two suns in the sky, both dim. But maybe it won't be much different from moonlight."

"I can stand that, Cap," Cookie assured his chief. "Think about it, Cap! If old Big's moon is as good as it looks—we got a whole world to ourselfs! Prolly got life a lot like home—"

"Don't count on it." Judson cut off the little man's enthusiasm. "Just as likely to be like Mars, or Venus. Maybe worse."

"We'll see," Cookie muttered.

"I just don't want you to be too disappointed," Judson soothed. "As we get closer, we can begin to gather some data. Then we'll know."

11

It was a long, tedious voyage, but never really boring, as the Solar System dwindled to a mere star, seen from a distance AutoSpace's probes had never penetrated. And ahead, Brownie grew more distinct on the parallax screen, and at last was picked up by the high-resolution nav sensors.

"She's just a little bigger than Sol," Judson noted, "and puts out a flux only about ten percent lower. It looks good."

"Old Big's an ice giant," Cookie commented. "But her moon's only one-point-three Earth-mass. The Gs will be a little heavy, but tolerable. We'll get us some big muscles, Cap, working in that."

Judson nodded. "I make it sixty degrees Centrigrade at high noon at the middle latitudes of Junior. Plenty of water, too. One big continent, the rest is sea."

"We better be careful where we set *Rocky* down, Cap," Cookie offered. "Prolly won't be able to move her in that G."

"I'm looking at the big plain near the West Mountains," Judson told his crewman.

"Prolly a lot like Nebraska, where I grew up," Cookie reasoned. "Only no bison, I guess."

"That was great dinosaur country a few hundred million years ago," Judson pointed out. "Let's hope we miss that stage—if there's any life at all."

"I know, Cap," Cookie griped. "Prolly nothing but bare rock down there. But it's more fun to think about green grass and shade trees, and maybe a bison or two after all."

"We'll know in a few weeks," Judson said, and was surprised at the curious sensation he felt below his rib cage at the thought. *Fear?* he wondered to himself, *or just excitement . . . ?*

Cookie spoke up. "Idear scares me, someways, Cap. Lord knows I want to get my feet on solid dirt again and breathe air ain't been in a can, but . . . there's so much at stake here. Like about the future, like you was saying. I wisht we was already there, down and safe."

And a month later they were. At a half-million miles, the broad plain the two explorers had named Nebraska had showed an albedo consistent with grasslands. They picked a spot near the convergence of two rivers of liquid H_2O. Air samples revealed an O_2 content of fifty percent, with the rest nitrogen, CO_2, and inert trace gases.

"Made to order, Cap," Cookie said contentedly. "Figures: made out of the same gas cloud as Sol and the System. Reckon old Brownie and Sol started out as a double star, and in those early times when everything was a lot closer together, something come along and split 'em up, sent Brownie out here. Brownie got a set o' planets outa the deal, just like Sol did. Then the biggest one broke up and made Big Boy and its satellite. That's how I dope it. Figures, don't it, Cap? And starting with the same raw materials, life had to cook just like it done back home."

The two men went eagerly to the DV screen for their first look at their new home—or grave.

"All I can say at this point, Murph," Judson commented, after a glance at the grassy plain, on which they had come to rest, "is that it looks that way. Once started up, it's reasonable that life took a similar course, because that's the only course it *could* take. We happen to have arrived at the 'vast-grassland' stage, like our own early Pleistocene. Should be plenty of game out there."

"You reckon we'll find something we can *eat*?" Cookie hoped aloud.

"Life on Earth developed as it did because it had to," Judson stated. "The same rules have to apply here. Local plant and animal tissues *could* be assimilable."

"If you're right, Cap," Murphy responded, "and I believe you are, it's not one chance in a zillion—it's a dead cinch! Let's go *out* and see."

Judson restrained the little man's eagerness. "This is what's known as a historic occasion, Space'n," he said quietly. "Comparable to Columbus setting foot in the West Indies," he went on. "We owe it to posterity to record the event." He activated the scan-and-record equipment covering the personnel hatch, then cycled it open. Daylight flooded in.

Cookie leaned forward and drew a deep breath. "Smells like Spring, Cap," he remarked and collapsed, almost falling down the ramp.

Judson caught the limp body and lifted it gently to the bench against the bulkhead, and a moment later had brought over the "noser," which only a few months before had been restowed after Cookie had used it on his captain. Now it was the cheerful little man himself who lay, his mouth half-open, breathing noisily but steadily, while the captain set the control for the patient's body weight and attached the sensors to forehead, chest, and tongue. The apparatus hummed and winked, then spelled out: *D. Body has inhaled a complex alkaloid of unknown structure; Rx: supply pure* O_2 *at ambient t and p.*

Judson quickly followed instructions, placing the oxygen mask on the small, monkeyish face. Cookie immediately stirred, made feeble motions with both hands and feet, then sat up, pulled away the mask, glanced at Judson and remarked:

"You here, too, Cap? What happened? Musta been fast to get the both of us that way." Then he looked around, frowned, and added, "Naw, this here is *Rocky*, Cap. Must of been some kinda dream."

He stood, shakily, and glanced out the open port, into the noonday glare. "Look out, Cap. Smells good out there, but I think there's something fishy . . ."

Judson took the small man's arm, urged him to sit. "You passed out, Space'n," he told the bewildered man. "Scared me. You said something about smelling the flowers, and—dropped in your tracks."

Cookie was shaking his head, "Naw, Cap, not me. I seen all them blue flars and went down to smell 'em better, and then I was flying. I can really do it, Cap," he enthused, avoiding Judson's grab to get to his feet again. "All you got to do is . . ." He hesitated. ". . . get yer mind right, arch yer back a little, and just lean into it." He leaned, and Judson caught his arm.

"Easy, Space'n," he said. "You got a good whiff of the local air, and went on some kind of trip."

"How long, Cap?" Cookie inquired earnestly. "I was flying for hours, seen Junior set and Brownie come up, kinda dirty red. Grass looked black. I come to this city, all lit up, deep twilight, it was, with just Brownie in the sky. Stars, Cap. Lots o' stars. Wonder if one was Sol? Coulda flew there . . ." The man's voice trailed off. "Guess I'm talking crazy, Cap, talking about flying—but it was *real*, Cap. I remember."

"We'll have to be a little more careful, Space'n," Judson told him. "Walking out there as if we were the last to arrive for the class picnic wasn't too smart. You got off easy. Now, you'd better get to your quarters and sleep it off. I've got work to do."

"It was great, Cap," Cookie moaned. "Just floated along, all I had to do was think, *I wanna go that way*, and there I was."

"It must be powerful stuff," Judson replied. "Let's hope it's not addictive."

Cookie, who had been edging toward the open hatch, turned away abruptly. "Naw," he said. "I ain't hot to try it again, right away. But it *was* fun, Cap, you'll see."

"We've got breathing masks in stores," Judson reminded his crewman. "Use one of these sample cases"—he indicated the racked equipment on the bulkhead by the exit hatch—"and get me a two-liter specimen of the local air. I'll run the analysis, and set up the masks. When you're rested, we'll go out."

"I'm all right, now, Cap," Cookie protested. "No need to wait—"

"That's an order, Space'n," Judson snapped.

Cookie said, "Aye, sir," and went about his job. Judson took the air specimen to the tiny lab area and soon isolated one cc of colorless, odorless gas of complex structure that failed to match any in the analyzer's memory. Its closest resemblance was to the psychoactive component of an extract from a substance refined from the truffle-relative used by Australian aborigines in their Dream Time ceremonies. Judson recorded it, filed the specimen, and went aft to inspect the scout car, which was a standard item of equipment on every deep-space hull of his design. It was a four-wheel-*cum*-air-cushion unit, with a single centerline cleated track; it had a full persplex canopy, seats for two, three-sixty trideo recording gear, and a 5-mm swivel gun. The gauges showed full charge on all energy cells.

Judson patted the prow of the brilliant-orange-painted car and spent the next half-hour studying the outside view on the DV screen in the hold. He saw the heavenly-blue blossoms, something like wild iris, he thought, spreading in a solid mass for hundreds of feet in every direction; beyond, tall, deep-green grass extended to a remote line of forest. At high mag, the trees were revealed to have thick, sharply tapering white-to-pale-green trunks and bushy chartreuse tops, like giant celery stalks. Across the grasslands, bright-colored patches were scattered here and there—more flowers, Judson decided, no two patches of the same color. A few isolated trees of more conventional appearance made pools of black shade here and there. Altogether a beautiful landscape, Judson decided. There was no visible evidence of animal life. Cookie came in, looking ruffled and anxious rather than rested.

"Looks OK, Cap," he commented after a cursory glance at the screen. "Air's OK, and no dinosaurs, so what are we waiting for?

"Funny thing, Cap," he added a moment later. "When I was flying, I seen roads."

"Did you see the rivers?" Judson responded calmly. "I meant to put her down close to the main branch, but I don't see it now—unless it's beyond the trees."

"Sure, Cap," Cookie reassured his commander. "Seen the two of 'em, converge just past the trees yonder like you figured."

Judson opened the cargo hatch, drew his first breath of (filtered) local air, and started up the car. Cookie took his place in the co-driver's seat; Judson adjusted seats and shock-frames, and eased the vehicle, on wheels only, down the ramp. At the foot Cookie climbed out to inspect the ground. He walked around, heedlessly trampling the beautiful blues, as they had named the azure blossoms, and declared the surface suitable.

They first drove in a wide arc around the ship, which Judson had put down in the vertical docking attitude. The air was clear, the sky cloudless, the ground firm and smooth.

"Probably an old floodplain," Judson decided.

"Or an old sea-floor," Cookie suggested.

"Which way was that road?" Judson inquired. Cookie pointed. Judson gunned the speedy car toward what he had arbitrarily designated as west, after setting the inertial compass. They hummed along, observing, successively, after leaving the area of beautiful blues, half-mile-wide patches of magenta, yellow, pink, and tangerine-colored flowers, all of the same irislike form and size, but strictly demarcated by hue. The grass was uniformly tall and deep green, showing no indication of ever having been traversed before by any living creature.

Once abreast of the turning of the long belt of celery-trees, Judson steered west by north for half an hour, then pulled into the black shade of a patriarchal elm-like tree standing alone. He popped the canopy, and the two men climbed down to stretch their legs in a normal G-field for the first time in many months.

"Not bad, Cap," Cookie remarked. "Not more'n ten percent heavier. Feels good."

"I'll race you to the pink patch," Judson replied, and dug off, Cookie complaining at his heels.

"Cap," Cookie said, when he caught his breath, "you know, you must be feeling better; you *look* better. You couldn't've run like that the night I picked you up at Headquarters."

"I feel fine, Space'n," Judson replied shortly. "I was spooked," he added. "When I overheard those medics talking about how I was dying, I believed it. That'll make you sick, Cookie. Don't ever believe you're dying. I've got an idea," he warmed to the subject, "that's what people die of. The Bible says 'three score and ten,' and so, after seventy years, people expect to die and they do. Now, look over there, Cookie." Judson pointed to the apparent termination of the distant line of trees. "I have a hunch the trees curve away to the north, instead of ending. Maybe they follow the river. Let's go look."

12

The trees, of mixed species at this point, the celery-trees tall and top-heavy, others low and gnarly, did indeed curve away. Judson drove up to the edge of the deep-shaded and predominantly deep-green woods, and they looked into its interior. There was little underbrush; shadowy aisles, splashed here and there with brilliant daylight, led back into intriguing vistas of primeval forest.

"Looks like a fellow could drive right through," Cookie commented, studying a broad passage that curved away toward the presumed direction of the river.

"Wonder if the river will turn out to be H_2O," Judson said. "Let's go find out." He steered the car, now on air-cushion and blowing up fallen leaves in a cloud, into the inviting opening at hand. Deep shadows closed over them, but there was sufficient diffused light to steer by.

At close hand, they saw that the trees were all smooth-barked and that the green leaves looked more like kelp than like any terrestrial tree.

The sound of the air filters changed, became deeper and more labored. Judson checked gauges. "Heavy pollen count," he noted. "We'll have to clear the filters." He paused to activate the automatic system that did so. A puff of brownish dust *whoof!*ed from the discharge stack. At once, nearby boughs stirred, some to dip their wet-looking leaves into the dissipating dust-cloud, others to shrink away, as if avoiding contamination. One low-sweeping branch brushed across the transparent canopy and whipped aside as if scalded. A drooping vine twitched, oriented its broad leaves to form a parabolic dish aimed at the car, and seemed to wait.

Judson studied the big-leaved plant; its glossy red stem, studded with two-inch black thorns, seemed to quiver with eagerness. *For what?* he wondered. On impulse, he tapped the button that would equalize air pressure in the car's pneumatic tires. The dish swiveled instantly to aim at the nearest wheel, the right front, then at the left front, then at each rear wheel in turn, after which it seemed to droop minutely; then it whipped its thorny tendrils around, over, and down at all four wheels simultaneously. Indicated tire-pressure dropped instantly to zero, and the car settled on its wide centerline track. Cookie had leapt back as the vine made its unheralded attack; he relaxed as it withdrew, reassuming its "alert" posture. Judson switched on the top-mounted searchlight and directed its beam to the center of the dish; the dish folded inward and was a randomly-oriented mass of drooping leaves again.

"Try the tight-talker, Cap," Cookie suggested. Judson nodded, switched off the light, and waited.

It took the vine a full minute to deploy its dish again. Judson gave it a kilowatt of low-frequency noise. The dish redefined itself, held steady. Abruptly, the in-talker crackled and emitted a tone, a deep, resonant *bonngg!*

"It's answering," Cookie said in an awestruck voice. "What'll we try next, Cap?"

In reply, Judson picked up the hand talker and spoke into it, slowly and distinctly: "Dit-dit-dit; dit-dit-dit-dit; dit-dit-dah."

Cookie looked at him in puzzlement.

The in-talker said, "Dit-di-dit; dah-dah."

"What'd it say?" the crewman asked. "That's that Morris Code, ain't it, Cap? Where'd it learn that, you think?"

"It didn't. Garbage; it's trying to imitate our cries, that's all."

"You mean it's intelligent?" Cookie demanded incredulously.

"Just mimicry," Judson replied, "like a myna bird."

"Let's get outa here, Cap, sir," Cookie offered. "Every time I start to thinking it's homey here, something spooky happens."

"My feeling precisely," Judson replied, and backed off a few yards, then steered through underbrush to give the sensitive vine a wide berth. He resumed the trail and gunned ahead toward the full sunlight gleaming between tree boles ahead.

"Looky there, Cap," Cookie exclaimed, pointing at the screen. "That's the river, all right!"

"Calmly, Space'n," Judson chided. "After all, a river is only a river."

"Sure, but—if it's water—well, we're gonna need water, Cap. Only got six tons aboard."

"Beside which," Judson came back, "you happen to like boating, and wouldn't be above wetting a line, either."

"You think we'll find us a fish-camp or like that, Cap?"

"Not quite, Cookie," Judson answered gently. "But if there are any autochthones, they'll have settlements by the water—even if they don't need to drink it, which I doubt; a river provides free transport and communications."

"So you think the river will be water, and the local life will depend on water. Right, Cap?"

"It seems reasonable," Judson assented. "Give a cloud of atoms like the one from which the Solar System aggregated, it follows that water will be fairly abundant, more so than any other fluid, except possibly petroleum. Water's an excellent medium for biochemistry, and any life that's compelled by the laws of nature to appear will make use of it. But we'll know in a few minutes."

Without any perceptible preliminary thinning, the forest ended and the car shot out of shadows into full sunlight on vivid grass. The river lay a hundred yards ahead, its surface choppy, sparkling with reflected starlight.

"Let's just call it sunlight, Cap," Cookie suggested. "From now on, this is our sun; this and Brownie."

" 'Sunlight' for Junior, and 'starlight' for Brownie," Judson proposed.

Cookie nodded. "How long before star-rise, Cap?" he asked.

"Junior will set in two hours, and Brownie rises a few minutes later."

"Neat," Cookie commented. "Just like it was planned."

"Only at this latitude and this time of year and month," Judson pointed out. "I ran it all through Big Box before I picked our touchdown site."

"Sure, Cap," Cookie reassured his chief. "I was only kidding, like. But it *is* pretty neat. This here sunlight is a lot like a eclipse; I was in one when I was a kid. How bright will Brownie look, Cap? Not too hot, I hope."

"Very red," Judson replied. "Like a gaudy sunset; it will blank out the Junior-light pretty well, but we'll have a slight double-shadow effect."

Judson had eased the car forward to the low bluff that edged the river. After a few minutes of inspection and discussion, the two men suited-up, popped the hatch, and climbed out for their first direct experience of the brand-new planet, where, they realized, they would spend the rest of their lives, unless by some miracle they found a supply of reaction-mass in micropulverized form to feed the big helix aboard ship.

"Cap," Cookie said fervently, "I kind of like it. C'mon, let's check out the river." He sealed his breather and jumped in.

Judson had already determined, using the analytical scanner aboard the car, that the river was indeed water.

The ambient temperature was seventeen degrees Celsius, and Cookie, cavorting in the flowing stream, reported it "just right."

After some discussion of pros and cons, Judson agreed that the little cook could safely swim for a few minutes.

"Loverly, Cap!" he reported. "Slight smell o' peppermint, but otherwise just like a mountain stream."

Judson cautioned him to avoid swallowing any of the strange water. "The analyzer's not sensitive enough to pick up trace elements at a distance," he reminded the gaily splashing Cookie, "so don't ingest even a drop."

"I mighta already swallowed a few, Cap," Cookie replied, unworried. "It's just regular water."

"Which way was that city, Space'n?" Judson asked his lone crewman. Cookie stood in hip-deep water and pointed upstream. "Right at the fork, Cap," he reported. "You should be able to see it from here: less'n a mile, blue towers and all."

"Let's go take a look," Judson suggested. The stream side trees, he noted, ended abruptly, with only two more, widely-spaced in sight. When Cookie was back aboard, Judson moved the car along the river's edge to the shade of the first, or second-to-last, tree. The grass was shorter here, though of the same deep green. There were no vines growing on the glossy blue-green trunk and branches. The plate-sized leaves stirred slightly, but formed no parabolic dish. Cookie was eager to get out and inspect the tree more closely.

"Might be some good timber there, Cap," he commented. "That straight trunk'd make us some clean twenty-footers. Prolly some nice color in the wood, too. S'pose it's blue like the bark, Cap?"

"No, bright orange," Judson said. "Look there"—he pointed—"where there's a chip of bark missing."

"That what that is? I thought it was just a orange patch in the skin. But yer right, sir. Blue bark and orange wood. Boy, you know my hobby's wood working, Cap. Got my shop set up in the aft lazaret, you remember, sir. Can't wait to cut up a slab o' that B and O tree."

"If we're going to be naming things, Cookie," Judson said, "let's give it some thought. This river, for example: what shall we name it?"

Cookie frowned. "Well, lessee, Cap. Guess we better give it a name that fits it. How about 'the Nonestic'? That's a ocean in them books about Oz I was telling you."

" 'The Nonestic River,' " Judson repeated. "Sounds fine to me. How about some lunch?"

"Wonder if a feller could catch him a fish in that river . . . ?" Cookie remarked. "Anyways, for now we got to stick to our H-rations. I loaded *Chicken Française;* that suit you, sir?"

They climbed out, and in the shade of the tree, beside the Nonestic, they ate their first meal on the new world. The air was sweet, the breeze gentle.

"I'd say we come up smelling like a gallon jug o' *Nuit de Juin,*" Cookie commented, chewing thoughtfully. "Only thing is, it *can't* be this good. We better keep a couple o' sharp eyes out."

"We'll proceed in a space'n-like manner, Mr. Murphy," Judson told the little man. "So far, so good. To the north, you said."

"The city, you mean." Cookie nodded. "But, Cap, it was only a trip—I mean, you said so yerself. Something in the air . . ."

Judson nodded back. "Just playing a hunch, Cookie. Let's take a look."

Using the air-cushion now, Judson drove slowly along the high bank, studying the exposed strata on the far side.

"My guess is, this is like the Grand Canyon, seven million years ago," he remarked. "The floodplain or old sea-bottom we're on is being uplifted, and the stream is cutting deeper. That exposed sediment across there doesn't look terribly old; the uplift is in its early stages."

"Jeez, Cap," Cookie commented. "I never did get that plate tectonic stuff. Planet must be pretty Earth-like if it's going on here, too."

"There are similarities," Judson conceded. "But we mustn't expect too much."

"I expect a herd o' dinosaurs any minute," Cookie returned. "Gotta be *some*thing wrong here."

Judson shook his head. "No, the dinosaur phase would be long past. But no time yet for the rise of an intelligent life-form. We hit it just right, Space'n."

"*If* the Captain's right about evolution being the same here, begging the Captain's pardon," Cookie said in mock humility; then, "Look there, Cap. The other river's joining. Look at the whitecaps. We got to have some pretty seaworthy boats to navigate the waters here, Cap."

"We'll build them, Cookie," Judson reassured him. "Now, look at that natural harbor just above the confluence," Judson urged. "Backed up by a plain big enough for a city of a few million. Represents an earlier level of the river; must have been an interruption in the uplift."

"We'd be mighty lonesome in a town that size with only us in it, Cap," Cookie mourned.

"Notice how the bluff curves back and rises," Judson contributed. "Natural defenses, even."

"Against who?" Cookie wanted to know.

"Nobody, I hope," Judson told him. "But it's better to be ready just in case."

"You think big, Cap," Cookie said. "Already got a war going, and we ain't even met anyone yet. But," he nodded, "thinking big is what made Private Space big enough to challenge AutoSpace and make it stick. Come to think of it, if them damn bureaucrats trace us out here, we might need a fort sooner'n we think."

"They'll be here," Judson told Cookie. "But not for some time, I think. Even after they find Brownie, they'll expect us to have gone for Eenie or Meenie, as more likely habitable."

"Yeah, we foxed 'em, Cap," Cookie agreed. "Or *you* did. I wondered why you was so strong for this big old moon, when we had heavy planets to choose from."

"This isn't getting a city built," Judson pointed out. "We'd better start with a couple of huts."

"So the big city I seen *was* just a dream?" Cookie guessed.

Judson nodded. "So it seems; but maybe we can make it come true."

"Now yer talking, Cap!" Cookie enthused. "With what we got under the hatches, there's nothing we can't build." He paused and looked thoughtful. "*If* we got the natural resources, here," he added dubiously. "We better find us some mountains, Cap, and a iron mine or two—and some coal, too. Remember, we got to go back to primitive technology. Our little high-tech stash can't stretch too far."

Judson was studying the graceful B and O tree arching its branches over them. He put a hand on a satin-smooth bole. "I propose a precedent," he said seriously. "We respect the life we find here; we don't cut down trees for their timber, for example."

Cookie glanced up at the foliage above. "Right, Cap. Too purty to cut down anyways.

"Instead of building our huts out here on the plain," he went on, "what say we find some caves in the cliff over there?"

"There should be some," Judson agreed. "Underground water always finds a way to flow downhill, and carves cave systems when it does."

It was a leisurely five-minute drive across the smooth grassland to the cliff-face. They halted a hundred yards from the vertical rise; boulders fallen from above blocked the way.

"No glaciers here," Judson commented. "These rocks have never been tumbled and worn. No striation in the bedrock." He indicated the exposed stratum at their feet.

Cookie nodded. "A glacier'd of come down the river valley," he pointed out. "Ground rises to the north. Woulda swept up all this." He indicated with a sweep of his arm the thickly-dotted field of broken stone.

"Cyclic glaciers on a planetwide scale are a peculiarity of Earth," Judson pointed out. "The precise combination of factors required is bound to be rare. There are ice-worlds, of course, like some of the Sol System's outer moons, but alternation of temperature and arctic conditions over half a planet can't occur very frequently. And Junior is free of that problem. Her ozone layer looks good, and water distribution seems to be adequate. No deserts that were visible from orbit, not even at the poles."

"Looks like we found ourselves a winner, Cap," Cookie said. He looked around at the halcyon landscape, up at the scudding clouds in the deep blue sky. "Good to know He's here, too," he commented reverently.

"Don't worry, Space'n," Judson replied. " 'Infinite' and 'omniscient' aren't limited. Let's get busy."

They unloaded the car's go-cart, an electric-powered three-wheel affair, and got aboard. Judson delegated the driving to Cookie, who, he knew, loved operating the little vehicle. "Just remember, we're not in the Recpark," he cautioned. "Take it slow and easy."

"Jeez, Cap," Cookie complained. "You ain't gonna backseat drive, are you?"

"Absolutely," Judson replied, "if you start to get too exuberant with this thing."

Cookie steered carefully clear of boulders, rocks, and fist-sized pebbles, as well as abrupt changes of level, and brought the cart smoothly up before a gravel bank of outwash from a capacious cavern above. They stepped off the cart, checked their lights and hand weapons, and climbed the detritus slope to stand before the black, shadowy recess under the overhanging brow of eroded stone. Gradually they were able to discern black ovals against the blackness: the mouths of caves, well-protected by the overhang.

"The overhang alone would have been good," Judson remarked. "Those deeper caves will give us luxury living, Cookie."

"Looks like Cro-Magnon in France," Cookie said. "The early humans done OK there, and they never had no closet space."

"More than closet space," Judson corrected. "Living

space with two walls and a floor and a roof. And storage, too. We're still smelling like a rose."

"We got the shelter-repair kits aboard ship," Cookie stated. "We can make some partitions, set off my kitchen, and so on. Got stuff to spray for floors, and plenty of lighting and plumbing supplies. Bet we find a spring handy, and tomorrow we'll have hot and cold running water. And wait'll I get my stove and oven set up in here. I'm getting a pretty good appetite on me already. I guess it's lucky, after all, that they had old *Rocky* stocked as a supply vessel for the Io Colony." He glanced at Judson. "Or, no, I guess it wasn't a accident, was it, Cap? It was *you* steered 'em that way. Guess you must of had a idear even a year ago, what was coming up."

"The odd thing, Cookie," Judson replied thoughtfully, "is that I didn't. It just worked out this way."

"Praise Him from who all blessings flow," Cookie said contentedly. "Guess we better go inside and see if we like the wallpaper," he concluded.

It was cooler in the shadow under the rounded ceiling. The floor was striated and pebble-littered.

"Don't look like any kind o'critter ever laired in here," Cookie mumbled. "Hold hard, Cap, and I'll take a look in the back room." He patted the energy-pistol at his hip and unlimbered his cold-beam handlamp. Its rays showed a deep tunnel, running straight back for some fifty feet before it angled abruptly downward. He advanced cautiously, encountered no sudden drop-off, no yawning pits. A few stalactites were in process of forming along one wall, and out onto the arched ceiling. He was able to dodge them while proceeding upright. When he reached the incline, he called back, "No bats, Cap; no cave paintings—and so far no *Ursus speleus*. Make a fair pantry. I'm going up, now, but if I find any side-branches, I'll come back. All right, Cap'n, sir?"

"Don't go more than fifty feet," Judson called. "We've got lots of time." Cookie grunted assent and disappeared up the deep slope. Judson went to the mouth of the cavern and shone his light in. It looked, as far as he could detect, exactly like any water-worn cave on Earth.

In the gloom of the entry, he could see a dim, bluish glow emanating from the passage up which Cookie had disappeared. No, not so dim after all, he decided as he approached it. Almost like sunlight streaming in; the cave must have another opening to the surface.

At a distance of six feet he noticed the first crystals: pyramidal, glowing a heavenly blue, all sizes from mere specks to a foot tall, clustered in the opening and extending out over the floor for a couple of feet.

Judson looked up through the scintillating passage with the white glare of sun- or starlight at the top. Cookie was not in sight. Judson called, eliciting an echo which seemed to reverberate for an uncommonly long time.

After the last "-ookie; -ookie" had died away, he called again, and amid the echoes heard Cookie say, "Over here, Cap." He looked in the direction of the voice, saw the man's grinning face above, peering down through a cleft in the rock ceiling.

"Cap," Cookie said, "I found the city. C'mon up."

13

As Judson made his way up the jagged-walled incline, he examined the mirror-bright facets of the crystals all about. Their inner glow, he realized, was merely light refracted from above. The small crystals crumbled underfoot; they were barely harder than table-salt. Judson did not recognize the mineral. As he reached the top of the short climb and thrust his head out into open air, he was astonished to see that the crystals continued, clustered thickly on the rocky substrate of uneven ground. They were bigger and bigger, ranging from the size of footballs to that of apartment houses, an incredible vista of glittering beauty.

Cookie hurried up along a comparatively clear lane among the blue facets. "Stretches all the way across the hollow, a good half-mile, Cap," he reported excitedly. "Some o' them fifty foot tall. Reckon this is what I saw, eh, Cap?"

"That was only a dope-dream, remember, Space'n," Judson reminded him. "But I suppose this *would* look like a city from above."

"Never told you what the 'city' was like, sir," Cookie said. "Sounded too much like that 'Emeral City' in the books, only blue instead o' green. Kinda disappointed. Would been fun if it *was* a town."

"Unless the townsfolk didn't happen to like two-legged aliens with a funny smell walking on their crystals," Judson pointed out. "It's just as well we're still the only inhabitants."

"Looks to me, Cap," Cookie stated, "like it must of been a lake here—or an ocean or whatever, and it evaporated and the dissolved minerals crystallized out. Never heard about no sky-blue mineral shaped like a traffic marker. You, Cap?"

Judson shook his head. "There's lots of possible soluble minerals, Cookie. Most of them will form crystals; I guess some of them form blue, pyramidal crystals."

Cookie nodded; "That's what I mean when I said about the traffic markers, Cap. Couldn't think of that 'pyramidal.' But it's almighty pretty, right? Let's make a rule: nobody breaks off any souvenirs, or chops a trail or anything. We leave it just as it is. We can call it the Sapphire City."

"Absolutely," Judson agreed readily. "Now we'd better get busy setting up housekeeping down below."

"Kind of a ridge along the cliff edge," Cookie observed. "Held the water back, so that's why no crystals along the edge you could see from below."

14

They returned to the outer cave, talked over what to bring along on the first trip back to *Rocky*, then climbed aboard the car and drove back to the recon car.

The battered old ship came into view as soon as they cleared the end of the line of celery trees.

"Ain't nobody here to mess with her," Cookie commented, "but I'm relieved to see she's still just like we left her."

Judson nodded. "I wish now I'd set her down closer to the caves," he remarked.

"You done real good, Cap'n, sir," Cookie replied. "We can keep the car on charge all the time it's not in use; we can make all the trips we need to. I better hook up a cargo-flat to her, right, Cap?"

Judson agreed, and half an hour later, with the first load aboard the flat, they started back to the cave.

"Remember that able space'n Barbie McLeod, Cap?" Cookie offered as he parked the cart on the slope as close to the cave as they could drive.

"Who could forget her?" Judson grunted. "Don't remind me, Cookie."

"I always wondered," Cookie mused, "why a girl who

coulda been a trideo star was pulling eight on, twelve off aboard ship."

"I asked her once," Judson replied. "Bad luck with her boyfriends. Had to get away, she said."

"Funny she didn't enter a convent," Cookie commented. "Instead of joining an outfit that was eighty percent male."

"She *liked* men."

"You're breaking my heart, Cap," Cookie mourned. "And we'll never see a good-looking gal again."

"Nor a homely one," Judson agreed.

"Lucky thing, I guess," Cookie remarked, "that neither one of us ever got married. But it's too bad, too, Cap, you got no kids to inherit Private Space and all the rest. Summerlawn—beautiful house."

"Never mind," Judson replied. "The hundred and ten percent inheritance tax will pass this session."

"Guess we better quit jawing and get this stuff inside," Cookie said, and climbed out.

"We'd better hurry up," Judson told him. "Looks like a storm coming up from the south." He waved an arm toward a shelf of black cloud that was already beginning to darken the daylight. The wind had become brisk, blowing directly toward the oncoming clouds.

"Sucking up air like a tsunami," Cookie commented. "This ain't no little line-squall, Cap."

Now lightning-bolts were winking in the shadow under the solid-looking cloud layer.

By the time all the supplies had been transported and stashed inside the cave, bitterly cold raindrops the size of marbles were striking the rocky ground before the cave, and already rivulets were forming and trickling down the gullies toward the broad grassland below. Thunder rumbled continuously. The wind whipped at the tall grass and threw down a nearby tree as if it had been made of straw. Inside the cave, a steady draft blew from the cave of the blue city sucked out by the torrent of air flowing past above.

"We got to get us a couple partitions up as soon's this blows out," Cookie was muttering to himself, as he struggled in the wind with a tarp, which was quickly ripped from his grasp. Down below, the many trickles from the cliff-face were converging into two major streams flowing to the river, where the new influx made brownish stains against the gray-blue of the wider river.

"Don't reckon this happens often, do you, Cap?" Cookie inquired, shivering.

Judson reassured him. "Not likely, or we'd see more erosion of the cliff-face. Look at the size of that runoff down there."

Cookie followed his gesture. The more southern of the streams was fifty feet wide and turbulent, tumbling car-sized boulders along. A section of cliff-face to the left of and below the caves dropped away abruptly, adding to the talus slope.

"Cap!" Cookie blurted. "You don't reckon this here cave will fall in . . . ?"

"Not a chance, Space'n," Judson told him in a definite tone. "If it collapsed every time it rained, it wouldn't be here."

"Guess that's right, sir," Cookie conceded, then, pointing outside, "Looky there, Cap. Sunlight coming behind it! Storm's almost over! Good thing. Hope *Rocky*'s all right."

"She's parked on bedrock," Judson reassured him.

"Unless one o' them rocks big as Headquarters gets blown up against her, she's prolly all right," Cookie said without enthusiasm.

In half an hour, the storm had passed, with a final spatter, and suddenly the sound of trickling water was audible all around. Judson investigated the tunnel leading up to what they had decided to call the Sapphire City, and found that, because of its position on a steep slope, the cleft opening to the surface held almost no water. He glanced out, saw droplets on the crystals, and small entrapped puddles; otherwise the vista of glittering blue mineral was unchanged.

While Cookie busied himself in unpacking and laying out materials for a partition shutting off the draft, Judson took a tiny specimen of the blue crystal and ran it through the analyzer.

Cookie's next project was to erect a wall across the cave's mouth, complete with a sturdy lockable door, "Just in case," as he commented when Judson twitted him.

The crystal, Judson found, contained both copper and antimony, combined in a way unknown to science, or at least to the analyzer's datafile. It was soft, crumbling easily into white dust, at six-point-two-oh pounds per square inch. It was insoluble in water or alcohol at ambient temperature and pressure.

"Good thing," Judson commented. "Nobody'll be fighting over who gets to make jewelry out of it. Conditions must have been very different here when it formed."

"Hotter and heavier air, hey, Cap?" Cookie guessed.

"Maybe just water pressure at the bottom of the sea that used to be here," Judson suggested.

Just then, both men heard a roaring sound from outside, and looked out in time to see the advent of a flash flood, advancing in a wall of black water thirty feet high, pouring along the shallow river valley at perhaps fifty miles per hour, bearing a ragged mass of smashed trees intermingled with pebbles as big as aircars. Cookie gulped. "*Rocky*—"

"She's on high ground," Judson told him. "I tucked her in close to a rock-spine, if you recall, well above the average grade."

"Sure, Cap," Cookie conceded. "When it comes to looking out for our command, yer way ahead of me. You ex*pect*ing this here flood?"

"Not precisely. Just regular drill: 'always take the high ground.' "

"Sometimes us swabbies belowdecks forget the hard part of all that rank and pay," Cookie acknowledged. "I never give floods a thought, just looking at the nice grass and the purty flowers and all."

"How about spraying us a floor next," Judson suggested. "These channels are real ankle-turners."

"Take half a hour is all, sir. Brought plenty o' the pave-quick; can build her up three inches thick."

"Just use enough to fill the gullies," Judson directed.

"What color, Cap?" Cookie wanted to know.

"No color," Judson replied. "Just translucent."

"Easy enough, sir. Give her a non-skid surface, eh, sir?"

"Exactly. No high gloss to slip on."

Twenty minutes later, the floor was in place, optically flat, with what Cookie called a "gym finish." Through it, the deep red-gray lava floor was visible. Judson studied the substrate for half an hour, noting tiny granules embedded in the basalt.

"Look almost like fossils," he commented, "but it's unlikely that a life-form could have developed that enjoyed swimming in molten rock."

Cookie agreed. "Still looks like no land-animal life, Cap," he decided. "Sometime we'll have to do some digging, see what we can find."

It was Judson's turn to agree. "But right now, let's get that kitchen of yours set up," he added. "Let's try some of the recon stuff; we ought to save our low-0 stuff for special occasions."

Thus began a routine of work on the cave, leisurely meals, and endless speculation about their new home.

"We got a whole world to ourselfs, Cap," Cookie remarked one day after a filling dinner of stew and fresh-baked bread. "Nobody ever had anything like this before. There's gold mines out there, Cap, and forests and oceans and everything a feller needs to make whatever we want. Too bad you wasn't a gal, Cap; looks like we're stuck with ZPG whether we like it or not."

Judson shook his head. "It happened once before," he corrected. "Maybe a hundred or two thousand years ago, when the first Homo sapiens became aware of his own existence. He had a virgin Earth to work with; in some ways his descendants did a magnificent job, in other ways we failed miserably. Let's try to keep the magnificent part and eliminate the misery."

"Do you think we can, Cap?" Cookie inquired earnestly. "I mean, is it possible? Can you have one side of the coin without the other?"

"We can try," Judson assured him. "What do you say we go exploring in the morning?"

Cookie was enthusiastic as they set out. "Better go back to *Rocky* and get a full charge on our plates first off," he proposed, by which time Judson had already headed back along the visible trail across the grass that they had made on the first trip to the cave.

After ten minutes on the exciter, the car's plates were loaded. They spent another ten minutes checking circuits and topping off the water tanks. Inside the car they were free of the lightweight but still encumbering masks. Judson mentioned that sealing the cave and filling it with filtered air would be the first priority on their return. Judson rejected Cookie's suggestion that he try a lungful of the local atmosphere, "just to see what it's like."

"Maybe you could take a trip like I did, Cap," he urged. "Save us some driving."

Judson dismissed that as unlikely, and they sealed the canopy and set out to the north, following the river's edge, just above the low bluff.

The landscape varied little in the first twenty miles; then mountains appeared far ahead, a row of jagged peaks, geologically young folds in the planetary crust. The patches of woods along the cliff-edge widened and became a continuous forest, with the grassland continuing on a strip along the river. The river on the other side of the stream appeared similar. The patches of flowers continued to dot the grassland. On the second day, Judson directed Cookie to pull up beside a chrome-yellow patch.

"I have a hunch, Space'n," he told his friend. "The narcotic content of the atmosphere might be coming from these blossoms."

"Could be, I guess, Cap," Cookie assented. "Want me to run a check on the 'X' concentration here?"

"My idea precisely," Judson said. "Pull up in there, and take a ten-cc sample six inches above the flowers."

Cookie did so, using the versatile external manipulatory arm. The sample was placed in the analytic unit, and revealed a high concentration of a complex alkaloid.

"It's one of the minor components of that first sample we checked, back aboard ship," Judson announced after checking the datafile via the radiolink to the ship.

"We were close to the blue, then," Cookie observed. "Prolly that sample was heavy in whatever the blue puts out. I got an idea, Cap," he went on. "Each different color flower has its own brand o' dope."

"Let's try the analyzer on them and find out," Judson suggested. After half a day of testing nine distinct color varieties of the lily-like blossoms, they had isolated nine gases, all similar in complexity, but no two identical.

"Quite a pharmacopoeia, Cookie," Judson commented. "If they're all as potent as Blue, we may have made a major discovery here."

"We better never let the word get out," Cookie contributed. "We'll have every hophead on Earth headed this way. How we going to find out what we got here, anyways?"

"We have two guinea pigs," Judson told him. "You seem to have suffered no ill effects from that first accidental lungful of Blue you took. If we're careful, we can try minute amounts and monitor our metabolic responses closely."

"Have to do that aboard ship where we got the equipment," Cookie observed.

"So we'll have to take along samples from each of the different colors," Judson said.

After three days of careful selection and sampling, they had one-liter specimens of concentrate from sixteen distinct colors. The next morning, when they went outside to inspect the car, which had been in continuous use for seventy-five hours, Cookie felt an itch and reflexively reached to scratch his nose, accidentally partially dislodged his mask, and took a good whiff of Magenta before he realized what had happened and slapped the mask back in place. He turned to report the gaffe to Judson and slipped, half falling. He found it unexpectedly difficult to get his feet under him again.

He looked up, and Judson was staring down at him. "Gimme a hand here, Cap," he muttered. "Seems like I got a sniff of this air and it made me dizzy-like. Can't hardly get my balance."

Judson lent a hand, and Cookie rose lightly to his feet. Judson was still staring at him—but staring *up* now.

"Cookie, what the devil are you doing?" the captain demanded.

"Me, Cap?" the cook came back in a shocked voice. "Nothing. I fell down, and you helped me up, is all."

Judson put out both hands to grasp the smaller man's wrists. "Space'n," he said seriously, "are you levitating, or am *I* hallucinating?"

Cookie looked down. "I was the one got a smell o' the stuff, Cap," he responded. "Reckon it must be me."

"Your feet are eighteen inches above the ground," Judson told his now frightened crewman. "No wonder you had trouble getting up. Now, careful, Cookie: can you control it? Can you go higher—carefully, carefully; and more to the point, can you descend?"

At once, Cookie's feet lightly contacted the grassy turf. "Sure can, Cap, what now?" he said cockily. "Can't say as I liked that, Cap," he added. "Made my innards feel bad."

"We have to go to the ship at once and get you in the monitor," Judson told him. "Are you feeling all right now?"

"Little space-sick is all," Cookie replied. "Feels good to have my feet on the ground. I heard about guys out in India or someplace can do that levitating like you said. Heck, it ain't so hard."

"Try to rise, now," Judson suggested. "Be very careful, Space'n," he cautioned. "If you should begin an uncontrolled ascent, it would be fatal." Cookie duly rose a foot off the ground. "Now," Judson said, "try to settle down gently." He watched Cookie's feet. Nothing happened. "Try!" he repeated.

"How?" Cookie wanted to know.

"Just think of yourself doing it. We're confronted with new natural laws here, Space'n. We have to use our intellects."

Abruptly, the cook's feet slammed to earth, staggering him. He winced.

"I said 'gently,' " Judson scolded. "If you'd been fifty feet up . . ."

"Sure, Cap, I get the picture. Cap, let's find some reaction-mass for *Rocky* and get the heck offa this place."

Judson shook his head. "I'm afraid that's still very unlikely in the foreseeable future," he reminded the shaken man. "Just stay away from sniffing any Magentas—or any other kind, until we know the effects. Now, let's get back in out of this and explore a little farther over to the east, above the bluff, before we knock off for the day."

"Cap," Cookie said earnestly. "I was just thinking: If we both sniffed these here Magentas—what you said—we could cover a lot o' ground in short order. Why don't we try it? I guess I can stand a little bellyache."

"That's a mighty poor suggestion, Cookie," Judson said. "We don't experiment with anything here except under tightly controlled conditions."

Half an hour's drive inland from the river brought them to the shore of a broad lake, dotted with wooded islands. A dozen or more were visible from shore, the far shore being out of sight over the horizon.

"I never saw this here lake when I was flying," Cookie said. Then he paused thoughtfully. "Funny thang, Cap," he resumed. "We both been talking about that dream like it was real."

"Everything you reported has been proved to be correct, so far," Judson reminded him. "So, in some sense it *was* real."

"Magic?" Cookie inquired incredulously. "You saying this place is magic like that Oz?"

Judson shook his head. " 'Magic' is simply what we've traditionally called what we didn't understand," he explained. "As for your dream-flight, I think what the local flower-gases do is enhance natural abilities. We've always had people who claimed to be clairvoyant—that's seeing things at a distance—and some of them have apparently proved it. 'Out-of-body' experiences, they call it. I think the Blue heightened your native human ability, and the Magenta improved your levitation. I suppose others will enhance other latent abilities, some we think of as physical and natural, others we've always considered psychic and *un*natural."

"I always been pretty good with a ninety-deck, Cap," Cookie responded. "You mean you think maybe pink or yellow will make me even better at doing a side-straight?"

"Could be, Cookie," Judson conceded, "but you can forget that; I don't plan to play cards with you."

"Yeah," Cookie came back, "but if I can get offa here . . ."

"You won't," Judson discouraged him. "Better give some thought to how we should go about exploring those islands."

"What for, Cap?" Cookie returned. "We got maybe a zillion square miles o' good high ground to look at, without getting our feet wet."

"Of course we could get out there on the blower." Judson pursued the point. "But it's not good spacemanship to put all our eggs in one basket; if the blower failed, that would be that. The car won't float more than an hour."

"Thanks fer asking, Cap'n, sir," Cookie said fervently. "I know you ain't got to have my permission, but I'd vote 'no,' all right."

"We're not aboard ship now, Cookie," Judson reminded his friend. "You're free to do as you please. You stay with me only if that's what you want. No hard feelings if you disagree."

"Me?" Cookie inquired incredulously. "When'd I ever have a better idear'n *you*, Cap? I ain't about to go off on my own." He thrust out his callused hand, and Judson shook it.

"Thanks, Mr. Murphy," he said seriously.

"Now we got that out o' the way," Cookie said, "let's

get on with it. I say let's go once around the shore—if we can; no telling how far that'll be. Least fifty miles," he offered, scanning the broad expanse of greenish-blue surface.

The ground near the lake was soft, water glistening among the grass-blades.

Judson drove slowly, using the center tread now, which imprinted a narrow strip of mirror-bright water behind them. He pulled up on a slight rise with a lone B and O tree. They relaxed and ate an M-ration.

"All looks the same, Cap," Cookie commented. " 'Cept for that tread we're laying, this could be the spot we started from."

"The tree's our landmark," Judson told him. "The trail will soon disappear: this is spongy ground."

"Sure," Cookie nodded. "What say I get out and cut a twig for analysis? Might have dope like the flowers."

"Go ahead," Judson urged. "Stretch your legs. But don't forget to keep your eyes open and your mask *on*."

"Sure, Cap. Won't happen again." Cookie grunted and stepped out on the soggy ground.

There was a sharp *beep*! from the sensor panel and Judson turned to it impatiently. "It's all right," he told the alert apparatus. "I *know* there's movement inside the D-radius, but it's just Space'n Murphy." He made an adjustment and the machine accepted Cookie's presence.

Judson glanced outside, failed to see his crewman, stepped out into cool shade and looked around. Cookie was nowhere to be seen. Judson circled the car, found not even a footprint. He called once; no reply. Puzzled, Judson walked around the cart again, glanced up into the broad-leafed tree, scanned the horizon. He was alone as no man had ever been alone.

15

Judson was reluctant to leave the spot, but as Brownie rose and Junior sank low, and near-darkness closed in on the plain, he told himself there was no point in standing here; he could be mystified in greater comfort and security back at the ship.

He climbed into the car, started up, swung in a wide circle, seeing no trace of Cookie, headed back along his outbound track and went fifty feet. Then the car fell silent and coasted to a stop. All instruments indicated "normal." Swell! Judson looked around at the featureless plain of grass; his eye was caught by something that moved. Surely *that* was animal life: erect, manlike animal life, in fact. The approaching figure waved and Judson saw that it was Cookie, advancing at a run. He opened up and climbed down to greet him.

"—seen you start up like you was going to drive off and leave me," Cookie was blurting between out-of-breath gasps. "Cap, don't ever scare me like that again, please, sir!"

"Scare *you*?" Judson echoed. "How the devil did you get out there?"

"Walked," Cookie replied. "If that's what you mean,

Cap. You seen me: after you tol' me I could explore over that way, when we seen the dust cloud. I taken off running, and you said, 'Slow down, take it easy, Space'n. We got all day.' I remember that, cause I thought we better find out what exploded quick and get outa here."

Judson was frowning at the smaller man, shaking his head in negation. "I didn't see any explosion, Cookie, or hear one. I wouldn't send you off on foot, alone, to investigate, if I *had* seen an explosion. I got out to look around, and you had disappeared. I called—"

"Reckon I was too far off; I never heard you, Cap," Cookie offered, "but I heard that cycler start up and I come back on the run. What do you mean, you never seen the explosion?"

"Calm down, Cookie," Judson urged. "There's something odd going on here—again. We'd better slow down and figure out what it is."

"I volunteered, Cap," Cookie explained. "No, you never *told* me to go; I wanneda go take a look, and you decided one of us hadda stay with the car, no good to risk *it*."

Judson shook his head. "You walked around the back of the car and never came back—until I saw you running just now."

"I walked over there, Cap," Cookie reported. "And I seen this gray, powdery stuff all over the ground, all around where the explosion was. Seen a hole in the ground, grass was all tore up in a spot ten foot wide. Looked as if something like a mine blowed up. We must be in a minefield, Cap. Lucky we never run over one. Let's get outa here, OK, Cap?"

"Not yet," Judson objected. "We've got troubles. The car stopped."

"Yeah," Cookie nodded vigorously. "I was never gladder to see anything than I was when you stopped, Cap. When you started to drive off and leave me, well . . . I shoulda known better."

"*I* didn't stop," Judson told the excited fellow. "The *car* stopped. Power died, all instruments reading 'normal.' Let's take a look." He went to the port access hatch and opened it.

Cookie rounded the vehicle to examine the starboard side. "Everything looks OK over here," he reported. "Don't see no smoke, no broke lines, nothing. Pusher coil's hot, but not overheated. Ought to be running, go-valve's open. Beats me, Cap, but you're the feller designed this here go-box. Whatta *you* see, Cap'n, sir?"

"Slow down and I'll tell you," Judson replied. "I see dust. Powdery gray stuff, packed in the air intake."

"Funny," Cookie commented, "I don't see none this side."

"It apparently choked off the cooling conduits to the coil, and the automatics shut her down."

It was the work of a moment to brush away the encrustation of oddly heavy gray powder, after which the machine started up easily; Judson reverse-flushed the system to purge it of dust.

"This place keeps scaring me, Cap," Cookie remarked. "Looks purty and peaceful, but it's full of surprises. Let's get back before it springs another one. That there dust," he added, "looks like what I seen yonder."

"Let's go take a look at that explosion site," Judson suggested. Cookie complained, but subsided. They drove over.

"Oughta be about here," Cookie said, peering out at the rippling grass, as the car slowed to a crawl.

"Where's the dust you described?" Judson wanted to know. Cookie was baffled. "Stuff was all over. Fifty foot from the hole, it was half an inch deep."

"Show me the hole," Judson suggested.

Cookie was unable to find it. "Let's just go on, Cap," he urged. "It's happening again. I walked right up to it. Black hole in the middle of all that gray dust. Gone now. Let's get outa here."

Realizing that the man, whom he knew to be rock-steady under fire, was seriously upset, Judson concurred. He backed the car, then turned and headed back toward the lone tree that marked the in-trail. At that moment, a tremendous explosion rocked the ground under the car, jolting both men, and enclosing the vehicle in a blinding dust cloud.

"Close, Cap," Cookie managed. "She musta blew right where we was sitting."

Judson drove on to the tree, and the men dismounted and examined the car for blast damage.

"OK this side," Cookie reported.

"The intake's clear," Judson told him. "Funny, packed full when it shouldn't have been, and clean after it ought to be choked from that dust cloud."

Cookie was already back inside the car. "We gotta get back, fast, Cap," he urged. " 'Fore something happens to *Rocky*."

Judson agreed. It was an uneventful half-hour drive along their back-trail to the river and on to the ship, still standing, apparently undisturbed, as they had left it.

Cookie heaved an exaggerated sigh of relief when they were inside again.

"I'll rustle us a good dinner, Cap'n, sir," he offered. "After all that, we deserve it. Got one bottle o' the Colony '64 left." He hurried away at Judson's nod, while Judson busied himself examining the car more carefully. He discovered a shallow indentation in the rear air-skirt, and brushed a few ounces of the surprisingly stubborn gray dust from the crevices on the vehicle's stern quarter, taking a sample for examination. The stuff seemed almost sticky, as if magnetized to itself.

16

After a superb dinner of Chicken Française, Cookie spoke up hesitantly:

"You know, Cap, I been thinking. I seen that explosion *before* it happened. That's how come . . . well, you know."

"I see what you mean, Space'n," Judson replied. "But that doesn't quite explain how the air ducts got clogged before the explosion."

"Wasn't just me, Cap, seeing things—that claryvoice you said about—it was *time* outa whack. We musta drove over there and got dust-clogged and *then* I seen it blow, *after*, and after that we was in the car and we both seen it blow. Stuff doesn't happen in a regular sequence like we're used to. Wouldn't of been no dust *before* she blowed."

"I'm surprised to find causality breaking down this close to home," Judson commented. "It appears Einstein and Planck and the whole structure of modern physics will have to be rethought."

"Not by me, Cap," Cookie objected. "I already went as far as I can go reading 'string-bag' theory and all that."

"*I* had to drop out before that," Judson admitted. "When I got to O'Brien's 'First Cause' work, my brain stopped working."

"Kinda hard to grasp," Cookie nodded, "all that about the result evoking the cause, and all. Course none of it makes any kind of sense on a small scale. Even limiting velocity, and that stuff about 'velocities don't add' and all. Looks like we got some rethinking of our own to do."

"I examined the dust from the explosion," Judson told his friend. "Strange stuff: it seems to be collapsed matter, like you'd expect to find in a neutron star; it ought to be heavy—a cubic centimeter should weigh a few thousand tons. In fact, it ought to fall right through ordinary matter as if it were gas, right to the core of the planet."

Cookie was wagging his head. "That's all *way* beyond me, Cap," he said. "Guess we're lucky after all, we found some pretty normal conditions first: water flows downhill, wind blows gentle, and temperature and G are just right. We lucked out, Cap. What do we do now?"

"We start codifying information," Judson told him. "First, we need to call up the aerials the mapping gear took on the way in, and map what we've seen so far, especially the site of the explosion. That's funny stuff, Cookie, that dust," he added soberly. "Nothing like it exists on Earth or anywhere else I've ever been. Must be core material from a large body that broke up. It's a collapsed crystal, all right. But it has mass without weight. That's why it was so hard to handle."

"Don't *get* that, Cap," Cookie grunted. "Might make good reaction-mass," he offered.

Judson nodded. "The ideal material," he agreed. "We may lift *Rocky* yet."

"Let's do it, Cap," Cookie proposed instantly. "I decided I don't care for this place. If I've got a say, I say we try this new fuel and get the hell outa here."

"We'll do some tests," Judson agreed. "If the coil doesn't blow, it might work."

The tests were conducted cautiously at first, in a ground-power unit at a distance from the vessel, using a single grain of the collapsed crystalline matter. They gradually proceeded to a full-scale run-up of the main coil after the tests, and confirmed their hopes. They had "fuel."

"So what do we do, Cap?" Cookie wanted to know. "Do we go back home and face the Council's music, or should we check out Eenie or Meenie while we're out here?"

"I vote we stay right where we are," Judson replied. "At least for the present. It's a strange place, but we can accommodate to it."

"Looky here, Cap," Cookie urged, pointing to the ship's chronometer. "Messed up," he declared. " 'Less I forgot all I know about this here panel, that first two digits is the year. Says 'ought-nine.' This is eighty-eight. If the clock's blowed, what else has gone?"

"I've been watching that, Space'n," Judson told him. "It's been gaining at the rate of about six weeks per day."

"Shoulda tol' me, Cap'n, sir," Cookie grumped. "Might coulda fixed it."

"It operates on the decay-rate of U-238," Judson reminded the excited cook. "There's nothing to fix. It's right."

Cookie made a production of scratching his head. "What that s'pose to mean, Cap?" he inquired aggrievedly.

"We've been here twenty-one years," Judson said seriously. "Time is different here."

"Can't be, Cap!" Cookie objected. "Ain't been *time* to be here no twenny years! Ain't fixed enough meals. Seasons ain't changed. We got a fifteen-degree axial tilt here, and we *gotta* have distinct seasons! Clock's just broke, Cap, is all! If it was twenny-one years, you'd be a old man by now, sir, and I'd be getting purty middle-aged myself. Nossir. Been about a month, maybe."

"It's all relative, Cookie," Judson soothed. "It's like inflation: time was when a hundred dollars was a lot of money, get you a good meal in the best restaurant.

Now it's a tip for a car-parker. So what does it matter if we call it a C-note or a buck?"

Cookie rubbed his jaw. "Ain't shaved that many times," he muttered. "But, hell, yer right as usual, Cap. So what do we do next? Didn't get far with the big exploring expedition."

"I think we ought to send out the whirlybird," Judson said. "Let it cruise at say, a thousand feet on an advancing search-curve and give us a continuous visual. We'll take shifts monitoring the screen."

"Good idea, Cap," Cookie conceded. "Lot better'n going out there to get blowed up by some time-bomb. What you figger it was, anyway, Cap, blowed up like that?"

"I don't have a theory, Cookie," Judson told him.

17

On the charting screen, they watched featureless grassland pass under the televideo eyes of the unmanned spinner. The river flickered by, a thousand feet below.

"I'm going to take it up to two thousand," Judson said. "We need a more panoramic view. This isn't much better than driving on the surface."

"Was jest gonna say so, Cap'n', sir," Cookie replied. The scene broadened and lost detail. Now both branches of the river stretched away into misty distances, and the blue glint of the Sapphire City was visible behind the cliff.

Judson set the screen on RECORD. "We can have lunch now and review all this later," he told Cookie. "We'll study the printouts in detail; then maybe we'll learn something useful."

Cookie grunted assent.

At that moment a filter seemed to appear across the screen. Judson adjusted sensitivity and focus in vain. The view became increasingly obscured.

"Fog, Cap?" Cookie asked, peering in puzzlement at the now formless greenish-glowing rectangle of the screen.

"I don't think so," Judson said. "And no malfunction, either." Abruptly, the gelatinous membrane covering the screen developed a nuclear dark spot, which coalesced into what seemed to be an enormous, insubstantial eye.

"Something's looking back at us, Cap," Cookie blurted. "I tol' you we should of got outta here before."

"It seems we were mistaken, Space'n," Judson replied. "There *is* animal life here. Maybe even intelligent life."

The veil obscuring the spinner's viewers had thickened and become opaque. Only blackness was to be seen on the screen. Judson sent Cookie to the fore-scanner.

"Find the spinner and give it full mag," he ordered.

A moment later, Cookie yelped. "Looks like a manta ray," he blurted. "Got the spinner, it's wrapped around it. Looks like a jellyfish—transparent-like. Just folded over the spinner. Didn't like the rotor, tried to shy away, but fin'ly it smothered it. Falling together—look out!"

Cookie came back to Judson's side just as the slave-screen flashed white and died.

"Some kind o' critter," he gasped. "It grabbed the spinner and covered it. Looks like we stay inside *Rocky* from now on, eh, Cap?"

"At least until we find out what we've got here," Judson told the excited Cookie. "Easy, shipmate. I'm going to zoom in." He went to the scanner and upped mag until the wreckage of the spinner filled the screen, enwrapped in a diaphanous substance like a curtain of clear jelly. The alien "eye" was visible, like the yolk in a frying egg, broken and fading.

"Looks like it's hurt bad's the spinner," Cookie commented. "Reckon we better go over and take a look, see what we can do, Cap?"

"I'm proud of you, Space'n, for being the first to suggest it," Judson told him. "If, as I suspect, that's a mentational life-form, we'd do well to help all we can."

As they drove down to the smashed and goo-entangled flyer, Cookie's enthusiasm waned.

"Might not be hurt bad, Cap, might be playing possum," he speculated. "Better not get too close." Judson agreed, and pulled up fifty feet from the longest outlying mass of faintly-greenish, aspic-like substance. At this distance, he could see that it was quivering, and making vain attempts to pull its substance back toward its main mass.

"Still alive," he commented.

"Look at that eye," Cookie blurted. "Tryna to put itself back together, looks like. See, the iris part is almost together, there's the pupil; all that stringy black stuff is prolly the retina, you think, Cap?"

"If so, it needs help to get it back in position," Judson told him. "We could get out there and wade in to where we could help push."

"I don't know as we oughta go getting *too* brave here, Cap," Cookie pointed out. "Thing might snap together and mash us right up with the spinner. Not a whole lot left o' that spinner, Cap."

"The thing didn't crush it, Space'n," Judson reminded him. "It hit the ground hard, that's all. Come on."

Suited up, they descended the short ladder to step down on grass littered with dislodged fragments of their recon aircraft. They went across to the nearest edge of the truly immense blob of alien protoplasm, and stepped up onto the rubbery, translucent surface. It showed no response, although it was still, clearly, attempting to draw its outflung tissues together. They went across to the shattered eye, and while Cookie went around to peer down through the cloudy tissue at the seemingly intact iris, Judson proceeded to the spot where the creature was attempting in vain to reconstitute its retinal rods and cones. Judson pushed aside a shelf of resilient matter leaking greenish fluid, and with his gloved hand thrust together two major clusters of the light-sensitive cells. Instantly, there was a general readjustment which brought the two fragments into a different, more subtle alignment.

"Say, Cap," Cookie who had been watching in fascination as Judson reassembled the shattered circuitry of the fallen alien, "that top part there: don't it kind of remind you of that matter-transmitter idea you been playing around with? You remember, you showed me the wiring setup on the tablecloth back at Mess."

"It does, a little," Judson agreed, "but it's incomplete. Still, if I provided a link to this big axion here, it might be functional—indeed, I dimly perceive a whole spectrum of outré abilities that might come into realization, properly innervated."

"Better not mess around too much, Cap," Cookie cautioned. "Can't tell what this thing might take a notion to do if it could levitate and do telekinesis and all that."

"I still have the situation under control," Judson pointed out. "I'll hold back the final vital link till the last."

Curious, indeed, a bodiless voice spoke from somewhere near at hand. *Inside my head!* Judson thought wildly. He turned toward Cookie to call a warning, but the wiry little chef was already halfway to him, running hard.

"Get back, Cap!" he yelled. "Thing'll get inside yer head, mess up yer brains!"

. . . these entities appear to be self-oriented, even conscious, and—can it be?—motivated by an impulse to assist me, who will undoubtedly destroy them the instant I can control my substance.

Judson had halted and caught Cookie's arm as he came up, panting. "I can hear it talking, Cap!" the cook gasped out. "Talking about killing the both of us!"

"I don't think it will," Judson reassured the man calmly, "once we've explained matters."

"What 'matters,' Cap?" Cookie yelled. "It said, 'I'm gonna kill 'em as soon as they fix me up.' "

Impossible! The silent voice sounded shocked. *They can read my mind!*

"Listen, Jellyhead," Judson said aloud, addressing he knew not what. "If we can read you, you can read us. We can help you—or we can destroy you." He lifted a detached fragment of jelly containing a small patch of retinal cells, clasped it in his fist. "I can crush this, or replace it where it belongs," he pointed out.

By all means, replace it. That's a vital portion of my optical cavity; without it, I have no connection between my ocular and my proprioceptive faculties!

"That's all very well," Judson replied coolly. "But as long as I'm holding it in my fist, you can't destroy us as you threatened."

No threat was intended, the alien voice protested. *I had no idea you could monitor my thoughts; I'd never have warned you. Consider now, do you really believe I'd have told you knowingly what I intended?*

"Certainly not," Judson agreed. "But that's where we fooled you. The problem is not that you warned us, but that you harbored the intention, and still do, to kill us for no reason, after we had demonstrated our goodwill by helping you—and *that* after you gratuitously destroyed our spinner, which we need."

That's a most complex and difficult formulation, came the reply, *but I almost, almost, do you hear, grasp a sort of twisted symmetry in it. I take it you desire to continue your miserable dirt-bound existence . . . ?*

"We do, indeed," Judson confirmed.

Cookie dithered nearby, muttering and squeezing his head with both hands. "I can't stand it, Cap!" he moaned. "It makes my brains itch! Let's get outa here." He aimed a kick at a blob of detached jelly, succeeded in spreading it on the toe of his boot in a quarter-inch-thick, clinging film.

He kicked his booted foot in vain, then desisted and jumped down from the quivering mass and ran off toward the car before pausing to turn and bawl at Judson:

"Come on, Cap, before it's too late! This Jelly-bag is likely to—"

"Easy, Space'n," Judson called in reply. "This thing is intelligent, but not very, and not in a way we're familiar with." Reluctantly, Cookie approached, and the voice spoke again:

. . . perceive your intent is to discontinue your ef-

forts to assist me. This is undesirable. I am at, or perhaps beyond, the limits of my self-reconstitutional capacity. Without your fortuitous presence, my existence might have been terminated untimely.

"It still might," Judson reminded the obtuse organism. "We have no intention of helping you kill us, so you'd better abandon that idea."

What a bizarre concept! To permit an intruder in my domain to survive! It's not done! I can barely grasp the concept!

"Try to grasp this one," Judson suggested. "Unless you convince me you have no evil intentions regarding me and my shipmate—and in fact will help us all you can—you'll die right here, in pieces."

This "justice" which you conceive, Jelly-bag intoned, *is not a concept inherent in the natural cosmos. It is purely an invention of your own tainted mind, an attempt to place an arbitrary stricture on the workings of nature. I see it in your world-concept, but I can make no claim truly to grasp it, nor can I undertake to "deal" in accordance therewith.*

"Well, at least this bag of jelly is honest about being treacherous," Cookie commented.

By no means, the correction came sharply. *I vouchsafe only what is in any case obvious, even to your impoverished intellects.*

"That's it, Cap," Cookie stated hotly. "No way can we trust Baggy here! It's too dumb to see we're its only chance."

You err, Baggy corrected. *I see all too clearly that I must "deal," or dissolve, all unfulfilled.*

"We can deal, Cookie," Judson reassured his crewman. "I'm still holding Baggy's IQ in my fist. I won't return it, unsquashed, until I'm satisfied it will hold up its end of the bargain." With that, he squeezed the blob of tissue, causing droplets of moisture to ooze out between his fingers.

NO! Baggy shrieked silently. *I am still linked by indissoluble bonds to my retinal nucloid. Replace it at once, undamaged!*

"No," Judson told the excited being. "I think maybe I'd better squash it." He exerted more pressure on the egg-sized clump of neurons.

I perceive you have no intention of so doing! Baggy said. *In fact, it is quite clear you have every intention of honoring the terms of your proposal, as soon as I have succeeded in convincing you of my own reliability.*

18

"That'll be a cold day at Venus docks," Cookie answered. "We know you never heard of truth, gratitude, honesty, loyalty, or justice, for openers, so what makes you think we'll deal?"

I'm a lot *bigger than you are,* Baggy replied cheerfully; at the same moment a cavity in his substance opened under the feet of the humans. They leaped clear, and the cleft pursued them until they scrambled down onto the grass, clear of the wounded creature.

"Get back," Judson commanded Baggy as Cookie paused to look scornfully at the expanse of quivering jelly from which they had so narrowly escaped. Cookie hesitated. Judson grabbed his arm and pulled him along. Behind them, a ripple formed in the glistening surface of the alien; it rose to a ridge, elongated to become a ten-foot pseudopod, came arcing over and down to strike the ground at the spot just vacated by the men, with a resounding *splatt*!

Judson gave the matter in his hand an admonitory squeeze, then paused to address the creature.

"You're slow, Baggy," he told it, "and you telegraph your intentions: I picked up your idea before you moved.

You'd better just give up your 'kill anything that moves' strategy and start talking business."

While agile of body, Baggy replied, *your wits are slow; you still don't understand that I alone can exist here. There can be no sharing of my lifespace, especially with such alien entities as yourselves.*

"Why not?" Judson queried, at the same moment that Cookie blurted, "*Yer* the one that's a 'alien entity!' "

One at a time, Baggy begged. *To cope with two such outré incomings simultaneously is quite beyond my powers.*

"Gee, that's tough, ain't it, Cap," Cookie spoke up promptly, as Judson said, "Talk to it, Space'n. Tell it some of your racy stories, while I give it Crumblnski's formulations on the mass of the menton."

Fools! Baggy blatted. *After I explicitly instructed you—*

"Forget it, Jelly-bag," Cookie cut in contemptuously. "You don't command nobody."

"Baggy," Judson addressed the alien earnestly, "you're facing the necessity for adapting to something new. I know this is a unique experience in your existence up to now, but you'll have to face it: you've encountered living beings who won't permit themselves to be eaten alive—or killed, either, even if you disapprove."

The response was confused telepathic noise; wordless gibberish that buzzed like a fly in a helmet, until Cookie yelled and pounded his ears. "Make it stop, Cap!" he howled.

Judson considered for a moment; then began to recite pop-tune lyrics, as fast as he could recall them. "Stop it, Baggy," he yelled as soon as the noise had diminished a bit. "Pull yourself together! Try! It's to our mutual advantage to cooperate! Don't destroy yourself! We can help each other!" As he spoke he compressed the tissue in his hand.

The cacophony faded to a fitful muttering, than dissipated.

"All right, Mr. Jelly-bag," Cookie shouted. "Don't you ever try that again!"

"You had both of us in your power," Judson said

aloud, addressing Baggy. "You could have constricted and crushed us. And *could* have engulfed us sooner than you did. Why didn't you do it?"

You would be of little use to me crushed; except possibly as a nutrient . . . Baggy pointed out.

"Exactly," Judson said. "So you see, you did, implicitly if not explicitly, deal with us. You decided to have the possibility of our assistance, as preferable to the loss of that option. And you'd find our tissues would give you a monumental case of indigestion."

Very probable, as to the latter, Baggy agreed. *As for your "deal," I perceive, faintly and obscurely, what you mean by the word. I allowed you to escape in order that I might obtain your assistance in reassembling my neural circuitry. Yes. So be about it! Do all you can, at once!*

"There's one aspect of treaty-making which has escaped you," Judson pointed out. "The element of volition is essential. If we help you, it will be because *we* decide to do so, not you."

But—I've already fulfilled my part of the "deal," Baggy objected.

"But prior to our acceptance of the terms," Judson explained. "You'll have to forget about being the supreme power, having it all your way. Our preferences are to be considered."

You mean had I offered to release you in exchange for your help, you'd have refused? Baggy demanded.

"Not necessarily," Judson conceded.

"He's got us there, Cap," Cookie put in.

"The point," Judson went on, "is *prior* agreement. A unilateral decision is not binding on anyone. Let's go, Space'n."

As Judson turned as if to walk away, Cookie hurried around to confront him. "Wait a sec, Cap," he pled. "We got a lot to lose if we fold now—"

"Don't tip your hand, Murphy," Judson ordered, and pushed past the distraught Cookie. "Leave the negotiations to me."

Cookie fell in behind him, casting a last mournful

glance at the great ruined organism spread over the grass behind them, with the wreckage of the spinner poking up from amid ruptured tissues.

Wait! Baggy hurled the command imperiously after them. *I insist you at least link up my arcuate fasciculum.*

Judson paused. "No insisting, Baggy," he cautioned. "Remember the rules: mutual agreement." He gave the alien tissue in his hand another squeeze.

I forgot! Baggy explained frantically. *The concept is so outré, so totally unheard-of. You must—no, excuse me, please try to understand: it is extremely difficult for me to put aside all that is reasonable and proper as I must, in order to so much as consider your fantastic demands.*

"I'll try," Judson agreed.

"Jeez," Cookie commented. "This guy and Priss Grayce'd get along good. He can't even make pretend he's honest."

"That in itself is a form of honesty," Judson pointed out. "It's involuntary, of course, because we're communicating mind-to-mind, which makes lying impractical."

"Yeah," Cookie breathed. "Gives us an edge, eh, Cap? We can lie all we want to."

"Won't work, Cookie," Judson told him. "He's getting the thought behind the vocalization, not the spoken words."

"Sure," Cookie agreed readily. "I was only kidding, sort of. What we going to do, Cap? Do we go back in there and see what we can do, and hope old Baggy don't eat us?"

"Baggy is no fool," Judson said. "If he wants the use of his arcuate fasciculum, which is I suspect, vital to his high-level mentation, he'll have to restrain himself. Come on." So saying, Judson returned to the edge of Baggy's tissue-mass and stepped up. Cookie joined him.

Now, if you'll hurry, Baggy urged, *my discomfort will be terminated the sooner. There,* he went on proudly, *I curbed the impulse to command you! So hurry! It itches!*

"We'll overlook the form of your last request on the

grounds that you're under great stress," Judson volunteered. He turned to Cookie. "Scout over that way, Space'n, if you don't mind," he said, "and I'll check this way. We're looking for a body of greater density than the somatic tissues. Report anything that's a likely candidate, please."

"Hey, Cap, it's rubbing off," Cookie exclaimed. "Old Baggy can't give no orders, and you said, 'please,' and 'if you don't mind.' I like that. Thanks, Baggy."

De nada, Baggy responded in a surly tone. *You're being quite . . . "unfair" is the symbol I extract from your vocabulary, and a strange one it is. "Unfair": remarkable, a concept unknown to the cosmos, yet well-developed in your petty cerebra. Your sibling has been unfailingly "courteous" to you, in spite of his greater natural endowments, which should, by reason, confer absolute dominance on him.*

"Yeah, skip all that, Baggy," Cookie urged. "Sure, Cap treats me good; and I treat *him* good. We're friends a long time. What's it to you?"

Once again, the alien explained, *I find myself struggling with the inconceivable. "Friends!" A weird conception indeed!*

Just then, Judson grabbed Cookie's arm and hauled him back; in the same instant, a massive pseudopod came up and over and smashed flat the grass where they had stood.

"Why, the dirty, lousy—" Cookie began to bluster. "Thanks, Cap; he'd of kilt us for sure!"

Remarkable! Baggy contributed, *You, Judson entity, perceived my impulse, which of course leaked, due to my lack of use of the fasciculum. And, instead of at once saving yourself, you lingered for point-two seconds to assist the Cookie entity, at risk of your own existence! How can such absurdity exist? What sort of beings are you?* The alien subsided, muttering subtelepathically.

"You said it yourself," Judson informed the confused creature. "We're friends. He'd have done the same for me, if you'd leaked on his frequency, instead of mine."

Cap, Judson recognized his friend's mental voice instantly. *Baggy's right; you risked yer life to save me—again. Any way I can square it with you?*

I've been wondering, Judson replied silently, *if we could use this channel between ourselves since Baggy showed it to us.*

"Seems like I'd rather talk out loud," Cookie responded, doing so. "Used to it, I guess, is all."

"Suits me," Judson agreed. "But I think we humans have been relying on a lot of superfluous vocalization all along. Consider how we understand even heavy dialects, and confused grammar and syntax; the idea comes across subliminally."

Cookie rubbed his chin with a *rutch*ing sound. "Prolly," he conceded. "I remember a feller, from Granyauck or someplace, talked like it hurt him. Always figgered out what he meant, though. Usually, anyways."

"Which brings us no closer to a resolution of the problem," Judson pointed out, aloud. "We need all the help we can get, and it seems our boy Baggy, here, is the only possibility. But we can't trust him as far as we can throw him."

"Maybe not, Cap," Cookie came back. "Maybe he's not the only possibility, I mean. Hey, Baggy!" He changed tone to address the huge alien. "Any more at home like you?"

I am alone, came the mournful reply. *Since the demise of my last sibling, I've had no one with whom to converse, to discuss the manifold mysteries of existence. Since his departure, I have roamed my domain far and wide and never another such as you have I encountered. Whence do you come?*

"Talks fancy, fer a gob of goo, don't he, Cap?" Cookie commented. "What's that 'wince'?"

" 'From where,' " Judson supplied. He turned his attention to the wounded alien. "We come from Earth," he said. "I'll visualize it for you." He formed as vivid a mental image as he could of the Solar System, seen at a distance against the backdrop of the Great Bear, barely distinguishable at this distance.

Ah, yes, the major world, eh? Baggy queried.

"No, that's a gas giant," Judson corrected. "That's all the detail you need."

I caught a flash of something, just as you dissolved your image, Baggy said, excitedly. *A glimpse of a green world, teeming with life-force!*

"Forget it," Judson advised. "It's a long way from here; you wouldn't like it. Acid clouds, rivers of glorp, crowded, noisy, and the ozone layer doesn't look good."

"Jeez, Cap," Cookie interpolated, "are things really that bad? I heard about some nuts getting up drives to save the Anopheles and stuff like that, but seems to me it's mostly pretty nice, still."

"Perhaps I'm projecting a little," Judson conceded. "Since AutoSpace finally got approval to fire the radioactive wastes into the sun, we may begin to get a little relief."

"Heard they planned, one time, to bury all that hot stuff, right in the U.S. of A.," Cookie commented. "Crazy! Load it on a Saturn X and fire it into the sun, and it's gone. Wonder why they didn't do it sooner."

"Politics," Judson told him. "Very little graft in getting rid of the stuff for good."

Judson entity, the alien called silently. Judson waited. *You're in grave danger, strange being—unless you can endure a severe battering, and prolonged immersion in water*.

"Heck, no!" Cookie blurted. "Whatta you talking about?"

"Calmly, Space'n," Judson admonished. "No doubt Baggy is referring to the flood which will sweep the valley within a few hours at most."

Cookie stared at him. "How do you know, Cap? No disrespect, sir."

"We saw the thunderstorms moving toward the mountains," Judson pointed out. "All that water is going to go somewhere—presumably downhill—that means along the river course. We need to move the ship."

Quite right, Judson entity, Baggy confirmed.

"Thanks for warning us, anyway, Baggy," Judson returned.

Regarding the appellation "Baggy," the alien remarked. *I find it curiously pleasant to have a unique designation. Thank you.*

"You mean," Cookie demanded, "you never had a name before?"

I had no need of one, Baggy pointed out. *There was only my now departed sibling, and of course I was the only entity available for him to address.*

"Cookie," Judson said, "I think Baggy has proved he's an ally, rather than an enemy. Right?"

"Dern right, Cap," Cookie agreed fervently, with an anxious glance upriver. "We better get moving, Cap. Get *Rocky* to high ground. What about our cave? Reckon that'll be flooded out."

"I don't think so," Judson responded. Then he addressed Baggy: "How often do these flash floods occur?"

Once in a Great Light, on the average, Baggy told him. *And the Great Light sinks low. You haven't much time.*

"It won't take long," Judson assured him. "But we'd better get busy reassembling you. Come on, Cookie."

They stepped back up on the rubbery gel and went to work: Judson went at once to the site of the retina and tossed down the fragment thereof which he had sequestered. The formless jelly-blob at once sank into the substrate and migrated to the gap in the partially reassembled organ, dithered for a moment, then rotated and socketed into position.

"So, Cap," Cookie blurted. "There's them there blue lines I said reminds me of them drawings you showed me that time.

Judson nodded. "I noticed, Space'n. As I told you, with just a little modification, that neural circuit could approximate my matter-transmitter/teleportation proposal."

"Let's do it, Cap," Cookie urged. "S'pose I just shove this here piece over here." He poked a gloved finger into the translucent substance and prodded the outflung filament of deep blue into contact with the nearby mass of the same color.

Judson added a few finishing touches, and the protoplasm shifted to accommodate the new linkage.

Remarkable! Baggy said. *Now if I can coordinate the whazz emanations . . .* At once, Baggy underwent a general reorganization. The Terrans watched in fascination as the pigmented internal organs and conduits shifted into new alignments, while great masses of Baggy's gelatinous substance came together and melded seamlessly and the surface on which they stood vibrated and stirred.

"Watch it, Cap!" Cookie blurted. "It might pull that same trick!"

"I don't think so," Judson replied unperturbed. "Baggy's no fool. He knows now we're more valuable as friends and allies, than as an indigestible meal."

There, Baggy uttered hesitantly, as his reassembly was completed, *does this mean we're "friends"?*

A moment, Baggy went on after a pause. *I perceive strange new potencies flowing from the curious suture you created in my farf-complex. For example:*

The huge mass stirred and pulled itself into an oblate spheroid like a balloon full of water. *That's a lot better*, came its voice, stronger now, Judson thought. Then the bag stirred, lifted itself clear of the wrecked spinner, and settled down a few yards distant.

"Hey, Cap," Cookie said uncertainly. He was rubbing his face and looking puzzled. "I've got a funny kind of feeling in my . . ." His voice faded off and his knees buckled. He collapsed and lay moving feebly. Judson became aware at that moment of a sensation under his scalp like the probing of insubstantial fingers.

Baggy! he said sharply, *stop it!*

But I was merely replenishing my vital energies from your abundant supply, the alien complained. *You recall I told you—*

I recall very well, Judson told the hungry creature. *But we have no vital energies to spare. You'll have to find some other source.*

But there is none! Baggy carped. *If I skimmed off just a little it would hardly reduce your IQs by more than a point or two, and perhaps occasion a trifle of nausea. Surely you'll not deny me!*

Judson drew his power pistol. *Stop it right now, or I'll be forced to redesign your nodes again,* he warned, taking aim at the dark mass within the gelatinous bulk.

But— Baggy protested, *—when you risked your lives to aid me when I was helpless, I assumed you'd be only too glad to allow me to strip you of whatever I could use.*

I've known a lot of people like you, Judson replied. *You interpret kindness as stupidity and courtesy as weakness. Now lay off—and don't ever try that again!*

Well, Baggy responded dejectedly, *I'll try to abstain, but I'll be operating at reduced powers, you understand.*

"Cap!" Cookie spoke up. "That damned thing tried to kill us!"

"Not quite. He only intended to reduce us to seasick imbeciles. But he won't try it again."

"But can we trust the critter?"

Certainly not! Baggy affirmed promptly. *This is not an occasion for such far-out concepts as "trust!" Let us begin on a firm basis of mutual advantage!*

Even Cookie agreed that was reasonable, and after a brief discussion, the alien reluctantly conceded that the Terrans' help, although already accomplished, should weigh in the balance of "advantage."

"Which leaves," Cookie put in importantly, "what you're going to do for us—aside from warning us about the flash flood, that we—or Cap anyway—knew about."

I take it, the alien said soberly, *that the extension of yourselves—a "spinner," I perceive you call it—a triumph of brute force over the pattern of Nature—is prized by you.*

"Dern right it was!" Cookie blurted.

"We needed it for exploration," Judson explained, "and many other tasks as well. Its loss is a heavy blow."

Then why not reconstitute it? Baggy demanded, withdrawing, as he "spoke," the last of his tissues from entanglement with the smashed machine, the fragments of which lay flattened and scattered across the trampled grass.

"Good idea," Cookie exclaimed, "if we had the machine shop at Lunabase and an unlimited supply of raw materials, plus a few off-the-shelf-items like the plasma motors and the solid-state stuff!"

Already, the alien had deployed dextrous pseudopodia and had righted the mainframe and with a few deft taps straightened the longeron tubes; now it was busily rewelding broken joints, using a pinkish energy that flowed from the tips of specialized pseudo-limbs. The reconstituted spinner was taking shape.

"Jeez!" Cookie gasped reverently. "Looky there, Cap! Sparky's Frame Shop in the Belt couldn't of done it that good and that fast! Old Baggy might be a valuable contact at that!"

"Hold on, Baggy!" Judson spoke up abruptly. "That member can't be welded until the wiring is back inside." The alien paused in its swift manipulations to brush aside heaped fragments and segregate the tangled conductors of the primary cable, which it quickly freed of kinks and entanglements, then sealed breaks in the insulating cover, and finally tested it with a pulse of the pink energy.

"Old Baggy catches on fast, Cap, don't he?" Cookie crowed. "Sparky hisself couldn't of primaried that better!"

"He had direct access to both your and my expertise," Judson reminded the cook. "Now," he went on addressing the alien, "you'll find the broken panels rather difficult to work with. The material was compounded especially to resist fracture and distortion. Now that the force of the impact has fractured and distorted them, they will have to be discarded; thus, no reshaping them."

Oh, Baggy commented quietly, *suppose I try this?* He had extruded a thick, short member with, Judson noted, a direct neural connection to the fasciculum, and with it, plucked a warped and cracked panel from among the debris and spread a thin layer of living tissue over it. With a sharp *pop!* the panel snapped back into shape, the fractures annealing instantly. Baggy handed the panel to Cookie, casually. *Will this suffice?* he inquired diffidently.

Cookie looked over the restored part and declared it factory-perfect. "Durnedest thing I ever seen!" he told Judson. "I done my time in fabrication, Cap, you know that, and I never seen nothing like that before! I'd of swore it was impossible! Them crystal-lattices don't knit easy. How you reckon he done that?"

"Suffice it to say, for the moment," Judson suggested, "that he did, indeed, do it."

"Go ahead, Baggy," Cookie urged. "Fix the rest of 'em—and then let's see what else you got in yer bag o' tricks that's gonna recharge the accumulator plates and all!"

Meanwhile, the alien had continued to clear the heaped fragments, sorting and straightening, pausing only momentarily over the complex molecular-array circuit boards, then proceeding to reconstruct the major subassemblies and install the repaired components on the mainframe.

"By Gaw, Cap," Cookie marveled. "She's starting to look like a Mark XIII again; I never figgered that was possible, hard as she hit."

"I had a hunch Baggy could be a valuable ally," Judson reminded him.

The busy alien, now resembling a thick, lumpy blanket covered with tentacles, humped and slithered around, under and over the miraculously reappearing machine. As a final touch, it extruded a delicate member that exuded a glossy black fluid with which it retraced the legend ROCKY III—NINE on the repolished prow. The transparent canopy was a trifle cloudy, Judson noted, but adequate.

Baggy withdrew. *I have done all I can,* he said in his silent way. Judson nodded and climbed aboard. Once in the seat, refinished to its original deep-blue luster, he noted, he actuated the startup sequence and was at once rewarded with the stir of the invisibly-mended rotor and the mutter of the starting coil, which quickly rose to the muted howl of the main helix. He tried the controls. The spinner lifted lightly; he steered it in a fifty-foot circle and put it down beside the murky-grayish-with-green-showing-through blob—at least a hundred feet in diameter, he realized in surprise. Cookie jumped in. "Looks great, Cap!" he exulted. "Old Bag done good!"

"Suppose you set up an autosequence in the car's box, Space'n," Judson said, "to return to the ship and restow itself. We'll ride the spinner for a while."

Cookie nodded and hurried away. Judson focused his attention on Baggy. "Are you all right now?" he wanted to know.

I will probably never recover full function, particularly in the fifth mentational range, came the reply. *But I seem to be capable enough of simple functions, but by way of compensation, I have the remarkable new capacities with which your intervention has endowed me. I presume the curious sensation I am experiencing is that denoted by your term "gratitude." So I shall delay no longer in returning to my patrol duties.*

I shall return after the floodwaters have receded, and perhaps we can further pursue the possibilities inherent in a "friendly" relationship. "Relationship!" it repeated, wonderingly. *How readily a part of my psyche seems to accept the concept—when I know perfectly well that the only valid "relationship" is that of predator and prey.*

"There are better ways," Judson assured the alien being. "You've just seen one. We helped you; without our help you'd still be struggling to reassemble your central nervous system, to say nothing of your somatic elements. We can do more together; give it some unprejudiced thought."

I shall try, Baggy promised. *But how*, he wondered, *does one divest oneself of one's prejudices? And selectively, mind you, for it would hardly serve me to lose my prejudice against consuming the blue salts . . .* Judson sensed a mental shudder. *Farewell, Judson entity,* the alien concluded, and abruptly spread itself in a diaphanous membrane hardly half an inch thick, Judson estimated. It rippled like a flag in the light breeze and was lifted aloft, to rise with a thermal updraft, drifting off rapidly to the east.

"Wait!" Judson thought urgently after the departing creature. "We need to talk! There's a question I need to ask!"

Calmly, Judson, came the only slightly attenuated reply. *I shall monitor your frequency with a fraction of my awareness.*

"Listen," Judson demanded. "Are there any other life-forms here? You told us you're the last of your kind, but what about other species?" As Judson spoke, Cookie was guiding the car toward the ship; the entry dilated, and the car shot up the ramp and inside. Cookie, who had trailed the car a few feet, came back, breathing hard.

One does not trouble oneself with such trivia, the alien was saying loftily.

"What trivia?" Cookie demanded.

"Us," Judson told him mildly, as Baggy rippled in to rest on the grass beside the two men. Judson gave Cookie an interrogatory glance.

"What *about* us, Cap? We're sure-bob another species, and it troubled to wreck our spinner all the same!"

That was a different matter, Cookie entity, Baggy told him testily. *You, and your spinner-unit here, were truly different: never before encountered. I needed to investigate.*

"So now you investigated," Cookie came back sarcastically, "what do you think? Are we good enough to be pals with, or what?"

The matter is settled, the huge entity told him reprovingly. *We are "friends." Your Judson-unit so stated. Now I really must be off, and I advise you again to evacuate this site instanter.*

"Just leaving, Bag," Cookie said as he climbed into the spinner. "Ready to go, Cap?" he inquired jauntily.

You have only a few seconds before this spot is inundated, Baggy said, and rippled aloft.

"He's right, Cap," Cookie said, just as Judson said, "Buckle up, Space'n. I can hear it coming."

"See it, too," Cookie exclaimed. "Looky yonder! Cloud o' dust and stuff boiling up. Must be *some* piece o' water!"

"It makes the Johnstown Flood seem like a leaky pipe," Judson concurred. By this time Judson had executed a hover-turn, and they were speeding toward the small-office-building-sized tower that was their link with all of life's necessities. A distant rumble was audible through the sound-deadening canopy; then the vehicle began to pitch and yaw.

"Seismic turbulence!" Judson gasped out as he fought the controls.

"Look out, Cap!" Cookie yelped. "Fissure opening up there, off the port bow! Might spit fire!"

"I see it," Judson managed, as he steered left above unfractured ground. "How's the flood doing?" he asked, too busy to look.

"Close, Cap," Cookie reported. "And coming faster'n the Monoroute Dispatch! It'll miss us, though; spreading as the valley widens out here. But don't waste no time, Cap. We need full boost to squeak past 'fore it reaches here!" He grabbed a handhold as the turbulent air buffeted the light machine.

Judson, steering the nearly unmanageable vehicle low above rutted, cracked rock that rippled like the shallows of a river, was fully occupied with attempting to maintain an approximate course toward the ship, which was now rocking perilously on its spidery landing jacks. Cookie uttered a wail as the vessel leaned, teetered, almost settled back, then toppled, the portside jacks buckling, holding for a moment, then collapsing to allow the space-hull to slam the rock with an impact the two men imagined they could hear above the howl of the wind around the tormented spinner.

"Port antenna's gone!" Cookie blurted; the complex-shaped housing over the ship's delicate pickup structure had bounced free of its attachment and gone end-over-end, amid a cloud of dust and a hail of flying fragments.

Judson steered into the dust-cloud and skidded to a halt beside the fallen spaceship, studying the open seams with a professional eye.

"We'll be able to salvage quite a lot," he told his crewman. "I'd say her main conduit is intact, and if we can get into the aft module, we'll be able—"

He broke off as a final ripple running through the rock flipped the broken ship back against a newly up-thrust rock-ledge—the edge of a giant uplifted slab—just as Cookie yelled, "Hey, no fair! Lay off already!"

After a moment, the dust settled enough to reveal only the serrated sediment-layers of the exposed slab-edge, the view unimpeded by the prostrate bulk of *Rockefeller III*.

"She's gone!" Cookie gulped. Judson eased the vehicle forward, until a ragged line was visible that was the border of a fissure running parallel with the uplift. The spinner settled to rest. Judson set the controls on auto-hover.

"She fell in that damn crack!" Cookie wailed. Both he and Judson jumped out of the spinner, ignoring the flying dirt and grit, and the trembling underfoot, and advanced to the edge of the rift. Nothing was visible in the unlit depths. The spinner hummed, a few feet over their heads.

"Deep!" Cookie commented. "Can't see nothing down there, Cap! She must've fell a long way!"

Judson checked the ground at their feet, took Cookie's arm, and pulled him back, just as the rock on which they were standing dropped without warning into the abyss. More dust boiled up. The sound of impact below was a belated and long-drawn clatter.

" 'Are, eye, pee,' " Cookie intoned solemnly. "Cap, didja know that don't stand for 'Rest in peace'? It's '*Requiescat in pace*,' that's Latin, see. Anyways, Latin or English, 'are, eye, pee.' "

"Nonsense, Space'n," Judson said. "We're going to

have some work ahead, but we'll salvage her yet. We *have* to," he added. "Maybe Baggy will help."

"Ha!" Cookie barked. "Old Baggy's long gone! He don't want to get drowned no more'n we do!"

Before Judson could reply, both men became aware of the alien's characteristic "voice" intruding among their thoughts.

Judson entity! You must withdraw from the low ground at once; the seismic activity is severe; the entire formation is being subducted!

"Can't hardly run back, Cap," Cookie remarked grimly. "Floodwaters'll—" He was cut off by the arrival of the subject of his prediction. Both men jumped for the edge of the rock ledge above the rift that had swallowed *Rocky;* foamy water smashed against the rock-face as they pulled themselves up. Cookie was first to run a few steps back from the edge.

"We're sunk, Cap!" he yelled, returning. "Ends about ten feet off; I durn nigh went over; seen lava down there! Should we drownd, Cap, or roast?"

Neither, unless of course you so desire, Baggy's insidious voice replied. *I have an idea. Be calm, but act quickly. There's no time to summon your spinner; you must clamber aboard me, and I shall take us all to safety.*

A foot-thick membrane of Baggy's jelly-like substance slapped rock behind them. Cookie dived onto its relatively cool and dry surface, Judson following less precipitately. Abruptly, as Baggy lifted off, water surged across the rock-spine on which they had taken refuge, even as molten basalt, glowing dull red, welled up to confront it in an explosion of steam. The alien rose to an altitude of ten feet, bearing the two Terrans out of the dust and the stink of hot rock. They looked around at the suddenly-clear vista of rushing water, above which their host hovered at a height of some ten feet, rippling gently. A cool breeze blew away the last of the foul air. No vestige of their last perch was visible above the flood. A cone of ropy black lava was forming, fed by a constant upwelling of red-hot fluid from below.

Cookie drew breath and offered a stagey sigh. "Jeez, Cap," he said fervently, "We don't need to come that close again! Guess we got to thank our pal, Baggy. Thanks a lot, Bag, old boy; you're OK in my book!"

"How far to dry land?" Judson asked the circumambient space.

Three miles, due east, Baggy told him at once. *A height of land, now an island; I shall take refuge there.*

Judson was looking down at trees, tossing and spinning in the turbulent current below, their root-systems above water.

"Guess we'll have wood OK, Cap," Cookie was saying. "we don't need to cut no timber, just slice up what the flood tore up."

"Good thinking, Space'n," Judson told him. "Look over there," he changed the subject. "Do I see our caves above water?" Indeed, to the west, the highest ridge of the bluff was above the flood stage, and the black dots of the cave-mouths were visible, high and dry.

"Take us there, Baggy," Judson requested.

I secure a thrill each time I hear my very own personal designation uttered, Baggy crooned. *"Baggy." How euphonious it is! Baggy! Baggy, Baggy! I dote on it—and on my new "friendship" with you, alien beings though you are! I feel gratified that I experienced the impulse to succor you!*

"Did he say 'sucker,' Cap?" Cookie inquired dourly. " 'Impulse,' he says. What if he hadn't bothered? Did you ever really think about it, Cap? What it would feel like to be dead? To not be here, to have the world go on without you?"

"Never did, Space'n," Judson said. "But I suppose it would manage. I hope so; after all, Earth is going to have to get along without our contribution."

"Serves 'em right," Cookie muttered. "But this here place is a lot different story," he went on, warming to his theme. "Without us—zilch!" He made a throwing-away gesture. "Old Baggy'da been done for if we never he'ped him."

"But of course, he'd not have been injured in the first place," Judson pointed out. "If we hadn't intruded our alien spinner into his pristine environment."

"Let's keep that one between *us*, Cap," Cookie suggested.

No need, Baggy's voice rang in. *I had already tempered my bounteous "gratitude" with that realization. Still, you* intended *me no harm—that's being the odd thing you call "fair"—*and *you* did *assist me afterwards. To include that datum in my rationalization is also "fair"—while,* Baggy continued in an admonitory tone, *to propose to keep from me the awareness of your culpability, voluntary or no, is hardly "fair." This is an anomaly in your psyches that I will need to investigate at length. You declare, and indeed believe in, an abstract principle, which you then proceed to violate—or at least propose to violate. But I perceive further that you entertain many elaborate fantasies that you treat as real, while knowing full well their insubstantial nature; while other fantasies, no less ephemeral, proceed to fruition, as your decision to come here, all the recollection of which I find neatly stowed at the barely subvocal level in your curious minds.* As Baggy droned on, the two men crouched on the rubbery membrane that was the alien's hide, buffeted by the wind of passage.

"Talks a lot, don't he?" Cookie remarked. "But what's all that stuff got to do with anything useful?" he inquired sourly. "Cap ast you to take us to the caves, Baggy-Baggy. How's about it?"

"Baggy-Baggy!" the alien thought-form echoed. *Even lovelier! Baggy, Baggy, Baggy . . .*

"We got aholt of a advanced case of narcissim here, Cap," Cookie muttered. "Listen to him with that 'Baggy-Baggy!' "

" 'Baggy' is pretty," Judson said. "Why shouldn't he rejoice in the name?"

"Ain't modest," Cookie charged. "You and me, Cap, we don't set around saying 'Clarence, Clarence, Clarence' or 'Cap, Cap, Cap' alla time."

"That's because we grew up with a name," Judson

explained. "One of the first intellectual acts of our lives was the recognition of our name. We accept it as designatory of that marvelous, totally unique, universe-centered entity, *me.* Poor old Baggy-Baggy didn't have that advantage. He was only a spore, drifting in the cosmic current, along with countless billions of his siblings, unnoticed, unappreciated, not unique even to himself. Now, with a name that belongs to him alone, he can fully appreciate his importance, he wonderfulness, his only-one-of-his-patternness, if you will."

"What if I won't?" Cookie grumped. "You sound like a press agent, Cap. Old Baggy's just a guy like you and me. Nothing special; prolly even back when all these here siblings of his was still around, they never figgered he was anything much."

They shunted me aside, Baggy mourned. *They failed utterly to realize what a marvel of sensitivity and aspiration I was. They thought of me by the symbol "XZLX," which is to say, "boring." Me, Baggy-Baggy-Baggy, they found dull! Glad they're gone, the dull, unappreciative clods!* Baggy lapsed into vague, formless subvocalization.

"Don't sweat it, Bag," Cookie comforted the anguished alien. "That's the story of ever'body's life."

You, too, are unappreciated? came the alien's astonished response. *You, alien creatures of a strangeness not to be conceived, also suffer from the failure of the universe to fully realize your special sensitivities? Yet you have names, Judson entity and Clarence entity. So, unlike as we are, we too are siblings!*

"Fine," Cookie came back sardonically. "Don't try to eat us just yet. How about landing us right in front of that center cave, on the slope."

Baggy at once swooped down, and with a final ripple came to rest before the cavern. The two men deBagged and went inside to stand on the smooth floor.

Even stranger, Baggy was ruminating. *How readily they enter the dark confines of the terrible place.*

" 'Terrible'?" Cookie repeated the word that had thrust into his mind like a stab-wound. "What's terrible about it? Cap," he went on, "you hear that? Baggy says this here cave is a terrible place! What's he mean?"

"It's only that his kind evolved as bottom-feeders," Judson told him, having grasped the gestalt from the alien's shocked mind. "Their predator always lay in wait in holes and jumped out at them; it's just a hereditary fear, like our own instinctive dislike of high places."

"High places don't worry *me* none!" Cookie declared stoutly. "Hell, what's higher'n a ship in orbit? I like it up there!"

"That's different," Judson told him. "There has to be a material connection between you and the surface far below. Like standing on the platform at the top of the Lookout at Lunaport; unrailed, you'll recall, and six feet square. You look down and see that spire tapering down away from you, and it's a rare man who wouldn't rather be elsewhere; whereas, if you're flying in an atmosphere craft, you can look down and enjoy the toy houses and roads without a pang, because there's no link to tell your monkey-brain it's a high place."

"OK, OK, I get it, Cap," Cookie blurted impatiently. "But old Bag was in a panic there. If he's that scared o' this cave, we oughta check it out better'n we done." With that he began a circuit of the newly erected partition, scanning both floor and ceiling for signs of incipient disaster.

"Looks good, Cap," he reported. "Good to be home. Cozy-like. How about some chow? Good thing we packed as much stuff up here as we done before she fell. Got three cases of the King Tuts."

Outside, Baggy was silently murmuring. *Baggy-Baggy-Baggy . . .* then, *Men.* He focused his thoughts on the Terrans. *I am so profoundly grateful for the gift of my euphonious name that I have utterly abandoned any thought of devouring you. Indeed, I pledge myself to aid you in any way I can. It is yours but to command.*

"Sure, we covered all that," Cookie replied offhandedly. "We're friends, right? Let's get on with it. Bag, you can clear all that scree away from the slope there, where we won't break an ankle getting in. By the way, since you ran outa siblings, what do you eat?"

"You'd better use the controller to bring the spinner over here," Judson told Cookie. "Probably we should have flown over in it, and declined Baggy's offer of a free ride."

"But he talked kinda urgent," Cookie reminded his captain. "Seemed like a good idear to get out fast. We got out OK, anyways. That's what counts."

He switched the wavelength of his controller to that of the aircraft and gave the "lift" command. Far below, they could see the tiny spinner hop up at Cookie's command and head up-valley toward them, above an expanse of choppy floodwater.

"Do you think that's gonna rise any higher?" Cookie wondered. Both men were now looking out past the cave mouth at the swirling shallows a few feet below. Judson glanced up the valley to the west, where he saw the glint of sunlight on a tongue of green water, foam-laced.

"Jeez," Cookie said reverently, "here it comes again."

"Probably an ice-dam in the high peaks broke," Judson guessed. "It's not as big as the first wave. I think we'll still be all right here. There's a lot of valley to fill before it reaches the cave."

"Yessir, but we're cut off up here." Cookie abruptly changed subjects to ask, "Where'll I set her down, Cap'n, sir?"

"As close as you can," Judson told him. Cookie parked the flyer on the little platform just above the water's edge. "Let's do a recee," Judson suggested.

They boarded and lifted off and flew slowly upstream.

I, too, shall go aloft until the inundation is complete, Baggy's unexcited comment came to them. The thick blanket of living matter that was the alien thinned to transparency, did its preliminary ripple, and drifted upward, riding the slope-current, keeping just aft of the spinner.

"Old Baggy don't levitate like I done that time," Cookie remarked. "He takes it easy, uses the air."

At a great economy of energy, Baggy told him. *One must conserve one's strength for emergencies.*

"If getting chewed up by a Mark IV spinner and clobbering in, and being about to be drownded by a flood ain't a emergency," Cookie demanded, "what in tarnation *is*?"

What is about to transpire, so qualifies, Baggy replied, calm as always. *Some event the nature of which is so strange that I cannot conceptualize it, will occur in a matter of seconds. Guard yourselves well, little friends! Now I must flee. Au revoir!* and he was gone.

"Wait a minute, Bag!" Cookie yelled belatedly. "Tell us a little more about this here event!"

"Let's lie low and observe," Judson ordered. "We might as well go back and get on with fixing lunch while we wait for this cataclysm."

19

"You know, Cap," Cookie remarked half an hour later as they were finishing off the hearty lunch of ham sandwiches and shrimp salad that Cookie had conjured from the compacted supplies on hand, "this ain't so bad. We got plenty of room, a nice dry cave with all the modern conveniences, good eats, and nobody around to give us no trouble. 'Cept for the cataclysm, o' course," he added, "unless maybe old Bag was kidding us."

"No," Judson objected, "he wasn't kidding: the concept wouldn't fit into his mind, even—and we both read him loud and clear—with no overtones of deceit."

"Guess yer right," Cookie agreed, and rose to begin clearing the table. "Better get cleaned up here, where we can end neat, anyways."

"It's not necessarily going to be fatal," Judson reminded him. "All Baggy said was 'an event so strange' he couldn't picture it."

"Said 'guard yourselves,' too," Cookie pointed out. "I'll take another look." He went to the cave mouth and peered out under the overhang, wagging his head doubtfully.

"Prolly won't have no warning," he predicted. "Jest

all of a sudden . . . *blap!*" He came back, looking dejected. "This here cave will prolly fall in when the quake hits," he predicted. "No point in going outside, though, 'cause if it's a big meteor strike right here in the valley it'll vaporize the whole square mile."

"Maybe it'll just be a shower of daffodils," Judson suggested. "Baggy couldn't visualize *that.*" In the momentary silence before Cookie could muster a reply, both men became aware of a screech: a high, thin thread of sound descending from the supersonic.

"It's a incoming!" Cookie blurted. "I'll never fergit that noise! Gonna hit close, too!"

"Easy, Space'n," Judson told him. "We were just talking about meteorites; maybe—" He broke off as the sound abruptly modulated, became irregular, a sort of *thump! thump!* that in turn became a roar that swelled, echoing now across the valley. Both men dashed for the entry and looked out and up to see a bright point glowing just below the gray cloud layer.

"Can't be!" Cookie blurted. "A *Lindy*-class coming in on emergency GDQ! Or I'm a dirt-crawler!"

By this time Judson had trained binoculars on the glowing object.

"She's on a get-down-quick all right," he told his companion. "But she's botched it; she's coming in broadside and burning off hull-metal."

"The poor slobs," Cookie mourned. "Picked a funny place to clobber in on, eh, Cap? Way out here, what you think they was looking for anyways?"

"That's easy," Judson said. "Us."

The out-of-control vessel went into a tumble as it grew visibly in size.

"Baggy!" Judson called suddenly.

You see? came the unhurried reply. *What could be stranger than a near-duplication of your own unheard-of advent here? Once was almost incredibly unlikely; twice within a brief time quite violates possibility.*

"Baggy," Judson said urgently. "Could you encapsulate, er, wrap yourself around the ship and ease it down?"

Why, Baggy inquired in a tone of wonder, *would I do such a thing? The heat alone would occasion some discomfort, and the energy expenditures would quite deplete me.*

"To save the lives of the passengers," Judson told the naïve alien. "Unless you cushion the impact, they'll all be killed!"

Could you not reassemble them, much as you did my own cerebral members? Baggy wanted to know.

"Absolutely not!" Judson replied. "Hurry, Baggy, it will soon be too late!"

I shall assess the situation and determine if any effort I might make could be efficacious, Baggy answered casually.

The *boom!*ing of the falling vessel was like thunder as it neared the surface. Judson saw a flash of white light from the underhull of the now dull-red-glowing ship.

"They got a lifeboat away!" he told Cookie. "Baggy!" he renewed his appeal to the alien. "You can surely catch the lifeboat and ease it down!" Even as he spoke, he saw a flicker of motion by the tiny boat: it quickly resolved into the greenish blob-shape of Baggy, folding over the boat, which it dwarved in size, immediately slowing the descent, then dropping down at a more leisurely pace toward the surface of the river, while the ship itself fell impeded.

"No!" Judson yelled. "Not in the water, Baggy! No," he added, "on *this* side! We'll come in the spinner as soon as you're down. And *easy,* Baggy, *gently!*" To his relief, he saw the angle of descent become shallower as Baggy steered across the turbulent waters toward the high ground near the caves.

"Damn fool'da clobbered into the river," Cookie commented. "Fer a feller with all his brains, he's awful dumb." As he spoke, the two men reentered the spinner. They were headed out over the water so as to get a better view of the landing-site, when a titanic blast set the spinner into a tumble from which Judson righted it barely in time.

"Ship hit pretty hard," Cookie commented. "Boat got

away just in time. We going to go look at the boat?" In response, Judson lifted the spinner so as to afford a view of the slope just exposed by the recession of the flood-crest. The lifeboat, a standard class-C commercial-type emergency capsule, three-man, was lying canted, still draped in the translucent folds of Baggy. As Judson and Cookie approached, the aft personnel port stirred, then jammed. A scanner had swiveled to look Baggy over, then a small heat-projector of the kind known as "gravel-buster" quickly swiveled and, after hunting over the alien's glutinous surface, selected the portion where the cerebrum was housed, and halted to focus on it.

"No!" Judson shouted. "Dammit, Cookie, we've got to stop them before they fry old Bag's brain for good!" He gunned the spinner ahead to hover just above the boat, in order to allow the occupants to get a good look at it; then he settled in beside the boat. At once, Cookie was out and pounding on the forehull of the boat. He listened, heard a response from inside. Then he began to tap out in what he called Morris Code, the words: DONT SHOOT. THE ALIENS ON YOUR SIDE. The focusing traverse of the gun ceased. From inside, Cookie read, in code, WHO ARE YOU? HOW DO WE GET OUT?

Cookie tapped out, SIT TIGHT. BAGGY WILL LET GO NOW, then, "Baggy! Get clear! They want to open up. They seem to be OK in there, so, thanks!"

As you wish. Baggy slumped and flowed aside, to assume a form resembling a giant, translucent cow-pie, with the undamaged lifeboat sitting to one side, slightly canted on the grass. Cookie went to it, rapped out ALL CLEAR. COME ON OUT.

After a few moments, the personnel port again stirred, this time rotating briskly to pivot open. An arm appeared in the opening, clad in a civilian-tourist-style shipsuit and holding a 2mm needler, aimed vaguely. The arm was followed by a neat feminine figure topped by an old-style fishbowl helmet, inside which a face and an abundant head of red hair could be seen obscurely. She stepped down, turned quickly at sight of the men, and brought the gun up more purposefully.

"Who are you?" her voice crackled from the suit's talker. "What are you doing here?"

"Lady," Cookie replied, "we live here. The question is who're *you*, and what in tarnation are *you* doing here, outside o' clobbering in a mighty expensive *Lindy*-class?"

"I'm looking for traces of Mr. Marl Judson," she said. "He'd be long-dead, of course, but we think he could have made it here, and there should be *some* evidence—the remains of his ship, for example." She broke off, sounding a bit breathless. "All right," she resumed. "I've answered your questions. How about mine?"

As the woman spoke, Judson had come toward her until he could look directly into her face through the grayish bubble.

"Barbie!" he exclaimed, and caught her hand. "Barbie McLeod, what in the world—?" He broke off as the woman stepped back, shaking her head.

"No, I'm Barbie Allen; Barbie McLeod was my mother," she told the astonished men. "She always—Never mind. She lived a full life, and she never forgot. When the Council fell—only a year after Mr. Judson disappeared—she determined to find out what they'd done to him. It was a strange story. An Admiral Coign helped a lot, but he warned her a search would be useless. Still, she persevered, and managed to keep Private Space out of the hands of AutoSpace—she was a director, you may know—and at last she and a few others borrowed—or stole—the ship and mounted this expedition. I insisted on coming; I'd promised her the night she died I'd do all I could to find Marl Judson—and here I am. Now, who are you?"

"Brace yourself, Barbie," Judson said solemnly. "I'm Marl Judson, and as you see, I'm alive and well. This is my shipmate, Space'n Cl—Cookie Murphy."

"But—how?" the girl stammered. "You'd be almost a hundred years old . . . !"

"Not quite," Judson corrected. "Fifty-six next February, if I've counted right."

"You haven't!" she cried. "You disappeared over thirty years ago!"

"Dearie, would you mind putting that gun down?" Cookie inquired nonsequentially. The girl holstered the weapon; then, as she stepped closer to Judson and looked him full in the face for the first time, she exclaimed, "You *are* Marl Judson! I recognize you from your pictures! Mother had a trideocube; you gave it to her once at a party."

"I don't remember," Judson replied. "I'm surprised she even remembered me."

"She remembered you very well," Barbie told him almost rebukingly. "Actually I'm rather surprised you don't remember her—"

"I do," Judson said. "I was just a distant admirer."

"Not so distant, Captain," the girl corrected.

"Of course we were shipmates," Judson conceded.

"She said you were the only *great* man she'd ever met," Barbie told him. "She'd be so glad to know you'd made it here—while AutoSpace has been fretting over you all these years."

"Beautiful Barbie," Judson mused. "I should have taken the time to notice her more than I did."

"She understood," the girl reassured him. "You were more than a busy man: she was content to worship you from afar. And then there were the reports you'd been arrested for treason—and then word got out you'd escaped, disappeared. So we're here." As she finished, a man wearing a breathing mask emerged from the port, half-behind Cookie, a big fellow, six-five perhaps, and well-muscled. He held a wire-gun, which he jammed into the little man's spine. Without turning, Judson struck down at the gun hand, sending the weapon bounding off into the grass. The newcomer cursed, gobbled an apology to the woman, and charged Judson, who leaned aside, tripped him as he blundered past, and chopped him at the base of the skull. The man struck face-first, skidded a yard, and lay moving feebly. Barbie jumped back with an exclamation, then,

"George, you utter fool! Now get up, if you can, and apologize to both these gentlemen!"

"He'll be out for an hour or so," Judson told her. "I pinched the cord pretty hard, but he'll be all right."

" 'Cept maybe his fingers and toes'll tingle some for a few years," Cookie contributed. "He got off easy, pulling a gun on me and Cap. Cap coulda kilt him jest as easy."

"I'm *deeply* sorry," Barbie said contritely. "I had no idea . . ."

"He was just being protective of you, miss," Judson interceded.

"Please call me Barbie, or Barb," the young beauty requested.

Judson nodded formally. "And you, I hope, will call me Marl."

She shook her head, causing her tawny mane to toss inside the fishbowl. "I couldn't!" she declared. "Please let me call you 'Captain,' like Cookie does." She moved closer to the latter, melting him with a smile like sunrise over the Himalayas.

"As you wish, Barb," Judson acceded gracefully.

Cookie went over and stirred George with his foot. "Come on, hotshot, let's see you get a couple of feet under you."

"Just let him rest awhile, Cookie," Barb said. "The poor thing has been under a strain." Her eyes strayed beyond him to the smoking pit that marked the impact of her ship.

"There were only the two of us at the last," she said, "after Crench and Benny killed each other. It was horrible! And—and—it was all *my* fault!"

Judson went to her and embraced her comfortingly, while Cookie patted her shoulder awkwardly.

"It *wasn't* your fault, Barb," Judson told her gently. "You can't help being the most gorgeous female alive."

She wailed, shaking her head. "But you weren't *there!*" she managed. "How could you know how it was?"

"I know how I'd feel if I was locked up in a luxury hotel like your late command over there, for a few years, with the object of every man's profoundest fantasies, and two smaller males. It's surprising George here lasted it out."

"Benny was worst," Barb told the two men, who listened attentively. "He openly threatened to kill George and even old Crench! But Crench fooled him, then Benny fooled *him*, and the bomb killed both of them. That was what disabled the ship. George managed to get us into a sort of approach orbit, and then we took to the boat!" She paused to shudder. "And then we saw that *thing*—like a manta ray as big as a city block, made of slime—and it caught us and we fell out of control, and—and then you came!" She broke into tears, clinging to Judson, who murmured soothingly.

"That *thing* was only our friend, Baggy," he told the distraught girl between her paroxysms of sobbing.

"He's really a very nice fella," Cookie told her, then, "Hey, Baggy, say hello to Barbie!"

Hello, Barbie, the alien dutifully replied. *Welcome to Judson's Empire. Don't be alarmed, be happy! You've arrived safely, and George is only playing possum, right, George?*

The man on the ground moaned and made swimming motions.

I see there's a slight obstruction in the motor-nerve path, Baggy remarked. *May I soothe it? I won't meddle, just touch it lightly. . . .*

George sat up, clapped a hand to the back of his neck and yelled, "No! Get out! I won't have—!"

Do be calm, George, Baggy urged mildly. The big man had scrambled to his feet and was looking wildly from Barbie, still in Judson's embrace, to Cookie, standing by, looking back defiantly at him.

"Calm down, boy," Cookie told George. "That's just our friend, Baggy, helping you. If he hadn't done that, you'd of been on yer back fer maybe six months, and you wouldn't of had no Barbie for a nurse, neither. I'm just as glad I ain't gonna hafta hand-feed you and turn you over every few hours where you don't get no bedsores. So shaddup and be grateful!"

"Tell him to get away from Barb," George snarled. "I've killed two men and I'll kill two more—" Judson's backhanded blow knocked the loud-mouthed fellow on his back again.

Barbie clung to Judson's arm and said, "Please, Captain, don't pay any attention to him!" She stepped over closer to George, still lying supine, his eyes open, blinking up at her.

"Now, you, George," she said sternly, "you just stop making such a jackass of yourself. I hired you to run my ship, and you did a pretty good job of it up to a point. That's all there'll ever be between you and me. So it was *your* fault Crench's bomb blew prematurely and wrecked the panel! I'm ashamed of you, damaging your own command, and nearly killing both of us. If I hadn't thought of the lifeboat, you'd still have been groping the remains of the panel and gibbering. Then you wanted to kill Baggy, without even finding out who he was. 'Voices in my head!' you yelled. What's so awful about Baggy's voice? I think it's nice—and it helped *you!*"

"Let up, Barb," Judson urged. "The poor slob has just about had all he can take: committed murder, lost his command, been scared out of his wits, lost his dream-girl, been knocked on his butt twice, and now this chewing-out; it's enough! Get up, George, and forget your big ideas. They stop here."

George snarled and looked up at the girl.

"I done it fer *you*," he grated.

She tossed her head. "You're a fool, George," she said scornfully. "We were lucky enough to find someone here who can help us, and your first impulse was to start killing." She laughed. "Pitiful," she concluded. "You're not fit to carry Marl Judson's baggage!"

George made an incoherent sound and launched himself at Judson's legs, netting himself a knee in the face. Cookie came around Judson to confront the now bloody-faced fellow. "You're done, mister!" he barked. "Cap give you a chance, two chances, and you think that means he don't know how to deal with you. Well," the irate cook went on, "*I* do! Come on"—he nudged the tall man's legs with his foot—"get on yer feet, dumdum!" As George scrambled up, Cookie gave him a hearty shove. "Git!" he ordered. George staggered but halted abruptly and pivoted hard, his left arm extended, the hand flat. Cookie ducked under the whistling arc and kicked his charge vigorously in the calf of the leg. George yelped and grabbed his leg.

"What does Cookie intend to do?" Barbie asked. "George is an awful jerk, but I can hardly stand by and see him murdered."

Judson shook his head. "Don't worry; Cookie has a better idea than that." As Judson spoke, Cookie was urging George on, who was limping now and expostulating vigorously. After a while the two halted and Cookie addressed the man at length, interrupting himself twice to silence the fellow by shoving a wad of grass into his mouth. Then Cookie came back toward the lifeboat, while George spat grass and shifted from foot to foot until he suddenly charged Cookie from behind. Cookie seemed not to hear him, but when the bigger man reached him, he shifted weight and did a hip-throw that sent the bigger man sprawling, to lie where he had fallen.

As Cookie came up to Judson, he said, "I told the sucker I'd maroon him acrost the river if he didn't lay off tryna make trouble." He spat. "Damn fool come up on me like a line cart with a broke axle. Reckon he needs a few minutes to think it over."

"Captain," Barbie said in her soft voice, "could we go to your ship now? I'd love to get out of this vac-suit and fix my face."

"Your face don't need no fixin', Mis Allen," Cookie declared. "Good thing, too. Ship's gone."

"Gone? Whatever do you mean?" the girl queried confusedly. "Surely . . . *my* ship is destroyed," she said. "So all we have is yours, Cookie. And do call me Barb."

"We moved some stuff to a cave yonder, Barbie-honey," Cookie contributed. "Not too bad. You can catch up on your rest."

"I'd like that," Barbie said, putting a hand on the little man's arm, like the touch of a magic wand, transforming him into a handsome prince worthy to be her slave.

Leaving Baggy at rest, and George skulking in the distance, the three squeezed into the two-man spinner and quickly darted back to the bluff and settled down before their cave.

"No curtains," Cookie acknowledged. "Nothing fancy. But it's dry and warm enough, and we got *food*."

As they dined, Barbie gradually took notice of the amenities of the setting. "I never thought I'd be dining on Beef Wellington in a cave with two such charming gentlemen," she cooed. Then, more briskly, "Captain, there's something I have to tell you . . ."

Judson looked at her expectantly. "That you expect private sleeping accomodations?" he inquired indulgently. "No difficulty; there are extra panels and Cookie can run up a couple of partitions for you in a jiffy."

"Don't be fatherly, Captain, please," she countered in a tone with a hint of desperation.

Judson patted her hand. "What's wrong, girl?" he inquired in a tone that implied that whatever it was, it would be corrected.

"Captain," she said solemnly, with a melting glance at Cookie, "there was another lifeboat."

Judson nodded. "A *Lindy*-class carries a Schedule three crew-slab. Automated. I was wondering; your vessel carried a minimum crew of thirty-five."

Barbie was nodding. "The trouble started over a month ago," she told Judson. "That was when George and I killed Captain Hill. We *had* to," she hurried on. "Hill went out of his mind: he started waving a pistol around and telling people they were under arrest; that we were all traitors, aiding a fugitive enemy of the State." She paused to nod toward Judson. "That's you, Captain. He'd got an idea he could curry favor by bringing us all back 'in irons,' was the expression he used. When he tried to invade my cabin, George shot him! I was grateful. Then, Crench and Benny took over the bridge and they had a bomb and in the end Georgie had to kill them, too! It was horrible! The ship went out of control and we were barely able to get her into a capture orbit for the planet; we almost went into the dim sun." She paused to shudder. "The strain was too much for George. He told me he was the only man left—that was after the crew gave up trying to get at us and packed off in their escape module, when it looked as if we'd go into the dim sun—and he said that made me his woman. The fool! Actually, I'd liked him pretty well up till then, but he tried to rape me. I knew I had to get out; I almost left him behind, but I relented and let him into the boat. We didn't really expect to find anyone down here, except maybe the crew, all of them eager to kill George, and probably me, too. I'm *so* glad we found you!"

"We didn't see any sign of the crew-slab coming in," Judson told her. "It has a good cruise in atmosphere, so it could be anywhere."

"We better do a rec first thing in the morning, Cap," Cookie spoke up. "Get old Baggy on it, too." He paused. "No wonder old George hated the idea of being left out there alone so bad. He kept saying he had something to tell me, that would 'be to my advantage,' he said, if I'd let him stay on. Damn fool!"

"George seems to be full of information," Judson commented. "Maybe we should have grilled him before you ran him off, Space'n."

"I can run him down any time and pick his brains," Cookie grunted. "Didn't want the skunk in reach of weapons, might take a notion to shoot us all in the back. Barbie *told* us he's a killer."

Judson turned to the beautiful girl. "Exactly how many more in the crew?" he asked her. "Tell me about their leaders—not necessarily the officers, it seems."

Barbie shuddered. "There are four women," she said. "They divided the men up among themselves. They were known as the Duchesses. They'd determined to kill George because he left his duchess for me—that was his idea, anyway. Then he killed these fellows who belonged to the other three women. They all have reason to hate him—especially Nelda; George was her favorite until he deserted her and came over to me. It was a general mutiny, you understand. The officers were *all* killed. George saved my life, actually; Nelda sent him to kill me, but he didn't do it."

"I think we'd better assume the slab got down intact," Judson decided. "The automatic let-down circuitry in those Class C's is the best, and we have to assume they'll be hostile; they'll assume any signs of human life are the people who got off in the lifeboat. We know they're gunning for Barbie and George."

Barbie shuddered. "It's all so terrible, people wanting to kill each other—even here, so far from *everything*!"

"Don't fret, Barb," Cookie said comfortingly. "We're on guard; they won't sneak up on us. We've got some defensive gear—even your lifeboat will be useful. Let's just get some rest and tomorrow we'll find these Duchesses—or what's left of 'em!"

"We'd better start observing blackout procedures," Judson ordered. "I'll put out the fire, and you, Space'n, be sure the hand-light system you've rigged is shielded. Switch off all you can; even a faint glow from around the cave doors will stand out like a nuclear flare in this wilderness."

20

They passed a peaceful night. Shortly before dawn, Cookie nudged Judson.

"Something outside, Cap," he whispered, passing a needler into his captain's hand. "Heard a stumble on the ankle-trip I laid out in the scree."

"He came up from the left," Judson told the alert cook. "Climbed down from the top of the bluff over that way, I believe, and tried a quiet sneak up on our blind flank, but your stumble stones fooled him. I think it's probably George."

"I hear you talking in there!" George's hoarse voice rang out suddenly. "I've got the lot of you trapped. You'll have to deal with me, or I can hose you down like rats in a dry tank!"

Shall I remove this disturbance, friends? Baggy's silent voice interjected.

Judson heard George utter a single "Who—?" before he was silenced.

"He's harmless, Bag," Judson told the alien. "Leave him intact, but look out for the weapon he's carrying—probably a light assault gun—that's about all he could have hidden."

"I frisked him down good," Cookie reminded Judson.

"He could have gone back to the lifeboat," Barbie pointed out. "Cookie, I guess you should have shot him."

"Naw," Cookie dismissed the idea. "We can handle this clown—we might even straighten him out and get some use outa him." He looked at Barbie. "You think you could sweet-talk him, once we got him tied up good?"

"I could get him to cut his throat with a dull knife, if I wanted to," the girl said coolly. "I don't want to see him—alive or dead."

"Cookie," Judson said, "suppose you keep the jerk talking while I go out the back way and drop on him."

"Easy, Cap," Cookie responded. "Let me do the dropping. Old fella like you—eighty-something, Barbie says—could get hurt.

"Hey, you, George," he called toward the outer darkness at the mouth of the cave. "What you got in mind, fella? Cap wants to talk to you."

Judson shushed him and nudged him toward the back of the cave. He touched Barbie's arm, and whispered, "Go into your cubicle and lie low," he commanded. "Here—" He handed her the handgun. "Try not to shoot Cookie or me."

"I usually hit what I aim at," she replied, and moved off into the darkness.

"George," Judson called, "we're willing to talk to you, but first you'll have to throw that Mark Two down the slope. Go ahead. Now."

"Like hell I will—" George broke off as an abrupt clatter drowned out speech. Judson heard Cookie swearing and snarling, and George's deeper-toned objections, all mingled with the sound of blows, then comparative silence, followed by a sound of feet sliding on rock.

"Mark Two's downslope, Cap," Cookie reported. "Hope this poor sucker ain't got his neck broke."

There were sounds at the improvised doors and by the dim hand-light, Cookie crawled into view, dragging George.

"That's insubordination, Space'n," Judson told the returned warrior. "You all right?"

"Heck, yes," Cookie grunted.

Judson nodded. "Can't have the cook risking his neck," he stated, then turned to the crestfallen George, whom Cookie had trussed tightly.

"What did you have in mind, George?" he asked the man. "If you want to join the party, that was a poor approach."

"Things I can tell you." George's speech was slurred. "This little slut here—" Cookie's boot in his mouth cut short George's speech.

"Try again," Judson said softly, "and keep it civil."

"Kilt them fellers herself," he snarled. "She's the one sabotaged the ship. Tried to reason with her, Crenchy and Ben and me—she shot them, but I made it inside the boat and fooled her."

"Who's Nelda, George?" Judson asked casually.

George spat. "My woman," he barked, "or *was,* till little Barbie kilt her. Got jealous; me and Nell was content together, till *she* tried to come between us. Coming around half-nekkid, tryna stir up the men. She never told you about that, I bet."

The George unit is lying, Baggy put in. *Yet another curious concept: having the ability to communicate, yet employing it to obfuscate communication.*

"George," Barbie said from behind her partition, "I never thought you'd turn against *me,* after . . ."

"Yeah," George replied contemptuously, "you thought you owned me, didn't you, you bitch!"

George's head struck the pavement with a gourd-like sound as Judson's open hand slammed him backwards.

The Barbie unit has a pleasing mind-flavor, Baggy put in, *quite different from all three of you "male" units. "She"—I have difficulty in conceptualizing the profound distinction embodied in the pronoun "she"—yet she is pleasing to be near, though her mind seethes with the socially-repressed need to reproduce.*

"Why, I thought you were *nice!*" Barbie protested. "You just keep out of my head, Mr. Baggy!" She looked appealingly at Judson. "Where *is* this Baggy person?" she demanded. "How does he speak that way, as if he were inside my head?"

"Baggy's aloft, at about a thousand feet," Judson told her, having plucked the information from the alien's unshielded awareness. "He's drifting with the wind, dozing, but monitoring the surface below for indications of the crew-slab: lights, for example. So far, nothing."

"That's how he usually spends the night," Cookie put in, "drifting at low altitude."

"So I perceive," Barbie replied. "I don't really mind the contact so much, if he'd just not be personal."

How could any male not desire to "be personal" with such as you? Baggy responded. *Such a fecund medium for motherhood of one's brood is not to be imagined. Your bodily attributes which so arouse your fellow humans are of course without force in my case, but the contours of your sweet mind, the frames of your world-concept are so appealing that my identity melts in the wish to merge with yours. That indeed would be "Heaven," if I may borrow the term in this context.*

"That's sweet, I suppose," Barbie replied coolly. "But I really can't have a hundred-ton amoeba leching after me. It's not practical—no, not even—" She broke off, confused. "Baggy, you *do* have a nasty mind! Find yourself a nice girl of your own species!"

You wrong me, Baggy complained. *I only . . .*

"Take it easy, Bag," Cookie advised. "We're all in the same boat."

"I'm tired of being nothing but a bone for men—and others—to wrangle over," Barbie announced. "I've got as much libido as anybody—but people killing each other—without even asking my opinion . . . I've had enough, dammit! Let's act like four people with a common problem, and start using our brains—I *do* have one, you know!"

"*I* always respected yer brains, Barb!" George burst out. "You know that! Gimme credit! I'm not like these two Johnny-come-latelys: I'm your real friend! Even if you was ugly," he added, not very convincingly. "Times

I wished your face'd get burned or like that, where nobody'd want you but me!"

"Thanks a lot," Barbie commented. "What makes you think you'd get me by default?"

"Stop it, Barbie!" Judson snapped. "I know it's instinctive, but you *have* to quit provoking us!"

"Ain't her fault," Cookie put in. "That architecture o' hers . . . Like Baggy said—a feller gotta want—"

"A fella better control himself, Space'n," Judson told him.

"Barbie," he went on, "give us a break, OK? Try not to be so damned appealing. Go put some clothes on, for example," he added, since she had appeared at her cubicle door draped inadequately in a blanket.

"We have to find that peel-off," the woman said flatly, ignoring the wrangling. "If those four bitches find us first—" She left the consequences to their imaginations.

21

At first daylight, the party of four set out: Cookie and Barbie in the car; Judson and George, with his wrists trussed, in the spinner. The plan was to quarter the area north, south, east, and west for a distance of thirty miles, the car taking the land south and west, the spinner across the river and into the foothills to the north.

With his radar adjusted to detect small, dense objects on the surface of the plain, Judson steered to angle north away from the river. Twenty miles downstream, he encountered a dense radar clutter at extreme range. He called Cookie and told him to "break off, mark, and rendezvous here soonest." Baggy intercepted the call and demanded an explanation of the order, which Cookie, being a space'n, had simply obeyed.

"It looks like a town," Judson told the inquisitive alien creature. "Why didn't you tell us about it?"

Baggy denied any knowledge of the sort of assemblage the image of which he plucked from Judson's mind in association with the word "town." *No such alien cluster exists here*, he asserted; then, after extending his awareness, he amended his statement. *None existed prior to the present. This is indeed an aggregation of entities of your own kind, together with the structures—another inconceivable concept—they have erected as shelter. I must investigate.*

In vain, Judson called after the impetuous Baggy to "wait, be careful, let us humans reconnoitre first." Baggy was incommunicado. Cookie arrived, zooming in to park the car beside the spinner. Barbie was first to report and request an explanation.

"We saw some perfectly idyllic country," she said, "lovely wooded hills and a lake. But before we could explore, you demanded we come rushing here!"

"Shut up, Barb," Cookie snapped. "Cap knows what he's doing." He waited for Judson to tell them about it.

George spoke first. "Damn radar's out," he grumbled. "Show a city size o' Blisterburg, where we know damn well there ain't nothing!"

"We'll go take a look before we get too convinced of that," Judson counseled. "Cookie, you better swap vehicles with me and do an orbit around whatever this is, at half a mile; stay in the ground-clutter."

"Swell," Cookie remarked glumly. "Bye, Barb, wish we'd had time to get acquainted. I already know all I need to know about this George. And I'll tell you fair, boy," he addressed the latter, "anything outa you except sit quiet and say yessir, and I gut you. Got that?"

"I didn't ask to go," George pointed out anxiously. "I'll tell you one thing: you smart guys better stay clear of that town. It's got to be the crew, probably put up the reserve emergency shelters. Just a squatter camp, but they're armed, and they'll be on the lookout."

"Don't you worry about tactics, Georgie," Cookie advised. "Cap can manage."

"Tryna help," George muttered.

Oh, Judson entity, Baggy's insubstantial voice spoke up. *There is a great confusion of entities' voices there, emanating from the "town." Many entities like yourselves, mentating at once!*

"What are they saying?" Judson demanded.

I shall try to show you, Baggy said dubiously:

"*—Mommy!*"

"*—get that crop in tomorrow for sure—*"

"*Keep an eye on that Francine; try something outa—*"

"*—knew I never shoulda—*"

"*—tryna kill us all!*"

I find, Baggy added, *that the ostensibly single town in fact comprises four hostile factions, each occupying a quadrant of the whole, and identified by symbolic colors: green, yellow, purple, and pink. They are, it appears, on the brink of mutual annihilation. How savage! And they're not even hungry!*

"All right," Judson shushed the alien. "We get the idea: just a bunch of people with problems, like everybody else. OK, Space'n," he addressed Cookie, "go ahead. We'll come up on the east tangent. Keep in constant contact."

"Aye—Roger, Cap'n, sir," Cookie acknowledged cheerfully and hopped off.

"Got the town in sight, Cap," he reported a moment later. "I see a few lights down there. Looks like no power plant, just fires, and maybe some hand-lights. About half a mile across, two streets with a plaza in the middle, rows of issue hutments, and looks like some sod houses, too. I'm holding eight hundred yards from the plaza, attitude two hundred. No radar down there, Cap, with no power plant."

"Don't count on that, Cookie," Judson ordered. "Get down to a hundred feet, just in case. Any sign of emplacements, barricades, anything military?"

"Can't see too much in this here Brownie-light, Cap," Cookie reported. "I'll be on the lookout."

By then, the car was due east of the village, at a distance of a mile. Judson called Cookie to rendezvous. The spinner dropped in a moment later, and Cookie came over to the car.

"I think I'd better go in on foot," Judson told him, "and make contact with somebody in charge."

"Good way to get shot, Cap," Cookie objected. "Anyway, if somebody's got to do it, why not me?"

"One man won't panic them," Judson pointed out.

"I'm elected because I've had some experience in diplomacy—such as it was—dealing with AutoSpace and the Council."

"Guess I *ain't* no damn diplomat," Cookie acceded. "Place is cut like a pie, into four parts: two main streets, cross in the middle."

"Did you see a likely point of entry?" Judson queried.

Cookie nodded. "Got a kinda wall around the place. Sod, looked like. Gates at three streets: the other's got no gate installed yet, just a break in the wall. I'd say there. It's the southeast one, over there." He waved his hand.

"Go to a hundred feet and keep me in view," Judson said. "But don't intercede unless they've got a rope on my neck. George, you go in the spinner. Barb," he addressed the girl, "Space'n Murphy will take good care of you."

"Captain," she started, hesitantly, then changed her mind. "Be careful," she said.

"Them Duchesses'll kill us first and negotiate later," George contributed. "Better try to get to Nell. She's the least nuts o' the four."

"I'll drop the car near the wall," Judson told Cookie. "I may need it in a hurry, so leave it there."

"Sure thing, Cap," Cookie agreed. "I'll be keeping a close eye. Light's getting better, and I'll follow you with the spy-eye."

"Good idea. So long, Space'n." And Judson was off. He drove in close to the rugged, irregular, six-foot wall, which, as Cookie had thought, seemed to be of stacked sod-slabs. Judson halted the silent car fifty feet from the irregular opening, beyond which a yellowish lantern on a pole shed a wan light in a packed-dirt street. The few buildings visible through the opening were issue five-and ten-man units, each with a patch of short-mowed and well-trodden native grass. Children's toys in bright plastic were scattered on the grubby lawns, clearly an effort by the far-from-home squatters to recreate a homey environment, even here, in drab prefabs, light-years from suburbia. Judson used the shielded talker to call the spinner.

"So far, so good," Judson told Cookie, hovering noiselessly overhead. "Looks like any base housing area in the system. No military installations in sight. Peaceful folks." He left the car, and moved in on foot, alert for any movement ahead. At the edge of the opening in the wall, he risked a look down the street, saw no one abroad in the predawn glow. Other pole-lanterns made feeble patches at the alley mouths along the way, with a pair of brighter lights flanking the central intersection. Judson eased around the crumbling earth-wall and went along its inner surface to the back of the nearest shelter. There was no light there, the building shutting off the dim radiance of the pole-lamps. In deep shadow, Judson passed behind the issue-gray hutment, crossed an open patch, and approached an open door in the next unit, a slightly larger ten-man, without tricycles. At the doorway, he went flat against the wall, listening.

"Baggy," he called silently, "can you focus on this spot, and tell me who's in there, and what's going on?"

I shall try, Judson entity, came the reply, sounding close at hand. *This is confusing; ten men's voices all at once, though not, of course, so clearly focused as your own. Carefully, now, my touch must be light, and filtered, so that only you, Judson entity, can read me. I've noted that those not expecting me react with powerful resentment.*

"Better not talk to me, Bag," Judson cautioned. "Except for essential information. If you leak once, you'll upset them, as you said, so just tell me if the road is clear before I go in."

"Easy, Cap," Cookie's audible voice came from the talker. "Old Bag's spilling over enough that me and Barb are picking him up, so tell him to tighten up."

I shall so endeavor, Baggy responded obediently. *But it* is *difficult. Wait, Judson! There is an entity—a man, if you will. He's in a strange semi-comatose condition; his mind leaks bizarre images.*

"Probably asleep and dreaming," Judson guessed. He stepped inside. It was a bare police-station sort of room. A man in bundlesome garments lay on a cot, looking as if he had made it that far and collapsed. There was a bleeding gash on his left hand. Judson went to him, examined the untreated wound. A bloody rag lay nearby. The man stirred, snorted, rubbed at his unshaven face, blinked, sat up, put a hand inside his ill-fitting coat, and said, "Who're *you*, mister? Never seen you before." His name-tag read COLSON.

"Easy, Colson," Judson soothed. "I'm Judson. I live here. Just dropped by to visit you people. Didn't notice your town until a few minutes ago."

The man stood, looking into Judson's face with curiosity, rather than hostility. "You one of Anastasia's Chosen boys, eh?"

Judson shook his head. "I'm on my own," he told Colson. "I'm not a crewman; as I said, I live here."

"Hey," Colson blurted. "They were suppose to be looking for a fellow name's 'Judson,' a big shot. Come here after him. You claim you're *him?*"

"I told you who I am," Judson said. "I claim nothing. I want to talk to whoever's in charge here. How do I do that?"

Colson snorted. "Hah! Alexandra's Block chief, and Olga's Sector boss. Which one you want?"

"Who's this Anastasia?" Judson demanded.

"You expect to see *her?*" Colson seemed amazed.

"I don't know," Judson told him. "Not yet. Tell me about her."

Colson flopped his hands as one baffled. "What's to tell? She's a *Daughter*. Don't nobody see her, 'cept her broads, o' course. And her Chosen, once in a while, even yet. She don't get around good since she broke her laig that time."

"What's her title?" Judson wanted to know.

"Told you," Colson grunted. "She's a Daughter. Only one left o' the eight."

"What about the Duchesses?" Judson asked.

Colson looked amazed. "Anastasia's Marlene's Daughter," he grunted. "That what you mean? Old Marle's been dead since 'fore I was borned."

"The other three Duchesses?" Judson prompted.

"Oh, I heard about them" Colson offered. "Marle kilt 'em all, years ago, just after Landfall."

"How long ago was that?" Judson asked.

Colson did another arm-flop, miming helplessness. "Way back," he said. "O' course. Don't you know nothing?"

"Not much," Judson conceded. "Try to grasp this: I wasn't aboard ship with you—"

"Not *me*, my grandpa!" Colson objected. "Hell, mister—"

"Judson," he snapped. "You were born here?"

"Where else'd I be born at?" Colson demanded. "Look, 'Mister Judson,' you got no business being here in the substation, anyways, whoever you are. I got a mind to—"

"Don't try it," Judson suggested. "All I want from you is a little harmless information."

"I got to report this," Colson blurted. He started past Judson, who put out a hand from which Colson rebounded with a jolt. He looked down at Judson's steel-bar-like arm and rubbed his mouth with the back of his wounded hand, said "Ow!" and looked at it.

"Sumbitch *got* me!" he wailed. "Thought I felt something. Sneak-thief," he explained. "Seen him from my place, next door. Came over to check it out, and he jumped me, hit me with something."

"It must have been a knife," Judson said. "That's a clean slash. Hold still and I'll dress it."

Colson complied, and Judson used his suit-kit to disinfect the open cut, then applied a sealer and a wrap-tight, then sprayed the hand with a pain-killer.

Colson thanked him awkwardly. "Feels better, Mr. Judson. Smarted some, I'll tell you." He stepped back and eyed Judson curiously. "Some pretty fancy medicine you got there," he commented, then, in a tone of puzzlement: "How come you helped me?"

"Why not?" Judson countered. "You're a human being in pain. Naturally I did what I could. What about the fellow who attacked you?"

"You got some fancy idears, Mister; you was funning

me about being this Judson," he stated, "but I *like* you. Reckon that was old Henry. Caught him once before, tryna steal whatever was loose. Damn fool. When Alexandra catches him, she won't leave enough fer Olga to cut into strips."

"Anybody else in this building?" Judson asked.

Colson nodded. "Sure; Daughter Anastasia's in her quarters right now, herself, 'long with her Chosen."

"I want to see her," Judson repeated.

Colson grumbled, but agreed to try. "She won't like it none," he predicted, "but you being a Stranger and all, I guess I got a duty to let her know." He led the way along a narrow, gray-walled, disinfectant-smelling passage to a door where a tall, lean fellow with a bruise over his eye, and dressed in a strangely cut shipsuit, stood leaning against the wall.

The man stepped out as if to block the passage. "Colson!" he grated. "You went nuts, or what? If you disturb Her Ladyship, clumping around her private quarters—" He stopped as his eyes went to Judson's face for the first time. His hand went to his hip, grasped an empty holster.

"Taken my gun—" he gobbled, advancing on Judson. "It was *you* jumped me, stoled my weapon—if the Chosen hada found me like that, it'd a been my butt!" He reached as if to grasp Judson's arm, but instead jolted backward, his hand to his jaw, then sat down hard.

"Jeez!" Colson exclaimed. "I never seen nobody move that fast! Old Richie here's a Top Boy, too! Hey, Rick, I never—"

"Skip that," Judson said, and hauled Rick upright. "Where do I find this Anastasia?"

"Over my dead body," Rick grated.

"That could be arranged," Judson assured him, tightening his grip on the fellow's collar.

"Naw," Rick gobbled. "Jest a manner o' speaking, in a manner o' speaking—" He broke off as Judson extended a foot to discourage Colson, who had taken a cautious step backward.

"Where is she?" Judson demanded as he moved Colson in line with Rick.

Both men spoke at once, one pointing along the corridor in one direction, one in the other. Judson thrust them aside and tried the door Rick had been guarding. It opened. A startled youth who had been thumbing a worn pictonews in a shabby ship's chair jumped up, yelped once, and fled. Judson let him go. An inner door behind the boy's chair attracted him. He found it locked, but a kick at latch level slammed it open.

A tall, wide figure loomed in the opening. He opened his mouth and Judson stepped in and drove a stiff left to the solar plexus, following it with an equally vigorous right to the same spot. Big Fella *oof!*ed and doubled over; his reflexive swipe missed Judson's jaw by half an inch. Judson held the big man off and allowed him to sag to the floor, snoring.

A smaller man darted into view from behind a screen. He halted abruptly and looked at Big Fella.

"Goody!" he squeaked. "The big ape finely got what was coming to him!" He looked up at Judson; he had a narrow, pinched face with rabbity teeth.

"And you're from Her Ladyship, sir, I presume . . ." he said nervously before backing away.

Big Fella was tough. His eyes were open and staring at the little man.

"Googie, you let this here feller past you, I'll see you get throwed to the Pool!"

Googie gibbered, backing away. "Now, don't do nothing hasty, please, sir," he appealed to Judson.

"Just show me where to find Anastasia and I'll go on my way," Judson told him soothingly.

"B-but that's precisely what I'm sworn not to do!" Googie objected. "And when Fella here catches his breath—I didn't mean what I said, Fella," he told the fallen thug. "Jest trying some tactics on the intruder, here." He shifted his gaze to Judson. "Pardon that, sir, but I have to allay Fella's antagonism; you understand. In there . . ." He pointed to a curtain-draped alcove.

Judson brushed past him and into a second dim-lit

room. A fat young woman with long black hair was sitting in front of a blotchy mirror, combing her tresses, which Judson saw were artificial. Her ample body was swathed inadequately in gauzy stuff.

"Googie, dear!" she spoke over her shoulder. "Do be more quiet. I distinctly heard voices! You know very well that's a Capital No-no." She wheeled on her bench to stare for a moment at Judson before throwing her brush at him.

"Who in the world are *you*, Old Fella?" she inquired in a pleasant tone. "If you're the new one Pratt sent over, Pratt is due for promotion. Come sit here." She eased her considerable bulk aside to offer room for Judson to share her brocaded bench. He stood his ground.

"You're Anastasia?" he asked.

She looked astonished. "Whoever else?" she warbled. "I told you you might approach, Old," she went on, patting the gold and pink silken surface beside her naked, bulging thigh. "It's so seldom one sees a manly fellow like yourself, even if you *are* a bit past your prime. Not *too* old, I hope," she continued, "for the honor to be bestowed on you."

"I never did care for the fat ones," Judson grunted. "I'm here about a different kind of relations—diplomatic ones. I represent the local government, and we hope to establish a peaceful, if not friendly, relationship with you people."

"Talk, talk, talk," Anastasia murmured. "I expected better of you, Old."

"The name is Judson," he said. "How about it? Do you open the gates to our ambassador, or do we hurl our massed divisions against your walls?"

"Just what *are* your mast divisions?" the fat woman cooed. "Let's stop all this gabble-gabble, while I slip into something more comfortable. Did you say, ah, 'Judson'?"

"This isn't about comfort, Annie," Judson told her sternly. "Better get Olga in here."

"That strumpet?" Anastasia yelped. "Whatever for?"

"I have to talk to her."

"Oh, more talk, eh?" Anastasia warbled, assuming as coquettish an expression as her porky features permitted, an effect not unlike a China sow in heat, Judson thought.

"Call her now!" Judson demanded. "Unless you'd rather have Alexandra in on this!"

Anastasia recoiled. "Report this irregularity, *now*, to *that* petty martinet?" She almost moaned. "You know how she treasures her prerogatives! She'd bring it before the Four; it would be the Trouble for you and perhaps for me as well. You know she has a following."

"OK, Olga it is," Judson said harshly. "Hurry up. I don't have all day."

"Why, it's hardly daylight," Anastasia purred. "Do come and sit beside me." She put her hand where Judson's thigh would have been had he complied, and made patting motions. "I'm *not* known for my patience, you know," she added, in a level tone. Then, raising her voice, "Oh, Googie! Do come in. And tell Fella I want him."

"They're busy," Judson told her. "I have to talk to somebody about avoiding needless bloodshed."

"Oh," Anastasia replied in a tone of surprise. "Then it's Olga you'll have to see. She's in charge of all that sort of thing, under Alexandra, of course." Anastasia shifted her weight, reached out with a plump, veil-draped arm to tap a key-panel with a fat, beringed finger.

There was a *thud!* nearby and a door beside the mirror opened inward. A tall, thin woman of perhaps thirty-five came through, executed an elaborate salute in a perfunctory manner, and looked from Anastasia to Judson. She had a hard, weather-worn face with a tight mouth and small pale-blue eyes. Her black hair was concealed under a helmet-like cap. She wore a short leather-like skirt and metallic-looking shin-guards. In her left hand was a short but efficient-looking sword, which she raised as if to menace Judson.

He knocked it from her hand, caught it, and dropped it into a fancy wastebasket beside the ruffled dressing-table.

"You didn't want to cut anybody's head off today, anyway," he told the indignant female, fending her off with one hand. "I'm here about peace, not war. Are you Olga, or just a flunky?"

The woman drew herself up, stooped to retrieve her weapon, and stared Judson in the eye.

"I am, by the Grace of God, Olga, Sector Boss under her ladyship Alexandra, the sworn vassal of the benign Daughter."

"At ease, Oogie," Judson suggested gently. "I intend to lead a diplomatic delegation into this town later today, and I expect to be assured they'll be welcomed as friends and allies."

Olga glanced at Anastasia before answering. "We didn't know anyone else lived here," she said stiffly. "In all the years of exploration, we've never seen—"

"Never seen the Sapphire City?" Judson interrupted. "You need some more observant explorers. How long have you been here?"

"Why, I was *born* here, of course," Olga snapped back. "And just who are *you?* Which Daughter do you claim as Noble Ancestor?"

"I come from a long line of bachelors," Judson told her. "Let's cut the nonsense. Is it to be peace or war?"

"I suppose there's no harm in receiving a delegation," Olga conceded dubiously. "How many in your mission? And your ambassador: her name?"

"Barbie," Judson told her. "We'll be here in about an hour. Party of four."

"A bold one," Anastasia commented, "to assume *that* name."

Be alert, Judson, Baggy's voice warned, then broke up into gibberish: *ugga-woo gefuslaple nole.*

"I didn't get that last," Judson subvocalized. "Your scrambler must be on."

Sorry, Baggy came back. *But you are in a situation of great peril. Armed squads are advancing from three directions.*

"Swell," Judson subvocalized. "Which is the fourth direction?"

"I warn you, fellow," Olga said sternly, looking puzzled, "none of your trickery."

"Nope," Judson agreed cheerfully. "Just good old brute force." He ripped down a beaded hanging, and used it to truss skinny Olga's wrists, then roped her to fat Anastasia, whose bulging ankles he also secured.

"No noise," he told the sputtering women. "We don't want Alexandra to hear about this, do we? Remember, just a peaceful diplomatic mission. We'll have Her Excellency's car, of course, and a spinner. Just relax and everything will be all right. By the way, you'd better go in and put some Band-Aids on Goog and Fella pretty soon. 'Bye, now." He went to the door Baggy had indicated as the one not being invested by the guard force and left the room, finding himself in a side passage leading back to the main corridor.

"Baggy," he subvocalized, in the way that was becoming as easy and natural as speech, "relay this to Cookie:

"Put the spinner down beside the car. I'll be there in a few minutes. We're going in, all peaceful. Tell Barb she's an Ambassador Extraordinary and Minister Plenipotentiary to the dizziest bunch of lady wrestlers in known space."

"If you mean those Duchesses," Barbie's words were relayed by Baggy, "I'm not interested."

"No fear, Barb," Judson assured her. "They've been dead for years."

"Then—who are you talking about?" she insisted.

"Their descendants," Judson told her.

"Babies?" Barb wanted to know.

"Three to four generations," Judson corrected. "I think I mentioned that time is strange here."

"I don't see how it could be *that* strange," Barb countered.

"Neither do I," Judson agreed, "but that's the way it is. I'll see you at the car as quick as I can get there. Baggy, which way looks clearest?"

There are no mind emanations directly in your front,

the alien told him. *Proceed with caution, Judson, and I shall be alert for any peril.*

"Don't worry," Judson reassured him, "caution is my motto until I'm clear of this place." He proceeded along the passage to an imposing door, which opened after only a moment of persuasion with a needle-beam. Judson stepped out directly into what had an amazing resemblance to a suburban street anywhere on Terra.

A child squatting by a mud-puddle looked up and inquired, "Who are you, Old Lad?"

"I'm just leaving," Judson told him. "Nice mud you've got there. Let's see you build a castle."

"Naw," the boy replied. "It's gonna be a jail—a *big* jail fer that Jusson."

"Oh," Judson commented. "Pretty bad man, is he?"

"Kilt his own private cop," the lad assured him solemnly.

"Maybe he didn't," Judson suggested. " 'Bye."

"Bye-bye, Old Lad," the child responded. "If he didn't, why are they all chasing him?"

"Because they enjoy persecuting their betters," Judson suggested.

"Then I'm on Jusson's side!" the boy declared. "Where did you say he is, Old Lad?"

"I didn't say," Judson corrected. "You'd better go home now; it's time for lunch."

"Yeah, Ma told me five minutes. How long is that, Old Lad?"

"Time's up," Judson supplied. "So long, pal. Spread the word Jusson's a good guy."

"I will," the kid said importantly.

"But don't tell anybody you met *me*," Judson cautioned. "It's a secret."

"OK, if it's a secret," the eight-year-old agreed and trotted away.

Judson went on to the gate, passing only a few individuals in the street, all of whom had an air of being late to an unpleasant appointment. The gate was unguarded. "Unless," Judson told Cookie via Baggy, "you want to count the slack-jawed girl asleep in the sentry-box."

"I don't," Baggy relayed. "Easy, now, Cap. I'm right outside. Hope you don't mind."

"You did just right," Judson reassured him. He opened the gate a few inches and eased out past its edge. The spinner settled in beside him.

Judson climbed in. "Wow," he commented. "I don't know what I expected, but it wasn't that. It's a full-blown matriarchy, apparently run on semi-military lines, and it's been there for at least seventy-five years."

"That's crazy, Cap," Cookie commented.

"Sure is," Judson agreed. With little further discussion on the matter, they returned to the car, where Barb waited, holding her wire-gun on the tightly-trussed George, who was whining, "—Come on, Barb, give a fella a break; got no circulation, hands are hurting bad. Jest cut this here line and lemme get out and walk up and down. You know I wouldn't pull nothing on *you*. You know how I feel about you, Barb."

"Your kind would feel the same about any female you were marooned with, dum-dum," she told him shortly. "Now shut up, before I get impatient and put a wire in your leg just to see you suffer."

Cookie took over the wire-gun and checked George's bonds. "Didn't like leaving you here with the skunk," he told Barbie, "but you done good. I heard him tryna weasel you." He delivered a mild kick to George's ribs. "Yer lucky it wasn't me," he told the complaining man. "I'd prolly of shot ye full of wire just fer fun."

"George," Judson addressed the man, "we're going in—you, too. You have one 'kind-of' chance: do exactly what you're told and I won't have to bury you here before we go in."

George twisted to look up at him. "Might's well be dead as sufferin' like this here," he mourned. Judson took out his power pistol and looked inquiringly at him.

"You call it, George," he told the treacherous fellow. "Common sense says to get rid of you now. Why shouldn't I?"

"Just what I was wondering," Cookie put in. "C'mon, Cap, gimme that weapon. I'll do it; won't bother *me* none."

"We have a use for Georgie," Judson turned to the handsome but bedraggled prisoner. "If he's very cooperative, that is. Now, George, here are your instructions." He held the gun aimed in the general direction of George's face and spoke precisely:

"You are a devoted and obedient slave to Barbie, whom you will address as 'Madam.' You are tractable, sweet-natured, and very boring."

"You nuts or what?" George inquired sullenly.

Judson jerked the neck-tether. "You are to behave yourself, by walking docilely behind Madam, and you will make no complaint, no matter what. Is that perfectly understood?"

"Well, I guess I got no choice," George conceded.

"That's what happens to people who adopt treachery and violence as a way of life," Judson told him. He handed George's leash to Barbie. "Watch the skunk," he advised her. She took the rope-end dubiously.

"Barb," Judson said, "I'd like you and George to ride in the car with me. Cookie, just hover on stealth mode at about fifty feet and observe. Don't interfere unless it's absolutely necessary. Got it?"

Cookie nodded and lifted off the spinner. At Judson's prompting, George entered the car. Barb followed, while Judson covered the prisoner; then he climbed in and drove to the gate, approached and gave an experimental blast of the alarm horn. At once, the chinless woman on duty emerged, aiming a home-made blowgun uncertainly. She wore a dirty pink armband, Judson noticed.

"We're friends," Judson called on the P.A.

"Advance, friend, and be recognized," she ordered in a high, thin voice. She pushed the inward-opening gate open and Judson drove through.

"Follow my lead, Barb," he said to the girl. He got out and hauled George forth, looking crestfallen.

"Don't havta get rough!" George snarled. Judson approached him, reached out to take a grip on George's neck to apply pressure to the carotid. George winced but remained silent.

"You don't get any second chances, Georgie," Judson

told him. "We're on a tightrope here. You do your part as directed and you'll probably survive."

Barbie stood beside Judson, holding the rope distastefully.

"He's your most valued slave, remember, Barb," Judson told her. "You don't go anywhere without him."

"What—?" Barb started, but fell silent as the buck-toothed guard came over to stare at her curiously.

"Who are you, sister?" the guard muttered.

"You may call me 'Madam,' " Barb replied coolly. "We are here on official business of the highest order of importance."

"Yes, Madam, par' me," the woman babbled. "I never known, I mean my instructions—"

"We will call on Anastasia now," Judson informed the female. "You may tell Her Ladyship that Madam Ambassador Barbara has arrived; then you may show us to quarters appropriate to Madam's rank."

"They don't tell me nothing," the guard blurted and fled. She looked back to bawl. "You wait right there, unnerstand?"

"Yer crazy," George remarked. "They'll shoot us down where we stand."

"I doubt it," Judson said, "not with blowguns." He hefted his power gun. "I bet they'll recognize this, and treat it cautiously," he added.

The skinny woman had dashed to the entrance to a building halfway up the block; after a brief dispute with a sentry there, he admitted her.

"Now what?" Cookie asked via handset.

"We await our honor guard," Judson told him. "It won't be long, I think."

Indeed, in less than a minute the door through which the guard had disappeared opened, and ten tired-looking men emerged, carrying one end of a litter. On it, under a fringed canopy, Anastasia, now draped in pink gauze and feathers, reclined on one fat elbow. She looked at Judson as if wondering when she had seen him before.

"The ladies here come in two sizes," Judson remarked to Barb. "Too fat and too skinny."

The matriarch and her escort approached. Her eyes were fixed on Barb.

"Whose Daughter are you?" she squeaked.

"I'm Barbara's daughter," Barb replied. "I am dispatched here as ambassador to you, My Lady."

Anastasia waved her bracelet-hung arm in a lazy motion. "Sure, that's OK," she piped. "Ambassador from who?"

"From His Imperial Majesty, the Emperor," Barb told her on cue from Judson.

"Never heard of him," Anastasia said carelessly. "Got a strange machine there," she remarked, studying the car. "What's it for?"

"I travel in it," Barb answered. Anastasia was looking up at the spinner just overhead. "Unless," Barb went on, "I choose to go by air."

"Sure, sure, I know all that stuff," Anastasia came back. "Me, I prefer my palanquin here, get a chance to size up the new meat. These boys are on probation for reserve Chosen, you know."

By now the litter was beside the group at the car. The bearers put it down and stepped back, awaiting orders.

Judson took George's tether and hauled him forward, glanced at Barb and whispered, "Now, Barb." She took the rope distastefully. Anastasia watched closely.

Barb took a step toward Anastasia and paused, extending the leash. "My lady," she said formally, "I have the honor to present to you, in the name of His Majesty, his primary Chattel. He is skilled in any aspect of the servitor's art. He answers to the name 'George.' "

Anastasia had been looking George over with interest. She waved her largest bearer forward. "Just check out the fellow's meat, Ralph," she ordered.

The man stepped in and threw a right jab, which George knocked aside. George followed up with a hard chop to the base of the neck. The clavicle broke with an audible *snap!* The bearer stumbled back, hugging his arm. "He broken it!" he wailed. "Can't carry no more, what's to become of me?"

"You know damn well the fate of failure," Anastasia told him coldly. He whimpered.

"We will be pleased to accept this slave as a token of mutual esteem," Judson supplied, and took the condemned man's unbroken arm.

"Be nice, and you may even live through this," he told the whimpering fellow, who gulped and nodded.

"Come here, George," Anastasia cooed. George griped and complied. Anastasia's plump and delicately manicured hand caught his sleeve and pulled him closer. She caressed his biceps. "Hard boy," she murmured. "I *loved* the way you dealt with Ralphie. I never liked him. Where *have* you been?"

"Like Majesty here said, Sapphire City," George grumbled.

"Francine," Anastasia called to a spidery little old woman with pink leggings and cap, who had been hovering uncertainly. "George here is the new Chosen," Anastasia announced casually. "Old Ralphie done let me down bad. Let a whole gang o' outlaws come in and rough up my person and Olga, too. Take him in and wash him up some."

Francine plucked at George's sleeve distastefully, but dutifully herded him inside the building.

"All right, dearie," the gross woman addressed Barb. "You done pleased me right good with that play-toy." She looked Barb over critically. "He take care of you OK, did he?" She wiped at her red-painted mouth, not a rosebud, Judson decided, but more of a red cabbage.

"He did what I told him," Barb told the matriarch. "Now let's get down to business."

"Sure, sure," Anastasia shushed her. "Like I said, I'm in a good mood. What's this here Majesty o' yourn want, anyways? And what's he prepared to give for it?" Anastasia looked distastefully at the hovering spinner. "Don't need no humming machine," she pooped. "Nor no 'ground-car' neither. I heard o' machines like them, but I like this here palanquin, I already told you!"

"I have no machinery to offer," Barb corrected her. "I came to establish amicable relations, that's all."

"Now, don't you go talking dirty, girl, in front o' my tote-boys here."

"Do you prefer war, or peace?" Barb asked indifferently. "It's a matter of little moment to the Emperor."

"Where's this here Emperor o' yours at?" Anastasia demanded. "Skeered o me, I guess, he don't come hisself."

"He's right here, My Lady," Barb said.

Judson stepped forward. "As Emperor of Judson's Eden," he said impressingly, "I of course leave routine negotiations to a trusted servant."

Anastasia glared at Barbie. "You mean to tell me you, a lady, take orders from this here male?" she squeaked.

"I am a *Civil* Servant, Your Ladyship," Barbie explained. "A most important post, not a mere servitor."

"Well, I reckon not!" Anastasia declared. "Funny kind o' place that there Starfire City must be. Think I seen a pitcher of it once. Blue, is it?"

"That's the place," Judson confirmed. "And my ambassadress and I myself are here to offer you an alliance, which will place all the facilities and population of the city at Your Ladyship's service—or, if you prefer, to loose these same potent forces in war to the knife."

"Reckon peace'd be some better," Anastasia mused. " 'Cept for Georgie, now Ralphie's gone, I got no fighters, cept o' course, my Gal Guard, and I need them here, to see to my needs."

"A most rational decision, Your Ladyship," Judson congratulated her. "Now, I think we'd like to go to whatever suites you've reserved for us, and afterward, Your Ladyship and myself can perhaps confer in private, to arrange details of the new accord."

"Francine," Anastasia summoned the aged flunky, "you can show His Imperial Majesty and Madam and that other little feller in the flying machine to the Pink Suite. Then get my dinner onna table." She shot a look at Judson. "Yer Majesty and Madam are invited to chow," she stated. She glanced up at Cookie, peering down from the spinner. "Yer driver there can eat in the kitchen with the help," she conceded, and waved to her bearers to move on.

Judson told Cookie to retire to an altitude of one hundred feet and set the autopsy to keep close surveillance of the immediate area. "We may be leaving in a hurry," he told Cookie.

"By the way, Cap," Cookie mentioned, "there's a guard force forming up back o' the big shed acrost the street there. Maybe . . ."

"Good idea," Judson agreed. He took a step after the departing litter and addressed its passenger: "By the way, My Lady," he said casually, "what's in the building across the way?"

Anastasia gave him a glowering look from under the plucked eyebrows that adorned her fat forehead. "That's that Ingrid's turf," she squeaked. "I don't pay no mind to them trash."

Judson nodded as if enlightened. "Then perhaps after my ambassadress has established amicable relations with Ingrid, you'd be interested to know why she's massing troops in her territory."

Anastasia sat as bolt upright as a quarter-ton of painted adipose could manage.

"None o' that!" she screeched. "We got a like armistice—that means a truce—no sneak attacks allowed!"

"That's why Your Ladyship needs the good offices of Madam Barbara," Judson told her. "I'm sure she can soon rectify the misunderstanding." With that he took Barb's arm and headed across the street toward the large structure in question.

Anastasia screeched again and George appeared, rolling his impressive shoulders belligerently.

"Where's the criminal at you want clobbered, My Lady?" he inquired loudly. Anastasia motioned toward Judson.

George halted, looking suddenly shrunken. "Well, you see, Lady," he began. "Seein' that he's the Emperor and all, I—"

"You got yer orders, Georgie!" Anastasia yelled. "Do it! *Now!*"

George gave Judson a sheepish glance and rushed him. Judson eased Barbie out of the line of attack and stepped back to allow George to trip over his extended foot. George howled and scrambled to his feet, one hand over his bleeding mouth.

"Just go away quietly, George," Judson told him. "You don't need to ride this one down in flames." He turned to Anastasia. "Don't blame the boy," he urged. "Our person is protected by powerful Ju Ju."

Anastasia snarled. "Yer person's about to get squashed!" she shrilled, and motioned to Francine, crouching nearby. The spidery little woman launched herself like a cannonball, and this time Barbie stepped in. She did something twinkling-fast with her hands and the old woman ricocheted off her and collapsed in a heap, sobbing.

"You see, My Lady," Judson announced. "It's useless. An alliance is better. You note I don't demand total subordination. You will retain your full powers within your accustomed jurisdiction."

"I bet that Ingrid put you up to this!" Anastasia screamed; her bloated face was a deep purplish-pink now. She flopped her gigantic arms in futility. George rushed in to comfort her and was knocked sprawling by an apparently accidental blow of her flailing arm.

"Some days, Georgie," Judson commented, "you just can't seem to win one."

George got to his feet, snuffling and wiping at his blood-and-sweat-covered face. Anastasia noticed him and ordered him out of her sight. "After all I done fer you—and Ralphie, too. Both of you turnt agin' me! Now, git! No, wait. I guess I'll keep you on—just as a lifter, you know—but not as my Chosen. Nope! You done blowed that. Looky at what you coulda had, Georgie!" She rolled her vast bulk on the litter as if displaying a trophy.

Judson and Barbie continued across the street. Behind them they heard George's voice, entreating. Anastasia's replies grew softer, ending with, "Georgie! Come here! I want you to carry that there left corner. You, Seymour, you git! Yer retired. Easy, now, Georgie."

Judson and Barbie arrived at the other side of the narrow street.

Behind them, Anastasia was still muttering: "—nerve some men got! Talking about 'subordination' and all—"

"You can skip that line, My Lady," Barbie said over her shoulder. "I'm hardly a male, and I'm telling you that His Majesty has refrained from subjugating you—or wiping your nasty little town out entirely—solely because of his benevolence!"

"Durn right," Cookie contributed via talker.

Hurry, Judson-and-Barbie, Baggy contributed. *I shall keep the Anastasia-unit immobilized.*

At the door set in the wall of the building behind which the troops were gathering, Judson paused to examine the lock, a standard-issue keyed unit, he noted. It was the work of a moment to insert a probe and release it. He edged the door open and looked along a dim-lit corridor identical with the ones in Anastasia's headquarters. Barb looked over his shoulder. "All clear, it appears," she commented.

"Should be a guard," Judson replied. He stepped inside, still saw no one, only an alert spy-eye. "Barb," he addressed the girl, who was close behind him, "you'd better stay outside where Cookie can see you. I'll keep in touch via Baggy. OK, Baggy?" he concluded.

I shall be happy to relay your thoughts, the alien agreed.

"Not all of them," Judson and Barbie said together. "Just what's clearly intended to be communicated."

I understand, sort of, Baggy replied. *Your minds teem with biological imperatives, which you are determined to keep secret—though you are well aware of the reproductive mechanisms—how gross!—involved.*

"Now, Baggy," Judson chided, "as a friend, you'll have to stay out of that area. That's taboo. Understand?"

"Baggy," Barbie remarked reproachfully, "I thought you were a *gentle*man!"

I perceive I blundered in scanning that level of your consciousness, Baggy apologized. *I shan't do it again.*

" 'Shan't'?" Judson echoed. "Where do you get your vocabulary, Bag?"

I found that item in your "boyhood reading" department, the alien explained. *I found it quite charming, somehow.*

"Go ahead, Bag," Judson approved. "It's harmless pedantry."

According to your files, Judson, Baggy commented, *two centuries ago, small boys of aristocratic lineage and contrary disposition employed this term when defying their elders; "I shan't!" they'd state, and stamp a well-shod foot.*

"Hey, Cap," Cookie broke in, "what's all this stuff got to do with penetrating Ingrid's fortress?"

"Beats me," Judson acknowledged. Just then, a shrill yelp sounded from somewhere along the passage ahead, followed by other shouts accompanied by the sound of running feet, and in a moment the vanguard of a stampede appeared, a mob of yelling women of all ages, accompanied by female guards in green uniforms, followed by a few men in drab and shapeless tunics.

"Can't stand it!" someone was repeating.

"Even My Lady can't get away with this!" yelled a burly man who had hurried up along the flank. He had been attempting to get ahead of the crowd at his heels so as to turn and address them, but he was knocked down and trampled. Twenty feet from Judson and Barb, the front rank veered into a side passage, and their cacophony receded into the distance.

A lone woman of middle age came trotting along well behind the rear rank, muttering to herself. Suddenly she saw the intruders and halted, her mouth open.

"Who might *you* be, Madam?" she yelled as she marched up to Barb, with only a glance at Judson. "Are you responsible for this outrage?"

Then she straightened her garment, a pale green tunic with dark-green shoulder-tabs. "I'm Mob-major Irene, Madam," she reported. "Pray excuse my people; they couldn't take the new surveillance technique, hitting us like it did without warning. My Lady Ingrid should have, begging your pardon, at least let me and Genevieve know."

"I am here precisely to see Ingrid," Barb told the mob-major. "You may conduct me and my aide there." She gave Judson an apologetic glance.

Irene bobbed her head in lieu of a salute and led the way back along the hall in the direction from which she had come.

"I didn't catch the name, Madam," she said over her left shoulder.

"You may tell Ingrid," Barb said, "that Barbara is here to demand a full accounting. I have already briefed Anastasia."

"You *what?*" Irene screeched. "You mean to tell me you been consorting with that tub of reject mock-blubber?"

Barb chilled her with a look. "Kindly remember to whom you are speaking, Irene," she commanded. "I shall overlook your inexcusable behavior for the nonce, but I shall be observing you *most* carefully. Now get on with it!"

"Wow!" Cookie rang in. "Hate to have that lady mad at me!"

"Never, Clarence," Barb returned.

"Hey, how'd you know—?" Cookie blurted.

"Lead on, Major," Judson suggested. Irene complied, leading the way down the same side-passage which had swallowed the mob, of which nothing was now to be seen or heard. Irene stopped at a bigger-than-average door and gave it a complicated triple thump. It opened half an inch and a surprisingly pretty girl peeked out.

"Oh, it's you, Irey," she blurted. "Listen, a minute ago I heard a helluva racket out here; sounded like a sheep stampede I seen onna window."

Irene nodded impatiently. "It's all right, Pearl; my command spooked—the new surveillance, you know. Never bothered *me* none!" Irene preened.

"You mean about that spooky thing poking around inside my brains, Irey?"

The older woman nodded. "This here is Madam Barbara," she changed the subject. "Got her Chosen, I guess, with her. Kinda old," she confided in a stage whisper, "but he looks like he could handle the assignment."

Pearl snickered.

"None of your insolence, Captain!" Barb told the major. "Get on with it!" She stepped forward and punched the door open, causing the girl inside to yelp and jump back.

"Stephanie!" Pearl called over her shoulder. Barb thrust past her to confront a wiry, bowlegged little woman who feinted a leg-block and threw a cut-throat, which Barb fended off casually, at the same time taking a chicken-wing which sent her attacker to her knees.

"Never mind, Stephanie," Barb said coolly. "Just announce me to Ingrid. Right now!" she added after a moment's hesitation, as she released her. Stephanie scrambled up, rubbing her sprained elbow and muttering. Then she scuttled to an inner door and through it, giving Judson and Barbie a despairing look as she disappeared.

Watch that one, Bag advised.

"Cap, don't get in too deep," Cookie contributed, via Baggy, who reproduced the cook's mental voice to perfection.

Pearl, whom Barb had thrust aside, wailed: "It's happening again . . . !"

"Baggy," Judson addressed the alien, "you'd better tighten your beam; you're scaring the natives with the leakage."

Sorry, Judson, Baggy replied contritely. *I shall be more careful.*

Barb went to the frightened girl. "It's all right, Pearl," she soothed. "Just the new technique, you know. We'll go in now." Without waiting for assent, she went to the door through which Stephanie had fled. Judson held it open for her. Inside, in a deep, forest-green gloom scented with a sleazy incense, they could see a tall, powerfully built woman of early middle age, quite beautiful, with elaborately dressed golden hair.

"My Lady," the scrawny Stephanie was saying, "I beg to report—"

"I can see them, Steph," Ingrid told her. "It's all right." Then, fixing a stern gaze on Barbie, "What are you doing here? Why do you burst in on me? Why, at the moment—"

"We know about the attack, My Lady," Barb interrupted. "That's why we're here."

"Oh?" Ingrid replied coolly. "What attack is that?"

Baggy relayed Cookie's urgent voice: "About a hundred armed females fell in in ranks now, Cap. Big shot fat lady giving 'em a pep talk. They got spears and—it looks like—some handguns. They're getting ready to do *something!*"

"Baggy," Judson communicated unobtrusively, beaming his words tightly to the alien, "poke around in the fat lady's neurons and find out what's up. And remember to shield your transmissions; you're upsetting these people."

I shall try harder. Baggy's voice sounded a trifle muffled. *It appears these units have aggressive intent directed toward the Anastasia entity and her retainers. A second body of warriors is assembling in the street to the west. They are to attack at once.*

"That's right, Cap," Cookie confirmed. "Good work, Bag. I didn't see the rascals, lining up under the eaves along the wall. Must be another fifty of 'em."

"There is little time to waste, Ingrid," Barb told the imposing matriarch. "This attack would be a major blunder. Call it off at once, or Anastasia will have your Chosen for dessert tonight."

"Never happen," Ingrid dismissed the warning. "Huey wouldn't go near that beached blubber-tub!"

"Not even with a hook in his nose?" Barb challenged. "Save him the indignity. Order your general to suspend operations until I can explain."

Ingrid hesitated, then told Stephanie, "Get up and pass the word to General Vanessa, Colonel. Quickly!" The wiry little officer darted away through the hangings.

Half a minute later Cookie called in: "Cap, something's up. They're breaking formation. Looks like the offensive is called off."

"Wisely done, Ingrid," Barb congratulated the woman. "I am here to convey His Majesty's decision that there is to be peace between you and Anastasia."

"Hey, Cap," Cookie announced via relay. "I just noticed something: this bunch on the east side is working out of old Annie's HQ. It looks like they were both gonna attack at the same time. We better forget this peace-making idea."

"Baggy," Judson communicated silently, "it seems that it was Anastasia's troops we called off. Better do the same for Ingrid's."

I had noticed the diversity of allegiances, Baggy replied. *I wondered if it was important*.

"Very," Judson confirmed.

"Kindly summon your Chief of Warfare, at once, My Lady," Barbie requested.

"What for? Places are all set—" Ingrid broke off. "I mean, what for? I've got no—"

"Never mind," Barb said. "I know all about the troops now in formations waiting the order to attack."

"*Counter*attack!" Ingrid corrected. "My sneaks told me the bitch is planning to jump my HQ by surprise! Today!" She glanced at an elaborate wall-clock. "Right now!" she finished. "I've got to hurry!"

"Yes," Barb agreed. "Hurry to cancel your offensive."

"Dunno why I oughta do that," Ingrid grumped. "Gonna have *her* bullies in here, invading me, any second now!"

"Baggy!" Judson called. "See if you can change her mind. Make her remember that Anastasia's troops are her devoted friends and allies."

"Hey!" Ingrid yelped. "I just remembered! Me and Annie got a alliance cooking, which her and her girls are my devoted friends and allies! Vanessa!" She dashed away and could be heard berating the hapless general.

"You get yer troops out there and greet them gals! Them are my allies now, I'm telling you. I don't want no unfortunate incidents, neither!"

I took the liberty, Baggy reported, *of informing the*

kitchen staff that a grand banquet is to be laid on for three hundred units.

"Say," Ingrid blurted. "I have a splendid idea: Pearl, you tell Stephanie to get the word to Maddy and them back the kitchen, to whomp up a big special feed for, lessee, three hunnert hungry gals! Ready in two hours! Git!"

"Do sit down," she cooed in an abrupt change of tone, indicating to Barb a low divan. "Yer Chosen, too, I guess," she added, less graciously. "Lordy, things have been happening so fast, I've forgotten where I am." She sat on her padded stool. "Got a big bash planned," she informed her guests. "I want you to come. Celebrating, you see? I just concluded a pact with old Annie, which she's not such a bad old slut, even if she is bigger'n a ore-boat load o' lubnite."

"That's odd," Barb whispered to Judson as he sat beside her. "Baggy told us about the banquet before Ingrid ordered it. Or did . . . ?"

"Probably," Judson confirmed. "Old Baggy is sharper than he looks."

I heard that, Judson, Baggy spoke up quietly. *So are you.*

"Hey, Cap," Cookie called, "I guess I missed some o' that. Something about this here Ingrid—not bad, that one, for a change—and Fat Annie being pals all of a sudden."

"Precisely," Judson replied. "Dinner will be served at"—he glanced at Ingrid's clock—"eight, sharp. Baggy," he shifted tone, "see to it he arrives safely and on time."

I shall, Baggy agreed. *First, there's the matter of bringing Ingrid's army around to greet their old friends of Anastasia's guard force. I shall be busy for a few minutes, assisting this understanding.*

22

"Captain," Barbie said urgently, "I have the feeling we're in some sort of institution for the mentally disturbed. I'd like to get back out into the fresh air."

He patted her hand. "Right away. We've accomplished what we came here for: we've got an alliance between two of the town's Sectors. Now we have to see about the other two. So let's get started." He rose, and Barbie addressed Ingrid:

"I regret, My Lady, that my duties require I go now. You will be hearing from me, regarding further consolidation of His Majesty's domains. Good day."

"What's that s'pose to mean?" Ingrid barked. "I don't know about this 'His Majesty' domains. I'm in charge here!"

"Can it be," Barb demanded sternly, "that you are unaware that you exist here under the benign indulgence of our Emperor?"

"The blue city," Ingrid gasped. "They told me it was deserted—the whole planet, they said! *We* were the first ones here!"

"Hardly," Barb dismissed the claim. "As for the Sapphire City, it is a mere adjunct to His Majesty's Residence. A back-garden decoration, one might consider it. As for Judson's Eden being on an uninhabited world, my very presence here today refutes that."

"Well," Ingrid changed tack, "I don't want trouble with this Emperor, nor anybody—"

"I had expected no less," Barb congratulated the statuesque blonde. "His Majesty's presence here in person is earnest of his commitment to full recognition of My Lady's rank and station as Princess of Green Quarter, ally of Pink and soon of Yellow and Violet Quarters as well. Congratulations; you have pleased His Majesty."

Ingrid looked from Barb to Judson and back. "You mean this feller is His Majesty? Why didn't you say so? As fer Yeller and Vi'let, I don't know them women. Can't claim to be allies—don't think I'd like 'em much."

"Why not?" Barb wanted to know.

She fears they plan to form an alliance to overwhelm her quarter, Baggy supplied.

A worried look came over Ingrid's handsome face. "Looky here, Madam Barbara," she said hesitantly. "I don't know who said that"—she turned quickly and scanned the room behind her—"but I got good reason to believe they're up to something! My intelligence chief, a gal they call Patsy, she infiltrated, and set in on a big-like meeting and heard it all!"

"Excellent," Barb commented. "It remains only for you to join the alliance, and consolidate the power of the city."

"Now, you're going along pretty fast, here, Madam Barbara," Ingrid objected. "I got this sacred mission from Daughter Sophia herself, my mother, you know." She looked expectantly at Barbara.

"I am aware of My Lady's impressive lineage," Barbara told her, "and of the traditional antagonism among the Miladies; but the time has come to initiate the new phase in the development not only of the city, but of the entire continent, eventually the entire planet. I'm sure you join with His Majesty in desiring that the city play a central role in that great renaissance, rather than being cast aside as a useless anachronism."

"I don't know what that last is," Ingrid supplied. "But the city's not useless, I know that much. I've got the trained personnel right here to start up the materials systhesizer over in Pink, if we could get our hands on the mines Yeller and Vi'let are holding for theirselves. It's pure selfish! Can't even use the ore, and Pink's as bad; grabbed the machines, and won't let my folks even look at em! Hadda train onna tapes! And my girls—and some fellers, too, all crammed to the eyebrows with all that expertise since they were little!"

"I foresee a great future for the alliance," Barbara predicted. "Now, I think his Majesty would like to perform his ablutions, and on to the banquet."

23

An hour later, refreshed and clean, and clad in fresh garments trimmed in green, the guests took their places at a long table, one of four in a vast and handsomely decorated room which occupied the entirety of a Class Two shed (utility). The food, all fresh and natural, no synthetic or stasis rations, Judson noted, was superbly prepared.

"Come on in and join the party," Judson said to Cookie, who had parked the spinner on the roof, after witnessing the mingling, at first hesitant, then jubilant, of Ingrid's soldiers with those of Anastasia. He appeared a moment later, escorted by two middle-aged female guards who marched him up to Ingrid and withdrew. The matriarch looked Cookie over and commented, "They haven't been overfeeding you, boy, that's for sure. You can set, right there that next table over."

Prince Murphy will sit beside his Emperor, Baggy interceded.

Ingrid jerked as if prodded by a sharp stick, rubbed her ears and said, "All right, Prince, I'll just scroonch over." She did so and Cookie sat down and pitched in.

"Aged to a minute!" he exclaimed, chewing a chunk

of the savory steak placed before him. "Real steer-beef, or I'm a cargo-hand!"

After the sumptuous meal, Judson, Cookie, and Barbara went to Judson's comfortable quarters, and Judson said:

"There are too many unanswered questions for me to waste any time putting them in words right now. Instead, let's sum up what we *do* know. A, there's something very strange about some aspects of what we're accustomed to calling 'time' here. The crew-slab which is the nucleus of the city landed a matter of hours ago, yet the city is close to a hundred years old, I'd say."

"But, at small temporal scale," Cookie contributed, "time seems to flow at its usual pace. Mighty strange. Reminds me of Crumblnski's work: about the temporal inversions and all that around a black hole. Only—"

"We'll work on the theoretical basis later," Judson suggested. "For now, we'll stick to the practical level."

Barbie spoke up. "I've read that time is only a construct of the human mind. We seem to experience it, so we think of it as an external phenomenon. But of course the captain is right. All we need to worry about for now is dealing with whatever we encounter. I think we've made a good beginning with the alliance. It's fortunate that Yellow and Violet are already in cahoots; now the Pink–Green accord can meet them on even terms, rather than being overrun one at a time."

"You done real good, Barb," Cookie congratulated the young beauty. "Tomorrow I bet we'll see the city unified into a going concern, four times as effective as any of the Quarters ever was!"

There was a perfunctory tap at the door before it opened to admit a small boy who advanced, bobbed his head at Barb, then stared wonderingly at Judson and Cookie.

"Her Ladyship honors you with a personal call, ma'am," he blurted, and fled. Ingrid was standing in the doorway.

"You folks better not go off half-cocked here," she warned in a businesslike tone. "Nelda and Rosie ain't dummies. You try to waltz into their HQs like I let you do here cause I was bored, and they'll gun you down and say 'howdy' later." She advanced into the comfortable room and sat in a chair facing Barbie.

"Look, dearie," she said in a weary tone. "I never did think all this fighting and sneaking around was a good idea, but I had my charge from Sophie, so I thought I hadda carry on. But maybe, now this here Majesty's here, we can work something out. Now, I got this secret tunnel; Marcy's people dug it, you know, back in Diana's time. But we never closed it up; we use it. Been slipping my people into Rosie's turf all along, know what goes on over there; they're ready to talk, only they're scared to."

"The trick," Judson said, "is to make them scared *not* to."

"How you gonna do that?" Ingrid wanted to know.

Judson gave Baggy a complicated cue, and the alien's voice sounded in each human mind within fifty yards of Judson. *The technique is simple enough,* Baggy said. *When presented with the totally unexpected, most people will tend to panic: experience provides no cue as to the proper response. When I announced to Annie's troops that peace had been concluded, they were so astounded by the manner of their notification that they forgot their habits and training and at once fell in with my commands. Rosie's people will respond similarly. We have but to appear among them, immediately after my manifesto, and all will go smoothly.*

"I guess *so!*" Ingrid breathed, watching Judson's face. "How'd you *do* that, feller?"

"His Majesty has many resources, My Lady," Barbara supplied. "If you will supply an honor guard and four soldiers, we will be glad to attempt your tunnel at first light."

Ingrid nodded and rose briskly. "I'm going, too," she declared. "I shall be here at first dawn, as Your Majesty suggests."

24

The grayish light of Junior was barely lightening the sky outside the single window when a peremptory rap at the door announced the arrival of Her Ladyship.

Ingrid looked serene, but at the same time excited. The flush in her cheeks made her classic features lovelier than ever.

"All ready?" she asked perfunctorily. "Let's go." Without waiting for a reply, she and her escort formed up. Flanked by half a dozen armed women, the party went along the drab passage to a massive pink-painted double door. Two guards darted forward to open it, disclosing a pair of pink-clad soldiers, who snapped-to and saluted. Behind them, Judson saw the rival matriarch on her gaudy litter. Anastasia's bearers steered their heavy burden deftly through the door, and the two powerful ladies stared at each other, then smiled and cooed. Ingrid directed her entourage on along the passage to a wide chamber painted pink, but with map-hung walls like a war room. The bearers put their burden down and departed.

"Now, Madam Ingrid," Anastasia squeaked, wincing as if the name hurt, fixing on Ingrid one eye that was nearly buried in doughy fat, "just take a look at the alcove across the room." She pointed a well-manicured but sausage-like finger. There, in a narrow niche, stood a man of burly physique, cradling a power gun. Judson stepped between him and Barbie.

"Come over here, Colson, and hand me that weapon," he ordered. Colson complied, moving like an automaton. He gave Anastasia a despairing look as Judson wrenched his gun from his hands. "My Lady, I never—" was as far as he got. Both hands went to his head. "I got voices in here, telling me I got to—"

"Treachery," Ingrid said coldly. "How did she smuggle *him* in *here*?"

I trust you don't resent my meddling, Judson, Baggy's familiar voice said apologetically.

"You did fine," Judson approved.

"I'm glad Baggy's on our side," Barbie remarked. "Even though he was shielding his suggestion, I had the damnedest urge to do whatever you said."

"You done good, Bag," Cookie applauded. Anastasia had flopped back on her lace-edged cushions and was fanning herself with one fat hand, until a servant stepped forward to assume the chore with a large pink fan. At Judson's gesture, Colson backed off into a corner out of Anastasia's line of sight.

"Like I was saying, madam," Anastasia resumed as if nothing had happened, "I'd like real good to please Yer Majesty, but I got my people to worry about. I can't hardly let my guard down long as we're like to be attacked any time."

"Ingrid would like nothing better than to conclude with Your Ladyship a treaty of eternal peace and friendship," Barbara assured her.

"Help me against the Yellow and Violet, too?" Anastasia demanded. "Not likely. They're all plotting to kill me!"

Glancing at Ingrid's impassive face, Barbara contradicted, "No, they're not. Not anymore, since you're never again going to send any more assassins into their Quarters."

"Who says I'm not?" Anastasia demanded.

"Your Ladyship," Barbara told her.

Anastasia looked astounded. "Why, I guess yer right, dearie," she murmured. "Rather be friends with them ladies anyways. Excuse me, I got work to do," she concluded, and heaved a sigh like a hot air balloon deflating. Her bearers reappeared as if by magic and carried her away.

"We didn't get much negotiating done, I guess," Cookie commented.

"We did enough," Judson corrected. "We've got her thinking of the benefits of peace—and more important, the disadvantages of war."

"You mean all them battle-ready divisions massing back at Sapphire City?" Cookie snickered.

"Every one," Judson confirmed seriously.

"This almost seems like it's too easy," Cookie commented, just as the wall-hangings burst inward and armed pink-clad troops burst into the pink-draped room, with effective-looking spears and shortswords at the ready.

Francine confronted Judson. "All right now, boy," she rasped, hefting her edged weapons. "Her Ladyship's had enough o' your crap, I guess. Yer both headed for the Labor Pool"—her glance included Cookie—"and as for Madam Barbara here . . ."

"Madam Barbara will attend to her own needs," Barbara interrupted, at the same time tripping the skinny little woman backward, while deftly switching the *gladius* from her grip. She turned to glare at the female soldiers. "Clear out of here, all of you," she commanded. "You should be in the courtyard, greeting Ingrid's people."

A chubby girl with apple-red cheeks spoke up:

"Seen Boy said we had a invasion on our hands. Where's Her Ladyship at?"

"You have your orders," Barbara responded coldly. "Now, git!"

Chubby got. Barbara said, "Thanks, Baggy."

You don't resent my interference? the alien's voice asked dubiously.

"You've been a big help, Baggy dear," Barbara told him. "Just keep monitoring these people and don't let any out-of-line impulses get out of hand."

"Out of line"? Baggy queried. *"Out of hand"? I don't understand, Barb.*

"Right now, one hasty move by some disgruntled individual could upset the rather precarious truce," Barbara explained. "Try to keep everybody calm."

By this time the crowd of confused warriors had been shepherded from the room by the apple-cheeked girl, who accompanied her shoves and buffets with a fine line of invective. Finally, she gave Barbie an awkward salute, said "Par'me, ma'am," and left.

"Like I said," Cookie remarked, "it's too easy."

"Not necessarily," Judson objected. "We're not out of here yet—and we still have the Violet and the Yellow to win over."

"It shouldn't be hard," Barbie contributed. "They all seem to be longing for peace and order, really. They were trapped in this armed-camp routine by tradition. All it takes is a nudge."

"I hope you're right," Judson replied.

In the other Quarters, Baggy spoke up, *the two entities called Nelda and Rosie are at daggers drawn. Their followers are preparing to attack each other.*

25

"This may be our best chance," Judson told the others. After asking Baggy for directions to the scene of the impending conflict, they followed his cues across the plaza and in through a muttering crowd of anxious-looking violet-uniformed females who stared at the intruders but did nothing. At a yellow-marked double door standing open, they entered boldly, went along a gray passage like that in the other Quarters, halting at a door behind which they heard raised voices:

"—*my* girls, dammit! I thought that was all understood!" a vibrant contralto was saying.

"Don't mean you can sneak your spies in here to try to stir up *my* gals!" came the indignant reply in a suety tone. Judson threw the door open and walked in. A statuesque redhead turned to stare at him with ice-blue eyes. Her fine features seemed more astonished than irate.

The shorter, stocky woman confronting the redhead threw back her round head and yelled, "Jake! Get yer butt in here!

"And here they are," she said to Red Hair in a quieter tone, looking the intruders over distastefully.

"Funny kind of snoopers you picked, Nelda: A old man, a little shrimp, and this fine-looking lady. What you think you'd accomplish with this bunch?"

"Listen!" Cookie demanded, stepping forward. "We're no damn spies, girls. We come here to help you!"

"Where'd you get the idea I needed yer help, Junior?" Fats demanded. "Nor Nelda, neither. We're doing good!" She advanced and took a casual swipe at Cookie, who ducked and butted her just under her well-padded ribs. She *oof!*ed and sat down, then disconcertingly burst into tears, squalling like an indignant infant.

"Here, you can't—" Red Hair started, but Barbie confronted her and said mildly, "We're not spies, Milady, as you well know. *You* didn't send us, and Fatty here would hardly spy on herself. Perhaps if you listened to us . . . ?"

"Surely, madam," Red agreed. "Just what—?"

"Try listening," Barb suggested. "You and your emotional colleague here have agreed on a truce. Now you're about to go to war because of a trivial misunderstanding. Tell me about it."

"Not so trivial," Red corrected. "Rosie here is trafficking with old Annie over the way. They're planning a sneak attack on me."

"Where did you get that idea?" Barb persisted.

"That Georgie told me," the redhead stated, as if that settled that.

"Call him in here, please, Milady," Barb requested.

The redhead shushed the still-blubbering Rosie and pulled a bell-cord.

At once, a hanging parted and George swaggered in. He gave Judson a defiant smirk and said, "That's the ones I told you about. They—"

"This man's a confirmed liar," Judson interrupted. "He's Anastasia's slave. He's only interested in making trouble."

Nelda turned to look critically at the big man. "That right?" she demanded. "You from Fat Annie?"

"I'm nobody's slave, Milady," George said unctiously.

"Except perhaps your own, if you'll accept my gift of myself."

"George!" Barbie said sharply. "You come over here and get on your knees and kiss my foot."

"Aw, Barb," George objected. "Don't be that way."

"You know this lady?" Nelda demanded. "Who is she? And who are *you*, Georgie?"

"Aw, *she's* OK," George reassured Nelda, "but these two fellers, they're spies and worse."

"You're still a damned liar," Judson told George in a flat voice that seemed to hang in the air as if debossed on sheet steel. George said nothing. Rosie whined.

Nelda stared at George expectantly. "You going to let this old fellow call you a liar to your face, George?" she demanded.

"Don't pay no mind to *him*," George suggested. "A old wore-out Poolbird like that. Hell, I wouldn't waste time on him."

Cookie had eased over beside the much bigger man. "Watch yer language, crumbum!" he said mildly, and stamped down hard on George's kneecap, continuing to rake down the shin to impact on the arch of George's flat foot, eliciting the *crunch!* of small bones breaking, a gush of blood from the exposed tibia, and a howl of anguish. As George leaned to grab his ruined leg, his face met Cookie's hard little fist with a meaty *smack!*

"Here, little feller, don't go ruining his looks," Nelda objected. Rosie had gotten to her feet to add her objections.

"Can't stand seeing trash like that mouthing off in front of decent folks," Cookie grumped. "Now, Cap, here, ah, Line-Captain Judson, that is, come over here to help you ladies out. You don't want to go and start no trouble now, right when you got a truce going. That's Georgie's work, I bet; Annie sent him to stir up something 'cause she heard you two ladies were making peace. So don't let him succeed. Shake hands, ladies, and make up."

Nelda and Rosie lunged to embrace each other, making cooing sounds and giving Georgie resentful looks.

"It *was* you, George!" Nelda accused. "I'm ashamed of you! Trying to come between my *dear* friend and me like that! You take him, Rosie. Now, we better get on with the joint review, before our troops start to get nervous about us being in here so long."

"Right, Nellie," Rosie agreed. She bustled away and Nelda followed. Judson let them go without objection. George was sitting on the floor, cradling his bloody leg.

"You ruint it!" he wailed. "Feller can't even walk, hardly. Look at that! The bone's exposed! And my foot's broke bad!" He tenderly caressed his foot, wailing.

"Too bad, Georgie," Cookie commiserated. "The old power kick is what skunks like you get."

"I was only following orders," George complained. "I hadda do like Annie said, or—Jeez! She can be mean, you know. Seen a feller they useta call 'Big,' had his ears cut off. Little feller name Googie hadda follow him around, handing him fresh bandages. Ruint his looks, and hurt bad, too. A feller with no ears looks like a gourd-head!" George cast an appealing look at Barbie. "Barb, you wouldn't let 'em cut *my* ears off . . . ?"

"What's the matter, you think that tub o' lard won't like you anymore?" Barb taunted the crestfallen treacher.

"Aw, Barb, you know I only . . ." he muttered and fell silent.

Judson, Baggy interjected, *I have observed a curious paradox which I feel is germaine to your mission here. Shall I report it?*

"Go ahead," Judson agreed.

These female entities are of two minds, Baggy supplied *Each lusts after peace and tranquility, while pursuing a course designed to perpetuate a mutual hostility.*

"Why is that?" Judson asked, aloud.

"Well, you know," George responded. "I hadda!"

"Not you," Judson corrected.

"Looky here," George went on, getting to his feet. "I can help you: I can get Nelda and that Rosie to make up like you said. Fat Annie talked a lot about them dames. Said they was really in league, and only pretended to be enemies to fake her and Ingrid outa position. I can do a sneak and get Nelda—she's the halfway pretty one—to do whatever you like. Then Rosie."

"You do that, George," Barbie commanded, giving him a look as ambiguous as a gold ring offered on a swordpoint. He gobbled and fled, with an apologetic glance back at Barbie, who pointedly failed to notice.

An hour later, having observed the amicable mingling of Ingrid's and Anastasia's combined forces with those of Nelda and Rosie, the peacemakers were about to leave the city when a messenger arrived at a trot to summon Judson to an "audience." He checked with Baggy, who reassured him that it was an innocent invitation from the four allies that he was free to decline.

"Don't go, Cap," Cookie urged. "I don't trust them women!"

"We can fly cover in the spinner," Barbie suggested.

After a brief discussion, while the young female messenger dithered impatiently, Judson decided to go along. It was a five-minute walk along peaceful but crowded streets to the rendezvous, in a tiny park-like area with smooth grass, a fountain, and stately celery-trees set among blossom-beds of varied colors.

Fat Annie and her almost equally plump colleague, Rosie, sat together on a marble-like bench, while the pretty Ingrid and Nelda strolled nearby.

As Judson came up, the lovely redhead and the beautiful blonde, smiling and gracious, saw him first and came around the fountain to meet him.

There was a sweet fragrance in the air, doubtless from the flowers, which resembled the wild ones that grew in great swatches on the plain, but were somehow more delicate in appearance.

"My ladies," Judson greeted the two lovelies, "I'm interested in the flowers. Are they bred from the wild ones outside the town?"

"Long ago, Your Majesty," Nelda confirmed. "By my revered Ancestor, the Founder Nelda."

"Is it all right to smell them?" Judson inquired.

"That is a privilege reserved for the Daughters,"

Nelda supplied. "Of course Your Majesty is now an honorary Daughter, so—"

Take care, Judson, Baggy cautioned. *Treachery is afoot.*

"That's an honor I must decline," Judson interrupted the redhead. "I'm not a daughter or even a mother. I'm a father."

"Indeed?" Rosie spoke up from the bench nearby. "Of whom, may I inquire?"

"Of me," Barbie's voice provided the answer.

Judson looked at her with an annoyed expression. "I just made that up, on impulse," he told her.

That was my idea, Baggy put in disconcertingly.

Barbie came up and hugged Judson's arm. "But it's true," she cooed. "Didn't you know, *really?*"

"I had no idea," Judson assured her. "I've been lusting after you just like all the fellows."

"Mother said she managed to get you drunk enough to depart from formality," Barbie explained.

"How could I forget . . . ?" Judson wondered.

"There may have been a little nemol in one of those drinks," Barbie amplified.

"Jeez!" Cookie commented fervently. "Cap, you mean you and Barbie . . . ?"

"So it appears," Judson replied; then, to Barbie, "I'm proud to be the father of such a wonderful woman." They embraced.

"All right!" Annie's harsh voice cut across the tenderness of the moment. "You reject the honor we was about to confer on you, hey? That's downright unfriendly, I'd say."

"Nonsense," Nelda spoke up. "No real man wants to be known as a Daughter." She moved closer to Judson, looking up at him warmly. "Where is this woman of yours now, this Barbie, Senior?"

"Mother died years ago," Barbie supplied.

"And she wasn't 'my woman,' " Judson objected.

"Never mind," Nelda dismissed the matter. "The question is, who is to be your protector now?"

Judson put up a hand in protest. "Let's not be in a

big hurry to get me married off," he pled. "I'm a confirmed bachelor."

"Surely," Nelda persisted, "you recognize your responsbility to pass along those royal genes of yours."

"I already did," Judson reminded her, and hugged Barbie.

26

After a week of mediating the petty bickering among the four matriarchs, and encouraging the increasing cordiality among the rank-and-file, with the timid males blossoming under the new equal-status rules and beginning to assume responsibilities and show initiative in methods of promoting the commonweal, Judson and his friends sat down to discuss their findings.

"It's apparent that the original Four Duchesses put aside their differences sufficiently to work out a division of labor here," Judson stated, "and allocated areas and resources accordingly."

"It's hard to imagine those four agreeing on *any*thing," Barbie remarked. "But there *was* a lot of unrest aboard ship because of the feuding. George and Crench and Benny weren't the only men who were rebellious."

"And I bet," Cookie contributed, "after they landed, the malcontents got together and made them old dames cooperate!"

"They must have," Judson agreed, "or *some*thing did; they picked the best possible spot for their camp, or town, and divided it up so each quarter had something useful. The spring's in Yellow. Pink has the iron mines, and Green is sitting on the best garden soil. Purple is where the coal is. They each had something the others needed, so they never resorted to all-out war, but with their habit of jealous female rivalry, they never got together and really built all they could have. When the ship's cargo was exhausted—the pre-fabs and all—they had to rely on the land. The seeds and animal embryos thrived, and they had plenty to eat, but technology declined."

"But now we come along, Cap," Cookie spoke up, "we can get things moving again. Hell, no reason we couldn't have a steel plant operating in a year."

"What about this strange time thing?" Barbie wondered. "What does 'a year' mean? If a few weeks to us can be eighty years to these people, what will a year be?"

"My guess," Judson said, "is that it will be whatever we think it is: the Strong Anthropic Principle. A grain of sand, a stone, a planet, knows nothing of time, which *we* perceive as passing. So—things take just as long as we expect them to—and 'long' is in terms of our idea of time. So let's get started. I think we can depend on the cooperation of the Daughters, now that we've shown them not fighting is better."

"Keeping them confined to Quarters for a while won't hurt any either," Cookie reminded him. "My idea, Cap, you recall."

"They do seem eager to get out and see what's going on," Judson agreed. "They may have some natural leadership abilities after all."

"I'm having great success with the mob-majors, crowd-captains, and bunch-lieutenants," Barbie contributed. "The group-colonels are less cooperative; they had plenty of rank under the old system, and aren't eager to change. I have one throng-general working with me: Martha. She's a great help. The colonels will come around in time. So I have a good basic cadre."

"We've got to take a complete inventory," Judson told the others. "And I have an idea: old *Rocky*."

"What about *Rocky*?" Cookie came back. "She's under a few zillion tons o' rock."

"Not if we get there in time," Judson corrected.

"What's that s'pose to mean, Cap?" Cookie demanded. "We *seen* her fall in that abyss, or whatever you wanna call it!"

"Perhaps we were mistaken. Let's go see."

"Crazy talk," Cookie snorted. "Cap, you been sniffing them flowers?"

Judson turned to Barbie. "I'd like you to stay here and keep things moving, Barb," he said. "They might start to slip back into anarchy if we let up the pressure."

"My idea exactly," the girl responded. "I'm as mystified as Cookie, though, Captain. How are you two going to excavate a buried deep-space craft?"

"Maybe we won't have to," Judson answered mysteriously.

The following morning, Judson and Cookie set out in the worn but still functioning ground-car for the site of *Rocky*'s disaster.

Cookie grumbled at the jarring ride. "Talking about time," he commented. "This here suspension knows it's getting old, and we can't do much long-range logistics planning if we don't know how long stuff will last. Hey, looky there!" He pointed to a slender spine standing alone on the plain. "Fer a second," he explained, "I thought it was *Rocky*."

"You're beginning to believe," Judson pointed out. "That will help. One day," he added, "we'll have to work on the math."

"Don't know *how* to do the math on that Anthropic Principle o' yours," the cook responded glumly. " 'If I think it's there, it's there,' is that it? Then how come I miss a step in the dark now 'n' again?"

"It's not quite so simple as that," Judson told him. "I'm groping as much as you are. Maybe . . ." His voice trailed off as they skirted the rock spine, and saw, sharply upthrust against the background of pale green, the unmistakable silhouette of *Rocky III*.

"But we put her down on bare rock, remember, Cap?" Cookie objected. "Now she's out in the grassy patch."

"Maybe we just *thought* we did," Judson conjectured.

"I remember just as plain," Cookie objected. "I was wondering why, and then we went out and seen them blue flars."

"Or did we?" Judson inquired. "Perhaps your little flight was the hallucination."

"Beats me," Cookie conceded. "But there ain't a mark on her, Cap! We musta come back here before she fell."

"About the time we witnessed the explosion," Judson estimated. "So while we were here, we were also a couple of miles south of here, looking at some strange gray, granulated matter."

"Let's go aboard," Cookie proposed, "and start salvaging, before some more impossible stuff starts to happen, and maybe we wind up buried with her." As he spoke, he pulled the car to a stop beside the port landing-jack, a space-burned and pitted surface of iodine-colored metal, reassuringly solid and mundane.

"Hey, looky over yonder!" Cookie exclaimed abruptly, pointing. Judson looked and saw a great mass of tree trunks, largely stripped of branches, heaped like jackstraws at a bend in the river.

"Timber!" Cookie gloated. "All collected for us! We can set up a cutter-beam to slice them mothers up into planks and start in building new houses outside the walls."

"First," Judson reminded him, "we have to inspect this old derelict vessel we happened on here."

Cookie stared at him. "Cap, you talk like you never came out here a-purpose to see— Well, I guess I could shut up."

After offloading the ship's three cargo flats, the two men spent the rest of the day loading them with the most urgently needed supplies and equipment, originally intended to resupply Io Base.

"Say, Cap," Cookie spoke up after stowing the last of the hundred cases of "mummy-dust"—as he (and others) called the dehydrated food—"if this here chasm never opened up like we seen and *Rocky* never fell into it, how come we remember seeing it happen? Hah?"

"That brings us back to our minds again," Judson pointed out. He pointed to his frontal lobes. "Our memories are patterns in here. That's all. These rocks here know nothing about what we think we remember, and are not constrained thereby."

"There you go talking fancy again, Cap," the smaller man griped. "It's spooky, is all," he explained. "I *know* what I seen! But here I am stacking mummified eats just like it never happened."

"Let's not demand an explanation; that's just words, anyway," Judson advised. "Let's accept the reality we're looking at."

"How do we know it's really reality?" Cookie wanted to know.

" 'Reality,' " Judson intoned, "can be defined as 'that which appears to be reality.' "

27

As the two men stood by the old ship, casually conversing, the hum of the seldom-used spinner became audible; the little craft came swooping across the rocky floodplain, hesitated, then veered sharply to land near them. The hatch popped and the young lieutenant Cookie had trained in its use jumped out, her short-cut black hair unaccustomedly unbrushed, the expression on her pert features anxious and eager at the same time.

"Marcy!" Cookie barked. "I *tol'* you no joy-riding in that machine! It's not getting any younger, you know!"

"I think Baggy's maintenance program is keeping it in good shape, Space'n Murphy," Judson remarked mildly. "Why not let the girl have a little fun with it?"

"Wouldn't call it fun, fellers," the girl put in breathlessly. "Come with *bad* news!" She paused as if to permit questions. Judson waited.

"Got a revolution!" Marcy wailed. "It's the Rejects," she added. "Got a few girls on their side already. I tol' Howie to fall dead when he tried that crap on *me*!"

"You know, Cap," Cookie commented quietly, "I always did think it was a bad idea, letting the incorrigibles stay inside town like we done."

"We could hardly have massacred them," Judson pointed out. "What've they done?" he asked the girl. "You did well to come out to let us know."

"Yeah," Cookie seconded, "done OK, Marce, but what'd these skunks *do*?"

"Started bothering people," the girl responded. She was staring up at the corroded tower that had been starship *Rocky III*. "Never saw this building before," she commented. "Why's it so *high*?"

"We'll tell you later, Marce," Cookie replied impatiently. "Go on, about this revolt."

She nodded. "Told people they were getting treated bad. Told fellers they ought to be in charge and told gals they were downdodden or something. Wanted ever'body to quit work and go throw stones at Headquarters. So I came out to tell you." She was still glancing uneasily up at the old ship.

Cookie, too, was examining the landing-jack beside him curiously. He scraped with his thumbnail at a pinkish encrustation around a bleeder-cap. "Never seen *that* before," he muttered. "Looky here, Cap," he went on, "some kinda lichen growing in here. Corrosion, too. Ain't been here a month."

"That celery pine looks pretty well grown for a seedling," Judson commented, indicating a two-foot-in-diameter tree growing at an angle from beneath a landing-jack.

"It's that funny time-business again," Cookie said. "Wish things weren't so strange here sometimes, Cap."

"We have to expect things to be strange this far from home, Space'n Murphy," Judson told his friend.

"Oh, sure, we always kidded about little green men and all," Cookie responded. "Solid gold mountains and oceans made of brandy or petroleum and like that, but this is *strange* strange!"

"We'd better get back," Judson said. "We can philosophize later, after we've got this revolt under control."

"Damn right, Cap!" the smaller man agreed enthusiastically. "Can't let a few troublemakers ruin everything everybody's accomplished so far."

Marcy was still looking up at the looming hulk of the mighty vessel. "Who built it?" she wondered aloud. "And what for? Way out here!"

"It was built on a planet called Terra, half a light-year from here," Judson told her. "In the Private Space shipyard at Mohave."

"How'd it get *here*?" Marcy demanded. "I heard about that 'Terra' in school. Spose to be folks' 'ancestral home' or something. Never did understand it."

"It brought itself here, long ago—" Judson started, but Cookie interrupted.

"Cap—the Chosen, here, I mean—conned it here himself, coupla months ago."

"I never seen it," Marcy objected. "You fellers wouldn't be funning me?"

"Ever been out this way, Marcy?" Cookie inquired.

Marcy admitted she hadn't. "But it's so high, I'd of seen it from the gate."

"We actually don't understand it ourselves," Judson told the girl. "But Cookie thinks it has something to do with Monidas' Formulation regarding the Strong Anthropic Principle."

"Take the spinner, Cap?" Cookie wanted to know. "Or the car? Spinner's faster, I guess. Getting rickety, though. Have the car up here in a second."

They settled on the ground-car, asking Marcy to return the spinner to its garage.

"Careful, fellers," the girl cautioned. "I heard some shooting while I was over the garage."

28

"Takes me back to the old days, Cap," Cookie commented as they approached the West gate on foot, after being fired on from atop the wall as they were parking the car by a clump of celery trees.

"No one shot at us that time," Judson pointed out.

"We'll get their thinking on that straightened out fast," Cookie predicted firmly. " 'The Rejects,' Marcy said: Old Fred with the sticky fingers, and Bud, thinks he's tough, and all them trash," the little cook muttered. "Kind of makes me mad, Cap, thinking about how the folks voted to let 'em live, give 'em the old Pink Quarter to live in, and let 'em earn food and all. This is the thanks they get: stirring up trouble. Folks deserve better."

"Our system still has plenty of kinks to iron out," Judson conceded.

"Remember back when we was the only ones here, Cap?" Cookie queried. "Or were we? Old Annie and Rosie and all claimed they was born here. How can that be?"

"Maybe some day our remote descendants will work

that out," Judson replied mildly. "Meanwhile, we just have to adapt to it."

By now the two men were in the shadow of the walls, and the desultory shooting had eased. The nearest gate was the West one, only recently completed. Marcy in the spinner had already settled down inside the town. No one had shot at her so far, it seemed.

"Wonder why they're shooting at *us*, Cap?" Cookie wondered. "Course, we always had a few soreheads wanted to hang on to some rank and all they had under the Colors, but this—coming out stirring up trouble and shooting at people—something musta happened. Bet that George got something to do with it," he concluded. "He's been quiet a long time, since you caught him stealing the spinner that time, and bent him some. We shoulda shot him soon's he got off that lifeboat. Hafta shoot him now anyways."

"First, let's find out what's going on," Judson cautioned.

After half an hour of cautious approach, Baggy suddenly rang in. *Captain, I suggest you permit me to warn Miss Marcy to lift off at once; a group of persons is forming up in a circle around her position.*

Easy, Bag, Judson cautioned. *Don't scare her to death.*

"Death"? Baggy queried. *I assure you, Captain Judson, my intentions—*

Just a figure of speech, Bag, Judson explained. *Dammit, don't be so literal. You know what I mean.*

Of course, Baggy confirmed. *I am to avoid any action which might result in Marcy's demise through fear.*

Just be careful, Judson instructed. *Anyone who's not used to you poking around in their thoughts would find it very unsettling. Try to sound like the voice of conscience or something.*

"What you think, Cap?" Cookie inquired anxiously. "That little gal gonna be OK? We better get over there to the garages fast."

"We will, Space'n," Judson told him. "Baggy has the situation in hand."

"Sure, but we gotta—" Cookie blurted, and started

up the rough-surfaced wall, clawing for toe- and finger-holds. Judson went past him, looked carefully along the weed-grown three-foot-wide trail at the top.

"All clear," he whispered, and turned to assist the smaller man up beside him.

"Lucky the sky's dark," Cookie panted. "Old Brownie won't be up for an hour. But we better keep low anyways. Looky, Cap. Lights yonder, near the garages." Then shots rang out. "Guess it's all over," Cookie mourned. "We're too late."

"Maybe not," Judson demurred. "I wonder where the fellows are who were shooting at us."

"Yeah," Cookie concurred, hugging the weed-grown earthen wall on which he lay prone.

"Look to your left," Judson said softly beside him. Cookie twisted his head to peer through the pre-Brownie-rise gloom.

"Looks like at least four of 'em," he whispered. "Wonder what they're waiting for?"

"In this light, they don't know exactly where we went," Judson told him. "Come on." Judson began to move off to the right, taking care to be absolutely silent. Cookie followed with equal care. At the first downramp built against the face of the wall, they eased off onto the sloping surface, changing direction in the process. Now the four sentries on the wall were clearly visible against the faint glow of the dwarf star just below the horizon. Abruptly, the men turned and moved off, away from their quarry.

"Break for us, Cap," Cookie commented. "We'da had our hands full taking four armed soldiers bare-handed."

They crept down the ramp to the level ground below. A dim, yellowish light glowed from a small window in the nearest wood-slab house. Inside, a pretty but worried-looking young woman stood by a table laid with plates heaped with food.

"Looks like dinner's ready," Cookie remarked. "Makes me remember we ain't et since Junior-set."

A door banged open near the window, and a solidly-built man came through it, scatter-gun in hand.

"Them damn vigilantes gone yet?" he inquired softly. "Come on out, fellers; we been watching you."

Cookie looked at Judson, who rose and said, "They went thataway."

The man snorted. "Blind as bats," he commented. "You fellers were lucky that time. Come on in and feed."

Judson went over to the big man, whom he recognized as a woodworker named Frank. They followed him inside and sat down to a hearty dinner made superb by appetite. Frank's wife, a sweet-faced girl named Edith, seemed a bit in awe of Judson. He sensed it and reminded her that they were after all cousins.

"It's a funny thing, Cap," Cookie remarked to him at a moment when Frank and Edith were out of earshot. "I know dern well I got six grandkids, and you and Steph got more'n that, so everybody in town's descended from both of us nowadays. Just can't get used to the idea. Don't seem like it's been that long."

"It hasn't," Judson pointed out, "at the level of our basic, inborn paradigm. We've known since Einstein that time on the sub-nuclear scale is mutable; why should it be immutable at the present-experience level?"

Cookie admitted that he didn't know. "It's kind of like living forever, ain't it, Cap?" he ruminated on. "We already lived a long lifetime, and I for one feel like I'm all ready to keep on going for another one."

"People die when they expect to die," Judson told him. "So do trees, and every other organism. It's a matter of morphic fields."

"I read some o' that 'morphogenic' stuff," Cookie replied. "But somehow I never felt like it had anything to do with me, personally."

"Since the Burman experiment," Judson pointed out, "it's been pretty generally accepted."

"Sure, but knowing trees grow leaves because other trees grow 'em is one thing; the idea I grow hair and fingernails because somebody else did it is something else. Anyway, it don't solve anything; what about the first tree in line, or the first hairy man? Where'd *they* get the morphic field from?"

"That's like asking 'Who made God?' " Judson replied rather wearily.

Frank came back into the cozy room and offered cigars and brandy, both rare items, but Judson declined politely. "I never got the habit," he explained.

"Funny about booze and smokes," Cookie remarked. "They taste terrible, when you're not used to 'em. Wonder how folks ever got past that to start the habit. Guess that's something like how the first tree grew leaves."

Frank prowled the house, listening, but reported all quiet.

"Some kind of excitement going on in town," he explained. "About an hour ago, there was gunfire and yelling from the direction of Town Hall. Then the spinner went out and came back, and more shooting along the wall. That's why I went out and found you fellas. What's up, anyway, Captain?"

"We've heard there's a revolution brewing," Judson told him. "Malcontents, trying to solve all their problems by destroying what we've built so far."

Frank nodded. "A wild-eyed character showed up here late yesterday afternoon," he said somberly. "All excited about overthrowing something he called the establishment. Wanted me to sign a piece of paper he had. I threw him down the stairs."

"You shouldn't have done that, Frank," Edith reproved mildly. "Could have hurt the poor boob."

"He was on his feet and shaking his fist in ten seconds," Frank replied. "Got his paper kind of messed up, though."

"They'll be back," Judson predicted. He silently signaled to Baggy.

All clear at the moment, the alien voice came back at once. *Marcy's safe. Still a small crowd by City Hall, but they're just milling around. Hold on—here's George. He's become quite feeble, and he's changed his head pelage to white, but he's still full of venom. Shall I quiet him down?*

"Nothing physical," Judson cautioned the creature. "Just suggest to him he ought to shut up and go back to bed."

"Captain?" Frank was repeating, Judson realized.

"Sorry," he said. "I'm afraid my attention was elsewhere."

"I've heard, Captain," Frank said, "that you have special sources of power. I always thought that was superstition."

"Not quite," Judson explained. "You know about Baggy, the original inhabitant of Judson's Eden . . ."

Frank nodded. "I had that in school," he agreed. "But I never took it literally. Magic, it sounded like. Do you mean, Captain, that it's literally true that there was an intelligent being here before you and Space'n Murphy arrived?"

"Not necessarily," Judson replied carefully. "We found him the day after we made landfall. Maybe that's when he began to exist—when we became aware of him."

"I got plenty o' that 'ego,' Cap; you know that," Cookie put in, "but I ain't got *that* much." The philosophical discourse was interrupted abruptly when a window exploded inward and a wrapped brick thumped on the carpet.

Judson waved the others back and advanced cautiously, listening. Hearing no telltale mechanical buzz or electronic hum, he nudged the paper-covered missile with his toe, then knelt and carefully unwrapped it.

" 'To all traitors to the People,' " he read aloud. " 'No collaboration with the oppressors will be permitted to live. Come out, big fellers, and save Frank's life!' " Judson crumpled the paper and dropped it into a wastebasket. He looked at Frank, then at Edith, who was crying and sweeping up broken glass. "We have to go, Frank," he said. "We can't bring you folks into this."

"We're in it, Captain," Frank stated flatly. "There's a back way out; the house dates back to the False Alarm, and my grandpa Eric was in the thick of that. Built the house as a kind of fort, with a 'monk's hole.' I used to play in there as a kid; never thought I'd ever really use it."

Edith reluctantly agreed to stay behind for a few hours, unless the attack on the house was renewed, then she'd meet them at a spot Frank designated in the Old Quadrangle.

"If it's the Rejects, as Marcy said," Judson remarked, "and we have no reason to think she's wrong, their headquarters will be in Pink."

"Awful run-down, nowadays," Frank commented. "Couldn't maintain any really big mob in there."

"They probably raid outside for supplies," Cookie pointed out. "You know there's been reports, Cap. That could explain a lot o' things."

"We should have taken action sooner, Space'n," Judson replied. "But I don't think it's too late to nip this, if not in the bud, at least before it's fully mature."

"First," Cookie stated, "we got to get over to City Hall and see if Marcy's all right."

"Precisely," Judson agreed. "Frank," he went on, "where does this secret passage of yours bring us out?"

"Plum Avenue, south o' the Square," Frank replied. "Three streets from the Hall."

In the darkness of Frank's basement, they made their way by the intense beam of a handlight, past the looming bulk of a masonry-built furnace and shelves stacked with Edith's home-made preserves, to a cluttered corner. Frank pulled aside a broken crate and a bicycle with a bent wheel to reveal a plain, wood-paneled wall. Just as Cookie opened his mouth to utter a complaint, Frank groped in a dark niche, and the panel said "click," and yielded to Frank's push.

"All manual," he commented. "No automatics to go dead. Been here a long time."

The passage was a concrete-lined tunnel high enough to walk upright in, barely wide enough to squeeze through. There was a faint odor of wet clay and mildew. Dark side-passages led off into deeper blackness.

"Say," Cookie said. "If we took this shortcut—" His words turned to a howl of dismay, which trailed off to a groan.

Judson turned back, just as Frank spoke up: "Stay away from the side-alleys—they're for the old ventilation shafts."

Judson, using the handlight, ventured a few feet into the aperture Cookie had taken, saw the gaping pit that opened at his feet. Thrusting the cold, white beam downward, he saw walls of glistening-wet concrete, stained with age and mildew. Far down, he could barely make out Cookie's frantically groping arms. He seemed to be wedged where the shaft narrowed.

"Space'n!" Judson called softly. "Are you all right?"

"All right as I can expect to be under the circumstances," the former chef called back in a severely strained voice. "Least I'm right side up. Legs jammed hard. Can't get a grip. Better drop me a line, Captain, sir."

"I've got a nylon," Frank told Judson. "I'll be right back. Keep it quiet."

In less than a minute he returned with a coil of the glistening white half-inch cable.

"I'll make a slip-noose," he suggested. "He can get it under his arms and it won't slip."

Frank dropped the rope, and Judson called down to Cookie, "Work it under your arms and we'll haul you up."

"No can do, Cap," the trapped man called back a moment later. "Too tight. I'll take a turn around my wrists and hang on."

"Better not discuss it any further," Frank pointed out. "The walls here run back of a residential block, and they're thin."

"OK, haul away," Cookie called unenthusiastically. "Easy, Cap. I think I got a broken leg."

Frank and Judson took secure grips on the slippery cable and at Judson's grunt, heaved on the rope.

A yell came from below. "Seems like my broken leg is caught where it twists it when you heaved."

"We can't talk, Space'n," Judson whispered down the echoic shaft. "We have to pull now," he added, and they did so. Cookie uttered a stifled yelp and they felt the weight shift.

"He's free," Frank whispered. "It's just hauling from now on."

Judson nodded. "He must have passed out," he guessed. The two men pulled up length after length of rope, coiling it on the floor. After some ten feet, the rope jammed. Judson looked down. "Cookie!" he said quietly. The latter was about fifteen feet down, jammed crossways. Judson could see the broken leg, folded grotesquely below the hip. Blood stained the injured man's clothing.

"Compound fracture, might have cut the femoral artery," Judson told Frank. "We have to get him up and stop the bleeding." Frank took the light and played it over the victim's agonized face, studied his position.

"Feller," he called quietly, "you have to use your arms to rotate yourself so your leg isn't in your lap."

Cookie flopped an arm and blinked at the light. "Can't do it, boy," he gasped out. "Seems like my back's bent some, hard to move." He was pushing futilely at the close-pressing walls of the shaft; it was clear he was jammed fast.

"I'll have to go down," Judson told Frank soberly.

"Wait a minute, Captain," Edith's voice spoke from behind him. "Better let me do that; I'm a lot smaller. Don't want *two* folks jammed in the Fool's Hole."

"Edie," Frank blurted. "What—?"

"Got tired sitting; no good for both of us to be all upset wondering if the other was still alive. Lemme past there."

Edith looked Judson up and down. "You're too durn big," she commented, and took a grip on the rope. "I'll go down. Lemme see him." Judson flashed the light down the shaft. and Edie remarked, "Mighty uncomfortable fella down there; I better hurry." Gripping the taut rope in both hands, she leaned over and went head-first down the shaft.

Moments later she called up, "Haul away!"

Judson and Frank pulled her up until she could grip the edge of the cleanly-cut shaft and scramble up beside them.

"He's OK now, you can get him up OK," she told them. This time it went smoothly, but Cookie arrived at the top unconscious and had to be pulled up by the arms and over the edge. He revived quickly, as Judson was examining his compound fracture of the femur.

"Dammit, Cap," he snapped. "That hurts!"

"That will have to be splinted," Judson told the others.

"Had the damnedest dream down there," Cookie reported. "Pretty gal kissed me. Musta been a angel; come floating down from above me, face-first. Then, here I am!

"Hey!" he interrupted himself, "we got to get moving. Marcy needs us right now!" He made a move as if to get to his feet, but fell back with a groan. "No good, Cap. Better leave me here and get to Marcy fast."

"Wait a minute," Judson suggested. "Let's see what Baggy reports." Then subvocally: *Baggy! Are you on top of this? How's Marcy?*

Marcy is quite well, Judson, the silent reply came back promptly. *She has taken refuge in the old sorting room. The persons attacking her have broken off the assault.*

"Well, that helps some," Judson told Cookie.

Frank and Edith were staring at him with awed expressions. Frank spoke first: "I always heard you fellers had some kind of demon you talked to," he blurted. "Always thought it was superstition. But I sort of *heard* that! Said some Marcy is all right. Edie, maybe you and me'd better go back now and see to the house."

"Just what I was thinking," Edith seconded. "Goodbye, fellers; good luck to you. I reckon you ought to get loose from that demon."

"Baggy's no demon, honey," Cookie said. "He's a native life-form. Usually floats around up just below the jet stream. Got good eyesight. He's been a good friend since our first day here."

"A native life-form, you said," Frank commented. "Where are his relatives?"

"All dead," Judson told him. "Or so he says. He reluctantly ate the last one some time ago."

"How horrible!" Edie put in.

"Nothing messy," Judson corrected. "Just a matter of absorbing his vital energies before he died out. It saved Baggy's life; cousin was a goner anyway."

"And that's your *friend*?" the girl demanded. "He doesn't sound like a nice person at all."

You wrong me, Edith, Baggy's silent voice spoke up, unshielded.

Frank uttered a resentful grunt. "Stay out of my head, dammit!" he growled. "Don't start on my wife—and leave our vital energies alone. We're gonna need 'em," he finished, motioning Cookie back as the lamed man attempted to proceed along the passage. "Listen!" Frank hissed.

Faint sounds were audible from the darkness ahead. Frank went flat against the wall, and Judson stepped back into the side-passage where Cookie had come to grief.

Frank took Edie's hand and pulled her over beside him. "Now, you'd better hurry back to the house, and get my popper, and bring it back fast. Can do?"

"All right, dammit," she acceded. "Try not to get killed meantime!"

"Cookie had better go with you, Edith," Judson spoke up, as Cookie protested. "We can rig a walking splint and he'll be able to get that far. We'll be back ASAP and go from there." They waited, heard no new sounds.

Using a length of vinyloid tubing, which Judson split open and fitted around Cookie's thigh, and then wrapping the leg tightly with strips from Frank's shirt, they managed to brace the injured limb sufficiently that Cookie was able to put enough weight on it to hobble, supported by Edith.

"I like this part," the old chef remarked, hugging the pretty girl's shoulder. "Let's go, Edie; tell me if I'm squeezing too hard."

"He's a tough old devil," Frank commented.

"That he is," Judson agreed. "But I have a feeling we ought to go back with them. We know Marcy's all right, so there's no reason to split up."

"Feel better myself," Frank admitted.

29

Back at the modest house, which they found intact, Judson contacted Baggy, who as always, was alert and ready to help.

"Try to get Marcy over here, Bag," Judson requested. The alien replied, *Nothing simpler.* After a five-minute wait, there was a sound outside.

"Sort of a 'pop,' " Cookie described it. "I better—"

"You better stay right on that bed," Judson told him. "I'll check it out." He went to the back door and opened it a crack. By Junior's pale, dull-red light he saw movement at the outer gate.

"Captain!" Marcy's voice spoke up. "I heard—there was—it was like the voice of Conscience, telling me to sneak down the alley and come this way. And it was right! Here you are, as I'd hoped. Was that—I heard . . ."

"That was our friend, Baggy," Judson confirmed. "Come on inside. What's happening back there?"

Inside, the girl was welcomed warmly, and put to bed at once by Edith. Marcy was delighted to rest, but was eager to talk. Judson sat beside the bed.

"It's that old George," Marcy told him somberly. "I don't understand. He's a feller, and has all the privileges there are. But I heard somewhere he once tried to kill you other fellers. Is that right?"

"It was a long time ago, Marcy," Judson soothed her. "He's been tried and restored to full citizenship. Just what is it he's doing?"

"He's out there in the street, with that white hair tossed up in a mane, yelling and threatening people and telling them to burn City Hall. He's got the gate to the Rejects' Compound open and he's forming those no-goods up into platoons or something, and sending them out to spread the enlightment, he calls it. What it is, is an idea that everybody is miserable, or ought to be because they don't all get to give orders; crazy idea! Says the ones who work owe it to the lazy ones to support them! Says people who work hard are bloodsuckers, exploiting something he calls 'the masses'! It's like he was talking about another planet! Nothing he says fits Eden."

"He never got over his resentment at not being allowed to kill Cookie and me, and drag Barbie off to the cave," Judson explained. "Poor fellow!" he added. "He wants to be a hero but he doesn't understand what a hero is."

"What *is* a hero, feller?" Marcy asked.

"I think a fellow who does what has to be done in spite of being scared and inadequate could be called a hero," Judson told her. "Even if what has to be done is only hoeing potatoes, or taking inventory in a shop."

"I always thought heroes killed a lot of people and were stronger and braver than anybody else," Marcy replied, glancing at Cookie. "That's why—" She interrupted herself.

"That's why you couldn't see why some folks called me a hero," Cookie supplied with a wink. "Too small for a hero, eh, Cap?"

"Take George," Judson suggested. "He's big and handsome, and—"

"And mean as a snake," Cookie finished for him. "He don't really want to *be* a hero, just wants folks to treat him like one."

"It's the same idea as wanting to destroy Testing, and put unqualified popular politicians in our toughest jobs," Judson decided. "That's Georgie, to the life."

"Let's find the skunk," Cookie said grimly.

"We will," Judson promised.

"What's a 'skunk'?" Marcy asked Cookie, taking his arm in a cozy way, looking up at his scarred and weathered face.

"Little wild critter back on Terra," Cookie explained. "Pretty little things, glossy black fur with a white rally stripe. But they throw a stink that'll stop a wolverine in its tracks."

"What a strange place Terra must be," the girl mused. "So many different life-forms, all living together. And some of them," she added distastefully, "eat the other ones. Why do they all let humans have their way?"

"It's all a complex web of interraction," Judson explained. "In the end, all of Nature works together for the common survival."

"But I read," Marcy blurted, "that we—humans, I mean—destroyed most of the natural habitat the other creatures needed to live."

"Man is a part of Nature," Judson told her. "Everything he does is natural. Downtown Granyauck at rush hour is just as 'natural' as the rain forest. So are a beaver dam and a beehive."

"But it's *different*," Marcy protested. "People paved over the land, and cut down the forests, and—"

"The planet's overcrowded with life," Judson said. " 'Every species for itself' is Nature's rule. The only exception is Man. We're the only critter on the planet that gives a damn about what happens to some other species."

"Still . . ." Marcy objected.

"*Some* species had to develop intelligence," Judson pointed out. "If it hadn't been Man, it would have been some other critter. Life needed intelligence to be able to colonize the planets before Earth was consumed. It's a long-range natural pattern, but we're as much a part of it as any other life-form."

No one seemed eager to conclude the conversation, which moved over many topics, while the dark hours passed. Near dawn, Judson rose and said, "I think now would be a good time to make our play. George and his friends ought to be at the low point in their circadian cycles, and off-guard, after six hours of quiet. Space'n Murphy," he addressed the injured man, just waking from a light doze.

"Yessir, just resting my eyes, was all," Cookie spoke up promptly.

"I'm going to give you a shot of U-for," Judson told him. "That will put you out for a few hours, so you won't get bored waiting for us."

"Dammit, Cap—" Cookie started, at the same time swinging his legs off the bed—or trying to. He grabbed his broken leg and lifted it back on the mattress. "All right, Cap, I got to face facts, I guess."

"The rest of us will get into Pink and do a sneak on Georgie's villa," Judson told him. "Probably catch him asleep."

"Then what?" Cookie came back hotly. "You gonna kill the sucker and then talk yer way out? Naw, I know that's not your way, Cap, but—"

"I'm going to talk to him," Judson explained. "I have a proposition for him."

"Dunno what that would be," Cookie commented. "He needs his throat cut."

"But," Marcy objected, "isn't George a feller, like you? Wasn't he one of the founders?"

"He was here, Marcy," Cookie agreed. "But he was no founder. He did all he could to kill the rest of us and ruin what we tried to build. Shoulda kilt him."

"How strange," the girl said. "Why would he do that?"

"He's a mixed-up feller," Cookie told her. "Wanted to be in charge, wanted to have power. Wasn't content to be part of a team. Had his ego all mixed up with his common sense. Tried to poison Baggy once; lucky old Bag don't eat like we do. All he done was give Bag a ache in the arcuate fasciculum. Baggy don't like him no better'n I do, now."

"But now, after you—you and Captain Judson—have given everybody a stable society to live in, built the city and laid out the fields and roads and everything, why would he want to wreck that? If he succeeded, he'd suffer as much as anybody."

"No figuring insanity," Cookie stated from his cot as the others prepared to take their leave.

"We'll be back in three hours, Space'n," Judson told the unhappy man.

In the narrow street, all was quiet. Judson led the way, via back alleyways, to an airspace behind George's villa, a grand house, built as an office complex, but converted to luxurious accommodations for one.

"George made things pretty nice for himself," Judson pointed out to the girl as they scaled the wall to descend in a formal garden. "He was a radioman aboard ship, you know. That's why we put him in charge of communications; had a job to do he knew how to do. He should have been a happy man, but no, he had a little power and he wanted more. Got to say which calls went through, set the priorities—that gave him a handle to start pressuring people, in a small way, at first: 'you supply me with the best cuts off that bovine, and I'll see you don't get any "circuits busy" signals.' Then he started dealing on a bigger scale, or trying to; told Veronica, over in Distribution, he'd see she got top priority on all calls, if she'd put him at the top of the deliveries list. She hit him in the eye and told me. I had to take his job away; put him in the relay station, doing routine maintenance. But he had a power base all the same, and used it to spread this dumb idea of his. Don't follow schedule, don't do what's expected of you; get together and pick a popular fellow to run things, who won't roust anybody in the middle of the night to do emergency maintenance. Damn fools!"

"Why didn't you stop him, Captain?" Marcy wanted to know.

"Hoped he'd straighten out," Judson told her. "I blew it; the conspiracy got bigger than I expected sooner than I expected. And actually, I have no authority; still I could have— I'm sorry."

Marcy hugged his arm. "You couldn't be everywhere at once, feller," she consoled him. "I think you're doing a grand job, being the Chosen. I'm glad *I* don't have to do it.

"He seems to have so many followers," Marcy went on after a slight pause. "Why? Why would anybody want to join in wrecking things?"

"Got their own reasons, I guess," Judson replied. "Sort of a vague idea that since the system here on Eden isn't perfect, it ought to be destroyed, and then maybe somehow something better will spring up to replace it. We know it's not perfect, and we're working on fixing what's not good. Tearing it all down won't help. Georgie thinks somehow he'll come out of the wreck in a better position. Figures he'll be the Big Boss to give orders and everybody'll obey because he was the one started the trouble, so they owe him. Damn fool!

"It's part of being human to forever yearn for free goodies," Judson pontificated after a short pause. "Georgie is just a severe case."

By this time the small group of counter-conspirators had crossed the garden to the high, stuccoed wall of the villa, where fragrant night-flowering vines clung to the wrought-iron work.

"Frank," Judson spoke quietly to the younger man. "You better hide the gals somewhere out of sight, then scout around front and report back. I'm going up. Just try to keep things quiet down here."

"*I* could climb them vines," Frank pointed out.

"Yes, but I'm afraid you wouldn't know what to say to Founder George. I'll be all right."

Frank went off with the two women, and Judson quickly scaled the wall to an ornate balcony where dim light glowed behind hangings covering glass doors. By putting his back against the glass, he could see, through the gap between drapes, the foot of an oversized bed, and a man's bare feet, tangled in silken covers. A moment later, the man rolled over, sat up, then stood and walked briskly across the room and out of Judson's line of sight.

Judson moved closer, managed to catch a glimpse of the broad-shouldered old man as he slipped out the door and was gone. At once, Judson tried the latch securing the glass doors; it resisted; he insisted. The mechanism broke with a faint *click!* and the door swung in against the heavy drape. Judson slipped past its edge and went to the chest of drawers beside the hall door. One drawer was slightly open. Inside, a leather pistol-holster was visible, empty. Judson went directly back to the balcony and watched until Frank reappeared.

"All clear," Frank called softly as soon as he saw Judson's face above him.

"Not quite," Judson countered. "He knows something is up. You and the gals had better get out of here fast."

Frank hesitated, looking puzzled. "What about you, Captain?" he wanted to know.

"I have work to do," Judson reminded him. "I'll be along."

Back inside, he rummaged in the drawers of a desk, found a reel of monofilament used for sealing letters. He went cautiously into the hall, tied one end of the gossamer filament to a doorknob across the way, led it back under the door and across the room to an inviting easy chair. After taking a lap of the line around his left wrist, he made himself comfortable and dozed off.

The sharp tug at his wrist awakened him, a moment—no, ten minutes later, he corrected himself—after a glance at the clock on the desk. As the hall door started to open, Judson rose and went silently across and took a position to the left of it with his back to the wall. George came through, brushing at his brocaded dressing-gown in an irritated way. Suddenly he brought his hand up before his face, cursed and turned—to find Judson confronting him.

30

"Damn you, Judson," George snarled. "This time you've gone too far—invading my personal quarters in the middle of the night!"

"That's not the half of it, Georgie," Judson told him quietly. "Your scheme is blown. It's all over."

"Me?" George protested. " 'Scheme'? Got no scheme. Just got tired o' the high-handed way you and that runt slave o' yours—" The back of Judson's hand interrupted the outburst. George licked blood from a split lip and felt over his teeth with the tip of his tongue. "All right, got tired o' having a mealymouthed dictator telling me what I wasn't allowed to do and what I had to do. Told a few folks and they agreed with me. That's all."

"You're about as good a liar as you are a fighter," Judson told the flustered fellow. Judson sniffed. "Yellowweed," he said. "No wonder you've got recruits. That damned stuff turns a man into a zombie ready to be programmed. And you tended to the programming, eh, Georgie?" Judson looked around at the luxurious apartment. "You used a considerable amount of other people's valuable time to furnish this place," he commented. "Where do you store the yellowweed? Not here—even *you* wouldn't be *that* dumb. But let's pass that for the moment. You've convinced your dupes that life can be a bowl of cherries if everybody stays sky-high on weed and duly elected bosses let everybody do whatever they like, without any interference from big-dome self-appointed technical experts. Suppose we put that to the test? We'll evacuate Pink of everybody who wants to go, and turn it over to you, to run your plan of government any way you like, say until the next eclipse. Then, if your plan works better, we all adopt it. Meanwhile, you get to stay here in your mini-palace with no hassle. And no more yellowweed in the water supply and no more recruiting."

"Ha!" George retorted. "You think I'm fool enough to believe you'd do that? As soon as—"

"You don't have a whole lot of choice, George," Judson said, and knocked him down. George complained, but made no move to get up. His eyes rolled fearfully up at Judson.

"Now you plan to beat me to death," he grunted. "Just what you always wanted to do. You won't get away with it."

"Put both hands up here, George," Judson ordered. "Wrists together." After some persuasion, the supine fellow complied. Judson bound his wrists firmly with the silken cord from George's robe. Then he bound his legs from knee to ankle, using a braided bell-cord ordinarily used to summon the servitors. Meanwhile, George kept up a steady stream of whining appeal, until Judson stuffed a lace doily in his mouth. Judson dragged him to the balcony and lifted him to the railing, then lowered him by the heavy rope on his legs. When George was safely down and in Frank's keeping, Judson followed.

"What do we do with this noise-box?" Frank asked Judson, as George maintained a steady stream of muffled expostulation. Judson stepped close to George and showed him a big-knuckled fist.

"Shut up, Georgie, *now*," he ordered, "or I'll have to knock your skull far enough sideways to put a pinch on your cord that will cut all your strings, maybe permanently." George subsided reluctantly.

"—Wait till my people get here," he trailed off.

" '*Your* people,' George?" Judson challenged. "I'll bet they'd be surprised to hear that. They no doubt think they're free citizens of their own planet."

"Hah!" George spat. "They're sheep, looking for an easy living. They'll do whatever I say. All I have to do is snap my fingers!"

"Better start snapping, feller," a deep voice spoke up from behind a flowering shrub. The burly man that went with the voice stepped into view, slapped his callused palm with the short club he carried, and faced George.

"I heard some o' that, feller," he growled. "Don't sound much like what you been speechifying about." He glanced at Judson as George shrank back, gibbering.

"Don't like having old George nor nobody else making a jackass out o' Big Willy McCann," he remarked. "Guess maybe I better throw in with you fellers."

"Welcome aboard, Willy," Judson replied. "Do you think you can put Georgie someplace where he'll stay quiet, without accidentally breaking his lousy neck in the process?"

"Nothing to it, Captain," Willy said and took a come-along grip on George's wrist. "Why you want to keep him alive, sir, if you don't mind my asking?" he inquired, not as if the matter were of much importance.

"Murder's against the rules, Willy," Judson told him as he cut George's legs loose.

"Yeah, but—" Willy responded, looking puzzled. "You're the Chosen—the top feller. You don't have to . . ." The big man's voice trailed off.

"I guess Cookie was right," Judson commented. "We'd better get all the way out of the picture. If people think I—"

"They don't, Cap, I don't think," Frank countered. "Just old Willy, here."

"We already have the Industrial Council to decide on the directions we go in our mining and manufacturing,"

Judson pointed out. "Why not extend that over the executive, too?"

"And have somebody like Georgie here get himself in power?" Frank objected. "Folks have got confidence in you, old feller. They respect you. I guess you know when duty calls. You've got an obligation to a lot of good people not to do the easy thing, and call it a democracy."

"Listen to the dictator, being *noble*," George sneered, before Willy's big hand closed his mouth.

"You done enough troublemaking, old feller," the seven-footer told him. "The captain said don't kill you; never said don't bend you some."

"Captain," Frank contributed, "I've never quite understood how the system works. I always thought you fellers gave the orders, but now, it sounds like—"

"We've been advisors, that's all, Frank," Judson explained. "We knew we had to have some kind of government, but we had bad experiences with governments, back home, on Terra. We hated to see that kind of stuff get started here on Eden. But we knew anarchy wouldn't work, so—"

31

Several weeks later, while Judson and Cookie were working on the chaos George's ideas had caused in Pink Quarter, Baggy abruptly rang in, prompting Cookie to respond impatiently: "Not now, Bag! We're busy!"

Very well, the alien replied. *I felt you'd be interested . . .*

Intrigued, Cookie reversed himself. *All right, come on; what is it?*

I have detected the mental emanations of individuals of your kind—humans, that is—at a great distance, to be sure, but approaching on a vector of—

Save the statistics till later! Cookie barked, while Judson waited patiently for the report to continue.

The vessel—for I assume a vessel, unless these humans are traveling exposed to the space environment—

Skip the pedantry, Bag, and get on with it! Judson put in.

Precisely what I have been attempting to do, Baggy came back a trifle huffily. *They are at a distance of one and one-half AU, proceeding at a velocity of .0001 light.*

"Well, Space'n," Judson addressed his compatriot.

"We knew the time would come, and here it is. Maybe it's just an innocuous survey vessel."

"Not *manned*," Cookie objected. "Risk human lives? 'Preposterous,' or so Priss Grayce said, when he was only a Councilman from Delaware."

"That was a long time ago," Judson reminded him. "And it appears they're on a beeline for us; I doubt that they're coming all the way out here to pin medals on us. We'd better get back to HQ, fast."

Fifteen minutes later, the two old spacefarers were in the usually quiescent Operations room, startling the on-duty watch dozing over their instruments. Judson pushed a fat fellow from his sagging perch in front of the DEW panel.

"Here—ah, sir!" the fellow objected. "You can't—Oh, it's *you*, Captain! My apologies, but of course that's the distant early warning beam, quite useless, nothing ever goes on there. So I'll just fetch the readouts, and—"

"Alert Section One of the Ready Crew," Judson barked. "Fast!" He manipulated the controls beside the small screen.

"But, sir—! They're asleep! It's off-watch!" Fatty objected.

"They've got ten seconds," Judson snapped.

The plump fellow rushed away, one hand to his forehead. The rest of the duty crew were gathering around, all talking at once:

"—a bogey—right there, one o'clock at lag distance—moving fast—this way!"

"—*never* light up!"

"Except for that rock, that time."

"That's what it is, another rock! Captain, will it strike Eden?"

A young girl trainee picked up a station-to-station mike and whispered softly into it.

The sound channel crackled and said, loudly, "You, there, dirtside! Speak up! Patrol Boss Nine-Three-Seven. I want final approach numbers, and docking codes! Now! And get the mush out of your mouth!"

"Why, sir," another, older girl grabbed the talker from the weeping apprentice. "As for approach, you'll need to bleed off velocity. I suggest you pick up orbit zero-one, do three circuits—" Her fingers were flying over the nav console keys.

"When I need elementary lessons in approach procedure," the harsh voice came back, "I'll be sure to notify you. Now let's have that let-down vector! I warn you—"

"Nine-three-seven," Judson cut in. "You can go to Hell. Maybe the Devil can teach you some manners, but I doubt it!"

"Cap," Cookie offered, worriedly, "is that—?"

"Probably not," Judson agreed. "But somehow I don't care much. Talk to Jodi." While Cookie went over to comfort the flustered teenager who had first spoken to nine-three-seven, Judson turned to Frank, who was standing by silently.

"You're a standby Security Monitor as I remember, Frank," he said. "I think we'd better put on a display. Run Practice Alert A with half-loads, starting now."

Frank nodded and hurried away across the room.

"Par' me, Cap," Cookie put in. "That's kinda risky. What if that hard-nose conning 937 gets spooked and starts to really get heavy?"

"He won't," Judson predicted. "He's too far from home."

"Look here, you—whoever you are," the talker blurted abruptly. "Perhaps you don't know who you're dealing with!"

"Never end a sentence with a preposition," Judson came back at once. "It's beneath the dignity of whoever *you* are, to commit solecisms."

"Damn your insolence!" the domineering voice came back.

Baggy, Judson subvocalized. *Can you give this hot-shot a little scare?*

Can I not, came the prompt reply. *I suspect a thousand-foot-wide manta ray invisible to radar and impervious to hardshots might suffice.*

"Wait a minute, Cap," Cookie suggested. "Before we

run these boys off, we ought to get a little information from them on conditions back home."

"I don't suppose," one of the young technicians remarked, "they'd have let *me* sign on for a trip to fabled Terra."

"It'd be a real one-way trip, Suze," Cookie told her. "You wouldn't want to leave home for good, would you, girl?"

"Why, I didn't mean *that*," she answered him sharply.

"Looky there," Cookie broke in, pointing at the long-range screen, which was rapidly flicking up-scale, adjusting to the range of a quickly shrinking red blip.

Thanks, Bag, Judson said silently.

"Man, that Bag is something else, ain't he, Cap?" Cookie exulted.

"They'll be back," Judson reminded him.

PART TWO

1

It was on the same day that the first transcontinental monorail was dedicated that Judson received a Priority Purple dispatch from Outer Security, notifying him that a flotilla of at least ten major space vessels was on close-orbit approach from Sector T (the direction of Terra). He and Cookie left the ceremony hastily and went directly to Operations, where an awed lieutenant showed him the Most Remote screen, where the fuzzy blip had now become visible. Even as Judson watched, it resolved into two squadrons of five units, coming in steadily.

"No doubt about where they're headed, Cap," Cookie contributed. "Nice tight formation. I think those boys mean business. Take more'n Bag's jokes to scare 'em off."

" 'Scare 'em off,' " Judson repeated. "Why, Space'n Murphy, I'm surprised at you!" he said playfully. "I'm eager to greet our guests, and find out what's been happening back on Terra and just how long we've been out here."

"Oh, Captain!" one of the communications lieutenants called. "I have something on my compound screen; not quite on-frequency. I'll just—"

The picture cleared up as Judson arrived in front of it. Though speckled with bright noise-spots, the three-D was clear enough: it showed a man in a regulation Navy blue uniform, with a seamed face somewhat in need of a shave. The insignia on his cuff was that of a fleet admiral.

"Ah, there you are!" he said brightly. "I'm Admiral Eagle. I was wondering why we were getting no response—but of course you wouldn't have the new hard-focus gear. But here you are; I trust you're receiving me adequately?"

"Five by five, Admiral," Judson responded. "Welcome to Eden. My operations officer will give you some numbers."

"Thank you; I was about to—"

"We're glad to welcome anyone who comes in peace—"

"—and with some o' that couth," Cookie put in amiably.

"Yes, well," the admiral temporized. "I've studied the Report of Contact of course; quite a hysterical document, that. I felt sure—"

"In that case," Cookie put in sharply, "why don't you fall out of that attack formation and take up a nice civil cargo-routine conformation?"

"Of course, merely standard handbook procedure," the officer explained. He turned away for a moment to issue orders, as on the remote screen the two squads deployed in attack columns shifted position, coming into line abreast.

"Some nerve," Cookie commented. "But, Cap, what if they *did* come barreling on in here at full gate? What kinda defense could we put up?"

"Why assume they're hostile?" Judson returned.

"I figure the gubment back on Terra—whatever it is—wouldn't send a battle group out here just to pass the time," Cookie stated. " 'Specially after we sent that first sucker home full of stories about how he was attacked by monsters."

"If it comes to open battle, we don't have anything to put up against Hellbores and Verbot Nine," Judson pointed out. "We have to balance the situation—besides which, we don't have any enmity for Terrans. We'll make them welcome."

He took over the shore-to-ship talker and patiently gave approach and docking information to a junior officer of the approaching fleet. Then the admiral took over. "Look here, fellow," he barked. "Put me on to your top person. It's hardly appropriate that I, as representative of the Concordiat Central Committee, should be dealing with an underling—"

"Gosh," Cookie spoke up. "We messed up, Cap. This here must be one o' them vee eyes of pee."

" 'Take me to your leader,' eh?" Judson queried mildly. "Oddly enough, Admiral, we don't have one."

"Don't waste my time with nonsense!" the admiral barked. "I assure you that Terra is not lightly to be insulted!"

"No insult," Judson corrected mildly. "Just the facts. We've found that the only policeman who can enforce laws effectively is the individual. We teach our kids to not *want* to break the rules."

"Aside from questions of criminality," the flag officer grumped, "there's the matter of administration of affairs. *Someone* has to be in charge!"

"In an executive capacity, for the purpose of coordination of our activities toward the common welfare," Judson recited, "we have a rotating chairmanship of a Coordinating Committee. This position is filled by one of the Group of One Hundred, who scored highest in Testing. The choice is made at random. The term is life. There are no perks."

"Sounds like nonsense to me," Eagle snapped. "Of course you have a president, or king, or chairman—you admitted you have a chairman; put him on at once!"

"I'm him!" Cookie barked back, giving Judson an elaborate wink. "Happens I was over here at Ops, checking on things, so if it makes you feel better, go ahead: what's this little visit in aid of?"

"If you are attempting to hoax a Fleet Admiral of

Terra, and thus to offer affront to Terra herself, I must advise you—"

"Now who's giving unwanted advice?" Cookie cut in hotly. "I asked you what it is you want here."

"Report has reached the Council," Eagle intoned, "that an earlier Terran Mission to NNGC 904-A-1 that—"

" 'Eden,' we call it," Cookie told him. " 'Judson's Eden.' Cap'n Judson here discovered it."

"As for this Judson," Eagle snapped back, "if you mean to refer to the notorious enemy of the state, one Marl Judson, Terra must refuse to recognize any traitorous conspiracy in any way connected with the criminal *or* his descendants or associates."

"How long since you last seen the captain?" Cookie asked lazily.

"The miscreant was hunted down and slain over two centuries ago," Eagle boomed.

"You're a liar, and a poor one," Cookie stated. "Got anything on a Space'n Murphy, a known associate of the captain?"

"An enlisted man, doubtless acting under duress, was with this Judson at the end and died with him," Eagle declared with finality.

"Where's he buried?" Cookie demanded. "That's a grave I'd be curious to see."

"The remains were completely destroyed in the explosion of the stolen vessel, *Carnesie II*," Eagle stated.

" '*Rocky III*,' " Cookie corrected, "and she never blew up. Where'd you get all this hokey information, Eagle?"

"You may address me as 'Admiral Eagle,' " the pompous officer snapped. "As for the stolen vessel and her occupants, it's common knowledge."

Cookie looked at Judson, who had stood silently by, listening to this exchange.

"That explains why weren't bothered until now," he commented, off-talker. "They published this bogus kill-report to save face, and after that they could hardly ask for funds to hunt us down."

"Last time, mister," Cookie addressed the admiral. "What do you want here?"

"Since you persist in this foolish pretence of speaking for the planetary authorities, I have nothing further to say," Eagle stated flatly.

"Watch that jet-stream at one-oh-five-one," Cookie advised. "We'll see you dirtside."

Judson turned to Cookie. "Space'n," he said seriously, "do you think you could whip up something in the way of a banquet for our guests?"

"Can I not?" Cookie returned with relish. "Just got the new veal aged and iced down, and the harvest is already in from Green Two."

Just then the ship-to-shore crackled and spoke, a different voice this time:

"You, there, the fellow who claims to speak for the planetary authorities: His Excellency the Admiral desires that you come aboard to present your credentials; he will dispatch a dinghy to collect you at once. Kindly note the coordinates of the pick-up point:" Numbers followed.

"Gee, fellers, that's right in the middle of Big Flat Lake," someone spoke up, pointing to the chart.

"Swell," Cookie commented. "I'll take the damn fool at his word and meet him there in a seine-boat. Take about half an hour, I guess."

"Kindly confirm soonest," the voice said, sounding other than patient.

"Tell his Ex he better wear his waders," Cookie came back. "Take a few minutes to get down there."

"C'mon, Cap," Cookie urged. "We don't want to keep this admiral's butt in ice-water *too* long, do we?"

"It's your party," Judson replied. The two men used an air-cushioned vehicle to drive out to the edge of the calm fifty-acre lake.

"Let's pull around to Green Point," Judson proposed. "We'll be within a hundred yards of the spot the admiral picked."

"It's funny how the Greens are so thick right here," Cookie remarked as they halted amid a flourishing stand of the heavy-headed blossoms, which ranged in color from almost black to a translucent chartreuse. "Rare everywhere else," Cookie rambled on. "Don't grow much in the greenhouse. Same soil, same moisture."

"Still, the plants themselves differ from their close relatives, the Blues, in their odd psychogenic effects," Judson reminded him. "The lab reports classify them as category Minus One: too potent even to experiment with."

The two men donned their standard-issue breathers.

"Be a shame if the admiral got a whiff, eh, Cap?" Cookie offered, coming to a halt ten feet from the water's edge. Judson also stopped, feeling the spongy ground underfoot.

"We'll take care to warn him, Space'n," Judson reminded him.

"Sure, sure," Cookie agreed. "I didn't mean anything tricky— "

"It never occurred to you, I suppose," Judson put in, "that warning him off would be the surest way of baiting him in."

Cookie was scanning the skies in the direction from which the skiff's approach could be expected. "Naw, Cap, not me. Why, this is a real Terra big shot we're dealing with; he said so himself."

The "incoming" light was blinking on the relay board, and Judson switched on the talker:

"—piece of impudence!" the admiral was saying. "Why, that's a lake down there!"

Cookie flipped the "talk" switch. "*You* picked it, Yer Ex," he reminded his guest.

"—could have mentioned—" Eagle was sputtering.

"I don't suppose he'd have listened if we had, eh, Cap?" Murphy remarked.

The approaching lander was in sight now, a disk which came sailing in across the grasslands, and dropped down to skim the surface of the placid water, its slipstream raising a rooster's-tail of spray. It slowed, dropped another few inches, touched water and skipped like a flat stone, skittering across the last quarter-mile to slide up on the grassy shore.

"That's *some* piloting," Cookie commented.

Judson keyed the talker; "You'd better stay buttoned-up, Admiral," he said. "Conditions here—"

"Not bloody likely!" the admiral came back sharply. "I want to talk to you fellows face-to-face and see if you maintain your stubborn attitude then!"

"What are we being stubborn about, Captain, sir?" Cookie inquired diffidently. "I forget."

"Existing," Judson told him.

At that moment, a hail from the beached flitter turned their heads. A small, dapperly-uniformed fellow with a compressed-looking face and a raised fist was standing in the mud beside his beached dinghy.

"It appears . . ." he growled, waving back another man who, black to the knees with muck, was attempting to offer him an arm. "Go back aboard, Harlow, and keep an eye on that three-sixty screen," he rasped to the persistent fellow. Then, "This treacherous turf is unable to sustain my weight. Kindly extricate me from this quicksand at once!"

"A fellow can't hardly go out there, Your Highness," Cookie advised the admiral. "We better go get us some pee ess pee."

"I respectfully suggest," Judson said, with exaggerated diffidence, "that you tell Harlow to bring you a breather immediately."

"Right away," Harlow replied, just as he ducked inside the grounded vehicle.

"Damn your insolence," Eagle commented. "I've already directed you to get me out of this!" he barked.

"Cap and me don't remember when we signed on to be your dog-robber, Admiral," Cookie told the indignant officer.

"Just what that fatuous remark is intended to imply is obscure," Eagle stated, as if settling a matter. "Now!"

"Sure, Admiral," Cookie said and turned and walked away.

"You, there!" Eagle barked at Judson. "Are you paralyzed?"

"Just fascinated," Judson corrected, eyeing Eagle

closely. "At your present sink-rate, I'd say a minute and a half before your cap floats."

Eagle made a convulsive effort and gained an inch toward firm ground while sinking two.

"I recommend, sir, you stop thrashing around," Judson offered.

"I'm not 'thrashing,' as you put it!" Eagle yelled. "I am calmly and expertly making such muscular efforts as are best calibrated to extricate me from this trap you've so foolishly laid, with the least possible delay!"

"What makes you think we laid a trap, sir?" Judson inquired, "and that we did it with the least possible delay? And if you're doing so well, you won't need any help, I guess."

"Sir," Eagle cried, staring at Judson in a manner which failed to reflect approval, "you are impudent!"

"One of my worst flaws," Judson agreed. "Still, *I'm* on firm ground and you're on your way to the hardpan, sixty feet down."

"You propose," Eagle demanded coldly, "to stand there and watch a fellow human die slowly and horribly?"

"So now we're fellow humans," Judson repeated. "We're getting somewhere at last. Let's go back, sir, to where you invaded our control zone without clearance, and insulted the Chief of Ops."

" 'Invaded'? 'Insulted'?" Eagle echoed. "Sir, you are suffering from delusions!" He made another attempt to advance and sank deeper, so that now only his upper torso was visible.

Cookie returned from the car with a coil of rope. He handed it to Judson, who threw a loop of it to Eagle, who grabbed it and heaved, depositing most of the rope in the mud.

"Hold on to the end, confound it!" the admiral barked.

"Hang on, sir," Judson advised as he and Cookie hauled the mud-coated dignitary to solid ground. He staggered a few steps, slapping ineffectually at the clinging goo, and bellied up to Judson. "You the one who claims to speak for the local authorities?" he demanded.

"You forgot to say 'thank you,' " Cookie observed.

"And for what, pray, am I to express gratitude?" Eagle snorted. "Having condescended to come ashore personally to convey an invitation to inspect my command, I am unceremoniously dumped in a hog-wallow!"

"You picked the spot, sir," Cookie objected.

"Why, I had nothing—!" Eagle started. "The approach was handled in a routine fashion," he grumped. "I have no time to double-check every determination made by my navigator, of course!"

"We tried to warn you off—" Cookie attempted, but was cut off.

"Therein lies your error!" Eagle told him. "No one 'warns' a Concordiat Naval Unit!

"Well," Eagle continued in a calmer tone. "I suppose there's no need for actual documentation; your presence is enough. I accept you as legitimate representatives of the local state, pro tem, so let's go aboard at once." He signaled, and the skimmer's hatch popped wide.

"Cap," Cookie offered, "reckon we better take it slow, now; we don't know what the admiral here's got in mind."

"Sir!" Eagle boomed. "Do you imply—?"

Baggy, Judson called silently, *do you think you could manage a big splash just offshore here?*

Nothing simpler, came the silent reply.

"By the way, Admiral," Judson addressed the officer. "If you'd just glance that way"—he pointed past the beached gig—"you'll see an example of our defensive marksmanship."

With a thunderous detonation, the calm lake erupted, hurling sheets of sand and water in a hundred-foot canopy, which collapsed, drenching the three men, the open hatch, and the surrounding grass, nearly washing the admiral's dress uniform clean of mud. He staggered back, gaping, as the surface of the water churned briefly and then stilled.

"A dastardly attack!" the admiral yelled. "Fortunate for you it was a near-miss!"

"It was a precision exercise, Admiral," Judson told him, "to illustrate the accuracy of our massed batteries!"

"Nonsense!" Eagle sputtered. "I'll wager that was a cyclic natural phenomenon which you knew was about to occur! I heard no incoming at all!"

Baggy, Judson merely murmured the thought. An instant later, a second explosion assaulted their eardrums, this time in the center of the lake, so that only a fine mist floated down over them.

"All right!" Eagle yelled. "Enough of your demonstrations! I assure you there'll be no treachery. Shall we board now? Mind my rope," he added. Without awaiting a reply, he turned and waded out toward the waiting boat, then paused and motioned impatiently, and the flat craft slid toward him.

"Reckon we're going," Cookie muttered. "No point in stalling around." He followed Judson to the waiting vehicle and climbed inside. The little boat was surprisingly roomy. Eagle indicated seats for the two visitors, while Harlow hovered solicitously. Without delay, the flitter lifted off, and in less than ten minutes, Judson and Cookie were watching with profound interest as the immense, iodine-colored hull of Eagle's ship swelled on the screen before them.

The metal was densely pitted by microstrikes, the bright work was dull, and the elaborate enameled nameplate spelling out *CND Judicious* was chipped and badly repaired. Still, the boat-hatch opened with precision to receive the returning gig, which came to rest inside a chamber like the Throne Room in Humungous Cave, on Io, as Cookie observed.

"Not quite," Judson demurred. "There's no trash lying around in the cave."

"Must be doing scheduled maintenance," Cookie deduced, observing the unstored equipment, open storage bins, littered papers, and other odds and ends scattered over the grungy deck.

"Just some stuff the fellows haven't got around to tidying up yet," Eagle explained. "Got to get *on* those boys." He glanced across the cavernous hold toward a dim-lit corner where three men were intent on a card game. "Hey, Jackie," he called. "Now, you, there, Chief Swayze. Come over here a minute, if you don't mind." The man ignored him. The admiral strode toward the group. They glanced up at him uncuriously; then threw down their cards in disgust.

"Told you fellers before, hoe this place out," the admiral complained without conviction. "Swayze," he continued, "I made you a non-com. So you got to do what I say."

A heavy-set, middle-aged man rose, hitched up his breeches and turned wearily to face his superior.

"Tol' em," he grunted. "Said they's tard, after that hose job they done, cleaning out the deep tanks."

"Never mind, Swayze," Eagle soothed the man's rumpled feathers. "It's just that we got visitors here today, and we like to make a good impression is all."

"Impression o' what?" Swayze demanded. "Slave labor, doin' busy-work?" He sat down and resumed play.

"Now, you gents don't care about trifles," Eagle informed them. "Let's go set down to a good feed, like I invited you."

They rode a creaky lift to the axial tube, walked along to the Officers' Mess, a small, unoccupied room with tables and a thick, gummy stink of sweat and mock meatloaf. Eagle led the way to a long table and seated himself at one end, motioning his guests to the bench along one side.

After ten minutes, a thin, nervous-looking fellow in soiled kitchen whites without rank insignia came in, looked around, and started back the way he had come.

"Hey, Jonesy," Eagle called. "You're the mess officer, right? How about a little service over here?"

Jonesy glanced up irritably. "Might give me a little *notice*," he remarked. "I have over two hundred personnel to feed, not counting . . ." He stared disapprovingly at the strangers, slapped with a damp napkin at food debris on a tabletop, and left the room.

"Old Jonesy's kinda nervous," Eagle explained genially. "Here Monday a week, the fellers staged a little demonstration, claimed the chow wasn't good enough, and pelted old Jonesy with hard rolls. Scared him some, I guess."

Cookie tugged at Judson's sleeve. "Kinda strange ideas about discipline the admiral's got," he muttered. "Kinda surprised: the way he conned his vessel in here and put that boat right down on a dime, I figgered this were real Navy professionals."

"I've got an idea his navigator is a computer," Judson returned.

"Not much to worry about from those AutoSpace Bureaucrats, I guess," Cookie concluded. "Sounds like they don't even feed good. And I'm hungry."

After half an hour, a man in colorfully soiled whites came in, carrying a steaming pot and pushing a tea-cart with dishes. He jostled Eagle, placing the soup bowls on the bare table, then ladled a greenish-black mush into them.

Cookie sniffed. "Smells like maybe turnip greens," he commented.

"Dandelion," Eagle corrected. "More nutritious, I'm told."

Cookie sampled the stuff dubiously. He swallowed with apparent difficulty. "No meat in this stuff?" he inquired of his host, who had already finished his ration, with apparent gusto. Eagle shook his head. "Tried some rats once," he told Cookie. "Turned out the exterminator-screens had mutated 'em. Tasted like spoiled fish. So we stopped eating 'em. Got to look out for the boys' health, ya know."

"I'm real glad," Cookie replied, poking at his mush. "Ever thought about not boiling yer greens so long?"

"The autochef—" Eagle began, but paused, frowning. "May be out of kilter at that," he conceded. "Hafta talk to Swayze. Get him to fix it. Swayze's pretty good at fixing stuff."

"Cap," Cookie said quietly, "I can't eat this stuff. Let's get outa here."

"Admiral," Judson addressed his host, paying no heed to the space'n's complaint, "I have the honor to invite you to dinner with us, in return for your gracious hospitality."

"Dirtside, you mean?" Eagle queried, looking surprised. "You set up to feed two hundred and six—that's all ranks?"

Judson glanced at Cookie. "Easy, Cap," Cookie asserted. "Already got the menu planned. Cook for a hundred as easy as for just the admiral here. Let's say sleep after next."

Judson nodded. "Our pleasure, Admiral. Am I to understand you intend to bring *all* personnel? No one on Duty Watch?"

"Sure enough," Eagle replied. "I's to leave any o' the fellers behind, they'd get pissed. Can't have that."

"Why not?" Judson inquired.

"Well, you know, they'd call a Deck Court, and I'd be taking a space-walk nekkid."

Cookie looked at Judson speechlessly. "Did I say 'discipline'?" he inquired.

"It figures," Judson told him. "Where all command decisions are made by computer, it doesn't leave much to base the concept of leadership on."

"Admiral," Judson said, as two men came over and took away the dishes, despite the admiral's mild objection as one plucked the spoon from his hand.

"Boys go off-shift here pretty soon," he explained to his astonished guests. "Can't have 'em running late and mess up the duty roster."

"Admiral," Judson began again, "our duties require that we return now. If you'll be so kind—"

"Well, Cap," Cookie remarked, as they waited for Eagle to rejoin them in the gig. "I never seen nothing like that before. I don't think we need to worry about these boys trying to get tough."

"Don't be too sure," Judson cautioned. "It depends on what's programmed into his Gunnery Chief." At that moment there was a heavy *thump* at the closed hatch, and the panel began to rotate, shearing the latch pins. Eagle's excited face appeared as the plug fell back.

"I almost forgot!" the admiral blurted. "Exec put the command on alert status; means if *we'd* launched, the aft battery'd have launched, too. Close call, that. Got to get Swayze to reprogram."

Judson and Cookie waited while Eagle summoned CP Swayze and mildly admonished him to reset the autofight circuits to allow the skiff to get away. "Like you done before, time Harlow and me went down there," he concluded his instructions.

Aboard the landing-craft, which was a little roomier with only three men aboard, Eagle studied the Owner's Manual before punching in his flight plan. "Got to stay clear o' that lake, or bog or whatever," he explained as he activated the surface-scanning Topar, which printed out a topographic map, with the nature of the surfaces clearly delineated.

"Forgot to check, last time," he said, forgiving himself the oversight. "This time I think I'll land in that blue town, yonder. Looks like a pretty town you folks built there. Like to see it."

Judson shook his head as Cookie seized his arm, about to object.

"I suggest you put her down on the ledge just west of the town," Judson said quietly. Eagle gave him an impatient look. "What for, mister? Town I wanta see."

"Cap," Cookie objected urgently, "if he dumps this tub right square in the middle—"

"The admiral knows best, Space'n," Judson replied gravely. Eagle nodded vigorously in agreement. He was peering into the approach screen, muttering subaudibly.

"—damn outrage: an official emissary of the Concordiat, coming in friendship, accorded a reception suitable to a space bum being escorted by port cops."

"Tol' you we're no cops," Cookie objected. "Cap and me are the Chosen here, close as we've got to bigshots. See, we don't like big-shottery, so we decided to do without it."

"Nonsense!" Eagle barked. "No society can operate without firm leadership! I—"

"If you're a sample of this 'firm leadership,' " Cookie muttered, "I guess we can get along without it."

"If you'd care to look to your left, sir," Judson addressed the visiting brass, "you'll notice a well-defined road running toward the river there."

"So?" Eagle demanded. "Looks like a cow-path to me!"

"Cap," Cookie appealed *sotto voce* to his friend, "we're getting no place with this fellow. I say, why waste any more time on him?"

"I think the solution to a problem is inherent in the admiral's visit," Judson told him. "Please be patient and think about that banquet we're laying on."

"Waste o' good chow," Cookie muttered. "But, OK, Cap. But I been wondering: Old Admiral here says two hundred crew in his entire complement for ten ships of the line. Seems mighty skimpy to me. Must be lying."

"AutoSpace doesn't need to risk human life, remember, Space'n?" Judson reminded him.

As the skiff descended on final toward the glittering blue spiral of Sapphire City, Judson diffidently called the attention of the admiral to the fact that there was no landing facility there. Eagle was indignant. "Why the devil not?" he demanded.

"Because, sir," Judson told him patiently, "it's actually not a city; it's quite uninhabited. Merely a natural mineral formation."

"Bosh!" Eagle dismissed the explanation. "I think I know a city when I see one!"

"Where are the streets, eh, Admiral?" Cookie inquired impudently. "Don't see any populace coming to rubberneck us."

"Doubtless you fellows imagine you're bringing off a clever coup, attempting to divert my attention from what is no doubt your capital. Won't work, I fear!"

"Cap!" Cookie blurted as the landing craft neared the tallest of the spires, near the center of the formation, "You ain't—!"

Judson calmly interrupted him to address the admiral. "We rather value this natural phenomenon, intact,

Admiral, to say very little of our hides if we attempt to come to rest in the midst of these fragile towers."

"Move off-side, blast you," Eagle ordered, watching the approach screens closely. "Over there! There's a ledge!"

"Too narrow," Cookie commented.

"The slope below!" Eagle commanded.

"Risky," Cookie commented. "Thirty degrees and loose talus."

"No more of these transparent excuses," Eagle decreed, as the boat tilted sharply, slipped sideways and came to rest with a tinkling *crash!* The admiral looked at Judson with an expression in which anxiety struggled with triumph. "There!" he announced. "We're safely down, just as I directed."

"Down," Cookie said dubiously, "but safe . . . ?" He switched on the lateral-view screens, saw a vista of chipped or snapped-off-short blue crystals amid which the boat nestled.

"How are we going to climb out of this?" he inquired rhetorically, as he scanned from screen to screen, looking for a likely point for debarkation.

"Curious sort of docking facility," Eagle grumped. "What are all those glass spires for?"

"There's no docking facility here, Admiral," Judson reminded the pompous fellow. "The spires are a natural formation: crystals of metallic salts, from aluminum to uranium. Remains of a dried-up sea."

"And how," Eagle persisted, "do you propose to extricate me from this ridiculous situation? Terra, I remind you, does not lightly brook mistreatment of her accredited emissaries!"

"Actually," Judson replied, "I don't recall having examined your credentials."

Eagle turned on him and pointed skyward. "You have only now been conducted on a tour of my credentials, dammit!" he spluttered. "All ten of them!"

Eagle made a round of the screen array, staring distastefully at each glowing panel showing the same uninviting panorama of blue crystals.

"Reckon the Sapphire City will never be the same again, Cap," Cookie mourned.

"You see?" Eagle blurted triumphantly. "You admit yourself it's a city."

"Just what we call it," Cookie explained. "First time I seen it, from above, it looked like a town to me—"

"And to me, as well!" Eagle declared. "I demand we debark at once and that I be accorded an appropriate reception!"

"Go ahead!" Cookie returned. "There's the hatch! Go on, climb out there, if that's what you want!"

"Easy, Space'n," Judson cautioned. "We're still responsible for the safety of our guest." He paused to communicate briefly with Baggy: *You see the situation, Bag: we're down in an inaccessible spot, trapped here, it appears. I'm going out, now. Keep an eye on me.* Then he cycled the top hatch and climbed up and out among littered blue chips. The view in every direction was exactly what the screens had shown: towering sky-blue crystals with deep indigo cores, many, nearby, chipped or broken off short. The rubble of the damaged spires filled the deeper abysses between spine-bases.

Behind Judson, Eagle spoke. "Well, how about it, mister! This is no city! This is nothing but rock! What kind . . . ? Valuable gems, eh? I suppose . . ."

"About like rock candy, Admiral," Judson told him. "Crumbly stuff. Rare-earth salts, mostly. Just what was left behind when an arm of the sea dried up."

"No wonder they wanted to keep this a secret!" Eagle told himself. "Looks like amethyst, maybe, or sapphire. Hell, that fellow called it 'the Sapphire City.' "

"Cookie was just indulging in a little fantasy," Judson explained. "Like 'The Emerald City of Oz,' you know."

" 'Oz'!" Eagle snarled. "That's some kind of kids' book," he snorted. "On the interdicted list, too. 'Fails to embody enlightened political principles,' like they say. Mere nonsense!" He clambered down beside Judson, breathing a little hard. After he had caught his breath, he commented, "Look here, whoever you are: we can work together on this thing; why, CINCFLEET doesn't even know my position within a few parsecs. Hell, my navigator had to work overtime to find the planet, with the sketchy trajectory Ops gave me! And—"

"Forget it, Admiral," Judson told him. "Aside from other considerations, there's no basis for a deal."

"Oh? Why not?" Eagle demanded. "We're both rational men—"

"A few moments ago you were saying I was crazy," Judson reminded him.

"Just a manner of speaking," Eagle corrected. " 'No basis,' you say. I disagree. Clearly you control these deposits, and I have the means of transport, and the official status—"

"You don't have anything we want," Judson explained.

Eagle planted himself in front of Judson. "That's preposterous!" he barked. "Terra has nothing this starveling world wants? What about Terran technology? Terran protection from natural disaster? And from piratical raids by outlaws like yourselves ensconced on a number of remote worlds and raiding both outlaw and legitimately settled worlds?"

"I'd like to know more about that," Judson commented.

"AutoSpace has succeeded in establishing viable colonies on more than a dozen habitable or terraformed bodies!" Eagle announced proudly.

"In two hundred years that doesn't sound like much," Cookie contributed.

"No, I meant the outlaw worlds," Judson explained.

"That, sir, is the Concordiat's most closely-guarded secret," Eagle boomed. "We don't know the precise locations of all of them, of course," he added, "or we'd long since have neutralized them."

"Are they all hostile?" Judson asked. Eagle nodded curtly. "By their very existence, they express hostility to an orderly development of the Arm," he pontificated. "Illegally settled, and maintained by piracy," he added, as if reciting a motto.

"How far is the nearest one?" Cookie inquired casually.

"Why, no more than—" Eagle started; then, "Never

mind that, sir! You tread on dangerous classified territory!"

"Suits me," Cookie conceded. "We can do a retiring search curve and turn it up, now we know it's there."

"You wouldn't dare!" Eagle barked. "I've told you the information is highly classified!"

"You also told us it's there," Cookie reminded the indignant admiral. "Can't expect us to just sit and do nothing about our neighbors, Admiral."

"Ha!" Eagle snorted. "I suggest that you first do something about extricating me, and yourselves, from this trap! Use the caller, man! Call for a rescue team!"

"I couldn't do that," Cookie replied. "Our boat coming in has damaged the city. Any more would be a disaster."

"The disaster with which you'd best concern yourself," Eagle grated, "is that of incurring the wrath of the Concordiat! Now! Unless you conduct me at once to a suitable place for the presentation of my credentials, I must warn you—!"

"Don't bother, Admiral," Cookie counseled. "Cap don't take kindly to warnings. Nor me, either," he added.

"Humpph!" the angry officer snorted, turning to Judson. "Do we have an arrangement, sir, or do we not?"

Baggy, Judson called silently, *You'd better get us out of here and back to town. Dump the gig over at Salvage.*

"Cap, look!" Cookie blurted, pointing toward a purplish-black cloud like an upside-down twister, which had abruptly appeared above the water. "It's coming this way!" the chef added, superfluously. Already, grit and dead leaves were stinging their faces.

Oh, Captain, Baggy called. *You'd best reembark. I fear you'd suffer injury if unprotected.*

Judson and Cookie hustled Eagle back into the boat, over his noisy protests. A moment later, the tiny vessel shook, grated on rock, and surged upward.

"Here, you fellows!" Eagle barked. "Why didn't you tell me this area was subject to cyclones!"

Easy, Bag, Judson cautioned. "But he's right, Space'n," he told Cookie. "We're a lot better off inside."

"If old Bag can set her down easy," Cookie worried, clinging desperately to his handhold, while Eagle bleated about his status as Terra's Ambassador Extraordinary and Minister Plenipotentiary. After a few moments, the noise and vibration ended abruptly with a gentle thump as all motion ceased.

Eagle made a show of looking around at the screens, which showed only the shattered blue crystals. At that moment, the boat was jostled into a level position. Eagle uttered a yelp and grabbed for a handhold. "The—the boat!" he squawked. "It's leveling itself! That's impossible! The power unit is crushed!" He pointed to the instruments, which showed a total loss of function of all systems. Then, on the screens, the view changed, showing the Sapphire City rapidly dwindling away below.

"It *can't!*" Eagle repeated. "This boat is inoperable!" He looked accusingly first at Cookie, then at Judson. "Another hoax!" he declared. "I demand you cease these futile efforts to delude me!" He made a move as if to open the hatch. Cookie knocked his hand away.

"How dare you strike me?" the panicked admiral demanded. "That, alone, means court-martial!" he announced triumphantly.

"Better'n trying to gather up your remains for a decent funeral all in one coffin," Cookie grunted. The gig continued smoothly on its way, Judson directing Baggy to put it down, gently, in the Central Plaza. A slight jar indicated their arrival.

"You done good, Bag!" Cookie exulted.

Eagle stared at him. "Whom are you addressing, mister?" he demanded.

"Oh, nobody," Cookie replied. "Just a manner of speaking, you might say."

Eagle *hrumph!*ed. "I demand we disembark at once," he announced. "I trust you've laid on suitable transport to your capital, since it appears this isn't it."

Judson called to Baggy again, thanked him for the

easy landing, and asked him to request a vehicle from the Motor Pool.

Be careful, he concluded. *You know how upset people can get the first time they hear from you.*

I've learned caution, Baggy reassured him. *I shall be circumspect. The dispatcher will think he's acting on a whim of his own.*

"—you fellows," Eagle was saying. "Actually, my discovery of this world will impress the Council most favorably."

" 'Discovery'?" Cookie queried. "Funny, me and Cap had the idea *we* discovered Eden."

"Ah, to be sure," Eagle concurred mildly. "But to accidently stumble upon a valuable parcel of real estate lying within the conic scheduled to be examined by AutoSpace within the century is hardly equivalent to the orderly inventory of those planets whose manifest destiny it is to be joined to the Terran Concordiat."

"How's the program going, so far?" Judson asked.

"Very well, indeed," Eagle stated.

"How many habitable worlds have you discovered?"

"Actually, none," Eagle vouchsafed.

"You call that 'very well'?" Cookie snorted.

"Except of course," Eagle continued blandly, "for those few seized upon by pirates."

"Discovered by actual explorers, you mean," Cookie decided. He winked at Judson. "Like us," he added.

"I suppose they've encountered some very strange life-forms," Judson suggested.

"Hardly!" Eagle snorted. "It has been determined by rigorous theoretical analysis that the likelihood of the appearance of life, let alone intelligent life, is of the order of one in ten trillion: a practical impossibility. No, we'll find no alien life-forms. They don't exist!"

"Suppose," Cookie countered, "I was to tell you there's an intelligent life-form here on Eden?"

"I should penetrate the lie at once," Eagle dismissed the idea.

Judson cycled the hatch open and saw a crowd waiting; they cheered as he emerged.

"Looks like word leaked out," Cookie remarked, giving the crowd a wave as they cheered his appearance. Judson held up a hand and the roar subsided.

"We have a guest," he announced. "Admiral Eagle, all the way from fabled Terra."

There was another roar as the emissary emerged. He beamed his gratification.

"Friendly folks," he remarked to Cookie as they followed Judson through an aisle which opened spontaneously through the crowd.

"It's quite a thrill for them to see a human they've never seen before," Judson pointed out. "One who isn't a known relative."

"Your people are inbred?" Eagle inquired, sounding shocked. "Curious: I see no gross deformities."

"No, we had a large enough founding population," Judson corrected.

Inside the public affairs building, Eagle studied with interest the instrumentations in operations, and demanded:

"Where did you fellows get this—and this?" He pointed to various technical installations. "All GUTS classified, top security items. How the devil did you manage to steal the Concordiat's newest and most closely-guarded technology?"

"No stealing, Mr. Eagle," Cookie told him. "Cap here is a pretty clever fellow. He invented this stuff. AutoSpace no doubt stole it from Private Space after Cap lit out."

Eagle sputtered. "You would accuse an official Concordiat agency of theft? Outrageous!"

"Then you tell me, Admiral," Cookie urged. "Where *did* AutoSpace get its space filter and the LRA gear, for example?"

"Why, the long-range assessor was developed by AutoSpace over two centuries ago!"

" 'Developed' by raiding Private Space's vaults after Cap and me took off," Cookie grunted.

"You suggest," Eagle queried, "that you people have

independently invented all Terra's most sophisticated space-related technology?"

"Just re-invented," Cookie countered. "Cap has a pretty good memory. Soon's we got our industries going, he got the fellows to run off copies of what he'd already patented back on Terra a long time ago."

Eagle frowned at Judson. "Are you claiming," he inquired incredulously, "that you hold in your mind the seventeen pages of abstract equations necessary to rig an assessor grid?"

"I 'claim' nothing," Judson replied. He paused at a desk, picked up a pen and on a pad of paper, quickly wrote out a line of odd symbols. Eagle goggled and snatched the paper. "The penalty for possession of these field equations is death on the spot!" he yelled.

"Better forget that, Admiral," Cookie told the upset official. "We're not in Concordiat jurisdiction here."

"You would defy the orders of the Council as enforced by the Navy of Terra?" Eagle boomed.

"Nope," Cookie reassured him. "We just ignore 'em."

"I confess," Eagle told them solemnly. "When I received my orders to seek out the destination of this escaped criminal, this Judson, whom you, sir, claim to be, in spite of—"

"I 'claim' nothing, Admiral," Judson told him. "Cookie told you my name."

"Very well, his descendant, then," Eagle huffed. "But as I was saying when I was interrupted . . . I was most dubious as to the validity of conducting such a search, so long after the fact. Now, of course, I understand: the equations are timeless. To leave them in the hands of pirates—" Eagle oofed as Cookie accidentally jostled him, treading on his bunions in the process.

"Par' me, Mr. Eagle," the cook blurted. "I guess talking about pirates and all makes me kind of jumpy. Lucky we're all honest citizens here."

"You think a veiled attack on my person will pass unnoticed?" Eagle demanded harshly.

"Attack? Me?" Cookie derided. "If I was going to attack you, Fats, I'd have done something like this—"

He jabbed his stiffened fingertips toward Eagle's short ribs, but instead encountered Judson's oak-like forearm. "Hold hard, Space'n," Judson said quietly. "I think the admiral would like to see the lookout room before he goes to sleep."

If Eagle noticed the by-play, he ignored it. " 'Lookout room,' you say," he murmured. "That sounds intriguing."

"Right over here, Admiral," Judson suggested, and led the way to a closed door, which he opened on a glass-walled space crowded with bulky equipment.

"Ummm," Eagle breathed, pausing in the threshold to cast an eye over the installation.

"A remote scanner, or I miss my guess," he commented, approaching a six-foot, cube-shaped item which was radiating heat and making a low buzzing sound.

"Late model, too," the visitor added. "With full texture-and-structure gear. And what's this?" He laid a hand briefly on a cylindrical accessory mounted atop this cube, jerking his fingers back with an exclamation.

"Running hot, Mr. Judson," he remarked. "Your Maintenance Chief must be malfunctioning."

"Cookie," Judson addressed the smaller man, "are you malfunctioning?"

"Not me, Cap," was the reply. "Hell, I'm not hardly functioning at all. Looker's got to run hot, Admiral," he shifted his attention to the big shot. "The whole secret of the fine-tuning. Cold vibristors won't cut it."

"Eh? Running a Looker hot, eh? And you claim it functions properly?"

"Like Cap told you, Admiral," Cookie answered sharply. "We don't 'claim' anything. Claiming is for liars, and you wouldn't call me a liar, now, would you, sir?"

"What's that?" Eagle came back, getting his indignant look in place. "Kindly refrain from taking offense when none is intended." He moved away to the front of the big scanner and peered at the Looker's ground-glass lens.

"Just as I thought," he barked. "False returns. Seems to indicate an incoming fleet."

"Scale's set small, sir," Judson corrected. "That's your crews coming down, I'd guess. The readout says two hundred and one personnel cases, at sub-atmospheric velocity, decelerating."

"Why, the cheek!" Eagle sputtered. "Young Harlow's taken a bit much on himself this time! I gave no 'execute' order."

"It's all right, Admiral," Judson soothed the excited admiral. "If they'll hand off to our ground-control, we'll have them down in Green Plaza in half a minute." *Baggy,* he went on silently, *steer the lead boat in to the edge of Green. See that they park in well-spaced rows, hatch-side up.*

"Well?" Eagle grumped. "Aren't you going to alert your Controller?"

"The situation is in hand, sir," Judson told him, indicating the adjacent ground-to-space panel where the incoming boats were now visible in orderly array, orbiting the landing site before peeling off one at a time to descend the final half-mile and settle in curved rows, adjacent to the Monument. A crowd began to form around them.

"What's that tower?" Eagle demanded, eyeing the memorial obelisk dubiously.

"It's a tribute to a friend of ours," Judson informed him.

"Eh? What's his name? Who is he?"

"He's called 'Baggy,' " Judson replied. "He's around somewhere."

" 'Baggy'?" Eagle snorted. "Are you ragging me again, Judson? Ridiculous name. 'Baggy' indeed!"

Judson, Baggy's voiceless voice came crisply to the captain, *I have taken a dislike to this Eagle! Did you hear him slandering my beautiful appellation? "Ridiculous" indicates "worthy of ridicule," does it not? I advise you to have nothing to do with this fellow!*

Easy, Bag, Judson soothed. *He's just not too bright, not dangerous.*

"Say," Eagle commented, watching the last of the boats settle in, in perfect alignment. "That Controller of yours works real good! Now I guess I better go over and tell the fellows whereat the banquet hall is. By the way, where is it?"

"It will be my pleasure to show you, sir," Judson replied. "Just fall them in in a column of twos, if you please, Admiral." *Thanks, Bag,* he added voicelessly.

The men and women had emerged from their transports and had fallen in smartly enough. All young and healthy-looking, neatly attired in their snappy uniforms, they presented an impressive appearance.

"What'd he do, this dead hero?" Eagle wanted to know, looking up at the fifty-foot stone pillar.

"He kept us all alive more than once," Judson replied. "And he's not dead."

" 'Not dead'?" Eagle echoed. "Never heard of putting up a monument to a live man."

"He's actually not a man," Judson mentioned.

"Very well, a woman named 'Baggy' is worse, if anything!" Eagle declared.

"He's not exactly a woman, either," Cookie contributed.

"Eh? One of those, eh?" Eagle snorted. "Hardly seemly, I think, to so honor a deviate."

"I don't think Bag's a deviate, either," Judson informed the confused visitor.

"Then what *would* you call it?" Eagle demanded.

"We call him 'Bag,' usually," Cookie answered.

"Well, Captain," Eagle changed the subject, "the crowd is pressing my people rather closely. Would you mind telling them to stay back, say, ten feet?"

The townspeople were indeed pressing close to the newcomers. Two hundred nubile, or virile as the case happened to be, strangers were hardly a common phenomenon. Every crew member was besieged by one or more young Edenites of the opposite sex. The orderly column had broken up into couples engaged in fascinated conversation.

"They're just making friends, Admiral," Judson pointed out. "Surely that's desirable."

"Bad for discipline!" Eagle snarled, even as an only slightly corpulent matron named Anastasia took his arm possessively. For a moment, the admiral appeared about to spurn the lady, but then he relaxed and even smiled as she whispered in his ear.

Then, abruptly, Eagle yelped, "Here, you fellows—what—where?" He looked anxiously at Judson. "My crew—where *are* they?" Anastasia patted him soothingly.

"They're just getting a little privacy, honey," she reassured him. "Like we ought to do. Come on, my place is just up the block here." He allowed himself to be led off, muttering. Once he started to break away to collar a shapely crewgirl, clinging to a stalwart local man, but Anastasia pulled him back.

"Let the young folks be!" she told him. "They need a little change of pace—yer folks as much as ours!"

2

At Cookie's urging, Judson sent out the word to move on and assemble at the banquet hall in half an hour. A gradual drift in that direction began. Eagle, mollified, went along with Judson and Cookie to the former warehouse, pressed into service and decorated for the occasion.

"They'll want to bring their new friends, Space'n," Judson told Cookie. "Can you handle it?"

"No problem, Cap'n," Cookie replied. "With just a little FHB we'll be fine."

"What's FHB?" Judson inquired.

"That's 'Family Hold Back,' " Cookie supplied. "Just a little: easy on the seconds, is all. I'll spread the word."

Additional tables were quickly improvised from trestles and doors from the millwork shop, and spread with heavy, snow-white linen tablecloths and set with fine procelain made at the Mudslick Potting Works, and solid silver from the mines in Magic Mountains. Eagle allowed himself to be seated, with Anastasia at his side, at the head of the central table. He leaned confidentially toward Judson, sitting at his right.

"My folks are hoping for a little fresh beef," he told his host, "and so am I. Fresh veggies, too. Mummy-dust gets tiresome after a while. Hey, we're not just having soup?" he exclaimed as a neat little waitress placed a steaming bowl before him.

"It's real good, sir," the girl supplied. "I helped make it myself."

"Never you mind that, Nancy!" Anastasia interjected.

Eagle dipped in a cautious spoon, netting a big chunk of tenderloin. He chewed tentatively, then smiled. "It's all right!" he declared, and stopped talking to eat.

"Cap," Cookie whispered, "this fellow acts like maybe we'd give him bad food."

"It's all he's ever had," Judson pointed out, just as Eagle was finishing his bowl.

"Not a bad dinner at all," the admiral admitted, as he started to push back from the table, just as Nancy arrived with a plate laden with crisp, golden-fried seafood. Eagle dropped back into his chair and looked around with an amazed expression. He opened his mouth, but instead of speaking, shoveled in a succulent forkful of the white-fleshed butterfish.

"At least he didn't salt it without tasting it," Cookie commented.

Eagle was chewing blissfully. "What kind *is* this?" he mumbled, still chewing. "Fine, fellows, really fine." Then he settled down to consuming every crumb along with the near-rice with gravy, the bright red Kong peas, and the tough, chewy, pizzlenut-flavored bread. Finished, he again started to rise, only to find Nancy placing yet another loaded plate before him, this time a small fowl, roasted whole and filled with a mealy and aromatic stuffing.

"You fellows have chickens out here?" he inquired wonderingly as he dug a butter-soft chunk from the breast of the eight-ounce fowl.

Cookie nodded. "Turkeys, too," he supplied. "Been breeding 'em smaller, for less meat, but better."

"Not bad at all," Eagle conceded, poking at the stripped carcass with his fork.

"Pick it up and finish it off, Admiral," Cookie urged. "That's what *we* do." He demonstrated, and Eagle followed suit, suppressing his running commentary in favor of chewing. When the assembled company had laid aside the last bone, Nancy returned with a twenty-pound loin roast, which she placed, steaming gently, before Eagle, then proceeded to slice off dark-brown-on-the-outside, pink-all-through slabs, which she put on Eagle's fresh plate, before adding a heap of tru-potatoes doused in rich gravy. Eagle hesitated, then cut himself a noble chunk, which sliced effortlessly, he absently noticed. A beatific smile appeared on his harsh features as he masticated.

"Damn fine roast beef," he managed. "Guess I didn't have to worry." He swallowed half a glass of black wine.

"We try to feed good," Cookie remarked. "Glad you like it."

"We *all* like it!" Eagle exclaimed, as he speared the last chunk on his plate. Nancy immediately refilled it, as well as his wineglass.

"A bit of the crispy, sir?" she inquired.

"Right, girl, and a bit of the other, too!"

"Say, Cap," Cookie whispered, "we better tell Bob to skip to the dessert. These folks aren't used to a full belly."

Judson agreed and passed the word. After a brief pause, Nancy reappeared with a magnificent chocolate cake, twelve inch-thick layers, with a thick, fudgelike icing. She cut a huge wedge for Eagle, who started to protest, then gave it up to inhale through his nose. "Lovely!" he breathed. "Is it *real* chocolate? Could one—?" He broke off as Nancy put a paper-thin glass of pale yellow dessert wine before him. He sipped it.

"Chateau d'Yquem, as I live and breathe," he commented. "How?"

"Starve the grapes," Cookie supplied. "Then let 'em stay on the tree till they're about half-rotten. Works good."

He sniffed his glass and sipped, then turned his

attention to the ice cream Nancy had placed on top of his layer cake. He tested it.

". . . why you fellows aren't fat," Eagle was remarking, as a large bowl of toasted and salted grich-nuts was placed before him. He bit into one and beamed. "A little like those Macphersons, or whatever," he commented, "only better." He glanced at Judson as if to ask, "OK if I take another one?" then noted that each diner had a full bowl. He settled down to serious grich-nut eating, lubricating the process with the sweet wine.

After an hour of feasting, Cookie told Nancy to pass the word that it was time for a stroll in the gardens. All rose, and filed out into an arcaded court, dim-lit by a crescent Junior, where fountains threw sparkling sprays into the glow of colored spotlights, artistically placed. Black-green leaves filled the spaces between brick-curbed beds overflowing with blossoms of every color. The delicate perfume of their pheromones filled the crisp evening air.

Young and middle-aged couples quickly filled the marble benches set at intervals along the tiled paths. Anastasia tugged at the admiral's arm. "Come on, honey," she urged. "I'll show you the nicest spot of all, over past the faun fountain."

"Got to get my crews back together," Eagle objected. "Scattered all over Hell's half acre here."

"This ain't 'Hell's half-acre,' honey," Anastasia explained patiently. "Let the folks have a little fun. Won't hurt 'em. Us, too." She led him off to the deep shadow of a pink-flowering arbutus. The bench there was almost invisible in deep shadow, and thus was unoccupied. Eagle sat beside Anastasia and turned his attention to her actually quite beautiful face, nibbling her ear, then kissing her warmly.

"Wow!" she exclaimed. "You got life in you yet, honey!"

"Damn right!" Eagle seconded. "What do you say we go up to your place like you said?"

She rose, took his hand, and led him away. He turned uncertainly to call, "Swayze! On the double!"

There was no response. He went back to where Judson and Cookie stood.

"Say, Mr. Judson," he appealed. "Maybe you could locate old Swayze and tell him to get his crews together. Back pretty soon," and off he went.

A young fellow, a husky black-maned bricklayer whom Judson recognized, came up to him and paused respectfully.

"Yes, what is it, Jim?" Judson invited. Jim spoke in a low voice. "Uh, Mr. Judson, sir, I was wondering: could I sign on with the fleet? Me and Gwendolyn got a good thing going here, and I don't want to lose her."

"Are you sure this is what you want?" Judson asked kindly. "You can't come back, you know. You'll miss Eden."

Jim nodded, looking sad. "I know, feller. It's not easy." His face brightened. "But Gwen—"

"*Vaya con dios,*" Judson said and shook his hand. "Of course, there's the little matter of getting the admiral's OK."

"Where is he?" Jim demanded.

"He'll reappear tomorrow sometime," Judson suggested. "Anastasia took a shine to him."

During the next half-hour, three more young Edenites sought out Judson to tell him they wanted to ship out with a new friend.

"Don't know if old Admiral can take 'em all," Cookie commented.

"If he can't find his crews," Judson pointed out, "he'll be glad to have all the recruits he can get."

By midmorning, Eagle had reappeared with Anastasia beside him. He was now arrayed in his dress whites, fetched for him by Harlow, with the big red-edged gold shoulder-boards and the blue-and-gold stripe down the trouser seams. He looked like a man well-content with life. He patted Anastasia's plump but shapely hip and came over to where Judson and Cookie stood under a flowering pizzlenut tree.

"You fellows don't seem to be joining in the fun," he remarked, looking around with an anxious expression.

"Still don't see my fellows and girls," he remarked. "I suppose they'll be along soon. You, there, McGillicuddy!" he barked suddenly, addressing a thick-set fellow with a brutal face and bowed legs. "Report!"

McGillicuddy turned his head slowly to stare coldly at his commander, but made no move.

Judson was watching without seeming to. He saw Eagle walk slowly over to the man, reach up and take a firm grip on one of his prominent ears, twist it cruelly, bringing McGillicuddy almost to his knees.

"You're getting a little ahead of yourself here, boy," Eagle told him sternly. He released his grip and McGillicuddy clamped a hand over the tweaked ear and looked sullenly at his commander.

"Got no call—" he started, but broke off as Eagle poked him in the chest with his forefinger. "Silence, you!" he ordered. "Now you come along with me." Eagle turned and strolled off along the path, stepped off in the deep shadow of a gorb-flower bush. McGillicuddy trailed slowly, rubbing his ear. Judson moved unobtrusively around to the other side of the shrub which sheltered the two.

"I'm disappointed in you, Mac," Eagle was saying. "You seem to be believing your own ham acting."

"Ain't no ham," the burly man objected. "Hired through Equity, same's you."

" 'The same as you, *sir*,' " Eagle corrected. "Your job is to get all teams in place in a coordinated manner. Have you bothered with that?"

"Aw, to hell with this," McGillicuddy blurted, and Judson heard a meaty smack followed by the sound of a heavy body falling.

Cookie had come up beside Judson. "What the heck!" he remarked softly. "Cap, you been holding out on me?" he went on aggrievedly.

"It wouldn't do," Judson cautioned him, "to let slip we had an idea something phony was going on."

"So you figured I'd act more natural if I *didn't* know," Cookie grumped.

"Something like that. How're your surveillance people doing?"

"Just like they ought to," Cookie reported contentedly. "Got all but four crew maneuvered into spots where they can't communicate with their team leaders. Mainly," he added, "they're enjoying themselves. Funny: these Navy folks think they're infiltrating us, and all the time our folks are isolating them, but both bunches are getting to be real friends. Even Anastasia. She told me Eagle's the finest fella she ever met."

"That's fine," Judson told him. "There's no reason for any personal antagonism. It seems things are going well." As the two men conversed in whispers, they were also listening to the snoring of McGillicuddy, and Eagle's departing footsteps. Judson and Cookie took a shortcut and encountered the admiral just as he returned to the spot where he'd last seen Anastasia.

"Ah, Captain," he spoke up at once, "have you seen—that is, the lady . . ."

"Annie's just getting you a fresh drink, sir," Cookie told him. "Here she is now."

"Oh, Admiral," the matron said as she came up, holding a full glass carefully before her. "I bet you never even missed me," she cooed.

"Did, too," Cookie corrected. "Just asking about you."

Eagle took the glass with thanks, glanced keenly at Judson, and drank it down at a gulp. "To Annie, here," he toasted, "and to a lot of lasting friendships formed here last night."

A young local girl hurried up to Judson and whispered, "Captain, one of the guests had a few too many; he's lying back of a foo-foo bush."

"That would be McGillicuddy," Eagle volunteered. "Good man, but doesn't know when to quit."

All five in the conversation group went along to where the man lay, profoundly unconscious.

"Quite a wallop," Cookie commented. Eagle glanced quickly at him.

"The rum, I mean," Cookie explained. "If you're not used to it."

"Excellent!" Eagle agreed, and put his empty glass on a bench. Anastasia picked it up and trotted away.

"Admiral," Judson said, "couldn't we dispose of this annexation business now? I think we'd both prefer—"

"It's not my preferences, or yours, Captain, which determine the course of events. It's Concordiat policy. That policy requires that I establish Terran sovereignty here with the least possible delay."

"That's just it, sir," Judson replied. "The delay, I mean."

Eagle gave Judson a hard look. "See here, Judson," he grated. "Don't you think it's about time we both dropped the charade?"

"Suits me, Admiral," Judson acceded. "You first: what's the idea of the Three Stooges routine? I'm afraid you overdid it just a little."

"I didn't expect—" Eagle started, then interrupted himself. "Your 'We're just a couple of simple country boys' number didn't play too well, either," he grumbled, then gave Judson a keen glance. "That artillery of yours," he mentioned. "Had to change a few plans when I saw that. We—"

"You didn't bring ten ships of the line out here to sightsee," Judson stated. "How far did you plan to go?"

"The Concordiat has a long memory," Eagle remarked. "CINCHS hasn't forgotten that your ancestor disappeared with a sprig of mistletoe pinned to his rear. My orders were to find out how he managed it and round up any surviving descendants and place them in detention." He paused to look around the fairy-lit garden. "That last part turned out to be impractical," he added. "But I still have my responsibilities to do what I can." He jerked his dress tunic straight, brushed cookie-crumbs from its front, and came to attention.

"Sir," he intoned, "I have the honor to notify you that you as chief conspirator here, are under arrest."

"Sorry," Judson told him. "That wouldn't be convenient."

"Didn't you notice, Admiral?" Cookie put in. "Your fleet is captured and all your personnel are under guard—and without a shot fired or a word spoken in anger."

Eagle turned stiffly to face him. "You—you wouldn't dare!" he declared.

"It's what they call a *fait accompli,*" the chef told him cheerfully.

"My command," Eagle blurted. "I have my command talker here"—he tapped a heavily gold-wire-embroidered lapel—"to call down a strike at any moment."

"Negative, sir," Judson countered. *Baggy,* he went on subvocally, *bring the admiral's flagship down—gently—in Pink Square.*

Right away, Captain, came the prompt reply. *Shall I use the watch personnel aboard, or intercede personally?*

Go through channels, Judson directed, then suggested to the admiral that they take a stroll.

"I have something you ought to see, sir," he explained. They left the park and went along the silent dark street to the wide plaza marking the border of Pink Quarter. Eagle looked around expectantly. "Well," he prompted, "what—? I mean to say, Mr. Judson, surely you haven't brought me her merely to admire the architecture? Interesting, at that: antique issue modules as modified by rude frontier construction techniques, plus the latest high-tech touches."

"There's something else," Judson admitted. Eagle strode out to the center of the intersection and planted himself as if to await the next revelation.

"Oh, Admiral," Judson called. "It's inadvisable to venture out there just now. May I suggest—"

As Judson spoke, a low rumbling sound rose from below the threshold of audibility. Eagle stiffened, looked around, then up. Barely visible, far above, a point of green light glowed, waxing perceptibly, then winked out. The rumble grew.

"What the devil!" Eagle snorted. "Sounds for all the world like—"

"It *is,* sir," Judson assured the admiral.

"Lost her main drive during let-down," Eagle barked. "Let's get clear of here!" he yelled, retreating from his position in the open. "That vessel will crash right on top of us!"

Judson went over to where Eagle was pressed flat in a doorway. "It's all right, sir," he soothed the admiral. "She's under full control."

Eagle gave Judson an accusing glare. "You talk, sir, as if you had expected this catastrophe!"

"No catastrophe," Judson corrected, then, *Baggy, you'd better show some lights. Be very careful, now, settling her in. I don't want any damage to the square.*

You quite surprise me, Captain, came the reply. *I shan't be careless.*

The two men watched as the vessel's running lights flashed on, a dazzling pattern of brilliant colors against the black sky; then searchlights speared down to light the square like a stage set. The dark bulk of the ship itself was visible only as a shadow blanking out the stars. The shadow grew; the rumble faded.

"This is impossible!" Eagle yelled, his voice echoing across the bright-lit plaza. "She's lost power, but she's falling like a leaf! What's going on here? What ship *is* that, Captain?"

"Watch her, sir," Judson suggested. The vast shadow blotted out the sky now. The sound of wind whistling across the square was the loudest noise as the reflected light began to show up the contours of the stern-plates and extended landing-jacks of a major space-vessel.

"My God!" Eagle blurted. "That's *CND Judicious,* my flagship. What—? How—?"

3

Displaced air whirled dirt into the men's faces. Without a sound, the million-ton cruiser floated down to settle onto the pavement with no more than a faint creaking from the landing-jacks to suggest her immense mass. Total silence fell as the disturbed air dissipated the last of its energy.

"I'm damned if I ever saw a smoother touchdown—and in atmosphere, too!" Eagle stated. "I didn't think Harlow knew his navigator that well. I've underrated the boy!" He started toward the ship, even as the aft personnel ladder extended to grate softly against the cobbles.

Eagle had halted by the port jack, and was speaking urgently into his lapel talker.

". . . ahead of yourself, mister!" he was muttering. "Display your aft batteries now: lock and load, but don't go near the 'execute' button until I personally give you the command. Is that understood?" He paused, nodded, then looked at Judson.

Freeze the armaments, Bag, Judson directed.

"Well, sir, you've placed yourself literally under my guns," Eagle stated. "A trifle too daring of you, to go so far as to actually to threaten me. 'Captive,' indeed! What have you to say now, sir?"

"Funny, Admiral," Judson remarked. "I don't see any gun ports opening."

Eagle wheeled to stare up at the tall column of the warship. "Harlow!" he barked. "Look alive, man! Carry out your orders!"

"Sir," the exec's reply was barely audible. "I . . . tried, sir, but it seems—"

"Harlow!" Eagle prompted.

"Admiral, I can't . . . sir, there's something—I can't really describe it, sir; I'm standing here looking at Gunner, but somehow I can't seem to utter the— Gunner! Arm aft batteries, code twelve! There, sir, I— But sir, Gunner doesn't respond! It's shut down spontaneously, sir!"

Eagle gave Judson a hard, flat look. "See here, mister," he grated. "I don't know what kind of game you're playing, interfering with a capital ship of the Navy, but—"

"*You're* in control of your ship, Admiral," Cookie reminded the irate officer. "You told us that. You've got your talker wired right into your fancy suit there—"

"Enough!" Eagle barked. "I'm at a loss as to just what it is you hope to accomplish, but you overplayed your hand when you couldn't resist showing off that fantastic precision artillery of yours. I've told you the 'bewildered rube' act will no longer play!"

Judson looked thoughtful. "You went a little too far yourself, Admiral, with your 'bumbling incompetent' routine: pretending you were stripping your ships of their entire complement. That's—"

"As to that," Eagle replied loftily, "the installed equipment is quite competent to perform all functions aboard ship. If I'd proposed to leave skeleton crews behind to man the craft in safe orbit, I'd have had a mutiny on my hands—"

"You're a liar, sir. Begging your pardon, sir," Cookie spoke up. "You have duty personnel aboard every vessel."

"How the devil do—would—you know that?" Eagle

demanded. "Treachery? An informer among my people? I shall deal harshly with him, I assure you!"

"You'll have to find her first," Cookie pointed out, forgetting the "sir" this time.

"Aha! A woman, eh?" Eagle snapped up the bait.

"Nope," Cookie told him. "We have our own sources." As the foolish conversation went on, the great ship's running lights blinked off and the searchlights dimmed. Eagle looked around suddenly, and up at the ranks of dark windows lining the facades fronting the plaza. "I suppose you have a marksman at every window," he grumped. "That's why you decoyed me here. Well, I can still order a salvo, you know. It seems you're outsmarting yourself once again, Captain!"

"Your big guns can't fire without taking you out along with us," Cookie commented. "Somehow, sir, I don't see you as the suicidal type. Now, our sharpshooters can nail a gnat's eye at two hundred yards." He glanced up assessingly at the four- and five-story buildings looming all around.

"A salvo would bring 'em all down," he pointed out. "Your ship would be buried to her bulkhead; she'd never lift off."

"It appears, gentlemen," Eagle said stiffly, "that we're at a stand-off. I propose an accommodation, as I suggested earlier. We both have much to gain if we do. So I put it to you: will it be peace and friendship, or interplanetary, fratricidal war?"

"The war's over," Cookie stated flatly. "We won."

"Now, just hold on, there," Eagle objected. "We haven't yet agreed on the terms of our arrangement! I came here in good faith to negotiate an acceptable accommodation with you fellows! We haven't even discussed matters yet!"

"Sure we did, Admiral," Cookie contradicted. "When you gave the order to clear for action and laid that aft battery on unarmed men—you said it loud and clear!"

"But I didn't open fire," Eagle insisted. "No act of belligerence has occurred! I insist that you respond to my proposal!"

"What proposal was that, sir?" Judson took over.

"Offered to spare us," Cookie contributed, "if we'd let him have all the sapphires in Sapphire City."

"Aha!" Eagle burst out. "You admit it's sapphire!"

"Admiral," Cookie stated judiciously, "you can have *all* the sapphires you can find in Sapphire City. How's that?"

"Now we're making progress!" Eagle declared. "As for my side of the bargain, I have a very convenient memory: I can forget I ever came upon this planet—except for that artillery, of course."

"They'd never believe you," Cookie said flatly.

Eagle stared at him. "The word of a flag officer—" he blurted, to be cut off by Judson:

"—won't be worth a jettisoned fat cannister, Admiral, when they see you have an entire replacement crew."

"What are you talking about, man?" Eagle demanded.

"Your original crew seem to have wandered off somewhere," Judson reminded him. "Luckily, we have lots of bright young folks who'd like to sign on."

"Preposterous!" Eagle yelled.

"Think it over, sir," Cookie urged. "We could put the rest of your squadron down all in a row, right down Blue Street, if we wanted to, and you couldn't find a crew member if your neck depended on it. Better take Cap's offer."

"Offer? I heard no reasonable offer, only vainglory and preposterous claims! 'Captain,' indeed! My command, I remind you, gentlemen, is intact, and I await your capitulation!"

Baggy, Judson called. *Vent off some waste gases, non-toxic, of course, in a tight jet directed at the seat of the admiral's trousers.*

There was a sharp click followed by a whooshing noise, then a loud hiss. Eagle jumped, whirled about and uttered a yell.

"Damn you!" he yelled, as he spun around furiously, but seeing no one behind him or anywhere else, he made an effort to recover his dignity, stamped over to Judson and Cookie, and barked: "You'll regret the day you set out to toy with a flag officer of the Concordiat! Now, enough of this horseplay! It's time to get down to serious discussion!"

"Oh, honeybunch, there you are!" Anastasia's voice spoke up from a side street.

Eagle leapt in surprise. "My dear," he cried, "I hoped you didn't—"

"She didn't see you dancing," Cookie reassured the rattled admiral. "She just now came on post."

He turned to Judson. "Lucky he was goosy," he commented to his compatriot. "Otherwise we might have had to get rough. And I'da hated that, frankly."

"Now, what—" Eagle said over Anastasia's shoulder as she embraced him heartily. "Oh, yes, about the terms of our accommodation: I suggest that after the jewels have been loaded—"

"Look, Admiral," Judson said wearily. "I've told you there are no jewels, at least at the mineral formation we jokingly call the Sapphire City; just useless salts. Pretty, from a distance, but valueless."

"I shall be the judge of that," Eagle persisted. "I doubt you'd have been so protective—"

"It's a tourist attraction, by overflight," Cookie supplied. "Like Grand Canyon back on Terra, and *Olympus Mons* on Mars."

"In return for a cargo-hold filled with the gems," Eagle plowed on imperturbably, "I shall omit from my report all mention of the personal indignity to which I have been subjected, as well as details of your potent, though deceptively simple-appearing defensive works—just the sort of provocation the Council most resents. Why, at Moosehead—"

"I heard," Judson interrupted. "Those boys showed what a small, well-organized force can do to resist interference by a bungling bureaucracy."

"And how did you hear that, may I inquire? Your isolation here—"

"Top secret material, I suppose, eh, Admiral?" Cookie suggested. "We monitor deep-space radio," he went on to explain. "Lots of clutter, but we can filter some intelligence, diffuse, you know, nondirectional."

Eagle was nodding, but caught himself. " 'Bungling' indeed! Piracy, sir! Chaos! Insurrection! They'll not long enjoy their respite, I can assure you! You'd do well, gentlemen, to disassociate yourselves as far as possible from the actions of such decadents!"

"Never met 'em," Cookie grunted. "Like to, though."

Eagle snorted. "I was on the point of offering, most graciously, I should point out, to overlook certain subversive activities as well as irregularities, to put it mildly, of protocol."

"Oh, you already got to where you whitewash your big report," Cookie told him. "What's new?"

"Then you'll agree to load the gems?" Eagle urged eagerly.

"Gold, now," Cookie commented thoughtfully. "Gold I could almost understand. It's solid, pretty color, works nice, doesn't rust. I'd like to have a big beer stein in solid gold, myself."

"Eh? You've been concealing a gold hoard, eh? Let me see that golden stein, at once." He paused only momentarily; but Cookie rushed in: "Them little blue stones," he sneered. "Even if they was rubies and emeralds, what good are they?"

"Rubies and emeralds, eh?" Eagle pounced. "Cut or uncut? Sizes? Quantities available and in reserve?"

"I'm afraid, sir," Judson put in, "you're getting carried away. Space 'n Murphy merely mentioned gold and jewels; he didn't say we *have* any."

"An entire planet!" Eagle muttered, smacking a fist with his palm. "It figures! Diamonds, too, I suppose, as well as other gems quite unknown on Terra. Let me see them, now, today. I'm *certain*, fellow, that we can reach a mutually agreeable arrangement—and beneficial, too: highly beneficial to you. Well, what do you say?"

"In return for all this hypothetical jewelry," Judson inquired, "what do you propose to give us?"

"Why, what else?" Eagle replied. "A favorable report, confirming your enthusiastic acceptance of Terran Concordiat sovereignty here!"

"So, we give you all our goodies in return for agreeing to be enslaved, is that the idea?" Cookie demanded sardonically.

"Precisely!" Eagle confirmed. "The use of the word 'enslaved' is of course an exaggeration," he added. "I doubt your annual assessment will exceed your planet's GNP!"

"I thought we'd agreed to drop the smokescreens," Judson commented. "Let's get serious. You like shiny baubles. All right, we'll see if we can round up some for you. But is the Council likely to settle for peanuts?"

Eagle snapped his fingers. "Poo for the Council! That silly gang of worn-out political hacks! It's me you have to deal with, gentlemen! Yes, I like the idea of heaps of cobochon-cut rubies, emeralds, diamonds; and gold: bars, heaped up and glistening, gold! I love gold; always have and never had any," he added in a less hysterical tone. "I want to see your treasury, fellows! I need to feast my eyes; then I'll get to work cooking that report!"

"Well, Cap," Cookie said in a tone of defeat. "I guess the admiral is just too sharp for us. We better give him all our jewelry."

"Never mind about fancy settings," Eagle butted in. "I'm going to pry the gems from their mounts and melt down the gold—silver, too, don't forget."

"And for your end of the deal," Cookie persisted, "you fake up your report and tell the Council we're all dead, right? And this planet's a poisonous wasteland."

"Well, just a minute now," Eagle temporized. "I said nothing about reporting anyone dead!"

"Just report a deserted world, is that it?" Cookie demanded.

"Probably the simplest way," Eagle agreed judiciously. "For their own good, of course. That pinpoint artillery of yours—"

"Yep, don't forget that," Cookie advised.

"That wasn't by any chance just a fluke?" Eagle wondered aloud.

Bag, Judson called silently. *Give the admiral another demonstration. Just blow the first fifty feet off the prow of his flagship—but mind you don't hurt anyone.*

"Say, Admiral," Judson continued, aloud. "Just glance up there at the prow of *CND Judicious* . . ."

Eagle glanced idly upward and recoiled against the wall as a blinding detonation enveloped the atmosphere-probe section of the vessel. When the dust cleared, it could be seen that the first three bulkheads and their sheathing were no longer there.

"My God!" Eagle blurted, then turned his attention to his lapel-talker: "Harlow! Report!"

The adjutant's tinny voice was barely audible:

"Sir, there's been an accident! No casualties, I believe—so far—but the reserve coil just blew off the probe module. The damage report—"

Eagle turned to Judson. "Sir, you dare to attack a capital ship of the Terran Concordiat?"

"Not an attack, Admiral," Judson corrected. "Just a demonstration. An attack would have blown her to hell."

"I shall have difficulty in explaining how I suffered battle damage on an uninhabited world!" Eagle blurted.

"Just put that report on the front burner and let it cook," Cookie suggested.

"Sir, you are impertinent!" Eagle blurted.

"Amazing!" Harlow's tinny voice came through excitedly. "The 'evacuate' order came through to the fore bay just a moment before the accident! That's all it was, sir, an unfortunate malfunction by Maintenance. I've spoken sharply to it, sir. And, oddly, Security says it gave no 'evacuate' order! I must investigate further, sir!"

"Easy, Admiral," Judson suggested. "I think there'll be no furthur malfunction aboard your command—for the moment."

"How the devil—!" Eagle burst out.

Cookie leaned close to Judson. "Cap, we're cutting it

awful close. If we manage to accidentally get old Admiral mad, he could—"

"I know, Space'n," Judson reassured his aide. "My strategy is to get him so confused he doesn't know what target to open up on."

"I guess there's a limit to how many tricks old Bag can do at one time," Cookie cautioned.

"So," Judson said briskly, for Eagle's benefit, "I think it's time to have done with the preliminaries and show the admiral to the Treasury."

"Right, sir," Cookie agreed. "Uh, Admiral, sir, you like to see the gold first, or what?"

"Rubies," Eagle barked. "Rubies are my passion. Though I wouldn't mind owning the Napoleon emerald."

"Good choice," Cookie approved. "Right this way, sir." He indicated the dark alley at their back. Eagle hesitated, but went along.

Judson paused only to direct Baggy to open all discharge hatches on the spaceship filling the plaza and order all personnel ashore.

4

As the confused crew members scrambled eagerly out of the confining vessel into the dim-lit square, they stared as if seeing a planetary surface for the first time, breathing deep of non-canned air. They paid no heed to their captain, but streamed past him and into the side streets, like starving animals heading for food.

Eagle turned away from the spectacle after one vain attempt to block off and speak to a petty officer who impatiently skirted him, ignoring his command to halt. The frustrated admiral turned to Judson:

"See here, mister," he barked. "I don't know how you've manipulated my people in this fashion, unless you've somehow spirited an *agent provocateur* aboard, but I've had enough of this nonsense about bribing me with rubies and gold to forget you exist!"

"My, oh, my," Cookie jeered. "No more sapphires, eh, sir?"

"That's another matter," Eagle grumped. He caught Cookie's eye. "Is it possible you actually don't know what you have here?"

"Cap," Cookie inquired innocently of his mentor, "do we realize what we've got here, or what?"

"Just what, Admiral, *do* we have here?" Judson put it directly to the visiting brass.

"Have you never heard of a controlled substance known to its devotees as 'Jazreel'?" Eagle demanded in a sarcastic tone.

Judson nodded. "I've heard it fries the brain," he supplied.

"Not quite so simple, nor so obvious," Eagle demurred. "Jazreel *is* a psychoactive chemical which has the effect of actualizing its user's most profoundly repressed impulses."

"That's why McGillicuddy smarted off to you," Judson remarked. "And why you slugged him."

"No comment," Eagle muttered. "I found some particles in my clothing after our visit to the deposit—or repository. Why in hell's name, man, are you manufacturing such hellish stuff and leaving it to lie in the open, accessible to all?"

"You catch on slow, Admiral, sir," Cookie said in a tone of forced patience. "City's a natural outcropping, just as Cap said. If that stuff is dope, nobody knows it."

" 'That stuff,' " Eagle intoned, "is worth a minimum of a million guck per ounce, uncut. You have uncounted tons of it!"

"Dope-peddling is an idea that never occurred to us," Cookie told the awed admiral. "Even if we'd known we had any dope to sell."

"Such a resource," Eagle pontificated, "is not to be neglected. Now." He paused repressively. "These are our final terms."

As he paused, Cookie demanded, "Terms of what?"

"Our understanding," Eagle stated coldly. "First, I *will* inspect the gold and jewel repository, then you will reveal to me all technical specifications for your artillery, as well as those of your long-range radar."

"That's all?" Cookie wanted to know.

Eagle shook his head. "By no means, sir. But I think that I would prefer a good night's rest before finalizing matters. Pray show me to quarters appropriate to my status."

Cookie stood before Judson and jerked a thumb toward the admiral. "This clown's got more brass than a nineteen-ought-nine Ford," he said.

Judson ignored this sally and ushered Eagle along the street to a large building, where they boarded a small lift; they rode up in silence. Eagle studied the unadorned car with apparent deep interest.

"I see no patent-data plate," he commented.

"It figures, sir," Judson told him. "There isn't one."

"No patent?" Eagle came back sharply.

"Correct," Judson affirmed. "Everybody knows a fellow named Jack Greenbaum developed this system, based on scanty data in the files."

"Cribbed from a Terran patent originally," Eagle snapped.

"Obvious idea," Judson corrected.

"Does no one attempt to make use of his work?" Eagle demanded.

"Sure, we all do," Judson agreed. "Jack was an ingenious fellow. Worked up a Model T, and a movie camera, and quite a few other things. He had a real knack for interpreting the old plans and specs. He was working on a biplane when he was killed in an accident."

"Anarchy," Eagle snorted. "But you have advanced WNF skimmers; of what use would a primitive biplane be?"

"That was before we worked out the WNF principle," Judson informed him.

"Just how long ago was all this?" Eagle asked bluntly, in the tone of one called upon to request his obvious due.

"Quite a while," Cookie contributed. "Remember that fufu tree in front of the Tower, here?" he inquired. "The one with the purple flowers," he amplified. Eagle grunted assent. "Very handsome tree," he managed.

"Was planted by Jack, after he got his first electric motor going," Cookie told him. "Kind of a memorial. Big, now. Long time's passed."

"Precisely how long?" Eagle persisted.

"We can't rightly say," Judson interjected. "We don't

have the neat timekeeping system Terra has, with a regular sunrise and moonrise and equinox and all that. We've just got Brownie and Junior. Very complex matter; no repeating cycle the average man would notice."

"That's absurd!" Eagle snapped. "Am I to believe you have no clocks, no calendar, no sense of history?"

"That's about it," Cookie agreed. "We've found we don't need to meter out our lives a minute—or a second—at a time."

"As a result," Judson contributed, "we don't feel compelled to age and die according to a preset schedule. At least that's our theory."

"Back home," Cookie amplified, "a kid starts out in a hurry to grow up: that's going to solve all his problems. After he's grown, he starts waiting to die. He expects to, when the calendar tells him he's eighty years old; he acts feeble, doddering around, stops driving, gives up and waits—and sure enough, pretty soon he's dead."

"Nonsense!" Eagle exclaimed. "Animals and oak trees die after a normal life-span, too, and they know nothing of calendars!"

"It's not the conscious awareness that kills you," Judson took up the thesis. "It's a deep cellular knowledge, the same time sense that tells birds when to migrate, females when to ovulate, bears to hibernate, and so on. There are ancient mollusks, related to the nautilus, which built their shells on a regular daily schedule. You can count the layers—twenty-two to a month. That's how long a month was to them. Every twenty-two days, their cells told them a lunar month had elapsed and it was time to seal off the section and start a new one. Our most fundamental mind-body structure tells us to age progressively until we can't function any longer. That made sense when our ancestors were animals like the rest of the fauna, to prevent overcrowding and starvation; the individual retained all his faculties long enough to reproduce and then became expendable. As recently as the Nineteenth Century the average life-span barely exceeded the breeding years—under forty. Here on Eden our built-in senescence equipment has no cues to work on, so it goes out of business. We've both got grandkids in the tenth generation."

"*That*'s what Eden has," Cookie told Eagle. "It's no secret, and it can't be exported. That's our treasure."

Eagle gave Cookie a stern look. "Very well," he intoned. "I see you're determined to persist in your folly. You leave me no choice!"

Judson and Cookie paused and looked expectantly at the admiral.

"The time has come," the latter declared in what he clearly hoped was an ominous tone, "to inform you that the scouting parties of destroyers which I have brought here are acting as skirmishers for the main party, consisting of twenty-five capital ships of the line. Our mission is to suppress certain disorderly elements which have repeatedly committed nuisances in this sector over the past ten years, in defiance of Concordiat authority. I found them to be unexpectedly resourceful, a contretemps requiring equal resourcefulness on my part. You, gentlemen, are that resource!"

"Say, Cap," Cookie spoke up. "Sounds like old Admiral here thinks we're a 'resource,' whatever he means by that. And all along I thought we were a free and independent world, by right of discovery and development."

"I shall require of you, at once," Eagle intoned, "your entire war fleet, complete with trained crews, provisioned for a cruise of indefinite duration."

"Time to give Bag the nod, Cap?" Cookie asked quietly.

"Now's the time, Space'n," Judson confirmed. Again he called to the alien ally, but this time received no response.

"Well," Eagle prompted. "I'm waiting. What is it to be? Orderly compliance, or war to the knife?"

Cookie took Judson aside. "Cap," he began earnestly, "I'm getting a little worried. This clown is too good to be true. What's he got up his sleeve?"

"I'm with *you*, Space'n," Judson replied soberly. "He's doing a gag within a gag. First he came on like a bumbling fool, and when we called him on that, he tried the 'Don't push me *too* hard, I might get mad' stuff."

"He's bluffing, Cap," Cookie contributed. "He wants something—I wonder what it is."

"He's being foxy, giving us the verbal equivalent of artillery preparation," Judson said. "We have to let him think he's figuratively pounded us to intellectual rubble, before he'll launch his first wave of the real stuff."

"Ha!" Cookie scoffed. "Cap, it's *too* easy. With old Bag and his bag of tricks—see, that's a little joke, Cap: " 'Baggy—bag o' tricks,' get it? Anyway, we can keep this paper-stacker so dazed he'll forget what he came out here for. We've got the ultimate secret weapon."

"Easy, Space'n," Judson cautioned. "This isn't a real battle squadron we're dealing with, true. It's just a warning. So let's be warned. We don't want any real hostilities; we couldn't afford that, Baggy included. So we play it carefully and make the admiral change his plans without noticing."

"Right, Cap," Cookie agreed readily. "No war. That means we're depending on Baggy. That's really all we've got, right? And right now he's busy."

"I'm afraid so," Judson concurred.

Eagle had halted and was eyeing them impatiently.

Cookie stared curiously at the arrogant intruder, but he spoke to Judson. "Let's give him a hotfoot, Cap," he suggested. "A lake of fire, say, with him all alone in the middle of it. No heat, naturally. Bag could do that, couldn't you, Bag?"

After a few seconds' delay, the answer came, dim if clearly enough: *Easily. However—*

All three men became aware, simultaneously, of a sudden sound which descended from the supersonic to become an audible shriek. They looked up, saw nothing. The disturbance seemed to come from just over a low rise in the ground. They felt the ground vibrate sharply underfoot, and a wave of hot air gusted past them.

"Take cover!" Eagle blurted, and went flat. Cookie

looked curiously at Judson. "More o' Baggy's tricks?" he muttered. "What's the point, Cap?"

Judson shook his head. "I don't think so." Silently, he called to the alien, but there was no reply. "Let's take a look." He set off in the direction of the blast, Cookie close behind him.

Eagle got to his feet and fell in behind. "Just a moment, you fellows," he called. "What do you—?"

Judson and Cookie ignored the indignant admiral, as Baggy spoke up suddenly, sounding distressed:

Captain! It appears I was in error when I told you that I am the last of my brethren! It seems that one, at least, has survived, long-lost in a cave where he took refuge from a hungry sibling, long ago! He has only just found his [or possibly her (actually, of course, the point is moot, due to—)] way out, quite famished, and at once detected my aura and is now attempting to drain my vital energies in order to survive, a course of action with which I sympathize, but which am unable to condone. I call on you, Captain, to take effective action at once—

"Cap!" Cookie blurted. "I got part of that; sounds like Bag's in deep trouble! What are we going to do?"

"—demand!" Eagle was just finishing his peroration. Judson brushed him aside, intent on the alien's distress call.

Bag, what can we do? he inquired of the circumambient silence. *How long can you hold on? We'll try to think of something.*

"Cookie," he went on aloud. "Did you get that? Any ideas?"

"We need more information, Cap," Cookie replied, at which Eagle interjected, "Information? What more do you need to know than that the might of the Terran Concordiat is ready to punish your insolence?"

"Skip that," Cookie told the irate fellow. Then, in an urgent whisper to Judson: "We've got to be careful, Cap. We're bluffing, and it looks like we can't count on old Bag anymore. Come on, let's see what—"

"I demand," Eagle yelled, scrambling to keep up,

"that you offer me evidence of your good faith, at once!"

"We have an emergency on our hands," Cookie informed him.

"Indeed you do!" Eagle seconded. "One which, I point out, you brought upon yourselves! Are you quite sure you're ready to challenge the Navy?"

Bag, Judson called. *How big is this fellow? Can you bring him here?*

It is quite immense, I fear, Baggy came back. *In resting mode, I'd say one mile in diameter, and with proportionate mind-power. I'm quite overmatched.*

"Wow!" Cookie exclaimed. "That's awful big, Cap! I don't see how—"

I shall make the attempt, Baggy's voice came through, sounding thin and strained. *There is one tactic which I hesitate to mention, but this is, after all, an emergency. The great perceptual ganglion is our vulnerable point, a fact I have so far been at pains to conceal, the protection of this weakness being my most basic instinctive compulsion. But now, clearly this consideration becomes secondary. I shall attempt a ruse to draw my attacker to your presence.*

"That's the stuff, Bag," Cookie blurted.

"Are you addressing me, sir?" Eagle bleated from behind. "I think you fellows are attempting to conceal something from me!" he complained, coming up beside the two, red-faced and out of breath.

"Admiral," Judson spoke up bluntly. "What is it you really want from us?"

Before Eagle could frame a reply, a shadow fell across the path. Judson glanced up. Junior's usually more-than-full-moon brightness was perceptibly dimmed by a diaphanous cloud of dull pinkish-purple tinge which writhed and flowed across the satellite's face, imposing deep twilight on the landscape.

Baggy! Judson called. *Is this—?*

Indeed so, Captain, the alien's silent voice replied at once, still clear, but noticeably weaker than only moments before.

You were going to tell me about the perceptual ganglion , Judson prompted. *You'd better hurry. You don't sound good.*

Baggy's failing voice gave Judson precise anatomical direction to the vital neural center, which, Judson learned, was a small patch of a bluish tone residing deep inside the amoeboidal form of the giant alien, which had now come to ground nearby, like a patch of fog, except that it threw back glints and highlights from a membranous surface. Eagle grabbed Judson's arm. "What the devil is *that*?" he demanded. He looked at Judson with an expression of fury, alloyed with fear. "I warn you, sir—" he began, but broke off as Judson drew the long-nosed power-pistol from the holster at his hip.

"Stand back, sir," he suggested, thrusting the excited admiral aside, then concentrated on studying the unstable anatomy of the immense alien creature. Baggy, he saw, was perched high atop the insubstantial bulk of his attacker, apparently just holding on.

Now! his weak voice came through. *A hardshot dead center will do the job!*

"Cap," Cookie spoke up. "You sure—?"

"No, I'm not," Judson conceded. He spoke to Baggy: *What were the fireworks all about?*

The reply was prompt: *It was necessary to draw your attention, and yourselves, to this spot, Captain*, Baggy came back, his voice sounding strangled. *I had no strength to bring this monster to you, so—*

"But that was before, Cap!" Cookie blurted. "Oh," he responded to his own objection. "The backwards time phenomenon again, I guess."

Judson nodded. *Baggy*, he called. *It occurs to me that it would be better to enlist Bitey as an ally, rather than destroy him.*

"Bitey"? Baggy came back. *You mean he's got a name, too, just like me? That's different! I couldn't destroy a fellow with an identity! Wait, I'll try to talk to him.*

Judson and Cookie waited tensely, while the great

mound of bluish fog heaved and rippled, spectral colors running across its surface, like oil on water.

"Well?" Eagle demanded, still prone. "Is this another of your attempts to divert me from my duty?"

"We've told you about our friend Baggy," Judson told him. "That's him, the little bump on top, I mean. The big part is a relative of his, trying to eat him."

"Barbaric!" Eagle expostulated. "Can't you *do* something?"

As they watched, the bump that was Baggy sank to the surrounding level, effectively disappearing, except that his internal structure was still intact dimly visible through the cloudy tissues.

Baggy! Judson called apprehensively.

I fear Bitey is too strong, Captain, his feeble voice came back.

Hold on! Judson urged. *He's trying to dissolve you! Don't let him!*

Beware, Captain. Baggy's voice was a despairing wail. *Bitey is becoming aware of you. He will attack as soon as he's dispatched the nuisance represented by myself!*

Tip him off that I have a crater-gun aimed at his favorite ganglion, Judson suggested.

"Better fire, Cap!" Cookie urged.

"No need," Judson countered. "Bitey is going to be nice."

"Here, you fellows," Eagle blurted. "What's going on here? That monstrous glob has ingested your friend. Now what?"

Judson ignored the importunate fellow. *Baggy!* he called urgently. *Are you—?*

I am still intact, the weak voice came back. *But I urge you, Captain, do something quickly. Bitey is draining me!*

Bitey! Judson called harshly, though silently. *Bitey! You must respond!*

Captain entity, a strange voice spoke up uncertainly.

"What's that?" Eagle yelled, clapping his hands over his ears. "What are you doing to me?"

"Forget it, Admiral," Cookie advised. "Bitey's just

coming up to strength. He's not used to it. Just learned it from Bag."

Speak softly, Bitey, Judson commanded. *You must cease in your attempt to ingest Baggy.*

Perhaps, Bitey's strange voice, now much moderated, came back promptly.

"He's breaking loose!" Eagle yelped. "See, the bump is back, and it's rising higher!"

Indeed, Judson saw, Baggy's relatively small mass was extricating itself from the overwhelming bulk of the strange alien.

Good! Baggy called. *Keep Bitey distracted!*

Let Baggy go, unharmed, Bitey! Cookie ordered, and saw Baggy pop free of his captor.

That was terrible! Baggy exclaimed, his voice stronger now. *I have much to teach this uncouth fellow before we can tolerate his presence among us!*

Bitey, Judson called. *Form yourself into a sphere and concentrate on maintaining a precise radius.*

The amorphous glob instantly contracted, assuming a globular form, the membraneous surface of which threw back a brilliant highlight, reflecting the harsh glare of the setting Junior.

"It's turned into a big ball!" Eagle blurted. "Captain! That thing was talking! I could hear it!"

Captain, Baggy came in, *I shall attempt to instruct Bitey—*

Stay clear! Judson warned. *Avoid contact, Bag! I think that gives him a big advantage!*

I had reached the identical conclusion, Captain, Baggy agreed. *First, I must show how to narrow his transmission band, and direct it precisely.*

Suddenly the glistening sphere lurched, and rolled toward the three humans. Judson caught an impression of intense hunger about to be appeased. He stepped before Cookie and barked, silently, *Bitey! You can't move! Stop! My name is "Cap." You couldn't ingest a fellow entity!*

The sphere halted, looming over the men.

Greetings, Cap, Bitey's uncertain voice said. *Pray*

excuse my impulse; I was of course not aware that you fellows were entities. Bitey's surface rippled, and he extruded a pseudopod which struck snake-fast past Judson to seize the arm of Admiral Eagle, who at once drew his ceremonial sidearm and fired a burst of .5 mm needles into the alien's translucent substance, splattering it. The ragged stump snapped back and disappeared into the surface from which it had deployed.

That smarted! Bitey said sulkily.

Damn right, Bitey! Judson assured the alien. *I warned you: don't try to consume any of us! Be nice!*

Just how, Bitey inquired confusedly, *does one go about "being nice"?*

Bag will show you, Judson told the chastised being curtly. Then, *Bag can you—?*

Of course, Captain, the smaller alien's voice responded eagerly. *It will be a pleasure! The joy of communing at length with a fellow Boog-entity will be exquisite!*

"What's a Boog-entity, Cap?" Cookie asked.

"It's what Baggy and Bitey are, it appears," Judson told him. "I suppose he'd have mentioned it earlier, but the subject never came up."

The nomenclature, Baggy explained, *dates back to that distant era when I was but a single cell, loosely associated with multitudes of my own kind.*

Baggy, Judson spoke gently. *Are you really sure there are no more Boog-entities around?*

A moment, please, Captain, came the reply. *I shall enlist Bitey's assistance in a wide-spectrum, long-range scan. First, of course, I have to show him how.*

"Look here, you!" Eagle barked almost in Cookie's ear. "I've had enough of this mysterious routine of yours. Your associate has an issue pistol. Tell him to use it, and eliminate this threat, at once!"

"Well, Admiral," Cookie replied, "I don't hardly give no orders to Captain Judson; wouldn't be polite, you know. He don't give me none, neither. And anyways, I guess if he hasn't shot Bitey yet, he's got a reason."

"Impudence! Insubordination!" Eagle huffed.

Cookie shook his head. "I'm not a subordinate, Admiral, sir," he reminded the angry fellow. "Never meant no impudence: just giving you the facts, sir, is all."

"Facts! Pah! You know nothing of the facts, you poor dolt! If you did—"

"Then why don't you tell me, Admiral?" Cookie suggested artlessly.

"I'll disclose no classified material to you, or to any other uncivil bucolic!" Eagle yelled.

Judson turned and remarked, "Admiral, there aren't any 'uncivil bucolics' on this planet; just an uncivil bureaucrat—and he's leaving."

"Cap," Cookie blurted. " 'Fore you give this poor sucker the boot, we better find out what all this 'classified material' is, eh?"

Judson nodded. *Baggy,* he called, *pick this fellow's brains, will you? Don't upset him, just let me know what it is he's concealing.*

Very well, Captain, Baggy agreed promptly, *I'll put Bitey and the survey on hold.*

Eagle clamped his hands over his ears and stared wildly about. "You can't!" he gobbled. "No, I didn't even *see* any cookies!" He babbled on:

"But, pop, I don't even know *how* to drive the flitter!

"She practically invited me!

"I was just looking out the window, sir!

"Don't tell, but I went *around* the water-hazard . . .

"But I couldn't help it; somebody pushed me.

"I worked on the requisitions all night, sir!"

He shifted one hand to cover his mouth and choke off the confessional stream. "Dastardly!" he barked. "Your brain-scraping techniques are surprisingly sophisticated, but scant good they'll do you! I have absolutely nothing to say about the rebellion and the invasion!

"I suppose the food was drugged," he added more calmly. "It was Anastasia! *She* slipped me the pink stuff, eh? In one of those drinks she so obligingly fetched me!"

"Nobody slipped you anything, Admiral," Judson told him. *Take it easy, Bag,* he went on, silently. *Skip all that juvenile stuff. More about the rebellion and the invasion.*

Sorry, Captain, Baggy gasped. *But there's so much here in the suppressed zone! Shocking!*

Stick to the subject, Judson ordered. *Don't pry in the man's private problems.*

That's going to be tricky, Captain, it's so complex and so tightly-packed. But I'll do my best.

Don't run it through his conscious, Judson specified. *Just read it and relay it.*

"*Bucolic frontier worlds!*" Baggy relayed from Eagle, whose purple face reflected his efforts to suppress his stream-of-consciousness utterance. "*Upstarts! In defiance of law and custom alike!*"

"Cap," Cookie spoke up, "I don't feel too good about this. Everybody's got something to conceal. We're kind of taking advantage of old Admiral here, wouldn't you say?"

"*—delivered their impudent 'ultimatum' on Flag Day,*" Baggy relayed. "*Damned insolence! Twenty-five derelict battle-cruisers and an odd lot of converted freighters! Called themselves the Cluster Defense Force! Damnedest bunch of uncouth scoundrels imaginable! Descended on Luna Admin Satellite One without so much as a conditional clearance from Outer Approach Control. Ignored our attempts to communicate, and actually fired on the Reserve Cutters when they attempted to intercept and board, as required by law!*"

"Whose law?" Cookie inquired, as if idly. "AutoSpace law, I guess."

"The term 'AutoSpace' is long obsolete," Eagle corrected sharply. " 'The Concordiat' is the correct nomenclature for our present form of government."

"Maybe these Home Guards figured they were being hijacked," Cookie suggested.

"You would find excuses for a pack of lawless ruffians who scoff at Terran sovereignty?" Eagle demanded, sounding indignant.

"I think the point Space'n Murphy's making," Judson contributed, "is that independent worlds like our own are under no obligation to comply with rules made on a distant planet—Terra, in this case—and to expect them to do so is naive."

" 'Naive,' " am I?" Eagle growled. "I'll show you some naiveté!" He turned to his lapel-talker, muttering angrily. "Ah!" he said after half a minute, "there you are, McGillicuddy! There'll be explanations to be made, Chief, and they'd better be good! I've been isolated here among the natives for over an hour! What? Nonsense! An hour at most! Assemble the landing party at the designated rallying point—the street where I've stationed the flotilla, of course, you insolent fool! Sorry, Mac, I didn't mean that! I'm overexcited, I guess! These locals are openly talking armed revolt! They even express solidarity with the rebels! Insufferable! I told you the Council was visionary, expecting assistance from this quarter! Execute!"

He stood looking expectantly along the street. A lone man stepped from a doorway and turned back to continue a conversation with someone behind him. When he made a gesture of frustration and started toward the extended personnel ladder of the nearest ship, a woman followed him, catching at his arm. He seemed to be about to shrug her off, but instead embraced her. Both were talking urgently:

"—can't *do* it, Jodi!" he blurted repeatedly, while she clung, looking up at him and repeating, "—you said yourself you hated it! You said we'd never part! And I told you I'd volunteer in your place! Heck, I'm as good a com man as old Eaggie's likely to find, even if—"

Both the young folk—barely out of their teens, they seemed—fell silent simultaneously and looked toward the group watching them from a distance of fifty feet.

"There he is!" both said at once. "We'll put it to him!" And, hand in hand, they approached. Eagle stepped forward, stony-faced. The couple angled past him.

"Ole feller," the girl spoke up first, "we—"

"Let me," the young man interjected. "Sir, Jodi and me—that is, I have decided, or I mean, may I have your permission—I mean your approval, sir, to take as my bride—"

"What Elmer's trying to say," the girl overrode him, "is we plan to get married. Any objections? With respect, fellers."

"What's this nonsense, Space'n?" Eagle demanded of the prospective bridegroom.

"I guess, sir," Elmer replied doggedly, "the nonsense is the idea of taking over this here world and turning it into another place for paper-pushing stuffed shirts to tell people what to do."

"Mutiny?" Eagle inquired in a tone of Interest, Mild, in an Unexpected Phenomenon (39-D).

"I guess that's supposed to be a 39, about an E," Elmer hazarded. "We only had time for the short course back at HQ, you know."

"To Tophet with HQ *and* the short course!" Eagle blurted out. "I've been told by no less a dignitary than Ambassador, later Undersecretary Sapsucker himself, that my mastery of the handbook is as complete as that of any senior officer of the *Corps*!"

"But you were saying about 'mutiny,' sir," Elmer reminded his chief, who roared:

"I guess I know what I was saying about, Elmer!" The admiral's gaze fixed on the young girl's pert features. "Doubtless, *this* person is responsible for your defection!"

"He never defected!" Jodi snapped. "Here he is, right here, ain't he?"

"He is indeed," Eagle agreed. "And I now call upon him to perform his duty by placing *you*, miss, under arrest!"

"She done nothing!" Elmer declared heatedly. Jodi was looking mournfully at him.

"We knew it'd come to this, Jodi, back when you near shot me, after we got accidentally locked in the storeroom together—or *was* that an accident?"

"Nope," the girl admitted. "Fact is, getting locked in with you was the best I could think of." After a pause, she added, "I was s'pose to help 'em trap you where they could grill you and then maybe kill you. I decided not to do it." She gave Judson an apprehensive look. "Could I see you alone a minute, Captain?" she requested diffidently. He nodded and took her aside. Cookie stayed close to Eagle. Elmer fidgeted.

"Captain—" Jodi said urgently. "I guess I goofed-up bad, not helping to kill Ellie and all—"

Judson cut her off with a shake of his head. "By no means, my dear," he told her quietly. "There's no need for murder, especially of a nice young fellow like your Elmer."

"You mean you're not mad?" Jodi gasped.

"Had there been a mass killing, I'd have been mad," Judson reassured her. "I never intended that our people should do anything more than distract the Terrans from their duties."

"But, Captain," the anxious girl persisted. "There's more! This peaceful infiltration, like Block Boss called it, is not all! I work up at Distant Early Warning, you know, and there's another flotilla half a light-sec out, a bigger one! Looks like this bunch"—she nodded toward the parked vessels—"was only an advance-guard, like!"

"That's preposterous!" Eagle burst out, addressing the space'n: "I assure you, Elmer, there's nothing—!"

Baggy, Judson called. *What about it?*

There was no reply for a moment; then, weakly, *Captain! It appears . . .*

"Cap!" Cookie barked. "Looky there! Baggy's—"

Judson glanced toward the spot where the gassy bulk of Bitey had lain, bulging, on the rock. He was gone.

"Just kind of disappeared, like!" Cookie blurted. "I was looking right at him!"

Judson called again, urgently, to Baggy. *Where are you, Bag? What happened?*

Cookie ran to the spot occupied moments before by the immense alien creature. He looked at the bare, lichen-crusted rock, then all around, as if he could somehow summon the vanished creature.

"Bitey's gone, and taken Bag with him!" he repeated.

"Look here," Eagle barked. "What's become of that gas-bag thing? I thought you said—"

"I did," Judson cut him off. "He's in trouble!"

"Captain, sir!" Jodi yelped, clutching at his sleeve. "What about this incoming bunch, Captain? Reason I came here—B Schedule says—"

"There's no occasion, yet, for B Schedule," Judson reproved mildly. "If and when attack is imminent—" His words were drowned by the sonic boom of a low-flying craft passing overhead below code minimum. It rocketed on over the horizon.

"What was it?" Cookie yelped. "Cap, I didn't get a good look. Heavy equipment, and old, that's all I seen!"

"That was a *Charlie Three*-class lugger," Judson told him. "Modified: gunnery emplacements on her equator, and a tail stinger—looked like a Bofors number sixty from a battle cruiser. Strange."

"It was *them*!" Eagle burst out. "That damned 'Planetary Defense Force'! Seems they don't feel quite the fraternal ties you fellows imagine. Now, no more temporizing! I must get my force aloft and in attack formation before the actual assault!" He hit the deck as a second huge ship roared past half a mile distant.

"What I was telling you about, Captain!" Jodi wailed.

"Got to get to my post, girl," Elmer told her, as he pecked her on the forehead and dashed toward the town wall.

Eagle turned to Judson. "This, sir, places a different complexion on matters, as I assume you agree?" His voice was drowned by the noisy passage of two more elderly cargo-ships. He fled, and Judson let him go.

"Number two recycler's about to go out on that last tub!" Cookie called as the *boom!* rolled away, fading to silence.

They watched as the four ships and a number of other, smaller ones smartly executed a rendezvous maneuver at the far side of the city.

"Looks like they're getting set to land troops," Cookie commented. "We better get over there."

Eagle had disappeared between two of his parked destroyers.

"I'll get back to post," Jodi said and set off at a run.

Cookie went to a ground-car parked at the curb and slid in behind the wheel. Judson joined him, and they sped along streets where people were still emerging from buildings to join those already there, staring toward the point where the new arrivals had disappeared.

"We'll stop by Center," Judson told Cookie, who braked hard and swerved into the side street leading to the administration building.

Five minutes later, having conferred briefly with the Officer of the Day, the two were back in the commandeered vehicle, speeding toward the landing site.

"In the wheatfields, eh, Cap?" Cookie queried, steering that way. "Ready to harvest, too." Then, thoughtfully: "Cap, you sure you done right, telling Bob to go to final alert and hold? Best time to hit 'em is when they just set down, and had no time to get organized."

"We're not going to hit them, Cookie," Judson told him. "At least not until we've talked."

"Got no call invading like they done," Cookie grumped. He glanced up as the first of Eagle's squadron passed noisily overhead. "Reckon he'll wait?"

"If he's half as sharp as I think he is," Judson replied, "he'll take up an 'Omar' formation at about fifty miles and open communications."

"You called it, Cap!" Cookie cried. "Sure as a snake bites! Look at that first echelon! Them boys know how to con them craft! Dern nigh fooled us, too, Cap: had me thinking they were damn fools! Smart tactics! But didn't do him any good. We seen through it!"

"Now we have a question to decide," Judson pointed out. "Are we on his side, or theirs? If they *have* a side. Maybe it's only a courtesy call."

"Doubt that, Cap," Cookie muttered. "Looky there!" He braked to a crawl as a tracked vehicle swung into the avenue ahead, its guns deployed. It advanced at flank speed, swerving in at the last moment to pull up alongside the unarmed car. A hatch popped and a tall, gaunt fellow in a patched coverall climbed out, cradling a crater-gun.

Cookie opened the hatch and the stranger stared down at him.

"You in charge here?" he inquired in a frontier dialect that his auditors barely understood.

"We'll do," Cookie replied promptly. "What is it you fellows want?"

The tall man climbed down, slung his weapon, and extended a callused hand. "Name's Pete," he stated, as if that were important information. "Had a idea we might find the swat-squad here. Only planet in a few lights," he explained. "Seen 'em in the distant screens last week, then they dropped out. You boys need a little help here? We knew you was here, been hearing your traffic for years. Meant to call before, but never got to it, seems like."

"No help needed yet, Pete," Judson replied. "I suppose you represent the Cluster Defense Force?"

"Heck, we *are* the CDF," Pete replied. "Heard about us, eh? By the way, we're wanting to be called the FDF now: Freedom Defense Force."

"Admiral Eagle had a few remarks to make on the subject," Judson agreed.

"Got to watch that feller," Peter told him solemnly. "He's not half the fool he acts like."

"We noticed that," Cookie contributed. "What about that Omar he's setting up on you?"

"He's got a couple surprises coming," Pete stated. "First, we're not a green outfit no more. We set down in a Brolly formation, just to sucker him in; we'll englobe his Omar before he gets his pickets out!" He glanced back toward the landing site, where Eagle's trim Navy ships were swarming, taking up the complex formation designed to blanket the grounded force like a vast tent. Just then, a pair of CDF ships launched vertically, penetrated the not-yet-quite-in-place tent, and fanned out, another pair following closely, and another, until they formed a thin but broad umbrella above Eagle's tent.

Pete ducked back inside his half-track. His voice came clearly to Judson and Cookie:

"Nice work, Grundy," he said into his command talker.

"Don't be first to fire, Pete," Judson suggested tersely.

Pete nodded, his eyes on the developing action. "Hold your fire, now, wait till— What's he waiting for?" he demanded, giving Judson a puzzled glance. "Damn fool let us complete our Brolly," he muttered. "There's just that one second when a Brolly's vulnerable, you know," he added. "When the bottom layer is braking on final; a volley then could break up the pattern, never get 'em back in alignment—but he passed."

"Maybe he's no more eager than you are to commit to an act of war," Judson suggested.

"Go to Phase Three, fast!" Pete ordered Grundy. "Yeah," he overrode the latter as he started to object. "I know we never went to Phase Two, ya damn fool! Do it!"

Judson nodded as the broad Brolly formation widened to a ring, surrounding the outnumbered Navy vessels' widely dispersed Omar pattern.

"Pull the string!" Pete directed, and the enclosing ring contracted, forcing the outermost destroyers to drop out of formation and descend to the surface. As the three men watched, the entire Omar collapsed and the ships dispersed, some coming to ground, others driving at full gate to penetrate the thin circle around them. Some of the CDF units broke out of place to pursue them.

"Break that off!" Pete barked. "No P and D!"

Grundy's aggrieved voice protested, but the scattering ships turned back. Eagle's fleeing ships came together in a tight hedgehog pattern and circled widely.

"So far so good," Pete gloated. "Run the damn Navy off the site!"

"They're not through yet," Judson cautioned. "How about a parley at this point, Pete? No need to commit to an irretrievable act of war."

"You don't get it, Cap," Pete responded. "*They* already committed that axe of war you're talking about!"

"Not here on Eden!" Judson retorted.

"You pals with the Navy?" Pete inquired.

"Not especially," Judson replied. "But whatever your problem is, it can be negotiated."

"I'm willing to talk to Eagle," Pete said heavily. "But how'm I gonna do that? He's pretty busy right now trying that double-Omar. Won't work," he predicted. "Old Sarnt Grundy ain't the patient kind. Nor Crebby neither, nor none o' the boys. They won't set around waiting for them ashcans to get in position. Look there—" he interrupted himself. "Breaking off and getting ready to do a full gaff—"

"Negative," Judson said firmly. "That's just what he's expecting; notice the flankers out to north and east. They'll have a gaff of their own out of atmosphere before—"

"I thought them was just stragglers!" Pete blurted. "But I see— Thanks, stranger. You kept me from goofing up purty bad, looks like!" Pete turned to look carefully at Judson.

"Who *are* you, Cap?" he asked curiously. "My guess is you felt a deck under yer feet a few times."

"This here," Cookie spoke up, "is Captain Marl Judson, brevet commodore, finest space officer ever told OAC to kiss off."

Pete thrust out his horny catcher's-mitt-sized hand again, caught Judson's, and looked surprised. After a brief clasp, he withdrew his hand.

"Nice firm grip you got there, Cap," he muttered, and put his hand in his pocket.

"Pete," Judson addressed the lanky stranger, "you'd better stack your vessels and back off to twenty miles."

"Broke shelf OK?" Pete inquired hopefully.

"Just so it doesn't collapse prematurely," Judson agreed. They watched while Pete talked to his captains, and the disreputable-looking ships of the FDF pulled up and away, to take up a tall, multi-tiered formation at the limit of visibility.

"Neat," Judson commented. "Pete," he queried, "where'd you learn your handbook close-contact tactics?"

"I was Academy," the rough-hewn bucolic replied. "Made it to Commander before the Navy realized it couldn't digest me."

"Better excuse me a minute," Judson said, and ducked back inside the car. He manipulated controls and spoke quietly:

"Admiral, Eden One here. The strange fleet has been IFF'd as a friendly force on a courtesy call. Please be so kind as to take up honor guard stations soonest and escort them in to locus fifteen-sixty on your chart."

"Like hell I will, Captain!" Eagle's voice came back irately. "Those damn fools have dispersed so I can hit them in detail! This is the opportunity I've been waiting for for over five years! Faking up an honor guard's not a bad idea, if they'd fall for it, but I've a better! Hit them now, while they're still stacking. That shelf of theirs will collapse like a house of cards once I take out numbers One and Seven. Over and out!"

"As you were, Admiral!" Judson barked. "I repeat: Friendly force! Do not attack! Form a Pagliacci and ground!"

"I appreciate your suggestions, Captain," Eagle snarled. "But I could hardly justify to the Council a failure to swat those damned dacoits now that I have the chance. I'm going to Final Red and may the devil take the hindmost!"

"Cap," Pete growled, "you sure I can trust that sucker? I got a bad feeling letting him lay out that Net, could be a trap! I better—" He broke off, addressed Sarnt again:

"Grundy, belay that last! As you were! Go to a Scoffer and Dip! Hit 'em hard! And hit 'em fast!"

Hearing this, Judson spoke quickly to Eagle. "Get your units on the ground soonest, Admiral! No fancy stuff, just go to ground! Do it! Now!"

Eagle's voice came back lazily: "I am not aware, *Mr.* Judson or whatever your damned name is, that I have turned over command to you. I shall by no means ground in the haphazard fashion you propose, but shall, instead, go over to the offensive and ground these damned pirates once and for all time!"

"Looks bad, Cap," Cookie thrust his head in the car to report. "I been watching with my nocklar, and looks like the strangers are going after the flat hammer and tongs, and old Eagle's shooting back! Uh-oh!" he added, scrambling back out to renew his observation. "Seen a vessel blow, Cap! Can't tell which side!"

"It was the damned Navy's," Pete yelled. "You saw that, fellers! The sneaky skunks turned on us and went into attack formation and got swatted for their pains! Go, Grundy! Go! That's it! Hit 'em high and hit 'em low and look at that yellow-belly tryna go to dirt! Strafe 'em, Sarnt!"

"Break off, Admiral!" Judson ordered. "Do not return fire! Hit the deck!"

"They ain't doing it, Cap," Cookie yelled. "Looks like the CDF got a little carried away, taking out that flagship so easy, and now they got a Navy Corjun all over 'em!"

Judson yelled across at Pete, still inside his command car, but was ignored. He climbed out of the car and went into the armored vehicle head-first. A moment later, Pete emerged, also head-first. He fell between the two vehicles. Cookie staggered back as the tall, lanky fellow slammed against him.

Pete got to his feet and told Cookie: "Get in yer jitney, little feller, and stay outa my way!" He implemented the order by grabbing the outraged chef by the neck and thrusting him inside the car. Cookie struggled to no avail, but slammed the door on Pete's arm. Pete bent the door, withdrawing his brawny limb, and turned back to his own armored transport. Judson had slammed the hatch: Pete climbed up on top of the tank-like half-track and to Cookie's surprise, secured a grip on a tie-down rail, braced his feet and wrenched it from its mountings with a single jerk. He got a finger under the end of the inch-and-a-half flint–steel cover of the air intake, jammed in the bar, and used it to pry up the cover. He glanced down inside, then put his arm in and at once went flat on the top of the car, his howl of anguish audible above the boom of battle in the near distance. Pete's face, almost black with effort, turned blindly toward Cookie. He got his knees under him, his extended left arm still at full length inside the ventilation duct. Slowly, he straightened his torso, gained an inch, almost went slack, then pulled again.

Cookie spun the talker dial to the inductance band, inched the car forward to make contact with the armored car, and yelled, "Cap! Let the poor sucker go! He'll tear his own arm off!"

Pete fell backward; his arm came into view, the bloody wrist clamped in a three-inch-wide loop of steel cable. The cable was visibly stretched a few strands broken and curled.

"Cut him loose, Cap!" Cookie urged. "Can't bear to watch this!" Abruptly Pete fell back, his arm free. The freshly cut cable-end was shiny against the darker metal.

"Thanks, Cap!" Cookie called. "I'll hold a gun on the sucker, but I don't think he's in a mood to give me no more trouble!"

Pete flopped over on his face and slid down the side of his car to the ground. After half a minute, he groaned, and groping with his better arm along the side of the car, got to his feet. He looked again at Cookie, ignoring the power pistol aimed at his head.

"I guess I got you to thank for that, boy," he said unsteadily. "Got a feeling old Cap wouldn't have done it . . ."

"You don't want to rile the captain," Cookie told the lanky Pete. "He told you not to start trouble, but you paid him no heed. That cut it! Now he's got yer tank here, and no telling what he's going to do. Dammit, Pete, you shoulda stayed clear of Eden!"

"Prolly so," Pete agreed, rubbing his right shoulder gloomily. Just then the tank's hatch popped and Judson climbed out. He went directly to Pete and told him to hold his injured left arm straight down at his side. Pete complied docilely. Judson put both hands on the shoulder and squeezed. Pete wailed. Then Judson doubled his left fist and struck the arm a sharp hammer-blow just below the point of the shoulder, eliciting a distinct *thunk!* Pete recoiled, but a wide grin spread slowly across his simian features.

"Feels good now, Cap!" he yelled. "OK if I move it?"

Judson nodded. "Raise it, nice and easy," he directed. Pete complied, still grinning.

"And don't try to break any more ten-gee cable for a while," Judson told him.

All three men looked up as a small car of the type carried on capital ships for ground liaison gunned into view at the far end of the avenue. Above, the two groups of fighting vessels swarmed like gnats, all formation abandoned.

"Looks like somebody survived that clobberin'," Cookie remarked. The car came on at full speed, pulled up in a cloud of dust and fumes, and sank as its cushion shut down. Through the transplex hatch cover they saw Admiral Eagle's red face, looking more furious than ever. He leaped out.

"I thought so!" he yelled. "Treason! Collusion! I had an idea I'd find you fellows in league with the enemy!" He had drawn his ceremonial sidearm, and yelped as Pete's long leg flicked out to kick the gun from his grip.

"You didn't want to shoot nobody, Eagle," the freebooter drawled. "You ready to surrender now, or what? Sorry about shooting up your personal yacht; old Sarnt got carried away." He grinned at Cookie as he turned his back on the flag officer.

"Now, you look here!" Eagle growled. "You, Judson, or whatever; I call on you to render assistance to a naval detachment in distress in line of duty."

"It wasn't your duty to try to pull an Omar on the FDF," Pete cut in. "We were ready to talk, but you fired on us. Naturally, we fired back."

"And you still are!" Eagle charged, waving an arm toward the stratospheric battle going on far overhead. Brilliant points of light winked almost continuously, the only visible evidence of the presence of the combatants.

"Call 'em off, Admiral," Cookie suggested. "Just end it, never mind who 'won.' "

"Pete," Judson addressed the tall man, "it's not too late to negotiate; will you talk to the admiral here, if he ceases fire?"

"Sure, why not?" Pete agreed readily enough. He wiped the back of his hand across his mouth. "Your move, Eagle," he grated, squinting upward at the arena of battle. "Sarnt!" he called urgently. "Stand off now; if they stop firing, you do the same, and if you don't, you got me to deal with! You got that?"

Eagle was back in his car, speaking urgently into his talker. He emerged, still red-faced, but calmer.

"All right, Mr. Judson," he grated. "I've given the requisite orders. I hold you fully responsible; if there's any treachery—"

"You can hold it right there, Eagle!" Pete cut in angrily. "Don't start talking about treachery until you see some!"

"Nothing is to be gained by this mutually destructive contention, here on this godforsaken world," Eagle stated. "Accordingly, I am willing to withhold the appropriate punishment for your unutterable impudence for the present. Ground your vessels and parade your crews to surrender all arms."

"Forget it, Eagle," Pete spat. "I'm willing to let your boys go home to tell your lousy Council that it don't pay to mess with the Freedom Defense Force. You can tell your captains to report to me, right here, right now, soon's they can get their dirt-boats away."

"Cap," Cookie said quietly. "We don't seem to be getting anywhere, trying to stop a war. Looks like we started one, instead."

Judson shook his head. "They're prepared to be reasonable," he told him. "Pete," he addressed the rebel chief, "what do you have to gain by being hard to get along with?"

Eagle cleared his throat noisily: " 'Pete,' he calls you," he accused. "You wouldn't by any chance be the miscreant known as 'Powerful Pete,' I suppose?"

"That's what the fellers call me," Pete confirmed.

"Why?" Eagle demanded. "Why do they call you 'Powerful Pete'?"

"Oh," Pete replied, "it's just a kinda nickname, you know. I'm really King Pete of Drygulch. You can call me that."

"I suppose," Eagle persisted, "that you boastfully gave yourself the name 'Powerful.' "

"Nope," Pete dismissed the guess. "Got it the time we brought in old Tang; 'Crubby,' we call him. He wanneda do a like contest: figgered he was a pretty tough fella. And he is: he had a track loose on his car; bet nobody could hold it up while he fixed it. So, just to kinda give the sucker a lesson-like in what ya might say humility, I picked it up—picked it up a little too high: toppled it over on its side. Old Crubby was pissed, b'lieve me. He trieda roll it back rightside up, and he on'y got it about halfway. But I come over and he'ped him some, and we been good pals ever since, and they started calling me 'Powerful Pete.' "

"Hah!" Eagle snorted. "You claim you can overturn an armored vehicle with your bare hands?"

"I don't 'claim' nothing," Pete objected. He was studying Eagle's half-track. Judson caught his eye and nodded. Pete stepped up to the blocky half-inch flint-steel-plated war-car, bent his knees, took a grip with his fingertips under the lower track-shield, and lifted. The car groaned and the steel rim buckled. Pete stepped back and blew on his fingertips. "Don't make 'em like they used to," he commented.

"Look!" Eagle blurted, confronting Judson and Cookie. "The fool is pretending to try! Well, Mr. Pete, I'm calling your bluff! Lift that car and it's yours!"

"That's no deal, Eagle," Pete growled. "It already belongs to Captain here." He glanced at Judson, who replied:

"Go ahead, Pete. It's not mine, but then, I don't need it."

Pete nodded and secured a new hold, this time under the exposed ram-rail. He twisted his neck to look at

Judson. "Arm's a little sore," he remarked. "Might not be able to do it."

"Hah! Excuses!" Eagle burst out.

Pete turned his head to look up at Eagle. "What if I lose?" he grunted.

"Then you acknowledge defeat, and surrender your entire, I hesitate to call it a fleet, to me!" Eagle told him with satisfaction.

"If he wins, Admiral," Judson put in, "then *you* do the surrendering. Right?"

"Why, as to that . . ." Eagle stammered. "All right! very well, why not? He can only lose. I risk nothing!"

"That's more like it," Pete remarked, and with a smooth lift, rolled the car over on its side. Eagle howled. "You damned fool! You've crushed my SR antenna! And the DV system is on the left side! My car is inoperable! Judson! You saw that! This fellow has vandalized Fleet property! I'm placing him under arrest!"

"Just how do you intend to go about that?" Judson asked him. Eagle's face was almost purple with fury. He went close to stare at the exposed underside of his car. "I see Maintenance at Aldo is remiss in its duties," he commented dully. He reached out to rub a fingertip on a dry grease-fitting. "No wonder my noise-suppressor was pulling three hundred volts! Damned scoundrels! I'll have a word to say to that Captain Oldtrick, the smarmy incompetent!"

"First," Cookie told him. "You got to survive, and get back there."

Eagle ducked, grabbed, and came up with the pistol Pete had kicked from his hand.

" 'Survive,' is it?" he barked, pointing the potent weapon at Pete. "Now we'll see, you thug!"

"Sure will," Pete responded lazily. "You notice I stepped on that weapon accidental-like, and the bore is prolly packed with mud pretty good. Better not squeeze it too hard, Eagle."

Eagle picked a lump of claylike soil from the near sight, rolled it into a ball and dropped it, then angled the weapon to peer down the bore.

Judson reached out casually and plucked the gun from his hand, dropped it into his pocket.

Pete took a step toward Eagle. "Time to teach you some manners, Navy-boy," he growled, and reached. Judson stumbled, knocking Pete's arm aside. As Judson had grabbed instinctively to retain his balance, his hand clutched Pete's good, or better, shoulder for an instant.

"Easy, Pete," he said. "You want the admiral in one piece, remember?"

Pete was rubbing his shoulder, looking thoughtful. "What's going on here?" he grumbled. His arm twitched, but remained at his side.

"Don't worry," Cookie put in. "Cap just squeezed the brachial nerve a little. You'll be able to move it in about an hour."

Eagle swaggered up to the disabled Pete, halted, gave him a contemptuous look, and spat. "I presume, you miserable oaf," he declared in a flinty tone, "you're ready now to bow to the inevitable."

"Guess so," Pete said and did a leg-sweep which dropped the indignant admiral on his rear.

"Been holding off on that as long as I could," Pete told Judson. "Hadda do it sooner or later."

Eagle had scrambled up. "That did it!" he yelled, turning to Judson. "I now call upon you, Captain, to arrest this malefactor at once and hold him in close confinement—locked in your car, for example—until I can convene a Court of Inquiry—not that there's any question as to his aggravated guilt!" He turned back to Pete. "No one lays hand—or in this case, a foot—on the person of a Fleet Admiral of Terra with impunity!" He shifted his weight and attempted to deliver a kick to Pete's nearer knee. The tall man simply turned sideways, grabbed Eagle's extended leg with his bad arm, and lifted. Again, Eagle fell heavily. Pete stooped, took a grip on his blouse-front, and lifted him to eye-level.

"Feller shouldn't try that unless he knows how," he commented mildly, and tossed Eagle back across the top of the armored car. Eagle began yelling curses.

"You stay right still, mister," Pete told him, "and I might forget about you."

"That's highly unlikely, you brazen scoundrel!" Eagle retorted, just as all four men became aware of the approach of a lone spinner showing Navy colors. It dropped in low, hovered, and settled down a few feet away. Immediately, Eagle began making hand-and-arm signals, and the transparent canopy popped open and two muscular men stepped out, carrying crater-guns leveled to cover all present.

"Here, Chadwick!" Eagle objected, at the same time sliding down off the car and groping for his misplaced dignity. "Point that thing off-side!" He stepped forward, moving well clear of the others, and grumped: "You took your time, I must say! Now arrest these fellows!"

There was a dull *bar-room* and soil spouted between the newcomers and the embattled three. A second spinner had come in on the tail of the first; it hovered, its hull-mounted blasters twitching nervously, following first one and then another of the potential targets.

"Don't move," Judson ordered Cookie and Pete. "Those damned guns respond to movement."

"Indeed they do!" Eagle exulted. "And—" He fell back as a second round dug a pit at his feet. "Chadwick!" he roared. "Take those damned things off auto! Fine-tune them to these fellows!"

"Sorry, sir," Chadwick replied, and went back toward the car to refocus his armaments. Pete, closest to the grounded flitter, eased an arm up below the guns' line of sight and tipped the hatch shut. Chadwick heard the vaultlike *thunk*! He yelped and turned indignantly to the tall man.

"You fool!" he blurted. "How—? Why—? Who—?"

"That's King Pete of Drygulch," Cookie supplied. Chadwick snorted and tried to thrust Pete aside. Instead, he rebounded like one who had walked into a wall.

"Stand aside, you!" he barked. " 'King,' indeed! How

dare you meddle with my dinghy? You're interfering with a naval officer in preformance of his duties!"

"When yer duties require you to call me a fool," Pete replied mildly, "I guess yer duties are due fer a change."

"As for that," the husky lieutenant snapped. "No offense was intended. I mean, I spoke without thinking; I shouldn't have used the word 'fool.' You have my apologies."

"Better just drop that gut-splasher on the ground," Pete ordered, plucking the high-powered weapon from Chadwick's grasp and tossing it aside. "Tell yer sidekick to do the same."

Chadwick took a step back, and motioned to his aide, who hesitated, then attempted to slip his weapon to his chief.

"Never mind that!" Eagle barked, one eye on the hovering spinner. "For the moment, we're forced to exercise restraint. This"—he indicated Judson—"is the local Chief of State, and"—nodding toward Cookie—"his Chief Minister. King Pete you've met. Capital fellows, actually, once you've come to know them. Laid on a delightful feast for me; many of my chaps and chips have formed close friendships—"

"But, Admiral," Chadwick butted in. "With respect, sir, isn't that fraternization with the enemy?"

"Depends on your definition of 'enemy,' " Eagle grunted. "Captain," he addressed Judson, "permit me to introduce Full Lieutenant Chadwick, a fine officer, and only nephew of Councillor Grayce."

"Old Priss Grayce is still around?" Judson queried.

"Third generation," Eagle corrected. "Our Harlow is the great-grandson of the original Chief of Council of that ilk. A powerful man," he added; then, to the lieutenant, "An imprudent man might have been inclined to align himself with one or other faction in the disagreement between myself and the CDF," he explained. "Captain Judson has not been so incautious. He has, in fact, done his best to dissuade the rebels from their folly."

"That right, Cap?" Pete demanded. "You siding with this sapsucker here?"

"By no means," Eagle contributed. "I merely said he has attempted to pacify you people. Certainly a laudable aim."

"Then, sir," Chadwick put in, "it still looks like I'd better arrest all these fellows, pending full investigation."

He made a casual grab for Cookie's arm and was thrown back against the war-car. In response he lunged again at the chef, who stood smiling insolently at him. Judson's outthrust foot tripped the lieutenant into the arms of Pete, who lifted him and asked Eagle, "What do you want me to do with this boy, Admiral? Seems like he wants to start trouble here."

"Chadwick," Eagle addressed the inverted officer sternly. "Go back to your spinner and just sit quietly."

Pete dropped the complaining lieutenant, who scrambled up, hurried back to his machine, and jumped inside, followed by his aide.

Eagle, who had been watching closely, leapt to stand in front of Pete, as the vehicle's stern stutter-gun traversed to take aim at the lanky king, now shielded by the admiral.

"Chadwick! Ordinary Space'n Chadwick!" Eagle yelled into his talker. "You are under arrest! Return to your vessel and enter confinement to quarters at once!"

"Do you think he'll do it, Eagle?" Cookie queried. "Him being a big-shot's nephew and all?"

"He's Academy-trained," Eagle grunted. "And he knows better than to defy a direct order of a flag officer!" The gun's muzzle depressed minutely and white flame stabbed from it, accompanied by a roar like an amplified death-rattle.

The megaquantum of raw energy scorched Pete's homespun sleeve as it grazed him, to score a deep gouge in the side of the armored vehicle beside him. A bright-glowing spray of molten metal ignited dry grass a few feet beyond the group. As if satisfied, the gun retracted and the port cover snapped shut.

"Admiral," the spinner's outside-talker spoke briskly.

"You're safe now, just walk away, they won't dare interfere."

"Try it," Cookie volunteered, "and I'll show you what a jackass your boy Chadwick is."

"Durn," Pete remarked, pulling up his sleeve to examine his blistered arm, the same one he had dislocated earlier. "Not too bad," he commented, gazing at the patch of raw and blackened flesh just above the elbow. " 'Less that thing puts out the short-wave stuff. Don't want no bone cancer popping up next year."

"It's clean," Judson told him, distracting the king's attention from the back of Eagle's neck. Pete spoke briefly into his field talker, and soon a car came soaring across the grassland toward the group.

"What's this?" Eagle demanded. "Treachery, by Gad! And after I had you under my guns and restrained them on the basis of a gentlemanly understanding!"

"You use that word 'treachery' a lot too loose," Pete reproved. "And the rest of that's all wrong, too. Just asked a couple of the boys to come over and keep an eye on Chaddie over there, so he don't get any ambitious ideas." The car arrived and disgorged an immense black man with filed teeth and white paint around his eyes. He was followed by Sarnt Grundy and a squat, mongolian-looking fellow with a lumpy Neanderthaloid skull covered with short bristly hair like an Airedale's.

"Crubby; Chief; Sarnt," Pete greeted the newcomers, then with a wave of his hands, "Gents, this here is Chief Umbubu from over Moosejaw, His Excellency Tang the Execrable, in from Drywash and Sarnt Grundy. They come to referee-like. Boys, meet Cap Judson and Space'n Cookie and old Admiral Eagle—you already met him, time he tried to bushwhack us off Aldo."

All of the men grunted and offered callused palms to be shaken.

"What's up, Pete?" the chief inquired. "These suckers the enemy, or what?"

"By no means," Eagle demurred. "There is no 'enemy.' We are, after all, not engaged in hostilities!"

"Then what was them up yonder?" Crubby wanted to know. "Shot the aft buffer plate right offen my *Rattler*."

"That *Rattler* o' yours is due for the salvage yards in the Belt anyways," the Chief pointed out. "No harm done, less you wanta count Eagles' go-boat, old Sally shot it up a little, *after* I give the break-off order, so it's not *my* doing!"

"Tell Princess Sally to report to me as soon as we get this here cleared up," Pete directed. "Got to talk to that gal."

"Better talk pretty," Crubby suggested. "She ain't broke nobody's arm lately. She's overdue."

"Maybe I'll let her be," Pete reconsidered. "Poor gal was prolly just tryna please, is all, and got a little eager."

"Most likely," Tang the Execrable agreed.

"An assault on units of the Fleet is not to be dismissed in so cavalier a fashion," Eagle said.

"You said about some good eats," Pete reminded Eagle. "Since we're all pals now and not enemies, why don't we go have a feast?" He glanced at Judson. "If it's all right with you boys, I mean, this bein yer planet and all."

"It is far from 'their planet'!" Eagle roared. "It is precisely the point of Terran sovereignty which is at stake here!"

"That's OK," Sergeant-Major Grundy contributed. "*You* can pervide the eats, Admiral, we're not particular."

"I have no 'eats' to provide!" Eagle responded heatedly. "However, I feel sure that Captain Judson will be only too happy to lay on a banquet in your honor." He gave Judson a pleased look, as if he had supplied a solution to a vexing problem.

"That'll take time," Cookie spoke up. "Couple days. Got the last one to clean up first, and I can't cook too good with a couple gangs o' stubborn jackasses shooting up the landscape."

"I'll be happy to conclude a truce, pending the conclusion of the festivities," Eagle volunteered. He offered his hand to Pete. "Your Majesty," he purred, "will show equal great-heartedness, I assume. . . ."

"You can skip that 'yer majesty' stuff, Eagle," Pete grunted. "The boys got enthusiastic the time after we showed them Bushwhack fellas who owned a piece o' loose real estate we call Iron Rock, and when they was well-juiced, they decided just being 'president' didn't seem like it was good enough; so they proclaimed me king. I never paid it much mind, never bought no crown nor nothing, just use the old title to impress the yokels sometimes. Like you, you know."

"Pah!" Eagle dismissed the explanation. "Do you agree to a cease-fire, or do you not?"

"Well," Pete drawled. "See'ns old Crubby's playing with the controls on that there gut-splasher again, I guess I'd be willing to go along."

"Don't need to, Pete," Crubby put in. "I locked my aft battery on his Nib's car there, and I got the fire-control right here." He showed the pack-of-butts-sized device in his hand, his thumb caressing the FIRE button.

"All right," Cookie spoke up enthusiastically, "a banquet it is! How many eaters you got, Pete?"

"Say about three hunnert, give or take them that's down with the *cafard*," was the reply. "You boys ain't got any rock-goat chops, I hope."

"Heard o' them critters," Cookie replied. "Toughern spike-lizard leather and taste worser'n cod liver."

5

"Looks good for now, Cap," Cookie said contentedly. "If we can get 'em eating, we got it made."

"My willingness to observe the civilities," Eagle reproved, "does not imply acceptance of impossible impudence."

"Lucky nobody's asking you to," Pete commented. "Look here, Eagle, after we single-handed, you remember, no help from the Navy, run them Ree back into Tip space, that Council of yourn, instead of giving us a bunch o' medals, come along and ordered us to report to the Navy yard on Luna—like *they'd* beat *us* in combat! Nacherly, we never done it, so they made the mistake of sending that Boy Scout troop out to try and make us. We never took 'em too serious, just nice Navy boys doin' what they was told: let 'em go with not hardly no casualties. But they wasn't satisfied! Sent out a full Ops Team after us and brought us to battle off Snodgrass, and got the tar whaled out of 'em! You boys are slow learners; you go by the book and we don't—so we always know what you'll do next—like the fake Omar you trieda pull on me just now. Couldn't leave well enough be! We stayed clear o' Terra, and the

Home Worlds, stayed out in Tip space till we discovered Judson's Eden here, monitored their high and medium bands is what we done, so we came out on a good-will visit and first thing we know we had you boys tryna pull a bob-war on us. Started in again with that 'disable all weaponry and report to Fortress Luna soonest' stuff again, too."

"Your existence as an undisciplined and uncontrolled force roaming Terra's sphere of interest is intolerable," Eagle barked. "Surely you can see that! Sooner or later, when you feel the need for fresh technology you'll turn to piracy and attempt to loot clients of Terra! Therefore, you are to be neutralized *before* the need becomes acute!"

"What you mean," Pete drawled, "is that Council of yourn can't bear to think there's anybody that's free and independent, not taking orders from guys like old Priss Grayce—"

"I've told you, Chairman of Council Grayce is long since dead!" Eagle boomed.

"No matter," Pete dismissed the objection. "There's plenty other windbags like him!"

"Your continued insults—" Eagle began, but Pete cut him off.

"You slang me and my boys," he said, "and when I come back disrespectful, you ack like I went and broke the pot at yer tea-party! Get realistic, Eagle! That little skirmish detail o' yourn can scare the pants off some bunch o' subsidized colonists on one o' them barely habitable worlds the Council is sponsoring, but that don't work with the CDF! Get it through yer head: you got to deal realistically with reality!"

"The reality," Eagle stated ominously, "is that no such rag-tag force as yours can, in the end, match the industrial might and technological superiority of the Terran Concordiat!"

Pete put a hand on Judson's shoulder. "I don't know," he replied, "Judson's Eden here has got technology that's way ahead of anything the Navy can field. Got some other tricks up their sleeve, too. You ever met that Baggy?" he inquired casually.

"I saw something which was represented to me as a monstrous alien of that ilk!" Eagle confirmed, sounding indignant. "Where's it gone?"

"Oh, he's around," Cookie replied vaguely.

"Hasn't run out on ye, has he?" Pete inquired.

"Hardly," Cookie dismissed the suggestion. Then, to Judson, "Where *is* he, Cap? I tried to have a word with him just now, and got no answer."

Baggy, Judson called. *It's imperative you respond, if you're able to do so. Can we help?*

Excuse me, Captain, the alien's feeble reply came. *I'm involved in an attempt—with Bitey's help, if I can persuade the rascal to align with me! She's stubborn, I assure you; can't see the need to exert herself.*

Where are you? Judson demanded.

Right here, Baggy replied. *I've distributed myself—and Bitey, too, in a film only a molecule thick—so as to be inobtrusive, though present, you understand. I perceived we were upsetting the Eagle entity. I didn't anticipate that so doing would interfere with my more material activities—such as . . .* The weak signal faded out.

" 'Right here,' he said," Cookie muttered, scanning the cobbled street around them.

"Drat!" Eagle exclaimed as his foot slipped. He regained his equilibrium and scraped the offending foot on the curb, freeing it of a slimy, colorless substance which clung like rubber cement. He detached the last strings with an impatient rake of his boot across the curb.

"Filth!" he barked. "Your streets are not so immaculate as they appear! Suppose we take another route?" He stamped off into an alley-mouth, still muttering.

"Here, Cap," Cookie spoke up. "This here Geopolitik's not so easy, eh? Every time we get Pete here calmed down, Eagle gets hard to get along with and vice versey."

Before Judson could reply, there was a yell from the alley where Eagle had disappeared. He reappeared, in full flight. "It almost got me!" he yelled, and stopped to point back whence he had come. "I nearly walked into it! That great, huge glob of filth, it attacked me! I barely escaped with my life! Grabbed my leg, shot out an arm, sort of, and caught me! I managed to extricate myself! Quickly! Your crater-gun. I'll—"

"Hold it, Admiral," Judson said and deflected the excited fellow's grab for his weapon. "It went for your *left* leg, right?"

Eagle was nodding vigorously, at the same time patting the offended limb.

"Would have had me, too," he elaborated, "had I not resisted so stoutly!" Now he was looking at his fingers.

"More filth!" he spat. "My leg is quite covered in slime! Faugh! The entire creature was made of unspeakable filth!"

"Not quite," Judson corrected. "You had part of it stuck to your boot, and it was simply reassimilating its own substance." Then, silently: *Baggy! You know better than that! Now, just recover your tissues quietly and inobtrusively. There's still some of you on the curb there—*

Of course, Captain, Baggy came in, sounding somewhat strangled, but stronger.

By the way, he went on, *you'd better call me "Baggy/Bitey" now; you see I assimilated the rude creature as she was attempting to devour me. She had suspended her auto-immune system momentarily in order to absorb me, and I seized the opportunity to turn the tables, and I absorbed* her.

I congratulate you, Baggy/Bitey, Judson offered. *Now, we still have a war to stop. And I think I'd prefer to call you "Biteur de Bagois" if you don't mind; still "Baggy" for short.*

Sounds rather elegant, de Bagois approved. *Thank you again, Captain. I wasn't really satisfied with "Baggy/Bitey," and I do love my old name "Baggy"; so euphonious! You've given me the perfect solution!*

"Hey!" Pete interrupted their inner dialogue. "What's going on, here? What was old Eagle yelling about?

Looky there!" He pointed to the gutter, where a translucent pseudopod of Baggy-matter was probing the stone-drain. "Looks like what's left of that jelly-glob thing, Baggy, I mean, you know. What happened to him?"

Did you hear, Captain? Baggy spoke up. *The estimable Pete referred to me as a "jelly-glob thing." Sheer poetry! Now I know how to introduce myself to new friends. Like these now approaching along the avenue.*

"You get that, Cap?" Cookie inquired. "Old Bag likes to be called a 'jelly-glob.' Glad he took it good, instead o' getting riled."

The approaching group was an ill-assorted lot. A squat fellow with a leather cap moulded to his flat skull swaggered in the lead. Behind him was a pretty woman with the look of a lady acrobat. A tall Sioux-warrior type was just behind her, then, abreast, a gorilloid fellow wearing yellow rain-gear and carrying a stout club in one hand and a seven-foot spear in the other.

Chief Umbubu went forward immediately to claim the spear just as Pete yelled:

"Hey! I never give no orders to you fellers to come over here!"

"Never give no orders not to," the girl responded spiritedly. "Got bored setting, so we decided to come over and see what's up. That Navy brass this Eagle feller? Why's he on the loose? Oughta of brigged him. Where's his crew at?" Close now, she glanced dismissingly at Judson and Cookie.

"Never you mind all that stuff," Pete urged as she advanced on him. "Got a bad arm here," he added apologetically, putting his right hand tenderly on his left shoulder, then, wincing, reversed the move and put his left hand on his right shoulder. "Hurt myself a little getting outa my car," he explained.

"Reckon that's why all these here enemies is running around loose," she said contemptuously. "I been thinking it over, Pete, and I don't see why I should be taking orders from you, or anybody. So I guess it's time to get you straightened up a little here." As she passed Judson she reached for Pete, but somehow tripped and fell on her face. She looked up furiously.

"How'd you do that, Pete?" she demanded.

"Did nothing," Pete grunted. His eyes met Judson's. "Gotta watch Cap, here," he muttered. "Looks like a nice quiet feller a little past his prime, but he don't like nobody to get rough. Cap," he went on, "this here is Princess Sally, out Jawbone way. Sal, meet Cap Judson." He reached awkwardly to help her up and hesitated. "Already got a broke arm or two, just about," he told her seriously. "Gonna be nice?"

She came to her feet in time to confront the Amerind and the Homo Erectus type.

"Boss," she greeted the latter, then, "Charlie, this here feller is spose to be some kinda stripped-down, home-made 'Captain,' name's Jordan or like that. Dunno about the other clown." Almost casually, she interposed herself between the newcomers and the introducees.

"Pete got a bad arm on him," she explained, "reason he ain't got 'em in arns."

"Which one?" the squat man demanded. "Arm, I mean?"

Pete reached out, caught him by the throat, picked him up and threw him back behind the Amerind type. "Don't matter, Boss," he grunted. "Now, all you boys line up nice and I'll give you yer orders; that's why you come over here, I guess." The four men complied, and Sally unhurriedly joined them.

Pete turned to Judson. "Cap, meet Princess Sally, next to her, that's Boss Nandy, ain't got much brains, but he's good-looking. That's Heavy Charlie Two-Spears next, awful good with a bow and error. Chief Umbubu here, you met, but he can play a git-fiddle with his feet and a Zalbian sqeeze-box at the same time and also blows a pretty good harmonica. Don't turn yer back to him. Captain Josh there, he got this thing about line-squalls coming up sudden. He can tear up a four-inch oak plank like it was a phonebook. Boys, shake hands with Space'n Murphy and Captain Judson; Sally got that wrong, ain't 'Jordan.' "

Four leathery palms were offered, and Pete tut-tutted. "That was a figger a speech," he remarked indulgently. "Old Cap here ain't about to fall fer that one. You, Boss, I'm making you responsible: nobody tries out this feller's meat; can't afford to have none of you disabled."

"Watch that there Cap Jordan," Sally told them bitterly. "He's a tricky one, ain't you, Sugar?"

Admiral Eagle stood aloof from these pleasantries. "Let's get on with the surrender," he growled. "King Pete, I assume you are empowered to sign the article of capitulation for all those oafs?"

"What's that 'Oaves'?" Five voices demanded in unison.

"Means 'persons of noble birth, natural lords, praiseworthy servitors of their people.' All that sort of thing," Eagle gobbled. "No offense."

"Nice of you to offer to surrender," Sally spoke up. "Save trouble all around. Tell ya the truth, my old tub, *Odie Colon*—ex-Navy garbage scow you know—she's about ready to tow in fer salvage. Never stood up good to the recoil on them thousand millimeters we scabbed onto the aft ramp. Glad to get clear o' this tumble."

"Ain't no worser'n my *Patronage*," Boss Nandy asserted. "Taken a near-miss up there, opened her dorsal plates and lost hull pressure. Some of us couldn't hardly breathe none there at the last, when we done that neat stack. Glad we broke off when we done."

"Ugh," Charlie said. "Paleface break arrow just in time. Old *Indistinguishable*'s getting to smell like a buffler-hide hogan after a tough winter."

"Ain't call *me* no 'paleface,' Heavy," Chief Umbubu complained. "OK with me if old Navy boys wanta quit. Getting low on hogjowl anyway."

"Then it's settled!" Eagle exclaimed. "No senseless war of attrition will be needed after all, to bring you fellows—what's left of you—to your senses!"

"What's left of us," Pete stated truculently, "is a intact fighting force. Where's yours?"

"Why, as to that," Eagle stammered. "My units are even now resting on the surface in 'ready' formation awaiting orders to annihilate your hulks. I'm sure Chadwick probably has everything under control."

"That's the boy you left in the spinner?" Sally inquired. "Seems like he run into a little trouble: stuck his head out and called old Chief here a 'damn Sambo.' Chief's easy-going, but that riled him some; he took the hatch off and fetched old Chaddy out. Bring him up, Chief." At her gesture, the burly black warrior came over, dragging the unconscious Chadwick.

"He's . . . not dead?" Eagle gulped, going to the limp lieutenant. He spoke sharply to him and Chadwick's eyes opened.

"The rock-hauler," he mumbled. "I never saw it!"

While Eagle soothed his second-in-command, Cookie spoke quietly to Judson. "I'm mixed up, Cap; who's surrendering to who?"

"About that big feed," Pete spoke up. "We better just bring top honchos. Some of the rank and file are a little uncouth."

"Good thinking, Pete," Sally contributed. "I ain't never et with them fellers and I ain't about to start now."

"Admiral Eagle," Judson addressed the Naval chief, "if we could see the surrender documents signed and sealed right away, we could dedicate the feast to the new era of harmony it will establish between the Terran authorities and the outlying worlds. Perhaps when Lieutenant Chadwick awakens, you might direct him to fax an appropriate document."

"Sure thing," Eagle agreed. "Usual terms: all small arms to be laid down, heavy armaments to be permantly disabled, coils to be perforated, all personnel to parade for close confinement. Leaders to be tried and sentenced IAW Code stipulations—"

"Hold hard, Eagle," Pete cut off the admiral's contented litany. "You agree to stand trial?"

"I?" Eagle's voice broke on the pronoun. "You imply that *I* am in some way culpable here? The surrender is to be unconditional, subject to the stipulations I have only now cited, as appropriate to the civilized conduct of warfare!"

"How soon can your boys do that parade you talking about?" Pete demanded.

"I fear, my dear fellow," Eagle began, but Pete waved the remark away.

"You can skip the 'dear fellow' stuff," the cadaverous CDF leader cut him off. "I ain't 'yer fella,' and I ain't 'dear.' So cut the crap and get Chadwick here busy faxing that paper Cap said about."

"I hardly think—" Eagle began, but Pete turned away. "You got maybe a minute," he said over his shoulder. "That's· about what you got left before my rearguard I got orbiting at ten miles bomb and strafe that flotilla of yours you got laid out so nice yonder."

"You wouldn't!" Eagle gasped. "Under a truce, even *your* degraded conscience could hardly countenance such treachery!"

"I heard nothing about a truce," Pete responded. "How about it, Cap?" He turned to Judson for counsel.

"He's right," Judson told him. "There was no formal armistice, but it was implicit in his break-off of action and grounding."

"Ha!" Pete rejoined. "We *made* him break off! Had him beat bad! On the other hand, I don't guess he'd of come over here to talk if he didn't *think* he had a truce. So—" Pete turned to his sub-chiefs "—I guess we oughta go along—we don't need no technicality to beat his bunch!"

"Well said!" Eagle congratulated the king. "I withdraw my hasty remark about your conscience! I'll have Chadwick get cracking on the paperwork." He went to Chadwick, who was landstill looking dazed but conscious not sitting up.

"Cap!" Cookie spoke urgently. "I wonder—"

I am here, Baggy's long-absent voice spoke up. *I trust you don't object, Captain, to my meddling a trifle with the intellectual processes of the Pete and Eagle entities?*

Welcome back, Bag! Judson and Cookie said silently in unison. *What—? Where—?*

I must apologize, the alien interrupted. *There was no*

time; I mean to say I was overwhelmed so suddenly, by—

"By Bitey?" both men supplied, shocked.

Not at all, Baggy rejected the thought. *By the demands of long-dormant instinct: the compulsion to reproduce! Bitey, you see, is of the opposite reproductive orientation to myself, and once she had enveloped me, it was necessary to spread myself—our combined selves, I should say—in a film one cell in thickness, after which the peripheral areas spontaneously broke down into individual units, each equipped with its own need to survive by absorbing its fellows. When a part of my brood was separated by adhering to the pedal member of the admiral, I lost my head—I regret the inconvenience.*

"That's wonderful!" Judson burst out. *Then you're not extinct at all! Congratulations, Baggy!*

The time to rejoice is not yet, Baggy cautioned. *The voracity of the young is quite beyond the comprehension of moderate individuals such as ourselves. Even I, when first we met, was intent on devouring any of my fellows I should happen upon. But from your example, I learned restraint, and thus it was that I did not at once attack dear Bitey, which would have ended the existence of Boog-kind for all time! Now, what about these troublesome entities, Pete and Eagle and their minions?*

Their differences can be resolved, Judson told the anxious creature.

Just what are their differences? Baggy persisted. *I could tweak Eagle's ego-gestalt—*

Don't do that—yet, Judson warned. *We can settle this rationally.*

"Hey, Cap," Cookie spoke up. "That's great, eh? Old Bag will have some company now!" He paused. "If they don't all eat each other like they done before."

No chance, Cookie entity! I, and thus we, my offspring being duplicates of myself both mentally and physically, have learned from you the awesome concept of living in amity with one's co-specifics! You are the great benefactors of all Booghood! And now it is pat-

ently our responsibility to assure that your own aspirations to peace and harmony are realized. Stand fast, Benefactors Judson and Cookie!

"That's swell," Cookie replied under his breath, but audibly. "But these two knot-heads are determined to start a war right here on Eden. No use just playing with their heads—their fleets will start shooting with or without orders if their bosses start acting strange."

"Indeed!" Eagle seconded. "My captains have orders to renew the engagement immediately if the rabble give any indication they don't intend to honor the surrender terms!" The admiral glared at Pete, who grinned impudently.

"You forgot to show me your surrender terms, Admiral," he remarked. "Get Chadwick on the ball. My boys are getting impatient; right, boys?"

Nandy nodded his flat head in eager agreement. Chief Umbubu showed his pointed teeth. Princess Sally turned to walk away. "While you gasbags are gassing," she called contemptuously over her shoulder, "I'm lifting *Odie Colon* soon's my crew-chief's got her seams tight; oughta be ready by now. Hang loose, boys, that's all the warning you get!"

"Stop her!" Boss Nandy ordered Tang, his voice blending with that of Pete, giving the same command to Chief Charlie, neither of whom moved, though Charlie remarked, "Hey, it's starting to rain."

"I already got this bad arm," Pete offered. "Otherwise—"

Sally turned and marched back up to him. "Yeah?" she challenged. "You'd what, yer Majesty?" She brushed at her face as if to wipe away a spider web.

"I'd ask you to take it easy, let's wait and see what old Chadwick comes up with." Now Pete was busy wiping at his face.

Sally turned to Eagle. "Get that log-room yeoman o' yourn out here!" she snapped. "Lessee what you got on yer mind!" She paused and a startled expression spread over her pert features. "What—?" she blurted. She wiped at her eyes and turned and walked away a few steps. At the same moment, Boss Nandy's gorilloid face writhed into a scowl. He raised a wood-hard hand and slapped himself on the back of his bun-shaped skull with a sound like a ballbat striking a watermelon and an impact which sent his flat leather cap flying. "Hey!" he remarked, and turned to Pete.

"Whosa wiseguy, Pete?" he challenged, and clapped both hands over his small, neat ears, while he squeezed his porcine eyes shut. "Lemme be!" he demanded.

Tang the Execrable was busy making motions in the air with both hands.

"Here, Crubby!" Sarnt Grundy spoke up. "Include me in on them spells, OK?"

"Hey, Cap," Cookie wailed. He was wiping his hands over his face, clawing at fine filaments of gluey substance.

"Stand fast," Judson ordered, then, *Baggy! What's this? I thought we had an understanding!*

Indeed we do! the alien's insubstantial voice came back, conveying distress. *Help, Judson entity! My young, poor little things, being denied sustenance, are dying by the thousand! Even now they call to me for aid! What can we do? If you remain adamant regarding the ingestion of the vital energies of humans, we are doomed after all!*

"Cap!" Cookie blurted. "It's not rain!" He was still wiping sticky matter from his face, as were Chief Umbubu, Tang, and the others, while Sally was deep in conversation with Nandy.

"Listen carefully," Judson instructed the others. "Our alien friend is in difficulty; the fluid falling on us isn't normal precipitation, it's tiny, new-born Boog, dead of starvation. We have to help them."

"How we gonna do that?" Chief demanded as the others nodded, seconding the query.

"Got no baby-bottles nor nothing," someone remarked.

"They feed on vital energies," Judson explained. "Like ours: we have to let them draw a little from us—just enough to survive, you understand. We'll hardly feel it." *Right, Bag?* he queried silently.

Captain! Baggy called. *I must rest now. I'm counting on you to find a solution to our malnutrition problem!*

But do hurry! I haven't much time. Already the former Bitey is disassociating from our common identity—and I had come to treasure the enhanced computing capacity with which she had endowed me/us! But I—pray excuse me: in my anguish I hardly heard your query, and I am computing rather sluggishly, without dear Bitey's full support—she found, at the penultimate moment, that she could not after all withdraw; she is now as dedicated to our union as I . . . Yes, Captain, my babies will restrain themselves—now mind you do, dears— The alien voice changed slightly for the admonition. Judson felt a faint stinging in the areas where the gooey substance still adhered to his skin. After a moment, a wave of incipient nausea passed and he realized he had staggered, but was all right now.

Easy, Bag! he commanded. *Better spread it out! That was too close for comfort!*

As you wish, Baggy responded. The assembled warriors were exchanging puzzled looks and instinctively forming a tight group, all facing outward.

"Hey, Cap!" Pete spoke up. "Just had a touch o' space-sick, never been spacey in my life! What—?"

"That was odd," Admiral Eagle commented.

Pete was holding Chief Umbubu at arm's length. "Not me, Chief!" he was telling the irate cannibal. "Bothered me as much as it did you!" He turned desperately to Judson. "Seems like your pal Baggy is chewing on my brains, sort of," he complained. "First he attacked us with this slime-blitz—and—" He looked down in disgust at his feet, now squishing in the layer of gelatinous matter covering the ground. "Wasn't 'spose to be anything like this," he went on. "Then when we was busy scraping off goo, he starts in mind-nibbling. I don't like it a bit!"

"Have you all gone mad?" Eagle thundered. "Judson! What's the purpose of this attack? Who's responsible?" To Chadwick: "Is that document ready, boy?" He turned back to Judson. "Look here, Mr. Judson, surely you don't actually intend to challenge the might of the Terran Concordiat? Any such treacherous attempt is, of course, foredoomed to failure! Your defenses, while impressive for so remote a colony, would collapse in moments under major attack, while your offensive capabilities appear non-existent. I urge you to reconsider this folly!" He wiped at his eye impatiently. "No more of that mental meddling, mind you! I won't have it! Now, where the devil's Chadwick with the surrender and annexation documents?"

"Saw it was raining and didn't want to get them wet, sir," Chadwick's mournful voice came from the car's external talker. "But of course, if it's your wish—"

"My wish is I'd never seen this infernal world!" Eagle roared. "Let's get on with it, my dear boy!"

Thus urged, Lieutenant Chadwick ducked out into the diminishing precipitation, and looked anxiously across at his chief, the faxed Articles tightly rolled in his hand. He hesitated, peering upward.

"Nasty weather, sir," he remarked. "It appears to be raining slime. It's all over the canopy."

"Never mind that, Lieutenant!" Eagle snapped. "A little slime won't hurt you!"

"Hey!" Heavy Charlie Two Spears barked. "Are them guys the ones hosing us down with snot, or what?" Without awaiting elucidation, he stepped into the path of the approaching Chadwick. "Just a minute, boy!" he growled. "What's this crud yer spraying on us?"

Chadwick shied nervously. "I have *no* idea!" he yelped. "And as a commissioned officer of the Navy, I resent being called 'boy' by you, or by anyone! My uncle—"

"Shove yer uncle!" Charlie proposed genially. "Hey, Boss!" he called to the squat anthropoid. "Junior here don't want me to call him 'Boy!' "

"What's old Boy gonna do about it?" Boss inquired interestedly, like a juvenile delinquent wondering how a grasshopper will react to the removal of one hind leg.

"Here, you ruffians!" Eagle interceded. "How dare you interfere with my ADC! His uncle—"

"Who we got here?" Nandy inquired, scratching his flat skull with a fingernail like a corroded banjo pick.

"Must have a famous uncle, hey? How about his aunt? Don't she rate a mention?"

Eagle growled, "Insolence!" and attempted to spin Nandy around by a grab at his boulderlike shoulder. Nandy half-turned, and threw the admiral six feet.

"That's enough!" Judson barked. "We're having a civilized Council of War here; there's to be no hand-to-hand combat!" He went over and took the documents from Lieutenant Chadwick's hand and unfolded them.

At once, Chadwick executed a stylish leg-sweep which dumped Boss Nandy on the lichen-covered stones of the trail. Immediately, Pete charged him with a roar and somehow tripped, as he passed Judson. He came up swinging, accidentally connecting with the jaw of Chief Charlie, who retaliated by kicking Pete behind the knee, from a supine position. Pete went face-first into the side of the armored car. Boss Nandy, having climbed to his feet, and Chief Umbubu both lunged to Pete's aid at the same moment, collided, and went down together locked in mortal combat. Tang the Execrable looked across at a short, swarthy man, who had quietly joined the group. "Well, Sam," Crubby remarked to the former rock-miner from Borax, "no point in you and me missing all the fun." With that, he uttered a screech and snapped a power-kick at Sam's knee. The joint went with a goose-bump-raising *crunch*!

"Sorry 'bout that, Sam," Tang said contritely, as Sam collapsed, howling. "Thought you'd get outa the way."

Sam, lurching to his feet, replied by bending his good knee as he doubled a hamlike fist, then straightening his leg to bring the fist up in an uppercut which flipped Tang end for end. The maddened Oriental bit the nearest leg, which happened to be that of newly arrived Commisar Objuck, who fell on him, fumbling out a switch-blade with which he jabbed in vain at the agilely dodging Oriental until Cookie kicked the weapon away, netting himself a deadly look.

"Cap," Cookie commented. "Looks like the Peace Conference ain't going too good."

"I've changed my mind!" Admiral Eagle spoke up,

wiping dispiritedly at the last of the gooey substance trickling down behind his ear.

"These chaps are altogether too uncivilized for me even to attempt to come to an accord with them!" He plucked the treaty documents from Judson's hand and tore them in two. "Chadwick!" he barked at his subordinate, who had flattened himself against the side of his spinner to avoid the melee.

"Admiral," he called hopefully. "I'd best return inside the gig, just to ensure it's not damaged, of course."

"You'll do nothing of the sort!" Eagle informed him. "If I were forced to report to the Councillor that his favorite nephew had shown the white feather, it would be the end of *two* promising careers!"

"Suppose we just don't tell him, sir?" Chadwick offered.

Cookie approached Judson and said glumly, "Looks like these boys ain't serious about wanting peace, Captain." He broke off as Chief Umbubu fell against him, muttering. Cookie pushed him away just in time to be knocked back by Charlie's leap after his adversary. Sam was standing to one side, feeling his bloody knee and muttering, while keeping his eyes fixed on Powerful Pete, who was now dabbling at a bloody nose and favoring his left knee. Sam mimed a lunge at Chief Umbubu, but instead kicked Pete in his good knee.

"Stop it!" Admiral Eagle bellowed, attempting without success to restrain Heavy Charlie in his attempt to throttle Umbubu, whose face-paint was now badly smeared. The chief managed to get his feet under him and throw Charlie, with Eagle attached, back into the free-for-all.

"Gentlemen!" the impotent admiral yelled, then paused to confer with himself. " 'Gentlemen,' indeed! A lot of wild animals, bent on treachery! Under cover of this pretended riot, they're isolating poor Chadwick from his pet spinner, and me from Chadwick! It's reprehensible!"

Princess Sally, who had remained aloof from the brawl, grabbed Eagle by the lapel.

"You're a fine one to talk about treachery!" she told him. "We know about that second echelon of yours! We spotted it as soon as we put our screens on you! You've suckered the boys into this little private agrument here, to keep 'em from joining up with the captain and Cookie." As she spoke she caught Cookie's eye. "Don't let this sucker fool you, honey," she purred. "That second wave will be hitting atmosphere any time now!"

"There *is* no second echelon, worse luck!" Eagle roared. "That's nonsense! I was on a routine exercise, breaking in green crews when I detected you people, intruding in Home Space! Naturally, I hailed you in the normal manner, but instead of heaving to like law-abiding subjects, you chose to attempt to elude me!"

"We're not 'subjects,' " Sally corrected. "You and yer squadron came on in battle formation, and we was busy, so we took off. That's all. We come here to see if maybe these folks would like to join up in the CDF, and the next thing, we find you boys'd invaded and the war was on!"

"Not 'war,' " Eagle objected. "Only a routine administrative contact, in spite of your efforts to resist the due process of law! War is what I am here to prevent! Now, if you could persuade your colleagues to desist, we can get on with the negotiation!"

"You might's well tell a sand-tornado to 'desist!' " Sally replied. "Here, Sam!" she yelled, almost in the ear of the burly ex-ice-miner. He responded by turning toward her, at which Tang dealt him a terrible blow to the side of the head. Sam went down and Crubby's sallow face grinned at the girl. "Could *I* he'p you, Sal?" he offered genially.

"Yeah, Crub," she asserted. "Get the boys to quieten down so's the admiral here can do his surrender speech."

Tang turned back and waded into the battle, which, for a moment, seemed to rage on, unchanged; then Umbubu appeared, on all fours, emerging from the eye of the battle, shaking his head. Heavy Charlie was ejected bodily from the chaotic struggle, and fell almost at Sally's feet. He shook his head and attempted to come to his hands and knees, but she kicked one arm from under him and his teeth *click!*ed as his chin struck the ground. Others were emerging from among the tight-packed combatants: Grundy, looking back over his shoulder and pounding his ear with the heel of his hand; Commissar Objuk, his turban shoved down to completely cover his eyes, groping his way until he collided with Boss Nandy, who turned on him with a snarl.

"Easy, Boss," the commissar soothed. "Just got to get clear where I can fix my head-rag, is all."

The decible level had dropped perceptibly by now, allowing all present to hear a youthful female voice calling: "Captain! It's important!"

"What's important, Tammy?" Judson inquired as he turned to the distraught girl just arrived, who had first to catch her breath before replying.

"Got another invasion is what's important, Cap," she said bluntly. "I'm on distant Monitor, and—"

"I know, dear," Judson soothed. "Tell us the details, please."

"Picked 'em up soon's I come on-watch," she told him. "Must be hunnerts of 'em. Just a few *big* vessels . . . but a whole flock of thousand-tonners around the big fellers. . . . Coming in fast on a SDBTP!"

"Thank you, Tam," Judson said quietly. "Now please walk back slowly and catch your breath. Don't worry. Keep it as quiet as you can so as not to alarm everybody."

"Word's already out, Captain," she explained. "Sorry about that, but it was on the big screen and everybody saw it! Got pretty excited; Chief told me to find you 'at costs' is what he said, but it didn't cost nothing, only run half a mile!"

"Cap," Cookie said, sounding anxious. "What do you think old Navy'd send the Home Fleet out here for?"

"I assure you," Eagle spoke up, "if, indeed, a major force is now approaching this world, it is *not*, I repeat NOT a detachment of the Terran Navy!"

Judson nodded and turned to Pete, who had also retired from the fracas to nurse a bleeding nose.

"Got two bad arms and a bad laig," he complained. "And now this here busted nose; spoils the fun some."

"Too bad," Judson commiserated. "Do you know anything about a major task force about to hit atmosphere?"

Pete shook his head. "Nope," he stated with finality. "Got all the boys with me, 'cept old Tinkerbell from Dyke Nine. He was having his hair done, he says. Whattaya mean, 'major task force?' "

"Sounds like all the Goliath class dreadnaughts the Concordiat owns, complete with their ancilliaries. The whole works."

"CDF's got nothing like that," Pete grunted. "Our heaviest hull is a converted garbage scow mounting two experimental not-approved-for-Concordiat-procurement hellbores. So who in Tophet can it be? Not the Ree again, I hope. We sent *them* worms home, sadder but wiser as they say."

"That's a thought!" Judson said. "An alien species!"

"Nonsense," Admiral Eagle put in. "I've explained to you that Autospace has determined definitively that no mentational alien life-form could be expected to exist here in the same volume of space occupied by Mankind. Absurd!"

"Then who is it, Eagle?" Pete demanded.

Baggy, Judson called silently, and was surprised to receive an immediate response, somewhat stronger than before.

Yes, Captain, good news! My poor babies are not after all dead, just depleted, Poor Dears; all they require is more nourishment and their mental abilities will return! I appreciate your efforts, but I experimentally fed a few thousand some of my own vital energy, and at once they joined with me at a level of mentation almost equal to my own former powers!

Congratulations, Judson exclaimed noiselessly. *But we have a new problem here, Bag: an unidentified fleet is on final approach. Huge force: looks like modern equipment, I understand. Can you . . . ?*

Nothing easier, Captain, the alien reassured him at once. *As you know, I monitor the approaches to my, excuse me*, our *world, and I had noted the intruders several milliseconds before you mentioned them. I was in fact about to broach the subject to you. What do you wish me to do—? Keeping in mind that my powers are still not up to their full potentiality, and will not be until my young have fed fully and can join with me at their full vitality. I* am *somewhat depleted after reproducing, you understand.*

"Cap!" Cookie spoke up. "Old Bag's right! I was looking at this here slime, and it's all tiny Boogs o' course, and they're *alive*."

"Excellent news," Judson remarked.

Not unless I can continue to curb their instinct for mutual predation! Baggy interjected.

"They seem to be quite content to co-exist," Cookie reported, poking at a gob of the infant creatures with a twig.

Happy day! Baggy caroled. *I find my young are in full possession of all my philosophical discoveries! They have no wish to eat each other! A new day truly dawns for Boog-kind!*

"Lamarck was right, it appears," Judson commented. "Inheritance of acquired characteristics."

Ah! Baggy exclaimed. *Heavenly! To know again my full powers as in the days of my youth when I was surrounded by my less alert siblings. Now to attend to these nosy intruders who are even now hull-down to the east!*

" 'Hull-down?' " Cookie echoed. "You mean . . . ?"

That is no moon rising there, Baggy pointed out, and Judson and Cookie, as well as the suddenly silenced leaders of the CDF stared in awe as a truly immense hulk rose with glacial sloth above the eastern horizon. Cookie used his binoculars.

"It's a vessel, all right!" he told the others.

Just then two men arrived on foot at a full gallop, a small, wiry fellow, and a tall cadaverous lout with a swarthy face buried in blue-black whiskers.

"Cap, Murph," Pete spoke up, "this here is Mean

Ernie and the Mad Ayrab. Howdy, boys, care to join in the deliberations?"

The newcomers ignored both introduction and invitation, but fell in behind Pete. "Who you want kilt, Pete?" they demanded in unison. Pete waved that away. "All pals, now," he explained.

The riot had by now fallen silent, as all involved gaped at the monstrous spaceship which was still emerging into view.

"Half a mile long anyways, Cap," Cookie muttered.

"Make that two miles," Judson corrected.

Soundlessly, the titanic alien ship approached.

6

Baggy, Judson called. *Can you give us a report? What is it? Who's conning it, and why are they here?*

A monitor vessel of the Great Fleet, Baggy reported. *It is the advance scout of a flotilla of one thousand capital ships, and they are here to conduct a reconnaisance of your—I mean our world.*

"Swell," Cookie commented. "All we need is an alien invasion to make it a perfect day! And that baby's just a scout-boat for the big boys!" As he spoke, all present noticed a number of bright flashes near the oncoming behemoth.

"My attack boats!" Eagle squawked. "Poor fellows! I told them to make a close pass and observe its gun emplacements, no hostile action! And—"

"And it swatted them like gnats," Cookie supplied. "Nice, friendly folks!"

Au contraire, Baggy spoke up. *They are of an alienness which makes your own curious kind seem like near kin, and they are of a malignancy undreamed of in my philosophy!*

" 'Malignant' how?" Judson demanded.

They have noted your cities and towns, Baggy replied, sounding shocked. *They propose to level them so as to provide even more breeding surface for His Magnificence. Tell Pete to scatter his forces; they are about to be destroyed; and Admiral Eagle's squadron must hide as well. Flee, humans, scattering is your only hope to avoid mass destruction!*

"They're attacking without provocation, without warning—just like that?" Cookie demanded.

Not so much attacking as simply eliminating vermin, Bag corrected. *Much as you might spray a nest of noxious insects. His Magnificence luckily, has not yet noticed me and my family. Farewell, entities! We shall meet again, I hope!*

Baggy! Judson called after the alien.

"The slime, I mean the young!" Cookie exclaimed, "It's gone!"

"What's going on here?" Eagle demanded. "Are we to do nothing about this unprovoked, murderous attack? I, for one, do not intend to remain passive! My main body is still intact, and will attack at once!"

"'Negative, Admiral," Judson interceded, catching the incensed officer's arm as he started toward his vehicle.

"So far, they've only scattered some annoying gnats," Judson explained. "Let's not attract their attention just yet."

A second titanic vessel hove into view in line astern of the leader. Both contrived to cruise slowly past the grounded fleets, ignoring both these and the city lying unprotected beyond them.

Baggy! Judson called. *What can we do?*

Simply observe, Baggy suggested. *No need to waste your pitiful forces against His Magnificence.*

Whose side are you on, Bag? Cookie sub-vocalized. *You sound like you admire these mothers!*

I am indeed impressed by their very bulk, Baggy conceded. *However, I can experience no fellow-feeling for their determination to sterilize our world in preparation for spawning.*

Just how do they intend to go about that? Judson inquired.

First, Baggy explained, *they plan to bathe the planet in hard radiation which will cause the dissolution of all organic compounds, and thus all life, native and foreign. Then they will remove all matter projecting above an arbitrarily designated grade and deposit it in the declivities, producing a sphere as smooth as a billiard-ball (a term I extracted from your pre-conscious).*

"Cap," Cookie spoke up, "that program doesn't appeal to me one little bit."

"Here," Eagle blurted, "what are you fellows talking about? What 'program?' "

"That of the invaders," Judson told him.

"Yes, yes, and how do you know—ah, just what does this 'program' entail?" Eagle gobbled.

"They're going to kill every living thing on the planet and then level the surface, to prepare it for breeding," Judson told him.

"I reckon," Pete spoke up, "they'll have the CDF to deal with before they get to do all that. Right, boys?" He turned to the motley crew now exploring their cuts and bruises, and tending each other's wounds.

"Sorry about that ear, Crub," Commissar Objuk was saying. "Never meant to bite it that hard. Hold still now, lemme get this regen-strip on there good. Don't want you going around with a ear like a beagle."

"You mean a bagel?" Boss Nandy asked.

"Said a 'beagle,' " Objuk pointed out. "Hanging down like that, I mean."

"Sure, Ob," Boss agreed. "No offense. What we going to do about these here whachamacallums?"

Both giant vessels had now come to rest on the surface, flattening trees and a few outlying buildings, and indeed deflecting the underlying rock. The men waited.

"Ruint that farm yonder," Mean Ernie commented. "I was a farm boy. I kind of resent that."

"Shall we hit 'em fast, Cap?" Cookie wanted to know. "While they're not expecting it?"

"Let's wait and see what develops."

"Reckon they plan to start destroying all life right now?"

Heavy Charlie grunted. "Heap mean folks, sounds like, worser'n Arrapahoes. We better go on warpath pronto."

"Negative," Judson decreed, and Eagle nodded in emphatic agreement. "We must attempt negotiation first," the admiral announced. "Look!" he interrupted himself. "They're debarking troops. Odd," he added. "Such tiny creatures for such an immense vessel."

The aliens swarming from the open unloading hatches were indeed small; no bigger than so many eight-legged washtubs, but with limbs which they appeared to use interchangeably as arms or legs.

"Look like great big spiders!" Boss Nandy spat. "Never did like spiders! When I was jest a small child—"

"You?" Sarnt jeered. "You wann't never no 'small child,' you ornery old devil! You was borned growed up and looking for trouble!" He put an affectionate arm around the Boss's impressive shoulders. "That's why you're my pal, Boss."

"Like I was tryna tell you," Boss objected, throwing off the embrace. "I was laying in my bed, or crib or whatyacallit, and this big old spider dropped on my face. I guess I yelled some! Pa come in and squashed it, broke my nose, that's why it's kinda flat now. Never taken to them spiders since."

"Sure, that figures, Boss," Sarnt Grundy acceeded. "But what do we do about these here ones?"

"Look!" Pete boomed. All eyes swiveled to stare as a large hatch cycled open. In the gloomy hold behind it, something stirred. A snout appeared; not that of an ore-boat, as Cookie first guessed, but a living creature, moving sluggishly on stubby but powerful limbs. The large, slit-pupiled eyes were visible as the scaled lids rolled back. An immense, fang-studded mouth opened slightly, no more than a yard or two. The beast lurched forward and half-slid down the thick ramp, which sagged under its weight until it scrabbled clear and out onto the grassy plain.

"Looks like a shark with a crocodile's head and hide!" Chief Umbubu declared. "Big juju! Boys, let's make tracks outa here, while these fellers here deal with their little problem." The Mad Ayrab Abdul's blow caught the dusky leader on the back of the head, sending him staggering. Abdul turned to face the other captains of the CDF. "First thing we do," he stated, "is we grab some o' them little fellers fer hostages, or involuntary guests like you could say, and see what big Daddy does." By now a second behemoth had emerged from the other strange vessel, likewise accompanied by a swarm of the tiny arachnoids, which crawled over the immense animals, some apparently grooming their warty hides, others stuffing vegetation into the corners of their cavernous mouths.

"Look here!" Admiral Eagle commanded. "You, King Pete! I'm making you brevet-commodore, and impressing your fleet, as an auxillary unit to Fleet Operations. All you other chaps, line up here! I'm swearing you all in as provisional ensigns in the Reserve!"

"Nix," Mean Ernie objected. "I already got the rank of captain in the Merchant Navy, and I demand—"

"Very well," Eagle cut in, "you'll all be captains. Now, I want your vessels prepared for action instantly, so you'd best all disperse to your respective commands at once! Dismissed!"

"What's that 'respectful?' " Mean Ernie wanted to know.

"He said 'respective,' " Pete corrected. "Now, you heard the admiral! Let's move!" With that, he commandeered the nearest vehicle and drove off across the pristine turf.

"What about you fellows?" Eagle inquired, turning to Judson. "I trust you'll not object to provisioning both my force and the reserves, in light of the circumstances?"

"Sorry," Cookie volunteered. "We got no war materiel, Admiral. Never needed any."

"No ammunition?" Eagle cried as if amazed. "But that fantastic artillery of yours . . ."

"I think I explained, sir," Judson offered, "that our friend deBagois supplied the firepower."

"Well, tell him to get busy and equip my vessels, and King Pete's, too, with the cannon!"

How about it, Baggy? Judson queried. *You remember the explosion you put on for us: how did you stage those detonations?*

Oh, yes, Baggy replied. *I recall; just foolishness, but I have a retentive memory, especially since you were so thoughtful as to rewire my cerebrum. Simply a matter of causing energy to flow from a small air-mass against the thermal gradient, into the adjacent atmosphere. As a result, low pressure and an implosion. Quite spectacular, but unsettling to one's nerves. I don't care to do that sort of thing anymore.*

But we need your help, Judson insisted. *We have to do something about these invaders!*

Interesting, Baggy replied silently. *I note that the large creatures have no manipulatory members, yet they are in possession of artifacts requiring considerable manufactory ability. It appears they have impressed into service the smaller life-forms which, though extremely dextrous, have little intellect. El Supremo breeds, protects, and sustains hordes of the tiny Geepers in a symbiotic relationship.*

As Baggy spoke, Judson noticed a resumption of the "falling-mist" effect, accompanied by an itch in his cortex. He rebuked Baggy sharply. The alien replied sulkily, *My little ones are in dire distress; having recovered sufficiently to resume levitation, they of course are attracted by the handiest source of sustenance.*

Both Cookie and Eagle were now complaining of dizziness, as were a few of the CDF captains.

You know better than that! Judson told Baggy sternly. *I suggest you send your spawn over to check out the new playmates.*

Oh, will it be all right if I/we snack on those fellows? Baggy responded, communicating pleased surprise.

They volunteered, Judson pointed out. *They came here uninvited, so they'll have to take their chances.*

The malevolence emanates only from the Geepers, Baggy *reported. The Supremos are quite amiably inclined, I note. So suppose I start with the little fellows?*

Good idea, Judson agreed.

The last of the moist film withdrew abruptly from the men's faces.

"Boys," the mad Arab spoke up. "There's somethin' needs takin' care of. We'd better get crackin' before these monstrous creatures start to waste the landscape. They'll prob'ly begin with the town there."

"True, Abdul," Chief Umbubu spoke for the group. "A bit of a sticky wicket, one might almost say."

"Don't get the wind up, boy," Abdul replied coolly.

"Ain't call *me* no 'boy!' " the chief responded hotly. "And don't know nothing about no wind being up. What about a modest wager, eh, old chap? Last one to dance on El Supremo's head is a rotten egg!" He sprinted toward the swarming Geepers; Abdul threw aside his djellabah to follow, and with a surprising burst of speed forged ahead of the long-legged chief.

"Teen guck on Boobie," Pete called through his damaged face as he got out of his car, and was at once jeered by Boss Nandy. Other wagers were quickly made and Judson agreed to hold the stakes. Meanwhile, the two charging CDF's had entered the fringes of the Geepers, which scattered to open a lane to the nearer of the two great crocodilians. Abdul was first to reach the monster, and without pause, he leapt up to a foothold on the warty hide just behind the lipless mouth and bounded up to stand above one bulging eyelid. Umbubu was beside him a moment later. Judson paid off the bets. El Supremo ignored the nuisance, except to blink, which sent Abdul skidding across the wading-pool-sized expanse of warty hide between the eyes. Umbubu went to his assistance and the two stood and waved to their comrades gaping below.

The dispersed Geepers were hurrying back to their stations closely ringing their immense masters.

"I dunno, Cap," Cookie offered dubiously. "I had a idea we could maybe deal with the little fellers, them being slaves and all, and isolate the big boys, but Baggy says it's the little ones plan to level the planet and breed. Old Supremo don't seem to mind the boys dancing on him."

"Didn't notice, most likely," Eagle contributed. "The ratio of size is about that of man to gnat."

Just then there was a stir among the tiny alien retainers. A small detachment formed up in a column and set out to crawl up the snout of their monstrous sponsor.

"They're going after Ayrab and Boobie," Sarnt Grundy's voice cracked on the car talker. "Boys, are we gonna let 'em do it?"

A resounding, "Heck, no!" was the response; in a moment, the frontiersmen had fallen in, in a ragged squad formation. Pete looked across at Judson and Cookie.

"You boys want a piece o' this?" he inquired casually, and without awaiting a reply, continued: "Cap, you can take the point with me. Space'n Murphy better bring up my combat car. Might need some firepower if we got them figgered wrong."

It was a short drive to the edge of the area taken up by the excited Geepers, who were scurrying about, busy with some activity not clear to the humans, appearing to be oblivious now of their approach. Suddenly, Umbubu whipped up the seven-foot spear which was as much a part of his persona as his blue-black hide, and poked experimentally at the vast, glistening eyeball beside him. The thick, leathery eyelid snapped down in a blink which almost trapped the spear tip, the chief working it free with some effort.

It appeared to those approaching that the chief rebuked the monster sharply; then he poked the spear at the nearest hide-fissure, at which the great monster twitched sharply; as he fell, Abdul caught sight of the approaching squad of Geepers. In an instant he was back on his feet, awaiting the assault. Instead of sweeping forward in an overwhelming wave, the Geepers halted and one crept forward, holding up four limbs in a universal gesture of truce. At the same moment, words formed silently in the minds of all present: *Peace, curious beings. We perceive you have come at last to rescue us from the clutches of the brutal Supremos. Kindly destroy them at once.*

"Hold hard, buddy," Umbubu said, hefting his spear, while looking over the immense, scaled hide of the vast creature on which he stood.

Right up under that forelimb ought to do it, the small voice remarked; and the leading Geeper moved another foot forward. Abdul caught him with a brawny arm.

While this mini-drama was in progress, Cookie pulled the armored car in close to the Supremo.

"Ease around to the right," Judson directed, and Cookie pulled up alongside the splayed hindlimb. He carefully aimed the turret-mounted infinite repeater at the point where the giant's lumbar vertebrae ought logically to be situated.

"It's not necessarily a vertebrate," Judson cautioned, "and definitely not a terrestrial vertebrate. Its anatomy could be more like a squid."

"He won't get far with his wiring cut and his insides outside," Cookie countered, "no matter how he's built."

"Hold your fire," Judson said. "Listen!"

Cookie nodded. "Like Baggy, only different," he commented, tuning in on the mental communication. "Said to kill the big boys, just like that," he mused, then, *Baggy! Where are you? What about these fellows?*

"Hold on Cap!" he interrupted himself. "This is different!"

Pay no attention to the hysterical demands of the treacherous Geepers, a vast, stony voice like an echo in a subterranean cavern boomed out silently.

Quickly! the lesser voices of the arachnoid cut in. *Destroy the monsters before—*

The car trembled as the ground vibrated under its tracks; the Supremo was moving, interposing itself between the car and the advancing horde of eight-limbed creatures, which were scattering now, attempting to circumvent the immense obstacle in their path.

Abdul and Chief Umbubu were left ignored by the small aliens attempting to approach the car.

"I don't like it, Cap!" Cookie blurted. "We're cut off from the little fellows. Should I fire?"

"By no means," Judson told him. "Listen!"

—*You see, it attempts to isolate you from us, your friends!* the squeaky Geeper-voice was bleating.

Withdraw, strange creatures, the big voice boomed. *Don't let them form their Circle of Power about you! Quickly now, before*—

The spidery creatures broke their ring to swarm over the immense reptilian creature. They clustered along the fissures in the horny hide, up-ended like feeding mosquitos.

Help us! Both voices clammered at once. The Supremo went to its knees, then flopped on its side, barely missing Abdul as Umbubu pulled him away. The two men came toward the car, unmolested.

The Geepers were reforming their circle, stretched out thinly now, but almost meeting behind the car. Cookie gunned it and backed clear of them.

Withdraw fifty yards, the big voice spoke up. *I think that will place you safely beyond their radius of effectiveness. Hurry! Then kill them all!*

"These boys want to play rough," Cookie remarked, as he swung around to take Umbubu and Abdul aboard. The two climbed in, breathing hard and both talking at once:

"—big mother damn near—"

"Guess I got to thank you, pard," Abdul's voice came through for a moment. "I guess I musta tripped."

"Ain't worry about it, Ayrab," Umbubu urged. "Anyone would have gotten the wind up a trifle with that behemoth falling toward him."

"Got no wind up," Abdul objected. "Just surprised, was all; I seen the big fellow step in and cut off the spodders, figgered he was OK; then he like to squashed the both of us."

"He'd have gotten a taste of the fang of the loyal Umslopogaas here," Umbubu responded, running a callused fingertip along the edge of the twelve-inch spearhead.

"Maybe it was just a accident," Abdul hazarded, doubtfully. "Prolly not."

All heads turned at a sound from the spot, a quarter

of a mile distant, where the heroes of the CDF were now mounting their vehicles and revving up aged engines. The little convoy fell into line abreast and advanced. The Geepers darted about excitedly, then formed a line of their own and awaited their arrival.

"Reckon old Pete's coming to our rescue," the Mad Ayrab remarked, as he and Umbubu climbed out of the war car while watching the advance and at the same time keeping a wary eye on the nearest Geepers. Chief Umbubu was similarly chary of the immense Supremos crouched near at hand, unmoving amidst the hubbub. Abdul spun suddenly and made a grab at the nearest Geeper which missed by an inch. The jittery creature leapt aside and spat a greenish substance which spattered on the Arab's knee. He howled and wiped a hand across the spot and howled again.

"Damn spodder burnt me!" he yelled, and pounced on another of the fast-moving creatures. This time he avoided its venemous expectoration and seized it by two of its rubbery limbs as if about to tear them off.

Stop! an anxious voice shouted silently.

Well done! another telepathic voice boomed. *Hold the vile thing, and allow me to handle the negotiation.*

"Hang on, Ayrab!" Umbubu urged, hurrying toward him as the captive Geeper threshed violently, spraying its poison. The chief ducked in and managed to seize a limb of his own, at which he tugged vigorously.

Release me, alien beings, the lesser of the two silent advisors urged. *We can help you!*

"Where did it get the idea we need any help?" Abdul inquired rhetorically. He gave the captive arm/leg a tentative tug. The small voice screamed silently. *Unhand me at once!* it demanded, but with a hint of plea in its tone now.

Abdul made eye-contact with Chief and both men applied pressure. "Easy, Chief," Abdul cautioned. "If'n we tear it apart it won't be able to call off the big boys for us."

Where did you get the absurd idea—? the voice of the captive Geeper began, then, *—if I do employ my* *influence to divert His Magnificence,* it gobbled, *will you release your grips on my person?*

Chief winked elaborately. "Quite, my dear fellow," he assured his victim. "We've no fell intent regarding you; we merely want to discuss the situation. Right, Abdul?"

"That's the idear," the Mad Ayrab agreed, and heaved hard on the limb in his grip. The voice shrieked and went silent.

Chief held up the feebly-twitching carcass, oozing yellowish fluid from the ragged wound where its limb had been rudely torn away.

Magnificence! a chorus of tiny voices wailed. *You have to protect us!*

With that, the Geepers broke off their advance and swarmed over the torpid bulk of the nearer of the two giant beasts, which reacted by attempting to roll over. The relatively tiny creatures dodged agilely aside, and the deep voice roared out: *Enough! Cease your torments, vile nibblers! I failed to notice Oogie's plight!* With that it raised its bulk on its stubby legs and lunged toward the men who were standing in a tight group, watching in fascination. The lunge fell short, the immense jaws snapping a yard from Mean Ernie, who picked up a handful of dusty soil and tossed it into the monster's nearer eye. The scaly eyelid snapped down too late. Blackish mud flowed from the irritated ocular.

Cease! the booming mental voice pled. *Cannot we unite against these pernicious Geepers?*

"What do you think, Cap?" Cookie inquired. "Are the Supremos the good guys after all?"

"I'm not sure the concept of 'good guys' is applicable in this context, Space'n," Judson replied. "We need more data."

During the confusion, the nearest Geeper had swarmed over the body of their dismembered fellow.

"Eegh!" Cookie burst out. "They're eating old Oogie!"

"Not actually," Judson corrected, as the heap of writhing Geeper paled and Oogie emerged, flexing his newly-mended limb joyfully.

"Hey, Cap," Cookie stammered. "Did . . . did I see— I mean—"

"Exactly," Judson confirmed.

The giant armored creature was down again, threshing ponderously, throwing up ridges of displaced soil in its struggles to rid itself of the swarming Geepers, which, however, retreated to the comparative shelter of the underside where they clung tenaciously.

"They're boring holes," Cookie noted, observing the thick orange-colored fluid oozing from a thousand tiny wounds in the warty hide. "No wonder old Supremo's upset, but he's getting some of his own," he called, referring to the smeared remains of half a dozen Geepers which had failed to escape the crushing weight of their victim.

"Their victim?" Judson queried. "Or are they El Supremo's victims? Odd relationship, it seems: not precisely master-and-slave, and not quite host-and-parasites."

"Whatever they are," Cookie responded, "it looks like our best bet is to let 'em control each other."

" 'Cept," Boss Nandy spoke up, "for the one that's trying to eat my ankle!" He kicked at a persistent Geeper, connecting solidly and sending the multi-limbed creature flying.

Good work! El Supremo's deep tone boomed out silently. *Help me destroy these confused nits, and I'll do what I can to protect you from my pal Troon here. She's ready to spawn, and temporarily immune to the damn things. Her juices taste bad. Benign dispensation of Divine Providence to protect a spawning mother during her ordeal.*

Don't listen to the great bully! a Geeper's tiny voice rang in. *They flatten our villages and won't stop until we supply them with servitors to carry out the work they're too clumsy to do for themselves. Like smelting ore and building the transports, for example.*

These feckless creatures, the big voice countered, *being morons or worse, though endowed with dextrous members in plenty, are quite incapable of coping with the forces of nature. Without my own intellectual virtu-*

osity to show them what to do, they'd still be subsisting at a pre-cultural level.

"So, the Supremos provide the brains, and the Geepers do the work," Cookie concluded. "Looks like they both need each other. So why are they enemies?"

"Let's check with Baggy," Judson suggested, and at once called the elusive alien.

Right here, Judson entity, came the prompt reply. *I see you've met the vile murderers.*

Where have you been? Judson demanded. *And why didn't you tell us about these fellows? You gave us to understand you were the whole inhabitant of the world.*

And so I was, until these voracious entities arrived from the inner world; the next planet in toward Brownie, that is. They quite took me by surprise, the Supremos, I mean. I'd been keeping surveillance over the Geepers, who seemed harmless enough; then their invading vessel appeared abruptly inside my alert radius. That's why I dashed off. They intend to devastate Eden, and populate it with their own objectionable kind. We must discourage them, Judson and Cookie entities! I think a strategic withdrawal out of squashing range would be wise.

"Good idea," Cookie seconded. "Before the big fellows take a notion to go over and roll on our transport."

Judson agreed, as did the CDF troops, and they hurried back to the group waiting by the cars. Eagle rushed to his spinner and yelled at Chadwick.

"Situation's getting out of hand, my boy!" he yelled. "Seems we're invaded by forces from an inner planet. I can hardly stand by and permit my annexation to be negated by these Johnny-come-latelies!"

Chadwick, still clutching the pieces of his documents, re-emerged from the spinner and hesitated. "Had I better amend the articles," he queried, "to include the capitulation of all foreign troops presently on-planet?"

"No, you damn fool!" Eagle roared. "Er, that won't be necessary, lad," he ammended the *gaffe*. "Terra does not recognize the existence of any extra-terrestrial powers, therefore to acknowledge their existence could leave the Council itself with egg on its face. Surely you understand. Otherwise, of course, your suggestion would have had considerable merit."

"No use putting band-aids on an amputated leg, Admiral," Chadwick sulked. "My feelings are hurt; you called me a fool."

"It was only a manner of speaking, dear boy," Eagle suggested.

"And a rude one, especially to a nephew of a Council Member, and a duly commissioned officer of the Concordiat," Chadwick saucily reminded his superior.

"Yes, to be sure," Eagle acceeded. "But no actual charges of treasonous incompetence in the face of duty have yet been lodged against you, so I suggest we turn our attention to the task at hand and carry on."

"Right, sir," Chadwick responded and executed a snappy salute somewhat marred by the floppy roll of faxed papers in his saluting-hand.

Eagle grabbed the offending documents and unrolled the pieces on the top of the armored car.

"Look here, you fellows," he addressed Judson and Cookie over his shoulder. "With all due respect, considering that you've twice been invaded here in the last few hours and are now confronted with not one, but two strange and hostile life-forms, do you still insist you're capable of existing as an independent world, outside the benign umbrella of the Concordiat Naval Forces? Eh?" He turned to look keenly at Judson. "Captain, I call upon you to give up this mad dream of independence and enter the community of mankind as a client world. You will, I think I can assure you, be accorded authority as the Council-appointed Governor. Taxes, you will find, will be light, barely covering the cost of Naval operations on your behalf."

"What do you think, Cap?" Cookie inquired as if in doubt. "Do we need some dirt-loving bureaucrat from Priss Grayce's gang to tell us what to do?"

"That, Space'n," Judson responded sternly, "was a severely prejudicial presentation of the question."

"What question?" Cookie replied and went up to

Eagle in a belligerent manner and was promptly knocked flat by a neat leg-sweep. The astonished space'n looked up resentfully.

"Wasn't set for that," he carped.

"Wasn't set for that, *sir*!" Eagle corrected him. "Now Space'n, get on your feet and do something intelligent to resolve the death-struggle about to eventuate yonder. King Pete's men will no doubt attack the monsters, and will be annihilated! Do something! If you people don't take effective action at once, *I* shall!"

"Better do what the admiral says, Cookie," Judson called. "I'd hate to see his units take another hack at the CDF. Their fleet would be wiped out, and we'd be stuck with them."

Cookie got to his feet and dusted ineffectually at his knees. "Just wanted to say, Admiral, sir," he spoke up hesitantly. "We can deal with these critters, with no help from your squadron."

Baggy, Judson called, *are these two vehicles the entire invading force, or are there more of them?*

There are another six units in synchronous orbit. Baggy informed him. *And of course, a very large reserve force is still in transit from the inner world.*

What kind of firepower do they have? Judson wanted to know next.

Virtually none, Baggy replied. *Their strategy is to land in overwhelming force and engage any resistance on the ground, avoiding space-conflict.*

"That's OK," Cookie commented, "if they can get the other side to play them rules. *We* don't hafta, Cap. We can lay back and bombard these two tubs, out of getting-rolled-on range."

"Here!" Eagle butted in. "What's this talk of bombardment? If you lay artillery fire on those behemoths, you'll annihilate King Pete, and his force as well! I demand you hold your fire!"

"Keep cool, sir," Cookie advised. "Nobody's gonna bombard the CDF."

"Certainly not!" the admiral snapped. "But since you

seem paralyzed, I shall commit my own force to action to salvage the situation."

"Who do you plan to attack?" Cookie queried.

" 'Attack?' " Eagle barked. "Who said anything about attack? I shall move my units in and extricate King Pete and the unfortunate Geepers from the clutch of the monsters!"

"With due respect, Admiral," Judson put in, "I'd advise against that."

"What? You imagine that I, like yourselves, will stand by, apathetic, while the monstrous invaders destroy smaller, harmless beings, including fellow Terrans? Never!"

"No, sir," Cookie put in. "Cap don't mean that." He looked to Judson for confirmation. "What *do* you mean, Cap'n, sir?"

Baggy, Judson called silently. *Please explain the situation to me. The Geepers are actively attacking both the CDF and the Supremos, with whom they had doubtless coexisted peaceably aboardship, while the Supremos have already crushed a number of Geepers and threatened the men of the CDF. What are their motives, and which faction deserves our assistance?*

The interspecies relationship is complex, Baggy came back. *While not quite a classic symbiosis, each relies on the other to an extent neither group will acknowledge. The immense Supremos possess a high order of intelligence, but, lacking manipulatory members, are unable to implement the concepts they perceive, while the deft and agile Geepers lack mentational abilities. Under the Supremos' direction they mine and smelt metals, fabricate spaceships, and provide all else that is needed for survival and progress on their barren world. They have come here, as you know, to breed, a process which is exceedingly difficult on their homeworld. The Supremos have lost control of their minions; those same minions find themselves trapped in the cycle of dependency on their giant mentors. Both wish to dissolve their relationship, but neither is able to do so.*

"So both of them are trying to con us foreigners into doing their dirty work for them," Cookie commented.

"See here," Eagle burst out. "Just why is it you fellows seem to go into a seance at irregular intervals and then make incomprehensible remarks, I have been unable to fathom. I asked if you expected me, a career officer of the Navy, to stand by and do nothing, and after looking vacantly into space for five minutes you make the absurd statement that 'both are attempting to trick us into laboring on their behalf!' If we don't join forces to destroy the monsters at once, it will be too late! I bid you good day, gentlemen!" With that, Eagle climbed into the cockpit of his scout-car and gunned away toward his grounded warships. Cookie made a move toward the armored car as if to follow, but Judson stopped him.

"He won't attack until we've drawn off Pete and his boys, as well as the Geepers, as he demanded," Judson reminded the space'n.

"Got no intention of drawing nobody off," Cookie snorted. "Old Eagle don't give the orders here!"

"Quite right," Judson agreed. "So I suggest we give some thought to precisely what constructive actions we *might* take, under the circumstances."

"That's easy," Cookie came back promptly. "We need to get a handle on these Geepers like the big fellas said, and let 'em work for us. Pete's fleet could use some Category One maintenance, for example."

"And how, may I ask, do you plan to establish that relationship? What have we to offer in return?"

"Breeding space, just like they wanted," Cookie supplied at once. "We'll let 'em know if they start any breeding activities without our say-so, they'll be sorry they ever came here."

"That might work," Judson conceded. "Meanwhile, what about the Supremos?"

"*They* ain't fixing to breed, I hope," Cookie replied.

"Let's go have a chat with the Geepers," Judson said. and started in their direction. Cookie fell in beside him.

"Don't forget!" the admiral called behind them. "You

need me! The rotted hulls of the CDF are negligible! I have the only effective fighting force on the planet, since you seem reluctant to employ your own artillery in self-defense!"

"We won't be needing you, Admiral, sir," Cookie called back. "No war, no Navy, OK?"

"Nonsense!" was Eagle's final word.

"How are we going to handle this, Cap?" the chef inquired interestedly of Judson.

"We'll talk to them, via Baggy, if need be," Judson replied. "But they seem to be expert telepaths. Let's say 'hello.' " He matched action to words by fixing his attention on the nearer of the giant alien creatures and concentrating on the idea of a benign meeting of mutually supportive beings.

How can we be of help? he asked, accompanying the query with a sense of an urgent desire to assist in the attainment of Supremo destiny, so long as that did not involve hostility to small, two-legged creatures.

Rid me of these nits! was the prompt reply. Once again, the hundred-ton beast flopped ponderously on its side and rolled, sending the last of the Geepers which had been probing its hide-fissures fleeing to join the main body, now formed up in an almost-complete circle, which broke and scattered as the huge Supremo rolled once again in their direction.

Help! came the small Geeper-voices, not quite in unison. *Earn the eternal gratitude of Geeperdom!* they entreated. *Kill His Magnificence! You see how it persecutes us! Look at our dead, lying crushed in his wake!*

"They've got a point, Cap," Cookie commented. "No doubt about Big Boy killing Geepers."

As the two humans neared the outflung line of spiderish Geepers, one darted in close, causing Cookie to shy and kick out. The sheep-sized Geeper reached out and touched his ankle.

"Ow!" Cookie yelped and grabbed the ankle. As he hopped on one leg, Judson shooed the Geeper away and came over to steady the steadily cursing Cookie.

"Let me take a look," Judson suggested.

"I ain't hurt," Cookie gasped. "But it itches something awful! I better sit down here a minute and scratch it."

"Better not," Judson counseled. "I'll use my Synapt on it." He rummaged in the kit at his belt, a standard-issue medical pack, and brought out a bright red cylinder, which he aimed at the purple welt across the cook's ankle.

"Ahh!" Cookie sighed. "That's the real stuff, Cap. I take back some o' them mean things I said about AutoSpace; making the kit mandatory was a smart move!" The flush faded quickly from the contact site, and Cookie pulled up his sock and got to his feet. "We better watch those damn spiders closer, Cap. If they ever came over us in a wave . . ." He let it go at that, then burst out, "Geeze, Cap, what a sensation that was! Like worms eating at me, mixed with fire! Get back there!" he barked at the eight-limbed creature which had stung him and still hovered near at hand.

"That's all you get, Sneaky!" he told the persistent arachnoid. "I'm on to you now."

You see, strangers, the big voice came in strongly. *The nits are not to be borne.*

We will restrain ourselves, alien entities, the Geeper voice rang in. *It was a foolish and counter-productive impulse which drove us to sample your essences. Give us your assistance and we will hold you forever inviolable.*

"Some deal," Cookie scoffed. "We help these damn things and maybe they won't try to eat us. I say, let's trash 'em!"

"Easy, space'n," Judson soothed. "I know it itches in spite of the Synapt, but the matter requires careful thought."

"Looks like Pete don't think so," Cookie grumped. "Him and his boys are saddling up, seems like; they musta bit *him*, too."

With dispatch, the leaders of the CDF manned their crude vehicles, and those of Eagle and Chadwick, as well as Judson and Cookie's own well-worn car. They formed up expeditiously as a column of twos and advanced directly toward the landing site of the newcomers.

"Better flag 'em down, eh, Cap?" Cookie suggested, but Judson shook his head.

The Geepers, still in their broken ring-formation, moved back, modifying their position to include the grounded vessels and the gigantic Supremos within their now almost complete circle. The two behemoths moved closer together and waited, immobile, for the arrival of the assault column. Some of the arachnoids, not included in the ring, scuttled up the ramp and into the nearer of the two side-by-side vessels.

"Uh-oh," Cookie remarked. "Looks like they're manning their defenses."

"That would be a mistake," Judson replied. "If they fire the first shot, that is."

"Couldn't hardly blame 'em if they did," the chef replied. "Pete's boys look like they mean business, coming on like that. Got the for'ad battery run out on the war-car, too."

"He won't fire it first," Judson told him. "Not if he's half the tactician I know he is."

"What's he pose to do?" Cookie queried. "Drive right into the enemy's guns and get blasted halfway to Seaside?"

"He'll wait to see," Judson replied. "Watch! I think—"

Just then a cloud of dust and gravel exploded from beneath the stern of the featureless vessel which had been boarded by the Geepers; its stern was suddenly enveloped in a curious bluish glow which extended probing pseudopods forward, following a faint pattern of yellowish corrosion-lines on the space-burned hull-plates, until the entire vessel was enveloped in it. It shuddered, then lifted abruptly, to hover fifty feet above the once-verdant wheat field. Below, the two Supremos turned and moved ponderously away, and the remaining Geepers scuttled for shelter in the lee of the other grounded ship.

Troon's voice spoke up: *Stop them! The ungrateful mites think to maroon us here on this inhospitable world! Fire upon them, strange entities, cripple them—quickly, ere they—*

With a dull *boom!* the immense vessel shot straight upward, leaving a column of dust behind it, like a cyclone in reverse. Pete's car, almost at the Geeper circle, swerved aside at the same moment that their formation broke and they rushed to enclose the Supremos in a new circle. Pete curved back, and Judson and Cookie watched as he came to a halt beside the scaly bulk of the Supremos, elevated his infinite repeaters, and fired a salvo at the rapidly ascending stern-tubes of the departing vessel, which was at once enveloped in yellowish-white fumes. Lightning danced along the yellow pattern of the huge hull and the ship abruptly lost momentum, lurched sideways and fell heavily from an altitude of two hundred yards to impact with a long-drawn *smash!*, which shook the ground underfoot.

Excellent! the Supremo-voice exalted. *Now, kindly stand by while—*

"Geeze, Cap," Cookie muttered. "Ole Pete clobbered 'em good—prolly *too* good."

"He did what was necessary!" Admiral Eagle barked. "Since he was acting in the capacity of Naval auxilliary, I daresay a Navy Cross is in the offing for his Majesty—and for a number of his subordinates as well. Pity . . ." He turned to give Judson a cold look. "That *you* failed to avail yourself of the opportunity to serve Terra."

"They might get a chance yet," Chadwick contributed. "Look, sir!" He waved a hand toward the fallen ship near which the surviving Geepers were once again forming up their line. "They're going to charge!" the lieutenant yelped. "Hadn't we better do something, sir?"

"Keep cool, boy," the admiral urged. "You have your sidearm: we'll take as many with us as possible." He glanced at Judson. "I see you've your weapon, mister; the time has come to make use of it." He took aim and fired at the advancing wave of arachnoids, sending up a gout of soil well in front of them, which they ignored. Behind the assault wave, the torpid Supremos were maneuvering ponderously.

"They're going to re-board!" Cookie exclaimed.

Indeed, the big voice chimed in. *We shall seize upon this opportunity to maroon the pests here where they shall surely fail to survive, unassisted.*

Help! came the small voice the humans had come to associate with the Geepers. *Detail, halt! This is unendurable!* the Geeper went on, and the advancing shock troops came to a standstill and broke up into agitated conversational groups.

Baggy's distinctive voice spoke up urgently: *Am I correct, Judson entity, in assuming you have no objection to our tapping the vital energies of the hostile Geepers?*

"Go to it, Bag!" Cookie exhorted. "Drain 'em dry!"

"Not quite dry," Judson corrected. "Leave them with sufficient vigor to carry out repairs on Pete's fleet."

I shall direct them to their new duties at once, Baggy confirmed. *But what of the Supremos? I feel sure they will expect the same Geepers to repair their own damaged vessel.*

"That'll just have to wait," Cookie stated flatly. By now the multi-limbed aliens had re-formed in a tight box formation and were moving off briskly toward the grounded units of the CDF, and Pete's column of vehicles had turned and were returning to the small group of observers.

"Looks like Spivey's Salvage yard in the Belt," Cookie commented. "Cap, you reckon them critters can really rehab them junkers?"

"I think so," Judson reassured him. "Let's go watch."

All present climbed into one or another of the vehicles once again present and fell into line astern of Judson and Cookie's aged car. By the time they reached the corroded bulk of Mean Ernie's *Objectionable IV*, the arachnoids had already disappeared inside. Moments later the hatches cycled open and a variety of objects came raining down, some bouncing off the roofs of the closely-clustered vehicles.

"That was a blim-blam rig!" Cookie blurted in a tone of astonishment, as a complicated machine smashed in front of him. "Musta been stole from Reno's Dive, which Reno'd skin the feller taken it, alive! Besides, it's a forty-year stretch on Io just fer possession!"

"That's good stuff them spiders is throwing around," Ernie mourned, as an "Imperial"-sized dream-box smashed on the ground a few feet away. Next came a shower of overaged ration-boxes, which burst on impact, spraying vile, well-rotted Class Two substances across the greensward.

"Ole Navy wastes a lot of stuff!" Ernie told the others. "Got them rations outta Salvage at Lunar Two, cook 'em up right and they'll tide a feller over, good!"

The next layer of ejected debris seemed to consist of laundry items, on which curious forms of lichenous growths had become established. A wide variety of trash, rubbish, garbage, dirt, and discarded packing materials followed.

"Musta stunk some in there," Cookie commented. "Guess the Geepers hadda plug up a little to get at the job."

"Had some nice yard goods and all in there someplace," Ernie mourned. "Meant to get them gals at Mother Trixie's in the Belt to run us up some new uniforms some day. Too late now," he concluded as bolts of vivid purple-and-chartreuse-checked fabrics fell into the soupy mess created by the combination of fluid ejecta and local soil.

Abruptly, a belch of dusky flame boiled from the port quarter trim jet orifices, then settled down to a steady blast of pale-green flames, accompanied by a stuttering roar.

"Them stern tubes been outta commission ever since old Bob fell in the mixing chamber, time he was cleaning lead and got drunk onna job," Ernie remembered. "Guess them spiders musta cleant old Bob's remains outa the filters. That's good, set her down smoother now."

Similar signs of activity were evident in and around the other units of the CDF contingent. Cap Josh muttered when his *Outrageous* burped and jumped ten feet above grade, to settle back off-balance. "Hey!" he yelled, making an abortive lunge toward his command. "She'll fall! Right on Objuk's vessel, looks like! Stop 'em!"

Sarnt Grundy's straight left jab to the jaw quieted the noisy fellow, and all hands watched impotently as the patch-scabbed converted ore-carrier toppled, impacting, as Cap Josh had predicted, squarely against Objuk's equally war-weary hull, christened *Spaceside II*, which collapsed, shedding insecurely attached parts as it fell. The Geepers surrounded the hulks.

"Just as well she's off-line now, Josh," Umbubu commiserated. "She'da never held together for a launch anyways."

Abdul casually blocked Josh's axe-hand directed at his dusky comrade. "—Don't go throwing off on *Spacey*!" Objuk was yelling. "She's got me through many a scrape, and she'll get me through this one! 'Can't launch,' eh, you flea-bitten savage!" He subsided reluctantly, as the Chief, looking embarrassed, mumbled his apologies. Meanwhile, the Geepers were swarming over the two battered vessels, occasionally huddling in little groups as if to confer, then darting off to gather again at the sites of major damage.

"Looky them!" Objuk blurted. "Look at that hull-plate! That's two-inch hardalloy, and bent double! They straightened it out! Maintenance Central at Clister couldn't do that! Crystallizes, see, and it'll shatter before it'll rebend! I seen all about that in a tape they made me look at, time I was in Max Security on Luna! Holy elephants! Look at that bunch by the broke landing-jack: they're putting that transmitter back together: had it wired together pretty good, but old Josh's tub busted—" He broke off to duck under a haymaker, and subsided, muttering.

The visible Geepers were busily extricating tangles of wire and tubing from the crumpled carcasses and laying them out straight before winding the intact strands on improvised spools. Bent metal was hauled clear and flattened, then stockpiled. The removal of shredded coilings revealed the ridged, bronze-black bulk of the main coil, ruptured in many places.

"Tough luck, Jukky," Sam Spewack remarked. "Once yer coil loses integrity, that's it."

"Like hell, you damn dirt-digger!" the commissar objected. "Just fix up them holes in the case, and—"

"—And once you've lost gauss, all the Pee Aitches of Dee at the Tempe think-tank couldn't get her running again!" Tang contributed. "Too bad, Jukky, with no command o' yer own no more, looks like you lose yer spot on the CDF High Command, so you better beat it now, before somebody notices a outsider listening in on our deliberations and like that."

"Oh, yeah?" the commissar retorted, "and who's gonna throw me out? Besides, old *Spaceside*'s gonna fly again!" With a wave he indicated the small, busy Geepers swarming over the broken hull, shifting shattered plates like ants moving leaves a hundred times their length.

"By gar," Terrible Tom Prouty spoke up, "looks like he might be right, Sam; looky there! Stitched up that thirty-foot gash neat as a gal tatting a doily! Now how they gonna get the main oleo tank back inside? Shoulda done that first."

"Calling me a liar, hey Tommy?" Spewack inquired lazily and dealt the ex-wrestler a terrible blow on the side of his bullet-head, which Tom shook, as if dispersing gnats. An annoyed expression formed on his blunt features.

"I got to teach ya yer manners all over again, Sammy?" He inquired wearily, and lashed out with a surprisingly long and limber leg to impact under the miner's ribs. Sam *oof*!ed and sat down.

"Now, you fellows," Eagle pled, "don't start clowning again, just when we're about to make some progress in pacifying these animals!"

Heavy Charlie put his hand over the admiral's face and pushed: Eagle staggered, but grabbed the muscular limb with both hands and with a deft motion, locked the elbow over his forearm and bent it backwards until Two Spears went to his knees with a howl.

"Hey, let's not have no more horsing around!" Boss Nandy grunted, just as he was felled by a haymaker aimed at Eagle from behind by Tang. Heavy Charlie expressed his resentment of this unilateral action by kicking the Mongol in the ribs, at which Chief Umbubu back-handed Two Spears across the face. Spitting tooth fragments, Charlie turned on Mean Ernie, who happened to be standing closest, and struck the smaller man a pile-driver blow on the top of the head, which left him face-to-face with Commissar Objuk, still muttering about "savages" and hull-plates. Ernie grabbed the politician's prominent nose and twisted, motivating Objuk to deliver a stunning sword-hand to the left clavicle, which broke with an audible *snap*!

"All right, that's enough, boys!" Pete yelled. "Way them vessels is coming back together, better'n new, we got to get ready to lift; still got the damn monsters to deal with, not to say nothing about the admiral, here!" He waded in, ejecting combatants left and right, until he was confronted by Sally, still on her feet and fighting mad.

"Don't you go messing with *me*, Pete!" she shouted in his face. "Got a score to settle with that Sam Spewack! Done tore my second-best frock here—" she indicated a rent in her blurb-hide garment which exposed an expanse of neatly-curved thigh. "Some o' the boys been aspace too long, I guess. Too bad! Step aside, Pete!"

Noticing that the princess was subtly shifting her stance in preparation for an emasculating shin-axe, Judson interceded, blocking the kick with his left hand, while catching her fist with his right.

"Let him go, this one time, ma'am," he suggested. "Old Pete knows all about tricky footwork, and his reflexes are tuned fine; your face wouldn't be so pretty after his fist landed on it." He thrust the only mildly-protesting girl back and deflected Pete's hammer-hand with his shoulder. Pete looked sulky, but accepted the *fait accompli*.

"Been wantin' a chance to teach that gal some manners," he muttered to an unseen judge.

Eagle was at Judson's side, speaking urgently: "—no hope of instilling any discipline in these Yahoos," he was insisting. "With your artillery and my command, we can eliminate the monsters and deal with the Geepers, too, before they've succeeded in putting these ruffians back in the space-piracy business! It is clearly expedient, as well as your clear duty to join forces with me now!"

"What about the big surrender and annexation, sir?" Cookie asked artlessly. "Good old Eustace or whatever got his papers all fixed up now." All eyes went to the admiral's gig, from which Chadwick was descending hesitantly, his eyes on the riot still in progress.

"Here, you fellows!" he spoke up. "You just *stop* that, right now! My uncle—"

The noise was cut off as if by a knife; the battling CDFers turned as one man to stare at the young officer; then a hoarse guffaw broke the spell. A few moments of knee-slapping and howling ensued, as hangnailed forefingers pointed to the lieutenant.

"His friggin *uncle*!" Spewack sobbed.

" 'Stop that,' he says! This kid is too good to be true!"

"That's enough of your damned insolence!" Chadwick's voice cut through the hubbub. "I am, by God, a commissioned officer of the Terran Navy, and I will tolerate no more of your infernal impudence! You! The tall Chinaman with the sheepskin vest! Stop that at once and come over here!" Tang, astonished at the show of firmness, abandoned his effort to remove a steel bracelet from the unconscious Mean Ernie's arm, and shuffled over to Chadwick; as soon as he was in kicking range, his limber left leg lashed out at the officer's middriff. Chadwick seemingly casually grasped the proffered ankle and gave the unshod foot a one hundred and eighty degree twist, dumping Tang on his rear. Before the astonished Oriental could muster a yell of indignation, Sarnt Grundy threw a straight left from which Chadwick leaned aside. Chadwick felled the noncom with a right hook which connected with Grundy's lantern jaw with a meaty *smack*! Chadwick turned to Admiral Eagle and came to the position of attention.

"Sorry about that, sir," he apologized. "Conduct unbecoming an officer, I know, but—"

"Quite all right, my boy," Eagle returned smoothly. "That right hand of yours is coming along. Look out for Abdul; he's creeping up—"

"I know, sir," Chadwick said, as he bent his right knee and snapped his left leg out behind him, catching the Mad Ayrab in the face, at which the latter's motivation abruptly deserted him.

"Hey, Sarnt!" he yelled, dripping blood from his head. "I got a idear: this here Chadwick's trickier'n he looks, so—"

"Way ahead of you, Ayrab!" Grundy cut in. He sought Pete's eye and called, "Say, Pete, what about this kid? He ain't—" His speech was cut short as the lieutenant knocked him down with a backhanded swipe.

"The next dirty animal who calls me 'kid,' " he said distinctly, "will suffer limb fractures. You first, Objuk?" he inquired as the squat functionary raised a hamlike fist to strike Chief Umbubu from behind. Objuk hesitated, unfolded the fist and put it away. "Who, me, Lieutenant?" he inquired in a tone of wounded innocence. "I was just—"

Chadwick hit him squarely in the mouth, breaking his rot-speckled front teeth.

"No lying!" Chadwick decreed. "And *no* more violence!" After knocking Objuk down, he found himself face to face with Heavy Charlie Two Spears, who attempted a casual grin which unfortunately looked like a grimace of ferocity. Chadwick grabbed the Amerind's dirt-stiff deerskin vest and drew him aside.

"This is hardly the time to make a tactical error, Charlie," he advised the seven-footer. "You can see that the balance of intimidation has shifted. I've brushed aside the bluster and bluff of these truculent fellows, and legitimate authority once more rests with the duly appointed officials." Charlie nodded, modifying his scowl to a sickly smile.

"Hey, Cap," Cookie spoke up. "Looks like maybe we had Chadwick wrong, here."

"Nonsense, Space'n," Judson dismissed his comment. "You're as aware as I that the course at the Academy includes techniques for deluding and neutralizing undisciplined forces. That was by the book, from the time he first poked his head out in the slime-rain."

"Guess so," Cookie subsided, as Chadwick moved among the CDF honchos, lining them up in ragged ranks. He turned abruptly to intercept Mean Ernie in the act of mimicking him. "Fall in, Ernie," he commanded. "You can save the show-biz for the Victory Ball, where I shall afford you the opportunity to perform on a stage, under a spotlight."

Ernie shook his head so violently that his genetically deficient features seemed to blur.

"Not me, uh, sir!" he blurted. "I'm a funny guy when nobody ain't looking, but I get this stage-fright something awful!"

"Well, we'll soon clear that up, won't we, Ernie?" Chadwick reassured the little man genially. "Two hours of stand-up, and you'll be an old trouper, I daresay."

Pete thrust himself before the abashed Ernie. "Leave the little feller be," he commanded Chadwick, who looked him up and down, and ducked deftly under a haymaker abruptly thrown by the king, countering with a grab for the other arm, which he held in a firm grip, while Pete shifted his stance, and suddenly threw himself backwards, pulling the lieutenant with him. Somehow, Chadwick's elbow impacted with Pete's throat as he fell. Pete rolled away, making ugly hawking sounds. Chadwick got to his feet, hauled the choking man upright, and took his neck in both hands.

"Have to get that cartilage reset," he muttered. "Sorry about that, Pete; you took me by surprise and I didn't have time to abort the reflex. Now, easy, just a little pressure here—try to relax. Yes, I know it feels like I'm choking you, but—"

Judson stepped in, gave Pete a sharp slap on the larynx and said, "Inhale!"

Pete did so, and stumbled away, holding his throat in both hands.

"Accident," Chadwick muttered.

"Sure it was, Lieutenant," Judson agreed, "just like you accidentally tripped Sally here before she could get that wire in between your ribs. Shame on you, Princess," he added, helping the girl up. "That would have been a serious mistake," he told her, and kicked her six-inch wire-sticker away. "No weapons in a friendly fracas, you know that," he admonished her.

"Shh!" she hissed urgently. "Don't let the fellows know. I'm ashamed, don't know what got into me. I was just—"

"Forget it," Judson soothed.

"I say, chaps," Umbubu spoke up from the sidelines where he had been examining his contusions, "would it be letting the side down if I went over and checked out *Macernuzahn*? It appears the little fellows are all done. Looks rather splendid doesn't she, with her black porcelain visible again, and the eka-bronze inlays all polished. I hope she's as ship-shape under the hatches."

"Go ahead, Booby," Pete grunted. "Matter o' fact, all you fellows oughta check out yer commands, see them spiders done a good job."

All present agreed readily, and as the veterans of the CDF began to struggle toward their respective vessels, Sarnt Grundy spoke up:

"All right, let's look good here, boys! You can fall in in a column o' ducks; you first, Boss, seein' yer tub is closest." He hurried up alongside the strung-out group and dealt the Ayrab a tremendous buffet on the side of the head. "Get in line there, you!" he yelled, and grabbed Mean Ernie, who ducked aside, but duly fell in line behind Cap Josh, who hastily aligned himself with the man ahead of him, who happened to be Commissar Objuk, six feet off-side. Grundy forcibly realigned his flock. "Now we got spit-and-polish vessels here," he announced. "We're gonna have a little military shape to us. Straighten up there, Chief! You, too, the rest of you or Cap Josh's line-squalls are gonna come up sudden!"

"One moment, Sergeant," Chadwick spoke up. "While your intentions are commendable, I must point out that your methods, including as they do, the use of physical assault, are not in accordance with established military procedure!"

"Eh, what's that, boy?" Grundy barked, miming incomprehension.

"I said 'no more use of assault, battery, and mayhem as instruments of discipline,' " the lieutenant translated.

"Still didn't get you, kid," Grundy snapped, and dealt Mean Ernie an open-handed slap on the back of his wet-dog hair-style. "*Git* in line there, Ernie, 'fore I hafta—" He broke off as Chadwick kicked him in the patched seat of his baggy ex-Coast Guard issue breeches.

" 'No violence,' I said," the lieutenant explained. "Like this."

He followed up the kick with a side-of-the-hand blow to Grundy's shoulder which set the non-com's arm to twitching violently. He halted and was shoved into ranks by Pete who remarked approvingly to those nearest him in the still ragged file:

"Seems like we got us a new honcho, boys. How about it? Old Lieutenant here got a better grasp of the realities than we figgered. Foxy, like the admiral. I say we elect him the See of Oh of this outfit! Any opposed? No! Motion carried. All right with you, sir?" he addressed the query to Full Lieutenant Harlow Chadwick, TN.

"It's rather irregular," the latter replied, "but inasmuch as you fellows *are* an auxilliary unit of the Navy, I suppose I could accept." He looked to the admiral for approval.

"Excellent choice, my boy," Eagle boomed. "I'm sure you'll whip these uncouth levies into shape in short order—"

"Don't ever call me 'my boy' again, sir!" Chadwick snapped. "Or refer to my command as 'uncouth,' either. Here, Pete!" he interrupted himself. "As my ADC, you may escort the captains to their respective vessels and see that all is made ready for lift-off within the quarter-hour."

"Good idea, Lootenant," Pete acknowledged. "Say, sir, OK if we skip the saluting the quarterdeck and the bosun's pipes and that? The boys are ready for action: don't want to remind 'em being in the Navy means more paperwork than combat."

"So ordered," Chadwick agreed. He turned again to the admiral. "Now what, sir? I remain, of course, at your command."

"Damn right, Harlow," Eagle confirmed. He was looking across toward his own neatly aligned ships, ranked along the highway beyond the formerly tilled land. "I wonder if these Geepers could—?"

Nothing easier, Eagle entity, the now familiar Geeper voices replied in ragged unison. *We do so love to be constructively occupied. May we get at it at once?*

"By all means," Eagle declared. He turned to Judson. "I'm still not quite accustomed to the idea of more-or-less intelligent alien life-forms here on 'Eden,' I believe you call it—to say nothing of ones whose only desire is to be helpful—and so efficient, too!" By now the group was under the looming stern of Boss Nandy's once-condemned passage liner, renamed *Patronage II*.

Cookie looked at his disturbed reflection in the gleaming hull-plates abaft the steering jets, and grinned, then laughed at the effect.

"Just like the fun-house over Off Limits by Clister Base, Cap!" he chortled, "only better! Look at old Admiral in there! Looks like a bow-legged midget with acromegaly! You look a little funny, too, Cap! And old Umbubu!" Cookie was slapping his thigh and howling, as the rugged troops of the CDF halted and gathered around to look at themselves, each jeering at the others.

"Harlow!" Eagle spoke up sharply. "You'd best restore order before someone takes offense and the riot resumes."

"My idea precisely, sir," Chadwick concurred. "Here, Pete! Stop that at once and fall the men in!"

7

An hour later, with all hands aboardship, and reporting "launch-ready," Sam Spewack, whom Judson and Cookie had accompanied aboard his sparkling new *Greasybread*, looked uncertainly around at the unfamiliar vista of polished surfaces and neatly ordered equipment.

"Fella can't hardly spit on a deck looks like that," Sam complained. "Don't feel comfortable aboard no more. Not homey-like," he amplified. "Don't hardly even wanta step on it," he added, sticking to the catwalk rather than descending to the polished deck.

"Your sensitivity does you credit, Sam," Judson commended the burly fellow. "But don't be concerned. In a few days you and your crew will have her back in her accustomed state of chaotic filth; she'll just function better than before."

"That part's OK," Sam conceded. "Never *did* like doing a blind Approach and Stacks without no numbers. But now she's in top shape, I wanna see what she'll do. You, Bully!" He barked at a freshly-shaven and combed lout awkward in clean and starched khakis, "Secure for lift-off, and let Buck and them know we do it by the book!"

"What book was that, Sam?" Bull wanted to know. "Ain't hardly never saw a book aboard old *Greasy* here."

"I'm talking the *Regulation for the Management of Fleet Vessels in Active Service*; AFM 222-5, you know."

"Don't know nothing about no Fleet Regs," Bull muttered, the last coherent words he was to utter until his jaw knitted.

The men watched on the close-scan screens as the other skippers entered their now-spotless vessels. Only a few Geepers remained nearby.

"Looky there!" Cookie exclaimed as the multi-limbed creatures closed in around Objuk, left behind as he struggled with a wounded knee to climb his gangway.

"They're cutting old Commissar Objuk off," the chef went on. "Ganging up on a disabled man—and waited till they thought he was alone, too, the sneaky rascals!" He lunged for the exit hatch, was pushed aside by Bull, and waited until Judson and Spewack had preceded him, to jump down, ignoring the ramp. "Damn!" he yelped. "Cap, done gone and spraint my ankle here!" He got up awkwardly in time to fall at Judson's feet as the latter stepped down on the turf. Cookie started off on all fours, but Judson heaved him upright, and between the Captain and Sam, he was able to hobble. As they approached the clustered Geepers now completely obscuring Objuk's prone figure, Judson holstered his weapon and said, "Hold your fire!"

"What for?" Spewack wanted to know.

Just then, Objuk got to his feet, thrusting aside the last few Geepers clinging to his wounded leg.

"Feels good!" he declared vehemently. "Don't know what the little fellers done, but they fixed my knee up good, when old Boobie done busted it." He pranced, stamping the formerly broken leg hard to emphasize its soundness.

"Thought I'd never walk good again, boys," he exulted. "Better'n ever! We got to thank them here Geepers some way!"

If you will permit us to serve you in our humble fashion—the Geeper voice began, to be cut off by

Objuk's yell, "Ain't nothing humble about giving me my laig back!" He noticed Cookie's pronounced limp.

"Here, feller, let 'em fix you up, too!" he urged, then, to the last of the departing arachnoids, "Help out old Space'n Murphy here, willya, before you go."

The spaniel-sized creatures paused, turned back and silently asked Cookie's permission.

"Sure, go ahead," he urged, lifting the aching limb as if to offer it. The nearest Geeper extended a leg and gently ran the tip over the damaged joint. Instantly, two others made contact with the first therapist, and a blissful smile spread over Cookie's face.

"Feels awful good," he stated contentedly. "Stopped hurting already—and feels like all the purty gals in town was loving me up at once. Prolly shouldn't be doing this," he advised himself. "Too much fun." He kicked out with the healed foot, shaking off the last persistent therapist.

"Git off there, now," he said, but his tone was indulgent. "Cap," he added, "I guess I know which side we're on, now. Say!" he went on, "Looky here, Cap!" He held out his left hand. "Remember that R-burn I had, wouldn't heal up? It's gone! Little fellows fixed that, too!"

Beware, strange entities! the big Supremo voice boomed out silently. *Lest the insidious mites form their Circle of Power and enslave you as they did my ancestor!*

"Cap," Cookie spoke up first. "What do you suppose that's all about? 'Enslave,' he said. Looks like now the Geepers are in charge."

"I've noted several times they've tried to form up a circle," Judson answered. "But somehow they were interrupted each time. Right now it looks like they've almost got it." He pointed to the seemingly patternless straggle of the creatures strung out at the base of the second vessel in line.

"They're tryna ring in *Greasy*," Spewack yelled. "Come on," he said, "let's investigate before they close the circle."

Buck and Bull followed Objuk as he trailed Judson

and Cookie to *Greasybread*'s off-ramp. The Geepers were now more neatly aligned, the tentacular limbs of each extended to touch those of his neighbors.

"Shoo!" Cookie barked, rushing at the nearest of the creatures. "Git back there!"

"Easy," the commissar objected. "These are my friends! You fellers don't know how bad that laig smarted fore they fixed it." He advanced toward a gap in the line of Geepers.

"Stop!" Judson barked. "Don't let them—"

Already the Geepers adjacent to the gap had reached out to grasp Objuk's wrists. He hesitated momentarily, then swung into alignment with the arachnoids.

Too late! the big voice rang out. *I warned you, entities! Now your associate is lost!*

"No, he's not lost, Dum-dum," Cookie contradicted. "He's right here, only he's holding hands with his pals the Geepers."

"Pals" indeed! the Supremo snorted. *In a moment you'll perceive the effect of the folly you've committed!*

"Oh, Commissar," Judson called. "Come over here, will you? We have to talk."

Objuk was gazing blankly up at the towering spaceship looming over them all. He ignored Judson's invitation, merely shuffled his boots as if to establish firmer contact with the ground underfoot.

"Objuk!" Cookie spoke up. "Cap'n's talking to you!" Still there was no response. Then Objuk, hauling his flankers along with him and creating a bulge in the now-completed circle, stepped over to the base of the nearest landing-jack and scanned its surface; then he reached up and touched the forward pitted surface and a foot-square rectangle hinged outward.

"Cap!" Cookie addressed Judson. "What—?"

"Stop him, Space'n," Judson rapped. "That's—"

Cookie went to Objuk and caught his burly arm, jerked him away from the access panel he had opened.

"Stay away from that, Mr. Commissar," the smaller man commanded. "What do you think you're doing? That's the remote test panel. You could—" He broke off as Objuk lunged against his restraint and thrust his hand inside the opening. At once, smoke belched from the adjacent steering tube.

"He's gone crazy!" Cookie wailed as all present leapt back an instant before a pale jet of flame licked from the tube. Even the Geepers seemed startled, scrambling back, and struggling to reform their circle, broken by Objuk's defection.

Cookie was struggling in vain to haul the dozerlike commissar away from the panel. "Cap!" he gasped out. "Seems like—"

Judson brushed aside the Geepers who had quickly readvanced to grab for contact with Objuk.

"Don't let 'em," Cookie managed, bracing his feet against Objuk's efforts. He managed to kick away a Geeper which had touched Objuk's ankle with a slender tentacle. He stamped on the latter, and Objuk broke free, only to be seized at once by two other arachnoids.

Do not allow them to reform their Circle! the Supremo barked. *You, Judson entity, do not link with the Cookie entity!*

"Thanks," Judson muttered. "I figured that out." Even as he spoke, Cookie, with a lunge, gained two feet, and reaching, grabbed Judson's arm. "Almost—" he stated.

"Let go, Space'n!" Judson commanded.

"Can't, Cap!" Cookie moaned. "It's like all in the world I want is to link up to form the ring of glory, and—"

Judson braced himself, doubled his fist, and struck his friend with a straight right jab to the jaw. Cookie's legs folded and he lay at Judson's feet, face down. "Sorry, Space'n," Judson said and yanked Objuk away from the panel. With a flick of his hand, he activated the RESET switch and slammed the panel cover shut. He tramped hard on the Geeper limbs still grasping Objuk's ankles, and hauled the semi-conscious man clear. Cookie sat up, shaking his head and looking around, bewildered.

"Almost had it, Cap!" he said in a strained voice.

"One more minimum time-unit and it would have been glorious victory once again to the Great People!"
"Take a deep breath, Space'n," Judson directed. "The Geepers had you in their Circle for a moment, and you have to shake it off. Help Objuk; he got a stronger dose."
"Sure, Cap," Cookie agreed eagerly. "Don't know what got into me, all that stuff about the Great People and all; felt kinda funny." He got uncertainly to his feet.
Well done! the big voice rang out. *Now you must destroy these vile treachers ere they destroy you, or, worse, entoil you as they have the Mighty Ones of Phoon.*
"How about it, Cap?" Cookie queried. "No doubt about them taking over a feller's brains. Felt awful!"
"No way, Space'n!" Objuk interposed, his hand on the butt of a well-worn issue crater-gun. "You leave them little fellers be!"
"No need for that, Commissar," Judson commented, and snatched the weapon from its owner's grip with a deft grab. Objuk yelled and lunged, meeting an uppercut which flipped him on his back.
Thus the mites subvert their victims, the Supremo observed. *Kill them all!*
You do well, strange entities, the Geeper voice rang in, *to ignore the exhortations of the malignant Troon. Were we not present to restrain their fury, the obscene monsters would already have devastated this continent and wiped out your kind! Now it will be necessary for you to destroy them utterly, before they can wreak their mischief on you all!*
"Nice folks," Cookie remarked. "Both kinds expect us to do their dirty work for them. Wonder why they don't do it theirselves?"
"Because they can't," Judson supplied. "The Supremos have been careful not to supply the Geepers with weapons, and the Geepers have covered themselves, too. They're forced to cooperate for mutual advantage."
"Sounds nutty to me," Cookie commented. "They

came here cooped up in the same hulls but they hate each other. That's why they lied to us about the big breeding spree."

That was no lie, but the very intent of the evil-doers! the Geeper and Supremo voices yelled almost in unison.

Eagle's armored vehicle was approaching. It halted.

"Here, you fellows," Admiral Eagle yelled from the open hatch. "That's enough conversation. I say *both* factions pose a threat to Terran interests and should be dealt with accordingly!"

"And how's that?" Cookie demanded. "How do you figure to 'deal' with them, I mean?"

"Watch me!" Eagle suggested. "Come along Chadwick," he barked and gunned away toward his ranked squadron, grounded neatly half a mile outside the city wall.

"What's *he* gonna do?" Objuk grunted. "If he plans on jumping my pals the Geepers, I'm gonna hafta stop him!" He dug a command talker out of the worn kit-bag slung at his hip and spoke urgently into it:

"Pete! All you boys! We got to stop old Eagle! Lift yer commands and rendezvous right here, soonest!"

All along the ragged rank of newly-polished vessels, activity was apparent as short-handed captains used remote panels to jump-start coil warm-ups.

"Hold it there!" Cookie yelled, and felled Objuk with a snappy back-of-the-knee snap. He grabbed the talker.

"As you were, Pete!" he yelled. "We don't want to start up the war again! Just rest easy until Cap and me figger out what way to jump here!"

Since you are unable to restrain the lawless element among you, Troon cut in coldly, *we must reluctantly take action.*

All eyes went to the immense creatures sprawled, torpid, beside their huge vessels. To the astonishment of the onlookers, the nearer of the two abruptly reared up, supported by the huge, muscular tail and the short but mightily-muscled hind limbs; it paused momentarily while its fellow did the same; then, incredibly, it sprang upward in a mighty leap and came crashing down on the first three Navy vessels, smashing ther flat. Without pause, it lunged and fell on two more The remaining Fleet unit's automatic circuitry lifte them barely in time as the next lunge covered the are where they had been parked. Eagle's car swerved an ran up alongside the behemoth. The fore turret ha swiveled to bear on the cliff-like flank of the vast animal

"Don't do it, Admiral!" Cookie spluttered impotently even as white fire lanced out from the car to pla ineffectually over the lumpy hide of the great beast. I humped itself back a few feet as one avoiding a nui sance, but showed no other response to the attack Eagle's car roared on, clear of the creature. A black ened spot showed against the grey-green where Eagle' light battery had impinged on it.

"Didja see that, Cap?" Cookie inquired incredulously "Old Troon took a full fire-gun blast at point-blan range! His innards oughta be blowed all over th landscape!"

I sense that your Eagle entity had some aggressiv intent, the big voice spoke up. *It is well that he took n offensive action, but only tickled me, or I should hav been forced to act; which candidly, I am reluctant t do. The energy drain is excessive, one gets quite tuckered out after only a few moments of projecting a Droon field. Perhaps I can prevail upon you to tickle me agai as your Eagle unit did just now. It felt rather good, an so therapeutic!*

Eagle's car was making a wide turn as if to make second run at the Supremo. Judson called him on th override band:

"Break it off, Admiral; new rules. The damn thing liked that last shot!" The war-car dutifully turned and came across to where the others waited.

A wise decision, Judson entity, the second big voice commented. *I shall approach; kindly restrain the violent one.*

They waited as the titanic creature came ponderously toward them.

I am Zox. I perceive that poor dear Troon erred in

destroying your artifacts, it said. *There will be no more such impetuous activity. The silly one imagined you were about—ha-ha—to attack us.*

Eagle arrived and cleared his hatch with a bound. "I guess I gave the big boob a sample of the good stuff!" he announced.

"Admiral," Judson said quietly. "Take a look."

"I've already looked," Eagle yelled. "Five units of my command smashed flat. It deserved all I gave it, and more!"

"Better listen to Cap, Admiral," Cookie spoke up. "He's tryna tell you, the big fellow soaks up that raw energy like it was gin! Loved it; wants more."

"You're insane!" Eagle yelled. " 'Wants more,' does it? Well, I'll give it more! Objuk!" He changed targets. "Why are you standing there? You fellows are an auxilliary of the Fleet now. Why haven't you deployed to avenge your comrades?"

"Well," the commissar temporized. "Seems like maybe old Troon's got us sort of at what you might say a disadvantage, like. Seem's you give it a full-discharge right in the belly-button, and it didn't hardly notice—"

Eagle stared in incomprehension, then whirled to look toward the grounded alien vessels. What he saw was his erstwhile victim lumbering steadily toward him.

"Captain Judson!" he barked. "The thing is apparently experiencing some sort of post-mortem reflexive activity. Seems to be creeping toward us!"

Silence the foolish one, Troon's voice boomed out silently. *It gives me a third-order node-itch to feel his feckless mentations! My ire is rising!*

Beware, strange entities! the small Geeper voice cut in. *You have succeeded in raising their latent aggression, a feat we Geepers never achieved. We will now withdraw out of range, and we urgently advise you to do the same. Ten miles should be sufficient, if it is not too seriously annoyed.*

Small strangers, Troon's mighty mental voice boomed out. *What is it to be? Will you tickle me again, or must I project my Droon-field?*

Eagle banged his ear with the heel of his hand "Damn!" he snorted. "There it goes again! Did you fellows notice? Every now and again I get this infernal itching sensation behind my ears, almost like someone whispering inside my head! Some kind of subtle attack by the monsters, I suppose! Look here, we can't take this supinely! We have to press home the attack! Objuk, get your vessel aloft! Captain Judson, you see to the rest of the auxilliaries, and you'd best range your artillery as well! I'm going back to administer the *coup de grace*. Ta!" With that he reentered the war-car, then popped back out. "Just a moment, there, Mr. Commissar!" Eagle barked. "Do you suppose you could put in a word with your clever friends, and have them refurbish my vessels as they did your own?"

"Sure thing, Eagle," Objuk called over his shoulder, before he disappeared inside the rattling ship. Eagle sped away to meet the advancing behemoth.

Abruptly, Judson became aware of a subsonic hum, which quickly swelled until it seemed to shake the very ground he stood on. The newly-repaired vessel beside him began to vibrate; small objects fell from it. Objuk stooped to retrieve a smashed convoy-light. "So you boys wanta play rough, eh?" he muttered.

"Just wait. I'll give you a taste of Hairy Harry and his Rocky Mountain Rockers!" he added, and ducked as a second fixture impacted a foot from his left boot. He looked up at the towering ship. "She's shaking like a wiggle-dancer on Io!" he yelled. "Gotta get aboard and see to my command!" he shouted, and dashed up the ramp.

"Getting noisy!" Cookie yelped. "Gotta do something, Cap!"

Just then, Eagle pulled up directly in the Supremo's path, elevated his fore battery a trifle and fired a full charge into the monster's gaping mouth. The between-the-bones buzz faltered for a moment and then resumed, more penetratingly than before. Eagle fired again and the pervading vibration died with a final rattle.

"Whoosh!" Cookie sighed, as he poked the tip of his little finger in his ear and shook it vigorously.

Half a mile distant, the city walls were wreathed in dust; as it dissipated in the brisk breeze which had sprung up upon cessation of the Droon emission, it was apparent that sections of the old construction had fallen, leaving gaps in the perimeter defenses. Beyond the wall, a number of the taller buildings looked shorter, their tops toppled.

"Cap, we got to get back!" Cookie blurted. "That there Droon is powerful stuff! And looky yonder! Old Eagle's last blast right down the esophagus never slowed it down! The noise stopped, but it's still coming on!"

We warned you! the Geeper voice chimed in. *Now, will you ally yourselves with us to neutralize the great scamps, or is it to be war with the Great Folk?*

"We don't want war with you," Judson informed the persistent creatures, "nor do we wish unduly to antagonize your shipmates."

"Shipmates," indeed! the noisiest Geeper scoffed. *The great brutes enslaved us with their Droon emissions and forced us to do their bidding! However . . .* The voice diminished to a tightly-beamed tone which Judson sensed he alone could hear. *However,* it went on, *we know the secret of their vulnerability. Just as they employ sound-waves in the Droon range to immobolize their opponents and destroy their artifacts, they are themselves susceptible to vibrations in the country-rock spectrum; I have already so advised the Objuk entity!*

There was a preliminary *crackle!* from the out-talker set in the aft hull, and a penetrating whine started up, rose in pitch and volume, then seemed to fade.

The commissar is focusing his transmission down to a tight beam, the Geeper announced. *Now, if he can direct it precisely into the great bully's snarf-node . . .*

Heads turned as Eagle gunned his car backward out of the path of the oncoming Supremo. The latter hesitated, pulled in its extended limbs and rolled over on its side.

Bullseye! the Geeper exulted. *I reviewed the vessel's*

tape library and selected Hairy Harry as the most potent candidate! As you see, I chose well. Luckily, Harry was a favorite of the commissar, so he had a wide selection of munitions from which to choose. The arrogant monster is done for, and its mate will succumb as well as soon as she's exposed to the Rocky Mountain Rockers unshielded! Potent weaponry! I think, Judson entity, that a new era of Geeper-Edenite co-prosperity is at hand! Now, fellows, let's fix up the hulls flattened by the enemy, it went on at wide-beam.

Eagle returned his war-car slowly to his starting point, watching the inert Supremo closely as he parked the car.

It appears, Judson entity, the leading Geeper voice spoke up again, *that destruction has been extensive. There are materials we shall require in order to replicate irretrievably damaged components: iron, for example, and copper, molybdenum, zinc and a host of others. Where do you suggest we acquire such materials?*

Baggy, Judson called in response. *How's the inventory coming? Can you direct the Geepers to convenient deposits of needed elements?*

Indeed, Baggy replied easily, *and to many unneeded ones as well. Gold, for example.*

"Hey!" Cookie spoke up. "Looky, Bag: I'll give you a mental picture of a big solid silver beer stein I saw one time in a pawnshop on New Barvaria." He proceeded to visualize the massive, metal bumper with its hinged lid. "Can you run me up one like it, in solid gold?"

Nothing simpler, Baggy assured him. *But solid arsenic would be even more handsome.*

"Belay that!" Cookie said loudly. "That's likely to give me a belly-ache."

"What the devil are you talking about, Space'n? I was simply securing my hatch against any repetition of the Droon. In any case, your tone is inappropriate for a space'n addressing an admiral." Eagle paused, then continued, "By the way, did someone say something about gold? I haven't forgotten our agreement, you know. Kindly deposit the gold right here, at once."

All right, Bag, Cookie beamed the words silently. *Give his Lordship a sample, but not right on top of him.* Before he had finished speaking, an ingot of dull-yellow metal thudded to the ground, half-burying itself, close enough to the admiral to make him jump back. Then he stared, bent, and attempted to lift the heavy bar.

"By the Great Hairy!" he blurted. "How did you do that, Space'n? Are there any more?" In rapid succession another dozen thirty-pound ingots dropped, apparently from nowhere, neatly aligned against the green sod. A massive beer mug settled in more gently atop the pile.

"That's mine," Cookie spoke up, and grabbed his prize. Eagle threw himself across the stacked bars, embracing as much of the heap as he could reach.

"I propose a fresh start, gentlemen!" he caroled. "Here we have a firm basis for a Terra-Eden accord."

"Better step back, sir," Judson suggested, and Eagle did so, a moment before a final gold bar impacted on the stack.

"Gad!" Eagle blurted. "You chaps must be more careful! You could have killed me!" He looked around craftily. "So that was your scheme all along, eh? To decoy me here and do me in secretly. Chadwick! You'd best bring along those articles after all. Hurry! I'm under attack!"

Chadwick scrambled back inside the gig, and re-emerged, carrying a set of freshly faxed documents.

"The Capitulation," he recited, "the Eternal Treaty, the Grant application, the Annexation Patent; they're all in order, sir, IAW Red Robin."

"What the devil's a red robin got to do with high matters of state, you nincompoop?" Eagle yelled. "Oh, I remember: the Supplement to Blue Baker Regs bear that informal nickname, I'm sorry I said 'nincompoop,' my boy. Over-excited, you know, after my near-escape from death!"

"You mean your escape from near death, sir," Chadwick corrected.

A small and exaggeratedly battered ground-car came

whining and bumping over a low rise and pulled ove
beside the ship. A tiny, spidery old woman in blac
bombazine hopped out, followed by an immensely obes
young fellow wearing a Buster Brown outfit.

"Hey, Ma," he bleated. "Wait up! Some folks ain't a
skinny as you, remember!"

"Here, Pete!" the old harridan yelled, her voice crack
ing with excitement, or something that made it crack
"I got a hot report you gotta have right now! Just got i
off the SWIFT gear!"

"Easy, Ma," the lanky leader soothed. "What's th
idea using the Shaped Wave Interference Front Trans
mitter without my say-so?"

"Had to, Pete," she responded, unabashed. "Got
hot flash from Benny out the picket station. Seems lik
the radio traffic has went and picked up. Lots o' jabbe
about 'Outspace' and the 'Presence.' Old Benny neve
knowed what it was all about, and me neither!" Sh
turned to the fat boy: "You, Bobby, you heard him; tel
Pete all about it, whilst I get aholt of the commissar an
check out some stuff." As she turned to go up the ramp
Pete grabbed her arm.

"Fellers," Pete addressed Judson and Cookie for
mally, "this here is Ma Kwikaid. Once wiped out
whole detachment o' revenue sneaks single-handed. Bi
Bob here's her boy, seems like one o' them revenooers go
to her that time. She was a lot younger then, eh, Ma?"

"Damn right, Pete," Ma agreed. "Worked out goo
at that. Bobby's a good kid and helped his ma ou
more'n oncet, like that time I ducked into a little plac
on Barbary in the Belt, for a quick snort, and three wis
guys lasooed me and was trying to string me up by th
left laig, and old Bobby, he throwed one feller out
third-story winder, and sat on the other two. One wen
out the winder had the shortest stay in the pest-house
I promised to give him his own command for a play-toy
not hardly room fer the both of us aboard my *Mombi*
anyways." She looked across at Eagle's remaining intac
ships. "One o' them there vessels will do good," sh
declared.

"See here, madam!" Eagle expostulated. "You appear to have no grasp of the meaning of 'government property!' I'm personally signed-out for every one of those units, and if they hit me with a statement of charges for even one . . ."

"Might eat into yer gold pile, eh?" Pete suggested. "Come on, Eagle, just one little old destroyer, make the boy happy."

Eagle sputtered, and the fat newcomer casually edged over beside him and pinned him against the hull of the war-car simply by shifting his weight. Eagle struggled like a fly impaled on a pin.

"None o' that, Bobby!" Ma spoke up sharply. "These here," her wave included everyone present not previously a member of the CDF, "are our new friends. Old Admiral here, he's gonna give you a brand-new destroyer he don't need no more, seeing he's rich. Ain't that right, Admiral?"

Eagle managed to extricate his head from beneath Bobby's back sufficiently to nod vigorously.

Ma nodded back and signaled Bobby to ease up, then turned and went up the ramp of the ship muttering about "checking in with Jukky."

"Oh-oh," Cookie remarked. "Look yonder, Cap. Better get on the horn 'fore them boys make a big arrow." He was looking toward the town, through the broached wall of which a party of ground-effectives was mustering, while air cover consisted of half a dozen spinners.

"Them's the new batch old Ziggy's tryna run off in the new plant," Cookie complained. "Ain't hardly been field-tested yet, not to say nothing about being signed-off."

Judson spoke urgently into his all-band talker and told the relief party to abort the mission and return to the city. The leader of the group, Ziggy himself, muttered about secret weapons, but complied.

"Just what I thought!" Eagle contributed. "You *do* maintain armed forces pitiable though they appear. One salvo from one of my smaller units, and they'd be history!"

"Sir," Chadwick spoke up, proffering the new documents. "I wouldn't do anything hasty, sir." He pointe off-side, where a second intimidating convoy had emerge from the north gate and was maneuvering to fall in o the flank of the first. "There's more!" the lieutenan said but Eagle hushed him, and he subsided.

"What about my hot news?" Ma demanded over th out-speaker. "You gonna listen or what, Pete?"

"I'm listening, Ma," Pete assured the beldame. "What it about?"

"Ha!" she barked. "That's the question, ain't it? I wa just saying about the 'Presence,' and 'Outspace' an all—" Her amplified voice boomed across the trample sward.

"No more, madam!" Eagle cut her off. "How yo became privy to the contents of the Extreme Lon Range Projection, I cannot fathom, it being classifie Galactic Ultimate Top Secret."

"Never seen no GUTS material," Ma objected. "Picke that offen the SWIFT like I said. Didn't say nothin about no privy!"

"SWIFT itself is known only to a few of us in the to echelon," Eagle grumped.

"Anyways," Ma persisted, "thang is, my C-14 chrono gear is messed up bad. Got to doing the twenty-yea maintenance schedule; hadda open the aft hatches fo that, o' course, reason Bob and me set her down lat here." There was a slight pause, then, "That's what needed to check with Jukky."

"Hey!" the commissar's voice replaced hers, boomin from the ground-talker. "Got a problem here, Pete! Ol auto-edit's went out on me! Done wiped half my tape here; set up to reprogram ever twenty-five standar years, that's for morale, ya know; ooney it done throwe out the rest o' my Hairy Harry's! Can't keep the pres sure on the monsters! Better unlimber my fore battery!

"Don't do that, Commissar," Judson countered. "To bad about old Harry being dumped into the dead stor banks, but you can retrieve him later on."

"Cap," Cookie spoke up anxiously, "what's going on here? AutoSpace never was too smart, but their C-1 timing gear was always dead accurate up to fifty thousand years. Funny Ma's and Jukky's done both gone out—"

"Maybe they didn't," Judson pointed out. "We know about the strange time effects here on Eden; maybe Jukky *has* been grounded for twenty-five years. Ma's only twenty out because she was ten minutes late joining up."

"What's that you say?" Eagle demanded. " 'Strange time effects,' eh? What's that supposed to mean?"

"There are no suppositions involved," Judson corrected. "I was referring to the fact that this planet, and this sector of space also, as far as we know, is not in chronological synchronicity with Home Space."

" 'Chronological synchronicity' is tautological, sir!" Eagle barked.

"Yes, but, sir, he's right!" Chadwick spoke up. "I'd been meaning to tell you, sir: all our chrono-gear is malfunctioning!"

"Nonsense!" Eagle yelled. "Our shipboard functional coordinator is one of AutoSpace's—or the Concordiat's finest achievements in precise engineering! I refuse to believe it has failed. If it had, we'd be hard put to operate the vessel, boy! Keep that in mind!"

"Oh, it's all right in the short-range, sir," Chadwick gobbled. "It's just that the main cruise clock says we've been in space for fifty-one years!"

Eagle commanded his junior to bring the skiff over. It arrived a moment later, apparently functioning perfectly.

"You see?" Eagle crowed. "Your maneuvering engines are in perfect sync!"

"Sure, sir," Chadwick agreed. "But as I said, sir, it's only the upper-range functions that are off. Did I make myself clear, sir? It's been fifty-one years since we cleared Luna Control."

Eagle looked imploringly at Judson. "The boy's gone mad," he stated sadly. "What will I tell his uncle? He was so set on the lad's having a big career."

"You can't tell him anything," Judson pointed out "He's doubtless been dead for several decades."

"Eh? What do you mean? Who told you that?"

"Councilman Chadwick was in his sixties when yo lifted, Admiral," Judson pointed out. "Add fifty-on years to that, and it's doubtful that he has lived past on hundred and twenty years of age."

"Fifty-one years," Eagle murmured. "Then how is i I'm alive, or even young Chadwick?"

"You're in Eden's curious field-effect," Judson tol him.

"B-but—after all these years—if this isn't just som silly hoax you're perpetrating—I'd have been in manda tory retirement for years—"

"And—" Chadwick took up the plaint, "my uncl persuaded me to go on active Naval duty by promisin me he'd personally see to it that I was promoted to fla rank within the decade. That makes me the senio serving admiral in the Fleet!"

"As to that, sir," the over-taxed Eagle replied in broken voice, "I can but defer to your superior rank. hereby hand over command to you, and shall observ with interest what disposition you make of this mare' nest! Lawless rogues running loose—"

He ducked under a casual swipe from Pete's lon arm. "—sorry about that; just slipped out, of course you're now noble spacemen of the fleet. Anyway no one, but *two* alien invasions, rebel forces in firm contro here on a world I desired to claim as Concordia property—nice item in my 201 file, that, Admiral. An spooky spiders doing depot maintenance on condemne hulls, other beings pounding my brains to a thin past with novel weapons! It's a nightmare, Admiral, eve without this time-scrambling! My command is sixtee years overdue for condemnation proceedings, unde the Rot and Rust Act of '73, and—"

"That's quite enough, sir," Chadwick cut off the flov of lamentation. "As to what I shall do, the first item i to assure Captain Judson, as well as King Pete, tha Terra has no intention whatsoever of attempting t annex this infernal planet. Consider, Admiral," he urged, as Eagle opened his mouth to object.

"If I should somehow manage to advise CINCFLEET that it was now responsible for the maintenance of Terran sovereignty on a remote world already occupied by potent alien forces and serving as a hideaway for rebellious units of the auxilliary, none of which can be reliably dated, to say nothing of explaining it . . ."

"Well, Cap," Cookie remarked in the momentary silence that followed Admiral Chadwick's pronouncement. "It looks like maybe we can get back to our inventory of Eden's resources, eh?"

"Why not?' Judson agreed. *Baggy,* he called, *can you cooperate with the Geepers in conducting an immediate survey of this continent? Later, we'll need your assistance in conducting both high- and low-altitude photographic surveys.*

My pleasure, Captain, Baggy came back. *I find the Geepers quite sociable, actually, as well as splendid sources of vital energies. Not malignant at all, once properly directed. I shall dispatch my young on a preliminary overflight at once.*

"If you could get the spiders to patch up my vessels, Captain," Chadwick proposed, "I think it would be well for me to lift my command with dispatch. By the way do you suppose I could take along a few breeding specimens of the Geepers, to be trained in Naval maintenance procedures?"

Judson addressed the proposal to the Geeper voices, who eagerly accepted.

"No unlimited breeding, now," Judson cautioned. "No attempt to take over Terran worlds."

Of course not, nothing like that! they agreed readily. *We're so glad to be rid of the Supremo's dominance that I'm sure we shall get along famously with you Terrans, who will supply ideas without exacting such burdensome disciplines as the great bullies did!*

The first units of the convoy from town were now pulling up alongside the row of parked vessels. A pretty young woman jumped down from the lead vehicle and came over.

"What's going on, fellers?" she inquired formally. "We saw them big critters coming toward you, and the brain-scramble went on, and after that lots of folks passed out cold when Hairy Harry came floating into town—"

"Sorry about that," Judson assured Patricia. "Just overkill; Objuk's beam leaked a bit, I suppose."

"Anyway things have quieted down in town ever since Old George disappeared. The new people have settled in well, and we was getting a little worried when the guard staff said you'd gone out-wall, and didn't come back. But I can see you've got everything under control, as usual."

"Hi, honey," Pete addressed the young officer. "I'm King Peter von Bülow, skipper o' that second vessel in line there; new in these parts and don't know nobody. Don't want to be head o' myself, but how about you having dinner aboard my command this evening? Autochef's just been overhauled."

"Thanks, Your Majesty," she replied prettily. "I've heard about you. A real hero, only the Council wouldn't give you any credit. Sure, I'll dine with you. My name's Patricia."

"Pete," Judson called as the CDF leader was about to stroll off after the girl. "I guess you know Eden is a free port to all units of the CDF, any time you need it. We're not going to join up, but you can consider us friendly territory. Meanwhile, you'd better report in to Luna base and get council confirmation on your status as an Auxilliary Unit of the Fleet."

"We'll do it, Cap," Pete agreed, and resumed his conversation with Patricia.

"Reckon you could find us all a gal?" Boss Nandy called after him.

"The rest o' you deck apes are on permanent sentry-duty," Pete called back. "I'll see what I can do after we got these Spreemers and Geepers out o' the way."

"These big fellows," Eagle spoke up. "I say, Admiral

Chadwick, wouldn't it be good tactics to get them back aboard their vessels, as soon as the little fellows have closed the seams in the one, there, and then take them in tow, back to the Belt, say, and release them on one of the larger bodies, Judson's Rock, say—" He glanced at Judson. "Most appropriate, in view of your presumed descent from Captain Judson, sir—so that council-appointed observers can see for themselves what a menace to Terran Space has been neutralized here? Instead of a mere starveling client world, dependent on Terra for protection, Eden will be seen as the first-line defense against all manner of hostile entities lurking, unknown in Outspace! The Council, gentlemen, will buy it!"

"Good thinking, Admiral," Chadwick approved. Judson nodded.

"Then there's the two inner worlds to see to," Cookie contributed. "I got a idea, Cap: if we shipped a few pairs of breeding Geepers to each one, do you think they could Terraform 'em, get 'em ready for colonization? Could send some of Baggy's offspring along to help out with the brains and keep us informed, and meanwhile, we got to get on with the big inventory."

"Quite a job we're taking on, Space'n," Judson replied. "At least three temporate zone continents to inventory: mountains, rivers, lakes, beaches, prairies, forests, mines, scenic views, and no deserts or ice-caps. We'll have to locate the mineral deposits, coal, oil, uranium, everything. It will take a while."

I'm quite thrilled at the prospect, Baggy put in. *And of course seeing and exploring the inner worlds still to come! I've tested the Supremos*, he went on, *and they're even more palatable than the Geepers; we can rely on them for sustenance until we learn how to live in harmony with them, on their lonely, hot planet.*

"Yes, a long time, Cap," Cookie agreed. "But time, it seems like, is what we've got plenty of."